The STEPPING *Series*

BOOK TWO

STEPPING ACROSS THE ENGLISH CHANNEL

KAT CALDWELL

Book Cover by GoOnWrite.com

ISBN: 978-1-964171-02-9

Ebook ISBN: 978-1-964171-01-2

First edition, 2025

Also by Kat

Historical Romance:
Aurora's Dilemma
Stepping Across the Desert
Across the English Channel

Contemporary New Adult Romance:
Coffee Stains

Mythological Christian Fiction:
An Audience with the King

Contemporary Fiction:
Bended Dream
Bended Loyalty
Bended Love

Para mi familia española.
Gracias por acogerme en vuestra vida.

Chapter 1

"IT CAN'T BE DONE." Philip stared at his friend, dead serious.

"What do you mean to say, 'it can't be done'?" demanded Lord Christophe Sutton, the Marquess of Candor, known to Philip as Cinch.

"You cannot invade England from the south." Philip waved his hand across his friend's walnut desk, his black-as-night mourning coat contrasting deeply with the white papers. They were seated across from each other in Cinch's study, where most of the work for Sutton Enterprises happened.

Cinch eyed him, folding his arms across his broad chest. "What about the Vikings?"

"What about them?" Philip asked, leaning over the desk and planting his palms.

He was lankier than his best friend, but since working with Cinch at Sutton Enterprises, his limbs had filled out, resembling an ironworker's more than a nobleman's. "They tried and ended up losing everything for it. Where are the Vikings now, in 1836?"

Cinch stood, chuckling as Philip turned to take a bow for winning the argument.

"I believe I deserve a glass of your finest for that." He and Cinch had been working for the better part of four hours, planning the next two quarters of Sutton Enterprises. They deserved a break. Philip strolled to the trolley where Cinch kept his bottles and a half dozen glasses.

"What's this?" he asked, picking out a tall, thin bottle with an amber colored liquid inside.

"Scotch. Falcon left it last time he was here."

Philip took a sip to appreciate the rich taste Cinch's brother-in-law had before pouring two glasses while his friend tidied up the papers on his desk. It was nice to be back in London and back to work after being away for his mother's passing.

"Would you like a nip, Henry?" Philip asked, holding up a glass of scotch.

Henry, Cinch's secretary, seemed flabbergasted as usual at the scene he had just witnessed. Even after three years of working at Sutton Enterprises, he seemed unused to the antics between Cinch and Philip.

"Oh, no, thank you, sir. I . . . I couldn't," stammered Henry.

"Cinch! Tell this young man to have a drink. He deserves it for putting up with you."

"Do as you please, Henry," Cinch said, glowering at Philip. "But do be warned that if you choose to start drinking at teatime, you are likely to become like Daucer, here. And I assume you are too intelligent to want anything like that to happen."

Philip wasn't about to allow Cinch the last word. He pivoted toward Henry. "Take a good look, Henry. I'd say, who wouldn't want to be like me?" He paused with his left side towards the bewildered secretary. "Come, Henry, take a look at me from this angle. It's my better side."

"Leave Henry alone. He doesn't understand your sense of humor," said Cinch, taking his glass of scotch. "I'm not sure I understand your sense of humor. You have no good side."

Philip waggled his eyebrows at his companions. "You simply don't have the taste of a woman. Neither one of you."

Cinch raised a hand to stop Philip from continuing. "Let's finish planning this trip. You are officially out of mourning in a week's time, are you not?"

Philip nodded. He had intended to sail to Spain on one of their boats in the autumn, but his mother's sudden passing changed everything. While he and his mother hadn't been close, she still deserved a proper mourning. She had given him life, after all. And he very much enjoyed his life.

"What is the status of our ships?" Cinch asked, appreciation flitting across his face as he sipped his scotch.

"That depends." Philip rustled papers to make room for his half-empty glass. "The *Lady Elizabeth* should dock in a few days from France. I received a letter from the captain saying he was simply awaiting the wind to pick up. The British Navy just signed the contract to once again use the *Queen Mary* to find ships illegally bringing slaves from Africa to the Americas. They will likely contract the use again and again. She's a fast one and was able to catch fifteen ships last year carrying illegal slaves."

Cinch nodded his approval. "The *Lady Elizabeth*, that one should be good to leave again a few weeks from now?"

A thrill ran down Philip's spine. He had never been to the continent before. Never been on a ship before. The very idea delighted him. "Certainly. I also heard from Clifton that *Prosperity's Pride* would be done with his repairs in two weeks' time."

"In London harbor in two weeks?"

"Yes."

"With that crew refreshed from almost two months of leave, perhaps it would be best for you to sail her over to Spain."

Philip marked the notes down. He tried his best to remain calm, but his smile was giving him away.

"Are you sure you wish to go this time of year? It won't be as nice as in the autumn," Cinch said, keeping his attention on the maps.

Philip narrowed his eyes, assessing his friend's sincerity as Cinch stood to stretch. He got his answer when Cinch chuckled.

"I thought you were serious for a moment," Philip said with relief.

Cinch came around the desk and patted him hard on the back. "I know how much you're looking forward to going, Daucer. Look here. I was thinking the best route would be to head to Royan, France. That's at the mouth of the Gironde River, where the wine barrels will be waiting to be picked up. From there, you will sail to Porto, Portugal. The barrels will be unloaded and taken down the river towards Zamora."

"I will go with them to visit my cousin," he said.

"Precisely," Cinch agreed. "Captain Margot will continue on to Tangiers to load spices and silks, then to Cadiz for oil and oranges, then to Porto again to recover you and the Madeira wine."

"Perfectly sound plan." Philip regarded the other two men and held up his hand solemnly. "I will remember you back here in the grey London weather while I make the best of my time in the vineyards of the Rioja."

"Toro," Cinch corrected. "Your cousin lives in the Toro."

"That's the town."

"That's the wine region as well, near the Ribera region," Cinch said.

Philip bowed to his boss. "Nevertheless, what stands is that I shall endeavor to taste each wine and set up our bridge and railroad project."

"Hopefully not on the same day," Henry said with a twitch of his lips. Philip snorted.

"Drinking each wine and doing business might not work well," Henry explained. His thin, dark eyebrows knitted in concern.

"Oh, you're serious?" Philip asked. "Can't believe you would think that way about me, Henry. I am nothing if not responsible. I only drink excessively at night, after business is over." Philip slapped Henry on the back hard enough for the young man to lurch forward.

"Speaking of the bridge project, see to it that you play well with the locals," Cinch said. "We need that bridge for the railroad."

"Have we finalized a contract on the steel?" Henry asked. He sifted through a pile of papers on his secretary's desk. Everything was so neatly stacked Philip wondered how the man could find anything. It was just one paper on top of another. "I have nothing here on it."

Philip set his empty glass on the mantel over the cold fireplace and looked at Cinch. He hadn't seen any correspondence about it either.

"Philip and I are meeting with a Mr. Finley later this week. We should be able to persuade him to enter a business contract with us," Cinch said.

"Will we?" Philip remembered Lionel Finley from college as an intense young man who was always talking about his latest business dreams.

"You can be charming when you wish, and I believe I have access to something he wants," Cinch said, rather cryptically. "Now, do not forget, you must make it back to Porto on time. Captain Margot will wait exactly one day, and then I will direct him to sail on to London." Cinch moved to stare out the large windows that overlooked the garden and said nothing for a few minutes. Philip waited, knowing his friend and when best to hold back his jests.

"You cannot be late to the ship," Cinch said, turning back to face Philip. His dark eyes were stern. "There is no time for a delay. We're taking a risk with the oranges."

Philip topped off Cinch's glass, clinking the glasses together noisily. "If I cannot be back in time, I will travel to Bilbao and take a ship from there."

"Where the fighting is?" Cinch asked dryly.

Philip scratched his chin. "Ah, yes, the war. Carlos should just surrender already. Countries have survived child kings and queens before."

"Yes, I'm sure he will change his thirst for the throne at your behest," Cinch said. Philip cocked his head as he considered the proposition.

"You're incorrigible," Cinch said. "Now, since we are finished for the day, I will ask you, have you given more thought to what you said during the funeral?"

"About what?"

"About marriage," Cinch prompted.

Philip sputtered, the alcohol twisting in his throat and keeping any fully formed words from coming out.

"I'm thirty-three," he croaked. "I'm too young to get married."

Cinch laughed. "That is not what you said at your mother's funeral. I remember my shock when you turned to me, your eyes wide and honest, and told me you should have gotten married while she was alive. That it was her greatest wish, and you shouldn't have been such a cad."

"Well, there it is. The lie in all this. I would never have called myself a cad. I love myself."

Cinch leveled his gaze at him. "I may have taken some liberties in the retelling."

Henry snorted from his desk producing a smile from Cinch as well.

"Oh, alright," Philip said. "It was a moment of weakness in my grief. I'm quite over it now."

"Ah, so you've decided against it?"

Philip threw himself into the high-backed leather chair near the fireplace, considering his friend's question. "I think I have. I am happy as a bachelor. And besides, I have not met a woman I could spend the rest of my life with. As much as you say marriage is great fun, I am not sure it's for me."

"I didn't use those words," Cinch said.

Philip waved towards Henry, who was ignoring the entire conversation. "Then it must have been Henry who said it."

Henry cleared his throat, his eyes never leaving the papers he was filling out. "I believe I said I very much enjoy being married to my wife. We're great friends, and I can't imagine my life without her."

"Ah, yes. And that going home to her was the better part of your day. Which I can sympathize with. Being stuffed up here in this office is a bit of a bore."

Henry sighed. Philip watched him, amused at the way he grated on the young man's nerves.

"Stop teasing Henry," Cinch said. "If he quits because of you, I'll make you be my secretary."

"Fair enough." Philip chuckled. "Please accept my apologies, Henry. Now, are you satisfied with my thoughts on marriage? It's bad enough I had to spend so much time with Theodore this year."

"Your brother? What has he done now?" Cinch asked.

"He has become more overbearing than he was before Mother died. Each time I tried to speak to him about the estate, he accused me of wresting it from him. Which is impossible to do legally, but law and facts have never been his strong point. And now he has given word that he is coming to stay in London. He sent trunks ahead of him."

Philip waited for his friend's wisdom as Cinch finished his scotch. But what Cinch said was nothing Philip expected.

"It would serve you right to fall in love with some poor woman while you're away in Spain."

Philip groaned, and Henry chuckled behind him. "I'm glad my suffering at the hands of your boss is entertaining to you, Henry."

"I do apologize, sir."

"You may go home, Henry. I fear Philip will only continue to use you as a distraction to my questions."

"If I am to endure more questions, I believe I need another drink," Philip said, rising as Henry gathered his things.

"Before I leave, my lord, will you be attending the House of Lords this week?" Henry asked.

"I supposed I should. We are voting on whether to send the Duke of Wellington with fighting soldiers to Spain, are we not?"

"Yes, my lord. I believe so."

"Very well. You may accompany me at the end of the week, if you wish."

Henry practically leaped out of the study. Philip turned to Cinch for an explanation.

"Poor chap loves being in the House of Lords. Believes we'll open it all up democratically one day and that he might get elected."

"That's asking England to change a lot in a short amount of time," Philip said, laughing as he picked up the scotch bottle again. "Which I doubt it will. But here's to England changing someday."

"I wouldn't mind not being responsible for what happens in the House of Lords," Cinch said. "Put that down. It's time for tea. My wife gets quite annoyed these days if I'm late."

"That doesn't sound like Rowena," Philip said, but he set the bottle down anyway. "She's such a calm woman. You know, if I had someone like her to pursue, I could consider marriage."

Cinch shook his head and said nothing more on the subject as they each put their jackets back on and left the study. They walked past the grand dining room towards the back of the house, where a more intimate room awaited them. Deep green paper lined the walls, and a fireplace with white marble jambs on either side held a steady fire stood in the middle, outlined by a myriad of books. Cinch had purposely purchased the corner lot, which allowed him to build a house with more windows than most London houses.

Tea was already set.

"Philip! I was wondering when you were coming to see us poor ladies," Rowena greeted him, her arms outstretched for a kiss on the cheek.

Philip leaned in over her protruding belly to kiss her. He wasn't sure how many months it took to grow a child, or when women stopped allowing men to see them. Both of his sisters-in-law had gone into hiding before he could tell they were even expecting, only to emerge months, or perhaps years, later. He never paid much attention.

"Uncle Philip," said a small, stern voice behind him.

He turned to find Eleadora, Cinch's daughter, staring at him, her hands on her hips. With her dark-as-night hair and olive skin, Eleadora favored her Spanish mother. There wasn't much use hiding that she was illegitimate, the product of Cinch's affair with a Spanish woman before he met Rowena.

Some, like Philip's sister-in-law, still arched their eyebrows at the little girl living in England with Cinch and Rowena instead of being sent to boarding school, but Philip was proud of his friend for loving her as much as he surely would the baby on the way. Cinch had made mistakes, but Philip still found him to be one of the most upstanding men he knew. And one of the few who owned his mistakes and didn't make others suffer for them.

"There you are!" he exclaimed. The little girl broke into a toothless grin. "How grown up you are in that dress. How old are you already? Thirteen?"

"Six," she said, shaking her head, but giggling when he scooped her up and twirled her around. "Are you having tea with us?"

Philip always marveled at how English she sounded. She had arrived in London speaking only Spanish just under three years before. She had captivated him with her big brown eyes and her affection for playing tag and fighting him off with a wooden sword. Play was wasted on the young, in his opinion. When Cinch's sister Emily was in town, he searched out Cinch's nephews at the park as distraction from ships, numbers, or business.

"I am. Much to your aunt's dismay," he said, eyeing Claire as she approached them. Eleadora grinned at her aunt. The spot where a tooth was missing added to her charm.

Claire patted Eleadora's head, but rolled her eyes at Philip. "Why are you always such a child, Philip?"

Despite her dry words, Claire smiled. Philip wished he could have fallen in love with her. She had been married off at a young age to Cinch's older brother, a womanizer and an all-around bastard. When he was found murdered at the docks, Claire endured the rumors and ridicule with her head held high. She was still quite pretty and not yet thirty. While they were close friends, she and Philip had no romantic attraction.

"Come try a cake and have tea," Eleadora said. "We can begin our Spanish lessons, so you don't befall grave mishaps while in Spain."

Philip suppressed a snicker at his goddaughter's lofty vocabulary. As he settled into the chair, she directed him to sit in, and obeying, Philip repeated words after her.

Chapter 2

"You all know my opinion on the matter," Tía Mercedes, Merce to her nieces and good friends, was saying in her sun-drenched drawing room on a beautiful November afternoon in Valladolid, Spain.

She paused, waiting for someone to beg her to continue. Carmen accepted the invitation with great enthusiasm. She loved how her aunt viewed the world from a different perspective than any other woman Carmen knew. Even her late mother, Mercedes' sister.

"On what matter?" Carmen prompted, ignoring the sighs from her younger sister, Isabel. It was something they had both heard so many times before, but while Carmen never tired of hearing it, Isabel did.

She and Isabel had arrived in Valladolid the day before from Toro. They were there to celebrate Isabel's husband, Jaime, receiving recognition from the Archbishop of Valladolid for his work as mayor of Toro. The ceremony promised to be long and tedious, but the dinner would be full of people Carmen hadn't seen in a long time. Mainly her soon-to-be fiancée, Miguel Perez.

She sat up straighter. Tomorrow evening would be the perfect time for him to propose formally, so they could prepare a wedding ceremony for that summer. Their relationship had been in the courting stages for almost two years due to Miguel's medical education. Carmen had been willing to wait, especially while Miguel studied under the King's optometrist, Dominguez, but now she was ready to be officially engaged, then married, and then mistress of her own home.

"Marriage is a game," Tía Merce said, starting her well-known dialogue to Carmen, Isabel, and the other ladies in the room. The room buzzed with excitement. Everyone but Isabel relished hearing the speech again. "And I believe I played that game well, even if I do say so myself."

"Tía," Isabel said, trying to sound as though they were all tired of hearing the lecture. Thankfully, Tía Merce wasn't one to listen to protests. She continued as though never interrupted.

"Marriage is a game that we women need to learn to play better. Men have had the advantage for centuries and we women have gone along thinking they have our best interests in mind when they are only thinking about themselves. It's about time we think about ourselves. They need us for their business and political dealings, which means we should start negotiating with them. Without us, they have nothing. Take you, Carmen. You have land that will be valuable to your husband. And Miguel is no fool. As much as he is concerned with treating people's eyes, he is concerned with being a landowner. Who has the most power in any country?"

The women replied in unison. "The landowners."

"Very good. And so, what did we do with you, Carmen and Isabel? We spoke directly to your father about your expectations for marriage and the land that will be yours upon your wedding day. It should be yours anyway, but I digress. I will not start that today."

Señora Villareal sighed as though with relief. Tía Merce snapped her head in the señora's direction, demanding an explanation.

"I'm not disagreeing," Señora Villareal said quickly. "I have just come to breathe deeply each time a topic arises that I cannot change."

"But we can change it. We must," Tía Merce said, her fist thumping into her open palm. Carmen could feel the heat radiating from her aunt.

"Whatever it takes," Carmen exclaimed. Tía Merce had her and Isabel repeat those words over and over during their adolescence.

"Hear, hear," cried out Madame Croyante, a daughter of a Spanish earl and the same age as Carmen's aunt. Her first husband had fought with Carmen and Isabel's father against Napoleon and, unfortunately, lost his life on the battlefield. She had moved to Valladolid to nurse her mother-in-law. Then she befriended Mercedes, who arranged a marriage between herself and a French count, a man much older than her but who had a fortune. Once the count died, Madame Croyante returned to Valladolid and reignited her friendship with Tía Merce. "Come now, Isabel, don't pout. We spoke at length about babies and your time of expecting. It's time now to have some fun at the expense of the weaker sex. We need some amusing things this afternoon."

"The weaker sex?" Isabel repeated.

Carmen looked up to allow her eyes a rest from her embroidery. The black circles that had plagued her for years hadn't stolen all her vision, but they forced her to center whatever she wanted to see. However, focusing hard on one small area was tiresome. And keeping all the stitches within the middle of the dark cloud surrounding her vision required so much effort. She set the stitching aside and allowed her eyes to relax. Nothing eliminated the black cloud, but relaxing her muscles helped stave off a headache.

"How can you call them weak when they are the ones who go out and fight for us?" Isabel asked, her voice slightly higher-pitched. Carmen squeezed her sister's hand, reminding her not to get too upset.

"Leaving us at home to defend ourselves," Madame Croyante said coolly. "You are recently married and to a young man who is respectable and hard-working. But regardless, you will soon find he is weaker than you. They spoil the children because they are unable to say no. They bed other women because they are unable to say no. They lose money on stupid business ventures because they are unable to say no. That is weakness, if you ask me."

Isabel scoffed but returned to her lace making without another word, probably silently defending her poor Jaime against what she would consider the foolish ideas of these older women.

Carmen left Isabel to her fuming and reached for a cup of tea, wondering if Dr. Miguel was weak.

"As I said before, men are playing a game, one in which all the chips lay in their favor. We all know that. We need only look at the laws of the country and the laws of the church to be reminded. We own nothing, we are not our own person." Tía Merce stood, so she could pace and wave her arms about as she was prone to do.

Carmen watched, captivated as always by her aunt's passion. "We owe it to ourselves and our daughters to start playing our own game. While it is wonderful that some people can find the perfect love match, as our beautiful Isabel has done, the cruel reality is that most do not. To most women, marriage is forced upon them by circumstances. Since we are not allowed to forge our own way, to educate ourselves and risk being smarter than the men, we must marry."

"We could run away to the Americas," Carmen pointed out, receiving a glare from Isabel, who knew that Carmen was only encouraging her.

"A wonderful suggestion," Tía Merce continued. "We could run away to the Americas. There are a few there making their fortune, are they not? But are they not men? What would a single woman do over in the Americas, a country founded by England? Are women freer in England?"

"No, Tía. I don't believe they are," Carmen said, covering her smirk with her teacup. She couldn't help reveling in the words she knew were coming. And Isabel's annoyance made it all the funnier.

"No, they are not. And we should not have to run away from our beloved country to be our own selves."

"What, then, are we to do?" asked Madame Croyante and Señora Villareal at the same time. Their voices resonated with the same excitement Carmen felt.

"Make a new game. Our own game," her aunt declared again, pounding her fist into her palm. "Those few women who find love aside, women should find the oldest man who is at least one step higher in station and marry him. First, it would keep a woman from having dozens of children because a man's, well, vigor, diminishes when he gets older. This would mostly benefit the poor women. Do you not agree, Madame?"

Tía Merce leaned toward Madame Croyante, who eagerly bobbed her head.

"Oh, yes. I certainly agree. My husband's vigor was just enough to give me one child," Madame Croyante said. "And while I adore my son, I do not wish to have more children. My sister married a younger man and had the misfortune of five children brought into the world in consecutive years after their marriage. After that, she moved to another room to cool her husband's vigor, though they recently had another child. She is exhausted. Her humor and figure are gone. I find her to be not just a bore now, but also bitter."

"I could not blame her if she is bitter," cried Tía Merce. "What carrying a child does to one's body is no small matter."

Isabel scoffed from her chair. "Babies are a gift from heaven. Besides, we shouldn't be speaking of the marriage bed when Carmen is present. Tía, you are her chaperone. You should take into consideration that she isn't yet married."

Carmen and Tía Merce exchanged glances. There were three times in her life that she spent alone with her aunt, and each of those times, her aunt took it upon herself to explain in detail what was meant by 'marriage bed.'

"I was never told before I married," Tía Merce had informed her. "And I was horrified to find out. I will do anything to keep you from the experience I had."

Carmen had at first been confused, then repulsed, and then apprehensive. Tía Merce had never denied that attraction between two people was possible and would lead to each person, even the woman, craving the interaction that went on in a marriage bed. Being a widow who refused to live with the confines of societal norms, Tía Merce had admitted to enjoying the act with a lover, but warned Carmen of the potential consequences if she and her lover were not careful to avoid a pregnancy.

"Your sister is practically engaged." Tía Merce said this as though it were an explanation, but Carmen knew to Isabel it would mean nothing. Isabel had married at the age of twenty after returning from Paris. Tía Merce had offered to speak with her about the wedding night, but Isabel refused to listen.

"Ah, I see," Isabel said. "You've already spoken to Carmen, using the excuse that you didn't know what was to come on your wedding night."

Isabel turned back to their aunt. They were too far apart for Carmen to focus on both, so she fixed her attention back on Tía Merce, whose face she could see.

"But then, perhaps the problem doesn't lie in the fact that you didn't know, but that your husband was old. In his loss of vigor, he also lost interest in making sure his bride was loved."

Carmen flinched inwardly at the ice in Isabel's words, but she could see her aunt smiling at them. Tía Merce tapped the tip of Isabel's nose.

"Touché, Isa. But then I had a different plan in mind other than the comfort of my marriage bed. I had a plan to be a comfortable widow when my husband died. And since he was already sixty-five when I married him, there wasn't long to wait."

"You speak as though you two didn't get along," Carmen chided, hoping to warm the air between the two women she loved most.

"Of course we got along. Alberto understood why I chose him. And I understood why he chose me. And once I was pregnant with his heir, he left me alone. It was why he wanted a wife, for which I do not fault him. We women are the only ones who can bring a child into the world, after all. It is the same as me wanting a husband for the sole purpose of being a comfortable widow."

"I would not be in the position I am in had I not listened to your aunt," Madame Croyante said. "I was fortunate to become her friend and for her to care enough about me to find me a nice old husband."

"You all speak of marriage as though it is such a horror to everyone," Isabel said, stomping her small foot as she stood. "I am happy in my love marriage. Jaime loves me and I am happy to give him, and myself, children."

"And that is wonderful for you, dear," Tía Merce said, calm and soothing. But Isabel wouldn't be soothed. Tía Merce and their mother had always encouraged them to speak up, and speak up Isabel would. Carmen could tell from her sister's energy.

"Carmen is set to marry a young man, full of vigor, as you would say. Would you have her not choose him? Would you have her choose an old man instead?" Isabel asked.

To Isabel, the only way to marry was if the couple loved each other, and she discovered that with Jaime. From the moment they saw each other, they loved each other. Their courtship had been quick and ferocious, with Jaime one time spreading flowers under Isabel's window and another time ambling through town loudly proclaiming his love for her. Within less than a year, they were engaged and married. Isabel was now pregnant with their first child. And she was almost two years younger than Carmen.

"I love my sister and do not wish to see her marry a wrinkly old man simply for the money."

"Not money," Tía Merce said. "But money means freedom in this world. And security. And there are exceptions, of course. Doctor Perez is a fine man and since he's a doctor, I believe he will treat Carmen well and allow her body to rest between children. The women I fight for are those whose husbands are not as educated or as kind. I fight for the change to our society where women are used as tokens in a man's game rather than as equals. That is what I fight for."

Isabel sat back on the couch, her face flushed and worn out. "I know, Tía. I'm just emotional."

Carmen touched her sister's forehead. "You always did get overly worked up about things. Have your tea and unwind. Let them have their fun."

Waving towards the sitting room, Isabel said, "Yes, go on and have your fun. I can see now that I won't bring you to my way of thinking."

"It isn't that, Isabel," Madame Croyante interjected. "We are quite proud of you and the match you made for yourself. In a perfect world, every woman would have the chance to make the same kind of match as you did. But since we aren't in a perfect world, we are merely advocating for more women to take up the reins of their future and keep them in their own hands as much as possible."

Isabel accepted a cup of tea from Carmen. She said nothing more and the conversation soon moved on to the gossip around town of a certain Señorita Ana María who had been married off quickly over the weekend. Carmen only half listened while she allowed herself to imagine the conversation she and Miguel would soon have about where their wedding should be, in Toro or in Valladolid.

Chapter 3

CARMEN WANDERED ALONG THE outer balcony of Señor Otera's grand house where the dinner celebration was to be held that evening. She had settled into her guest room, but instead of resting like Tía Merce or Isabel, Carmen decided to change for the evening ahead. She was too excited to rest.

Miguel had sent a message ahead, saying to meet him in the garden before dinner so they could speak.

A shiver ran down her spine as she gazed down from the second-floor balcony to the inner garden that was surrounded by the house. It was larger than any in Toro, according to rumors, and boasted a rose garden—no easy feat in a region prone to droughts. Carmen squinted. She dipped her chin, shielding her eyes from the sun, and finally spotted the green leaves of the rose bushes and the blooms poking straight up. It was the perfect place for Miguel to propose.

Hearing the echo of people gathering in one of the great rooms below, Carmen hurried down the stone steps and into the courtyard garden. Her light green dress, made of the shiniest silk she could find, rustled with her movements. Turning the corner on the stairs, Carmen was careful not to scratch the gigot sleeves that ballooned over her arms.

No one felt prettier than she did at that moment.

She touched the tiny pearls that outlined the bodice as a footman went by, suddenly conscious of her dress's low cut. Carmen considered changing, then decided against it. Maybe she wasn't married, but she also wasn't a schoolgirl. She was a grown, respectable woman, and husband or not, she deserved to wear the latest fashions from Madrid.

At the bottom of the steps, Carmen crossed into the open courtyard, noting the appealing crunch her silk shoes made against the tiny pebbles that dotted the winding path. A few people were admiring the roses, but Miguel was not among them.

"Carmen," called a female voice. "How wonderful to see you. I wasn't sure if we'd have a moment to catch up with each other."

Carmen pasted a smile on her face as Señora Otero, a petite woman with black hair and small eyes, marched up to her. "Señora Otera, nice to see you again. How are the grandchildren?"

"My grandchildren are well, dear." She then peered to her left and right as though about to burst with a secret. "But don't you want to know how my son Juan is doing?"

Juan was an attractive young man willing to do everything his mother said. When Señora Otera instructed him to pursue Carmen as his wife, he did so, clumsily and without passion, simply following his mother's orders. It had been a sad state of affairs to watch. Miguel, thankfully, was more independent than Juan.

She smiled tensely. "Of course. How is Juan?"

"Juan is getting married." Señora Otera's voice dripped with false sweetness. Able to relax again, Carmen was sure her expression brightened. "Congratulations, Señora Otera. I'm very happy for him."

The corners of Señora Otera's lips drooped before she straightened her spine and gave Carmen a small nod. "Yes. Well. Thank you, dear. Oh, I see Roberto. You-hooo, Roberto!"

Señora Otera left quickly, leaving Carmen alone. Exactly what she wished for. Miguel should arrive soon and would find her waiting for him.

Heavy footsteps crunched behind her, sending her nerves aflutter. But it was a footman, not Miguel. Carmen had a difficult time hiding her disappointment, though when the footman offered her a glass of cava, she accepted it with a murmured thank you. The young man clicked his heels together in response before wandering off through the growing crowd.

With a few sips of sparkling wine to give her courage, Carmen continued walking, nodding in greeting to those nearest her. There was no reason to appear like a young, eager debutante when she was well past that age.

A cold breeze caressed her shoulders as the sun started to set. Piano music drifted through the air. The smell of lechazo and fried potatoes wafted out from the kitchen.

"Good evening," Carmen said to each couple as she passed. Everyone was headed into the house. Ahead, Isabel motioned her towards the library where appetizers were being served, but Carmen signaled back with a small shake of her head.

Miguel still had not arrived.

All she needed was the ring and the call for celebration. She had her answer ready. *Sí.* Of course. He was the perfect man for her.

Carmen rolled back her shoulders in the darkening courtyard. As though listening to her thoughts, the footmen lit the lamps in the courtyard garden and on the balcony above her.

Carmen drew in a deep breath and started walking again, slowly and deliberately, feeling the pebbles beneath her shoes, listening to the soft breeze, and noting the floral and earthly scents. Not a hint of rain in the air.

She allowed herself to dream about how Miguel would ask her. She imagined he would approach her slowly, lift her hand, or perhaps, brushing her cheeks with his fingers, he would tell her how he had always known she would be the perfect wife for him, how grateful he was that she waited so patiently while he attended the university and set up his practice, and that now was the time. He could not, *would not*, wait any longer to make her his wife.

Carmen sighed happily at the image. Though nothing, not even sunlight, lessened the black circles framing her vision, the more light there was, the better she saw. For that reason, they would have a morning wedding on a gloriously sunny day so she could see as much of the festivities as possible. They would laugh and dance and sing. Her father, Jaime, and Miguel would twirl her around the garden. They would eat cochinillo or perhaps even bring in fresh fish from the north of Spain. Wine would flow freely, and all her cousins and friends would celebrate their long overdue matrimony.

To the right, a door opened, chatter and music spilling into the courtyard. Carmen took a breath and strolled through the roses. Footsteps crunched along the path at less than half the rate her heart was beating.

"Carmen?"

Miguel. Her hands suddenly shaking, Carmen swallowed.

"Over here," she called out. Miguel's footsteps continued behind her, then paused before she could find the bench.

She didn't wish to, but if he were to be her husband, she might as well get used to asking him for help.

"Hello, Carmen."

His voice sent a thrill down her spine. She turned slowly, noting the rush of happiness that surged in her at seeing his handsome face.

"Hello."

Miguel stepped closer. "Can I speak with you?"

Miguel must be as nervous as she was. His tone was cool. "Of course. Certainly."

She reached out, stumbling to find the bench, but her nerves had gotten the best of her.

"Let me help you." Miguel grasped her upper arm lightly, and together they walked four more steps until he released the pressure, indicating she should sit. She liked that he had experience working with people with poor vision and blindness. Every time her father guided her to a seat, he would say, "Sit." In the same tone, he spoke to his favorite dog, Elvayra.

"Thank you," she said, then laced her fingers together in her lap and waited. But Miguel didn't say anything. He stood still, his image in Carmen's eyes slowly being consumed by the darkening evening. Soon, he would be able to slip away without her knowing, except for the sound of his feet stepping on the gravel.

"You seem tired this evening, Miguel," she said, ignoring her own determination to stay quiet. She couldn't help it. Silence made her nervous.

"Yes," he said, sinking onto the bench next to her. The breeze could barely reach her now with his body blocking it, but it did allow his cologne to waft towards her. It was a new scent. Perhaps something he picked up in Barcelona.

Soon she would travel with him to all the places he went. Barcelona, Madrid, Paris, Berlin, London.

"Carmen, I must speak to you about something," he said. Carmen straightened her spine.

"Of course, Miguel," she said when he paused, as though expecting a response from her.

"It's about my trip to Madrid."

"Oh." Carmen licked her lips and groped for a better answer. A husband would share details about his trip. She didn't wish to appear bored even before the marriage started. "I would love to hear about it."

"I hoped to have better news for you. I really did, Carmen," Miguel blurted, then stood with a strange, deep groan. "For once in my life, I wished my calculations were wrong, that someone in Madrid, anyone, even Doctor Fero, would laugh at me and show me just where I went wrong."

Doctor Fero was Miguel's nemesis. The man always seemed one step ahead of Miguel in the world of medicine, despite them being from the same year at the university.

"I thought you didn't share your equations and findings with Doctor Fero."

"I would have, Carmen, had I thought he could tell me I was wrong."

Carmen raised her eyebrows at the comment, but said nothing. If she married a doctor, it wouldn't be the last time she struggled to follow the conversation.

Miguel picked up her hands from her lap, kneeling before her. She could see his face more clearly, illuminated by the lights from the house, though not the details. Thankfully, she had his face memorized. She didn't wish to have a furrowed brow when he thought back to this moment.

"Carmen, I can't cure you." Each word came out slowly, as though a lead ball was falling from his mouth.

"What do you mean?" Carmen asked.

"Your sight. I can't cure you. Surgery will do nothing. I asked everyone. I presented my findings to each doctor who would speak with me. Everyone told me my conclusions were correct. There is a doctor who performed surgery on two patients like you, but they woke up fully blind and have not yet recovered. It's been over two years now."

Miguel squeezed her hands sympathetically, but Carmen forced a bigger smile onto her face.

"It is called retinitis pigmentosa. The black circle around your vision will complete itself. Though not everyone goes blind, there is no cure to better your vision."

Carmen swallowed against the lump in her throat. She had suspected she was incurable. She had not known, however, that Miguel was striving to find a cure for her, even after he had mentioned last year that there probably wasn't one. "Well, then, we'll just have to enjoy the years I have with some sight. I'll continue learning as I must how to move about without sight, and perhaps someday there will be a new discovery."

"There are theories that your vision will deteriorate further as you get older. I, for one, see no evidence of that."

"I will stay the optimistic one who believes in miracles. You can be the scientist in our marriage." Carmen willed herself not to blush. He was a scientist and would be her husband.

Miguel pulled away from her. The air shifted in the empty space, cooler, dryer, quieter. She heard him muttering, the sound muffled as though he were holding something against his mouth. She imagined him combing his fingers through his hair, as he often did when thinking.

"I came here tonight to tell you, Carmen. It isn't easy for me, but you must understand."

"Miguel, please. It isn't your fault you can't cure me. I understand. Not everything can be handled by science. I will continue to pray that God brings you a solution, but even if He doesn't, this is not all terrible. Didn't you just say I might not lose all sight? This is already better news than I thought I would receive a few years ago. Your treatments must be helping, and with you by my side—"

"Don't you understand, Carmen?" he asked, frustrated. Carmen snapped her mouth closed. "I can't marry you."

The words froze every part of her, chilling her like a December morning frost.

"What?" Surely, he'd meant to say something else. He had meant to say he couldn't marry her this summer. Which was still disappointing, but she could try to understand.

"Are you listening to me, Carmen? I can't marry a blind woman. I can't be an ophthalmologist with a blind wife. Not even a partially blind one. How would anyone come to see me? How could they trust me for their surgeries if I can't even cure my own wife?"

"But surely people would understand? Do doctors never get sick themselves? Are their wives always healthy? And you just said I might not go completely blind."

"Carmen, please, I don't mean to hurt you. The problem is, I want a wife who can be my companion in the house and the laboratory. I want my marriage to be a partnership where I can rely on you for certain things. You were going to be my greatest accomplishment, but now, well . . ." When he spoke again, his tone was softer. "You will need help when we travel, and I can't be by your side all the time."

"I can still travel," Carmen interrupted, floundering to make sense of his argument. "I'm not afraid."

"Carmen, please. Know that I'm sorry. Please know that I'm doing this for you as well as for me. I cannot marry you. I'm sorry."

He brushed her cheek with his thumb before she heard his heels sharply strike the gravel and his footsteps carry him away. Carmen sat still for a long time.

She sat until the appetizers were finished. And the champagne was gone. And the dinner gong sounded.

She sat on the bench as though frozen in time until Tía Merce came to find her and ushered her into the house.

Chapter 4

THE DELECTABLE MRS. TURNER had her lodgings at 15 Newcastle Street in London. The house was situated on the edge of the new Mayfair district, only a few streets over from her former lover's house, the Baron of Grantham, who had died the previous year. He had been twenty years Mrs. Turner's senior.

Mrs. Turner herself was not yet thirty and had the misfortune of marrying the second son of Sir James Turner, a young man who died of consumption early in their marriage. Word had it that the young man reveled in card games and visiting the rather seedy parts of town. When he died, Alice was left with considerable debt as her young husband also liked to dress modernly and buy himself nice trinkets.

Forced to leave her husband's family home and given only one hundred pounds a year, Alice had few choices. She could become a nurse to a noble family, live with her brother who was said to be an alcoholic, or become a mistress.

Being a beauty, she chose the latter.

Philip chastised himself inwardly. It wasn't all that straight of a line for a widow like Alice. She had, in fact, tried to marry again. The problem was that most men worth having were not on the market for a woman in debt. And with young virgins coming onto the market every year, the men had their pick. Another strike against Alice was that she had failed to bear a child during her five years of marriage.

After one season, according to Alice, of failing to find a new husband worthy of her, she met the baron. For the first month, she had assumed he was seeking a wife. Then she found out he had one stuffed in a house up in Scotland. A wife he never saw but was married to all the same. Seeing no other option for herself and the baron being quite generous with her, Alice became his mistress.

Philip had encountered her before the baron died, while he was still paying for her house, though he was too sick to make his usual visits. Thinking about the baron in the lovely Mrs. Turner's bed revolted him, but there was no sense in denying what already was. Mrs. Turner wasn't the only mistress he'd had, though so far, she had lasted the longest. Perhaps because she understood that there was no chance of marriage between the two of them, which allowed them to make peace with what their relationship was: sexual.

"Hello, darling."

The purr stoked Philip's anticipation as he was shown into the cozy sitting room where Alice always received him. It held a dark blue velveteen couch that she was proud of, heavy brocade curtains, and two oriental rugs that were gifts from her short time as mistress of a sheik visiting London for a year. Or so she told him. Philip didn't know if he believed her, but she had a talent for weaving interesting stories.

She crooked her finger towards him. "Come here. I've missed you."

Alice was sprawled out on the couch, holding a book, though it was just for show since the book was upside down and the only light came from the fire. Philip had to admit it was working. He had never fantasized about coming home to a woman waiting for him, but now the whole aesthetic aroused him.

He towered over her, forcing her to thrust her head back to look up at him. "Hello," he murmured. "I've missed you, too."

Her lips, moistened with oil, begged to be kissed, and he couldn't deny them. She'd been gone a long time, and he was in dire need of her company. The moment his lips met her soft mouth, every fire within him raged.

"My," she breathed as he finally let go. "I see you have missed me."

Setting aside her book, Alice stretched her bare legs from underneath her skirts while Philip shrugged out of his coat and threw it to the chair.

He yanked off his cravat and tossed it as well.

"No time for that," Alice said. "Come here."

She pulled him hard until he fell on top of her, then wrapped her legs around his waist. He knew, as well as she, that after so long apart, their lovemaking the first time wouldn't last very long. He gave in without any further ado.

⁂

"When will I see you again?" Alice asked from the pillows. She watched him in the mirror as he struggled with his cravat. Through the mirror, Philip watched her draw the sheets taut over her breasts until her nipples poked through. His mouth salivated, but he glanced away. It was almost two in the morning and time to go home. He'd spent long enough giving in to his carnal desires.

"Perhaps in a few days. I leave for Spain in three days."

Alice shot up, the sheet falling away, her hair tumbling over her shoulders. "Spain? Why are you going to Spain?"

He winced at her piercing trill, his fingers once again fumbling with his cravat.

"Damn it," he murmured, tugging the piece of fabric off to start again. "I have business to take care of in Portugal and then in Spain. I'll be leaving next Monday."

He stopped short of saying that a delay due to the spring London weather was a possibility. With a decent enough cravat now tied, Philip retrieved his coat. Alice flung the sheet aside before stalking across the bedroom. She yanked her pink silk robe from where it hung across a silk Chinese room divider that depicted a lovely, tranquil rice paddy. Alice was anything but tranquil.

"Pet, what's wrong? Why are you upset?"

"Because you're leaving in a week," she said, puffing her lips out. He tried to gather her to him, but she pushed him away, keeping her mouth just out of reach. "And I just got back. I'll be bored and lonely without you. And you know how expensive I get when I'm bored."

She leaned in then, but he didn't kiss her. Threats for money turned his stomach, and she knew it.

Alice hugged her arms to her chest and pouted. "Maybe I'll go with you then."

"Go with me?" Philip was stunned. The idea of traveling with Alice left much to be desired. He could imagine her shopping while he was working, flirting with the men around her, and how would he explain her to his cousin? No, their relationship was best confined to London. "You can't go with me. It's a business trip."

Alice slithered up behind him, pressing her breasts against his back, her long nails gently scraping against his neck. She brought her mouth up close and nibbled his earlobe between her teeth. The touch sent a shot of electricity between his legs, but he held firm.

"Dearest love. Won't you be sorry not to have me with you? I have never seen Spain or Portugal. I'll wait in your hotel room until the evening while you go about your business."

"No," Philip said, firmer than he meant to, but he was tired suddenly. "There will be no time, and you know full well I can't have you tagging along. Imagine what my brother would say if he found out. It's simply not done, and you know it, Alice."

"Well," she said, pulling away from him. She picked through her perfume bottles before choosing one to rub on her arms and naked chest. "If you're going to leave me alone, I will have to find my own company."

Philip adjusted his simple knot–it would have to do–and turned to her. "Find company where, exactly?"

Alice shrugged an elegant shoulder, partially covered by her robe. "I visited with Georgina Totting yesterday. She is Lord Hastings' mistress now. You know of him?"

"I've heard of him." Philip dropped his defense on her petty threat to find company elsewhere and waited.

Lord Hastings was what society would call a rival to Mayfair. They grew up together and were eager to create a better London. Mayfair was ahead of the game, what with his connections to Wellington giving him a hand, but Hastings had found success in Bath. Rumor had it that Great Pulteney Street had his money behind it, as well as the neighborhood that led out from it. Philip and Cinch had invested in a small way in the design and still bemoaned not putting in more money when the opportunity had appeared. But Alice knew none of that. He figured the best way to get information from her was to play slightly ignorant. "Is he looking to invest in London now?"

Alice turned. Her knowing smile caused something akin to dread to churn low in Philip's gut. "He's here, and he's talking to people about your neighborhood. Mayfair wants it, of course, but he's going to have trouble getting it."

"Certainly, he will. No one in my neighborhood wishes to sell so they can be pushed out of London."

"You should speak to your neighbors more, Philip," Alice purred. "Lord and Lady Montague are never in their house and are looking for money. So are Lord and Lady Blackwood. Lord Robert Pembroke already sold and convinced his friend Lord Albert Bicking to sell. And do you know who Georgina saw when she was at Lord Bicking's for tea?"

"The prince?" Philip asked, already bored. While his neighbors' actions concerned him, he wasn't about to show it to Alice.

Alice waved his comment away. "Theodore Daucer. Your brother. It appears he is looking to sell your family estate."

Philip clenched his jaws. It had taken him four months after his mother passed to sort out the finances. The money he had sent during the five years prior had not always made it to the creditors. No, apparently new shoes and couches were at times more important to Theodore than reducing the family debt.

Alice ran her fingers up his lapel and gave a light tug on his cravat, perfecting the knot instantly.

"That's preposterous," Philip said.

Alice shrugged. "When I told Georgina that it wasn't Theodore's house to sell, she said something about the will not being in order."

Philip stiffened. "What do you mean? Though the manor has been in the family for years, I assure you it is his to sell as he pleases."

Alice burst into giggles. "I wasn't talking about the country estate. I was talking about the London house. She said Theodore sounded very optimistic about his chances."

Philip laughed bitterly. Theodore had always thought the London house should have been his. But his brother wasn't going to take the house from him, regardless of his optimism.

Philip leaned in and kissed Alice hard on the mouth. "You're a gem. Knowing this will help me fight my brother off, once and for all, hopefully."

"I'm a gem but not worth enough to take to Portugal," Alice said, pressing her ample chest into the air. Philip whipped out his wallet and set down enough for three new dresses.

"Keep yourself entertained, but not too entertained," he said, snaking his arm around her waist and towing her toward him. He kissed her again, then grabbed his hat and marched to the door. He couldn't afford to let his biology lure him back into the bed. "I'll see you when I get back."

Alice said nothing as he left the house, probably counting the money he'd laid out. It was a strange business, this having a mistress.

"Morning, sir," a constable said from his corner post.

"Morning," Philip said, still distracted by what Alice had said. Just for fun, he envisioned marrying Alice if only to spite Theodore, but the image of such an action made him shudder. There was nothing amusing about being attached for life to a woman who thrived on manipulation, no matter how delectable she was.

They couldn't spend the entire marriage in bed, after all.

Chapter 5

PHILIP FLICKED HIS SHIRT sleeves out of his jacket as he made his way down the hallway of his family's London townhouse. The March morning was as damp and foggy as any other that time of year, but the weather wouldn't deter him. It was the first day out of mourning since his mother passed. Not wearing the black cravat, black gloves, and black armband gave him a lightness he had not felt since before the funeral.

Philip paused at the top of the stairs. High above the staircase hung a painting of his great-great-grandfather that glared down at him as always. Philip saluted him as he did every morning. A man had reason to be dour back in the seventeen hundreds or whatever year his great-great-grandfather lived. But a man at the top of health, living in London in 1836, only had reason to be glad. He was a businessman and a gentleman, after all.

The poor men in the factories or in the mines might feel differently about Philip's mood, but part of his mission in life was to ease those men's burdens as well. It was why he was in business with Sutton Enterprises. Part of the reason, anyway. He and Cinch had changed the working lives of all those employed in their paper company, their mines, and on their ships. Despite complaints from the other businessmen who said Sutton Enterprises was causing the country harm by raising wages too high, Philip was proud that their employees were paid above average wages and were given decent housing. Improving their station made them happy to work with Sutton Enterprises, as Philip was glad to discover.

Philip breathed in deeply, cherishing his freedom deep in his bones. He was free of mourning clothes and would sail to Spain in just a few days' time. Life couldn't get any better than it was at that very moment.

The only thorn in his side was the news Alice had given him about Theodore trying to get his house. But after looking over the will, Philip was certain there was nothing Theodore could do to take the house away from him. It was, and always would be, his.

He started down the stairs. Perhaps he could see the building his solicitor said would be perfect for the hotel he wished to one day build. It would be the talk of the town, and people from all over Europe, and possibly America, would come to stay there. Another dream that had been placed on hold in the last months.

The image of a luxury hotel unfolded in Philip's mind. After he returned from Spain, he would focus on the hotel.

At the foot of the stairs, Philip found himself face to face with the stoic figure of Felix, his butler and most trusted staff member. Felix was the thinnest and most honest man Philip knew. He'd been his father's butler in London and chose to stay on when Philip inherited. With dull blue eyes and a face that was always expressionless, it was hard to always tell what Felix was thinking, but waiting for Philip at the bottom of the stairs was a sign something was wrong.

"Good morning, Felix," Philip said slowly. He glanced past Felix and saw no emergency, but Felix wouldn't stand there for no reason.

"Morning, sir." Felix coughed. Then cleared his throat.

Philip waited, but the butler said no more. "Out with it, Felix."

"Right, sir." He cleared his throat. "Your brother arrived early this morning. Lady Daucer is also at the breakfast table."

Philip gripped his chest and leaned into Felix. The man stood firmly in place, as he always did when Philip practiced his theatrics.

Between receiving his older brother, Theodore, and being stabbed, he would rather be stabbed.

"Sir." Felix stood still as Philip straightened his jacket.

Just a few days before, he had received a letter from Theodore informing him that young Oliver, his son, had broken his finger. This, apparently, had caused much distress on the part of Meredith, the boy's mother and Philip's sister-in-law. Philip had assumed this meant they would not be coming any longer into London. Evidently, he had been wrong. Philip's eyes flickered towards the dining room, then back to Felix, whose gaze was still fixed on him.

"Right then. Did Theodore say why he was here so early?"

"He did not, sir." No surprise there. Theodore didn't believe in talking with servants.

Felix shot a look at the new maid, Rebecca, navigating the hallway with a tray of tea, most likely for his brother.

"What is it, Felix? What do you know?"

"There is talk, sir," Felix said, making sure they were alone before continuing, "that Theodore has a meeting with Lord Hastings this week. There is talk that he is trying to sell this house. Or move into it. The rumors contradict themselves." Felix coughed. He didn't like bringing uncomfortable news.

"How interesting." The fact that the rumors about Theodore and this house were running through the downstairs of the old houses wasn't a good sign. The other bad sign was Theodore, allergic to anything that seemed like work, taking a meeting with men who had a reputation of working unless the meeting was to benefit him greatly. Being a sort of dandy who paraded about London in his latest fashion, perusing for the latest gossip, Theodore wouldn't normally be invited to a mid-afternoon meeting with the Duke of Wellington whose hands were always stirring the pot of London, not only in the city's political happening but also in its business and social realm. And sometimes outside of England entirely.

Philip was glad then that he had employed a chap named Gregory Wilcox the day before to investigate what Theodore was up to. Wilcox was one of the many detectives Sutton Enterprises used to find out about the business dealings throughout London. His need to hear what Wilcox discovered grew intensely now that Theodore was in his house. Unfortunately, he might have to wait until after he got back from Spain to receive the information.

"Thank you, Felix. I am aware my brother has been making waves about London. I'll take it from here."

Philip tugged at the cuffs of his jacket before turning on his heels and marching into the dining room.

"Good morning, Philip," Meredith said. It reminded him of the scratches on the blackboards at Eton.

"Good morning." Philip stood appraising the two of them. Meredith's sapphire eyes pierced him in the eyes, then moved about his person, investigating his clothing. She gave no nod of approval or frown of disapproval, but instead looked away as though bored before picking up a scone to butter. Meanwhile, Theodore hid behind a large newspaper, as though Philip would believe he had suddenly taken to reading. What was more annoying than his pretending to read was Theodore sitting at the head of the table. Philip's seat. Philip considered telling him to move. In his mind's eye, he seized Theodore by the collar and hurled him into another chair.

Instead, Philip plopped himself down in the second chair, the squeaking floor pulling a grunt of disapproval from his brother. Theodore found everything about the townhouse disagreeable, which was why he usually stayed somewhere else during the season. The London townhouse was their father's first purchase in the city. Small, with only four bedrooms, it had been built at the turn of the nineteenth century. Theodore preferred newer things. Grander things. And always found everything around him disagreeable, especially things belonging to Philip, who lived with more voluntary financial restrictions than his brother. Theodore thought Philip should remodel the house, buy newer things. "You are rich, after all, aren't you?" he would ask.

Philip never bothered to answer him.

Despite his dislike of the house, whenever in London, Theodore acted as though it was his. Philip was convinced this was just to annoy him. Theodore had always been the type of firstborn who dangled his luck of the draw birth order over him and Wyle. When Wyle became a minister, Theodore focused all that energy on Philip. He was, after all, the one who decided to choose business as his life's work. As a kid, Theodore's bragging used to anger Philip until he decided on a more amusing manner of dealing with his brother— teasing him. Since he took everything seriously, it wasn't difficult and gave Philip a good laugh at the end of the day.

Philip cleared his throat, then again, louder, falling into a coughing fit as he pulled his chair closer to the table. Bodily sounds were a pet peeve of Theodore. What wasn't? Philip cleared his throat loudly from imaginary phlegm. Childish, perhaps, but personally entertaining.

"Do you need to excuse yourself?" Theodore asked, peering over the rim of his glasses as though the minister of something important.

"Not at all." Philip yanked out a handkerchief and blew his nose as loud as he could muster. "Just a bit of dust. Nothing some tea won't cure."

Meredith glanced up from buttering her scone. "Perhaps we should eat outside, then."

"He's not sick." Theodore rolled his eyes. "He's pestering me. Just like he did when he was a child. Still acting like a child. You're thirty."

He was thirty-three, but no sense in correcting that statement. Philip shrugged and thanked Mrs. Brax, who delivered his tea. She was the head housekeeper, stood no more than five feet tall, but had the strength of an ox and more knowledge than all his Cambridge professors combined. Since it was a small house, there were times that Mrs. Brax filled in where they needed it. Her presence brought Philip a sense of ease and comfort. He liked her enormously, liked all his staff members. When Mrs. Brax lowered a plate before him with one piece of toast and one boiled egg, Philip thanked her again.

Theodore set his newspaper down and glared at Philip.

"What brings you to my abode so early in the morning?" Philip asked, holding off on the rumors about the house. He had to tread carefully with Theodore.

"We sent trunks ahead, so it shouldn't come as a surprise. As a lord, I have a few things to do here in London. Duty and all that," Theodore said, biting into his toast. A bit of butter hung on the left corner of his mustache.

Seeing the dandy get messy was always worth Philip's time. His day would be made if he watched his brother leave the house with that butter still clinging to his hairy lip.

"I had thought perhaps you changed your minds. What with young Oliver almost cutting his finger off."

"He didn't cut it off, it broke," Meredith hissed through her teeth. "We had planned to visit here for a while after our stay at the seaside, but we sent the children ahead to the estate."

Theodore waved his wife's words away as he chewed loudly on his toast. "Where were you yesterday?" Theodore asked. "Felix told us you came back late."

There was no reason to bring up Alice, so Philip only told half the truth. "I was working." Theodore blinked. "At the port. There was an issue with the ships."

"I do not think, even as the youngest son of a nobleman, that spending all day at the docks is very becoming," Meredith said, glaring directly at Philip as she said it. Theodore nodded in agreement with his wife.

"Strange," Philip said. "You don't disapprove of spending the money my work brings in."

Theodore shot him a weary look before saying, "I hear you are leaving for Spain in the near future."

It surprised Philip that his brother was so well-informed. His trip to Spain was not a secret, but Theodore rarely bothered to know what Philip was up to.

His surprise must have shown on his face because Theodore said, "I know more than you think, brother."

Philip washed the toast down with a gulp of tea before speaking. "It's well-known information in London. I'm not surprised, you know. Weather holding, I will leave on Monday."

"And you'll be gone for how long?" Meredith sounded polite, but since she had never asked Philip anything about his activities, he couldn't help but be suspicious.

"I will be gone for four or five weeks," Philip said. There seemed no reason to lie about the length of time. "Why?"

"I have business here. With Lord Hastings and a fellow named Nash," Theodore finally said. "Do you know him?"

Theodore ignored his wife's warning glance, but Philip had seen it. And to him, it meant Meredith was somehow behind the issue with the house. Which made sense. As boring as she was, she wasn't stupid. For years, she insisted that Theodore should have inherited everything, claiming Philip's ownership of the London house cheated her children out of their futures. That might be a fair argument, were it not for the money Philip set up for them to inherit from both the estate and

Sutton Enterprises for when they were older. Despite he and Theodore not getting along, he wasn't heartless against his niece and nephew. He simply didn't believe it necessary for them to inherit this London house when it was his.

"I believe I've heard the name."

"He's a lawyer. Meredith and I are, uh, planning our will. Father had a good idea when he did it. And you never know, right, dear? We want our children to be well taken care of and not end up in the hands of certain people."

Philip assumed his brother was talking directly to him with the 'certain people,' but he didn't care. He certainly had no intention of volunteering to take the children should Theodore and Meredith die. Children were fine to play with like he did with Eleadora and Emily's children, but Theodore had raised two children without imagination. "Sounds like a morbid, though solid, plan. Strange though, I thought you said Father was a ninny to have made a will. You didn't seem happy about it at all. At the time."

Theodore deigned to look at Philip then. "I did think so. You're right. I still don't believe Father needed a will, since everything should have gone to me. Young Teddy, of course, will inherit all the land and the estate, but I want to make sure my daughter has her dowry set out for her."

For a moment, Philip actually liked his brother.

But then Theodore spoke again.

"What I am trying to avoid are the mishaps that Father made by writing his own will and not understanding the letter of the law."

Hoping to sound uninterested in the conversation of the will, Philip changed the subject. "I hear you have a vote coming up in the House of Lords."

Theodore grunted. He wasn't one to care much about showing up for his vote.

"Did you hear that Mr. Finley is back in London?" Meredith asked, still arranging her scones. Philip hadn't seen her take an actual bite yet.

"Lionel Finley?" Philip asked, feigning surprise. "Is he back for good or merely visiting?"

"Who is Lionel Finley?" Theodore demanded.

"He's the second son of Viscount Faldrige." Meredith closed her eyes briefly and took a slow, deep breath before going on. "Mr. Finley fled England ten years ago. There are rumors that he put a young lady in a very compromising position. Whoever the lady is, her family did well in covering it up, though the rumors have narrowed the woman down to about four possibilities. One of them being your friend's sister-in-law, the former marchioness of Candor."

"Claire?" Philip asked. Now he was surprised. "I doubt it."

A yelp, followed by the sound of silverware clattering to the floor, suddenly drew everyone's attention. Rebecca, the young maid Philip had brought into London from his travels to the north of the country, was scurrying up from the floor, red-faced and stuttering. The tray she had been carrying was on the ground, the silverware scattered. She rubbed her wrist as she finally rose and stared at the mess.

"Why are you standing there?" Theodore barked. "Pick that up!"

"Yes, my lord," Rebecca said, dashing to gather the silverware. "I'm sorry, my lord."

"Don't worry about it, Rebecca," Philip said, rising to help her.

Theodore choked on his tea. "My god, where is this girl from?"

Rebecca flushed a deeper red and impossibly tried to move quicker. Her hands visibly quivered.

"She's from the north. Near Manchester," Philip replied coldly. He signaled to Nathaniel, his footman and carriage driver who came rushing in, to help gather the silverware.

"Her accent is atrocious. Do not allow her to speak while in my presence or Meredith's. Philip, why do you hire people who can't be understood?"

Rebecca tucked her chin as she hurried from the room.

Philip glared at his brother. "That was cruel." Theodore ignored him. "You don't get to tell me who I can and cannot hire. This is my house, and I will choose my staff and where they work."

Theodore leveled his gaze at Philip, probably thinking it was intimidating.

"We have a reputation to keep. We don't run a charity here, and there's no reason to be bringing in orphans from the north."

"This is my house. I may hire whomever I wish."

Theodore sputtered before finally speaking. "You must start taking your role in society seriously, Philip."

Mrs. Brax entered, carrying a fresh teapot. "I am sorry, sir," she murmured as she filled their cups.

"No reason to be sorry, Mrs. Brax," Philip said, still glaring at his brother. "Accidents happen. And the girl is just learning her station."

"You have no conscious idea of how to manage a house." The accusation came from Meredith.

Philip's irritation rose. "There is no right or wrong way to run a house, Meredith. I am of the opinion that treating my servants as humans gives them the dignity which they deserve."

Meredith scoffed. Theodore pointed one of his sausage fingers at Philip. "You shouldn't have this house. You're going to allow them to run it into the ground."

"Who?" Philip snapped. "Do you truly believe being good-natured and treating those who work for you as humans means I do not know how to be a manager? Theodore, I have helped build a business with Lord Sutton over the past six years. I managed factories and mines and several ships. I know much more about how to—"

"You are dismissed," Theodore growled at Mrs. Brax, interrupting Philip's dialogue. Philip gripped his knees under the table to keep from yelling at his brother. Or tossing the teapot at him.

Philip pushed his chair back, towering over his brother, who pretended not to notice. "I have business to take care of before I leave for Spain."

Without looking up, Theodore nodded. "Just so you know, when you come back from Spain, we will need to have a conversation. About this house."

Philip drew himself up. "Really?"

Theodore smiled smugly at Philip. "You studied economics at Cambridge, but your field of studies explains why a certain part of the will has gone unnoticed by you. Law is different from economics. Meredith and I understand that since we are drawing up our will now. The law must be followed to the T. Do you agree, dear?"

"Yes, very much," Meredith agreed. "If it isn't followed, society falls into chaos."

"What conversation are you wishing to have about the house,

Theodore?" Philip asked, his patience wearing thinner by the second.

"The townhouse, Philip, is not bequeathed to you, but to you, your wife, and subsequent children. There is a comma between the word 'you' and the words 'your wife', which acts as the word 'and' according to the law. Which means, brother, without a wife, the house is not, in fact, yours."

Philip turned to hide his surprise and forced himself to march through the doors as though Theodore had said nothing interesting. But in fact, it could change everything.

Chapter 6

"WHAT ARE YOU GOING to do?" Cinch asked.

Philip looked up from where he was staring at the floor. The two of them were sitting near one of the fires in a quieter corner of their club. Philip had no idea how much time had lapsed since he finished his story, but his brandy was gone. And he didn't remember drinking it.

"I don't know," he said grimly. The more seconds that ticked by, the more pessimistic he grew. Theodore wasn't going to give up easily. Meredith wasn't going to let him.

"I would like to figure out what they are planning," Philip said finally.

"They are planning to take your house away from you. It isn't hard to understand. You already know that much." The voice came from the doorway, not from Cinch.

Philip swung around in his chair to find one Mr. Lionel Finley smiling gallantly at him. He would have recognized him anywhere, though a decade had passed since they'd seen each other last.

"My god, your accent is atrocious," Philip murmured. "And what kind of hairstyle is that? Do you never cut it in America?"

Finley laughed, a deep belly laugh that also sounded very American. Certainly not English. He pushed back his chin-length hair and took a seat. "Nice to see you again, Philip. How long has it been?"

"Ten years, has it not?" Philip said, leaning in to shake Lionel Finley's hand. For a second, his mood lifted. "Since the Putney Ball when you fought Cinch's brother."

Finley grinned. "Sorry, Candor. I didn't mean to seem so proud. Don't mean to speak poorly of the dead, but he deserved that punch he got."

"He got everything he deserved, unfortunately," Cinch said grimly. "He was found dead at the docks a few years back after getting himself into a fight with a man he couldn't beat. It would be easy to feel sorry for him if he had lived a better sort of life."

Something flashed in Finley's eyes, but Philip resisted the urge to call it out. Cinch settled back in his chair and resumed their previous conversation. "Let's get back to what you know about Philip's situation here. You walked in, heard barely a sentence, and yet seem to know everything about it."

"I know your brother is after your house."

"Yes, yes. Theodore suddenly wishes to be part of London," Philip said dismissively, though he tried to keep it cordial. He liked Finley, but the idea that he knew more about the situation didn't sit well with him.

"He's been working hard to be one who can buy a house in Berkeley Square, where Grosvenor is building more houses. The ability to exchange your house puts him up higher on the list of those who will be chosen." Finley paused a moment before adding, "The house to exchange more or less guarantees him a spot in Berkeley Square."

Philip huffed. "Grosvenor offered the same deal to me a year ago."

Finley leveled his gaze at him.

"You're in on the scheme, aren't you? Is that how you know?"

Finley acquiesced with a half nod. "It isn't a scheme. It's building a part of the City of Westminster as London grows. I wanted to invest, but was not allowed in. I've invested with Hastings in Bath, though."

"Getting himself a place in Berkeley Square almost assures him access to other investment possibilities," Cinch said.

The thought hadn't occurred to Philip that his brother would want to take over his financials. Not that he minded. Philip had long complained that Theodore needed to take more responsibility for the estate and his own money. But he hadn't thought his brother would stoop so low as to take the house their father gave Philip.

"Cinch is getting to the heart of the matter. Your brother wants to invest with Mr. Colin Maxwell in a scheme in India. With silk, to be exact. Since the good investments through the tea have already been taken. I haven't been able to figure out what the project is because everyone in it is awfully tight-lipped to men like me."

"Men like you?" Philip repeated. "You mean those with atrocious accents?"

Finley flashed a grin at him before going on. "Outsiders is what I mean. These men are like a secret society. They don't want new money involved. Theodore wants in because a chap named Rosslyn has been grooming him to get in on many such schemes. Maxwell needs to fund this, and Rosslyn seems to be his man that goes about finding such funds. There are rumors Maxwell is mixing his business and this scheme with politics and favors."

Trying to think, Philip rubbed his temples. Men mixing politics and favors wasn't anything new, but this sounded a lot like a plan in which Theodore would walk away poorer than before, not richer.

"At any rate, since coming in on the Berkeley Square deal, Theodore has been around several places lately. Just the other night, he was playing cards with Mr. Maxwell—"

Philip groaned. "How much does he owe?"

"Nothing," Finley said simply. "He won. At least he was up when I left."

Philip gaped at Finley. First, because Theodore never won. And second, because nothing made sense.

"Well, then, fine. He can pay for his own investment without needing my house."

"Which is what he is doing," Finley said. "Did I not mention that part?"

Philip stretched his fingers and tried to understand where Finley was going. He didn't have to wait long.

"The other day, I was invited to a meeting in which a membership to a new club was proposed to me. A gentleman's club called Spector's. It won't be attached to political affiliation but will be exclusive. One must own property in London, in the center, and a select few neighborhoods."

Finley paused, and Philip had to admit the man had him on the edge of his seat.

"Don't you get it, Daucer? Your brother was at that same meeting. Because he is in the center of London society, or at least moving at a rapid clip towards it. He can't lose this house deal, or he will quickly be cut out."

Philip jolted forward. "It's Meredith. She's the one who wants to be on the inside of London society."

"Possibly," Finley said.

Philip eyed Finley, trying to remember the wording of the will. "For my youngest son, his wife, children, and subsequent children."

"What did he say?" Finley asked.

Cinch shrugged. "I think he's finally gone mad."

Fear pierced Philip right through his heart. "He means to take it away from me because I'm not married.

Finley nodded. "Bingo."

"Bingo?" Philip repeated. "This is a serious matter. One that might require me to chain myself to the opposite sex and you say 'bingo'? What is that word?"

Finley continued as though Philip had said nothing. "Do you know a man named Nash?"

"Only that my brother is meeting with him," Philip said. "And I have Wilcox investigating him."

"He's a solicitor. Lord Hastings's solicitor. And he's the kind of man who figures things out for the benefit of the men paying him."

"I believe that is what a good solicitor does, Finley," Philip said. Finley ignored his tone.

"Since the use of a will is still fairly new in London, I'm quite sure Nash thinks he can get the decision to be repealed. And without much fuss. The language in the will is open to interpretation, especially by someone who could claim to have known your father better than you. And if that person is also a judge who your brother could find a way to maneuver onto the case, I'm betting the whole thing could go in his favor within a few months' time."

The entire world deflated around Philip. The only thing in his favor was Theodore's laziness, and with the season coming up, he'd probably get distracted with a new wardrobe, which bought Philip time. Hopefully enough to figure out a solution.

It all felt unjust.

Cinch eyed him, then broke into a grin.

"What?" Philip couldn't help the biting tone in his words. He didn't see anything funny about this situation.

"There's only one option then," Cinch said, still grinning. "To get married."

Finley and Cinch both chuckled as Philip feigned holding back the contents of his stomach.

"I really wish you wouldn't find this so amusing," Philip said. "I don't find it amusing at all."

"Listen, Philip," Cinch said, "there's nothing fair about it. But if this is the one thing that gets you thinking about taking a wife, then I'm all for it. I believe it will be good for you."

Philip scanned the wood-paneled room, his vision wobbling from the amount of alcohol he'd consumed. This room was empty save the three of them, but Philip could see into two other rooms papered in red and ivory. Men sat in semi-circles of high-backed chairs with clouds of cigar smoke billowing over them. He squinted when he spied Viscount Hathaway sitting in one such chair.

"Marriage," Philip repeated. "Is that really what I'm going to do? Get married to keep my house?"

"You should be thinking of marriage anyway," Cinch said. "You're thirty-three. You can't be a bachelor your entire life."

"I could," protested Philip, but even he wasn't completely convinced. He wasn't fiercely opposed to marriage. He just wanted a good marriage. One like Cinch had. "Well, if you think I should get married, perhaps I will go speak with Lord Hathaway there. He's the one with the handful of daughters, isn't he?"

Finley's laughter faded. "You're not going anywhere right now, Daucer," he said, clutching Philip's arm and pushing him back into the chair.

"Why not? Might as well get it over with. That man has so many daughters, he'll be glad to get rid of one of them."

"You can't just demand to marry a man's daughter. You'll make a poor impression on him," Cinch said. "And besides, just a few months ago you told me Hathaway's daughters talked too much and know nothing about anything."

Philip opened his mouth to reply and found his tongue was suddenly double its size. He needed another drink to bring it back to right.

"I think you've had enough," Cinch said, motioning to the footman. "I should get you home. You leave for Spain in two days."

Philip's body swayed with drink and fatigue. "I'll go home because I want to go home. But know this: if I'm not going to marry for love, I might as well go against all my principles and marry as our ancestors once did. Strictly business. From now on, I will be on the lookout for such a woman."

"Such a woman?" Finley repeated, amused.

Philip waved his hands, his body following. He rubbed his temples as though to rub away the effects of his imbibing. "A woman such as one willing to understand business."

"God help that woman, Philip," Cinch said.

Chapter 7

THE SUN BROKE THROUGH the clouds, warmth pouring over Carmen as she slid on her gloves. Partly down the front path, she turned to admire her home. Her maternal grandfather, who loved French architecture, had designed the majestic two-story building. The dry Castilian vineyards in the background finished the picturesque setting, though arid Toro looked nothing like green France.

Don Suárez had built it following his father-in-law's plans when he married, though it took years to finish. Some in the village whispered about it being too opulent, but Carmen adored it. True, it reflected her father's considerable wealth compared to the village farmers, but she admired how he had returned to his childhood home, built up the land, and gave work to others. Most didn't know it, but when the King gave out land to the officers that helped them win the war against Napoleon, her father chose Morales de Toro. He could have chosen any place, but he wanted to help his childhood home.

"Where are you going?" Rosa, her cousin, asked, huddled against the doorway unprepared for the cool spring day. Rosa was ten years older than Carmen and Isabel and had never married. She had lived with them since her mother died years before. "Isabel will be here for lunch this afternoon."

"Vale, Rosa. I'm going out to find my father. Toward the bodega." The center of Morales was nestled under two large hills lined with vineyards two kilometers from the manor. The bodegas were on the other side of town, tucked inside the cool dirt of the hills.

Rosa heaved a sigh. She might be a poor relative, but Rosa was like Carmen and Isabel—bullheaded, with no problem showing when she was annoyed.

"Do you need anything in town?" Carmen asked, trying to calm her. She slipped on her rose-tinted glasses before tying her hat down low on her eyes.

"Will you even arrive in town?" Rosa asked.

Carmen laughed. Walking was her objective, not entering the tiny town of Morales de Toro, and Rosa knew it. Carmen loved ambling amongst the vineyards, even if they were still dormant.

"Perhaps not. But if I arrive, would you like me to get you anything?"

Rosa shook her head. "You will be back by two? You know how your sister will have my head if I don't have you pretty and perfect before lunch."

Carmen waved her hand, but Rosa glared at her until she acquiesced. "*Vale, vale.* I'll be here. I'll be sure to bring Papá back as well. You do know that Isabel is not my mother? You know that, yes?"

"Isabel is with child and much more anxious than you. You should be here when she arrives." Rosa spoke as though the last authority on the subject. Carmen laughed.

"You're no fun to tease today, Rosa," Carmen called over her shoulder as she continued towards town.

"Be back before three," Rosa called back, but Carmen didn't answer. Rosa liked having the final word.

Bare grapevines wove their way around the wooden fences that bordered the path to her childhood home. Planting them was, as the stories went, the first thing that her mother did when Don Suárez was gifted the land in Morales de Toro.

Señora Suárez, born the second daughter to the fourth Marquess of Liolá, spoke three languages, having spent much of her childhood at schools in Belgium and Switzerland. When Carmen was young, the family spent most of their year in Madrid, where her mother hosted the nobility and royalty of Spain. Back then, they only visited Morales de Toro, where Don Suárez was from, during the summer. He would return for the spring planting and pruning, a month ahead of Carmen, Isabel and their mother.

When Carmen was fifteen, they left Madrid for the country house with Señora Suárez complaining of her throat. By the time they arrived, Carmen's mother was feverish. By midmorning the next day, she barely moved or spoke. Less than a day later, she died.

Don Suárez buried his wife in the small chapel cemetery of Morales de Toro. And everything changed.

Within weeks of burying their mother, Don Suárez sent Carmen and Isabel to Valladolid to live with their aunt so he could mourn without them. When Carmen was nineteen and Isabel almost seventeen, their aunt escorted them on a year-long tour of France and Germany before returning to Valladolid when they were old enough to come out in society. It was in Valladolid that Isabel met Jaime, and Carmen noticed her vision declining into something more than simply needing glasses.

That first year the black cloud started invading the edges of her vision, Carmen saw four doctors. None of them had any good advice. One wanted to bleed her, which Tía Merce refused to allow, and the other three suggested staying out of the sun. It was one afternoon of chance that Carmen quite literally ran into Doctor Miguel Perez while walking through the old university.

He was standing in front of the Palacio de Santa Cruz, admiring the architecture while Carmen was focused on the ground. The two collided hard enough for Miguel to drop all his books. Carmen stooped down to get them, too embarrassed to stop herself from apologizing repeatedly. Miguel was kind enough to guide her to a bench nearby until she accepted that he was fine. They spoke for an hour about him studying medicine at the university and her helping with her sister's wedding preparations. When he noticed how much she touched her eyes, a bad habit she had back then, he asked to look at them.

"It's nothing," Carmen had told him. "I keep thinking I can rub it away, but I know I can't."

"May I?" Before waiting for her answer, Miguel tilted her chin towards him, murmuring to himself in words Carmen didn't understand. She was too busy trying to calm her heart, which had sped up at Miguel's gentle touch.

With her chin in his hands, Carmen scrutinized Miguel's face as he studied her eyes. His, a deep golden-brown, held a warmth she hadn't observed in other doctors. His hair, as with many Spaniards, was dark brown with a wave that accentuated his youth. The skin around his eyes and mouth was smooth, unlike most men in Morales who spent their days under the sun. He reminded her more of the men she had met in Paris and Berlin.

"I would like to see you in the clinic," he finally said, breaking Carmen's investigation of his facial features. His fingers dropped from her chin, and Carmen instantly missed the warmth.

"Clinic? At the university? I don't know." Going alone to visit him, though he was a doctor in training, didn't seem appropriate. Especially when he was so handsome.

"Alright, then, what if I come by and treat you at your house?"

Carmen calculated the risk before nodding. Tía Merce wouldn't mind. She was almost sure of it.

They parted, Miguel with the address in hand, and within a few months, they were courting. Their courting had been a gradual, inevitable occurrence. As though it were meant to happen.

Carmen blinked hard, shaking away the memories. Perhaps more than that, it was a courtship that hadn't considered several factors. Like how Miguel actually felt about her. In hindsight, Miguel had always been more attracted to his job than to her. She'd just been too blind to see it.

Carmen laughed dryly. What a joke. Her, a half-blind girl, with a heart too blind to see that the man she wanted to marry didn't love her.

She tried to focus her eyes and thoughts on the distant rolling lands of her home. To the left were fields of grains, and to the right, vineyards. There were few trees in this area of Castilla Y Leon, which made the summers perfect for grapes and difficult for humans. Still, she had grown fond of her land and welcomed the new laws permitting her to inherit it. If she was married.

Carmen kicked at a stone in the way of her path, breathing away her frustration. While she was glad the laws in Spain had changed a little, meaning they now allowed the firstborn daughter to inherit land and property as well, it didn't go far enough. The daughter had to be married after all, which directly affected her. It should have been changed to state that a daughter could inherit everything. But of course, that might ignite the rage of some man or another.

It wasn't just the engagement Miguel had broken. He had put her future in danger. A bruised ego and heart could mend, but if she didn't marry, she would become a burden to her father, especially if she lost more of her sight. And when he died, her entire life would depend on a cousin who cared nothing about the vineyards, or the wine she and her father were making, or her, for that matter.

"*Buenas tardes, Señorita.*" Señor Lopez grinned at her as he arranged his boxes of fruit for the evening customers. Carmen had taken a short path that brought her to the last few streets of the town.

"*Buenas tardes.*" She plucked two oranges from his first box, handing him the coins before placing them into her bag. "Have you seen my father?"

Señor Lopez gestured towards the stable where a young boy, Pablo, was leading a horse named Angel. "He's just over there, waiting for Pablo to get the horses ready."

"Horses? Is someone with him?" Carmen could distinguish between Pablo and the horse, but she couldn't find another person, blurry or not. A shadow falling on her left side made her jump back.

"Good morning, hija," Don Suárez said. "The other horse is for you. I thought you might come."

Don Suárez hadn't let her ride during the last three years due to her failing eyesight, too afraid she'd fall off and die. Isabel had stirred up his fear, and Carmen had been powerless to stop it. Once the idea was in her father's head, it stuck.

"Where are we riding to?" Carmen asked, eagerly stepping on the wooden box Pablo set out for her.

"The bodega, of course," Don Suárez said. "We need wine for lunch."

Carmen grasped the reins and hoisted herself onto Angel, needing only a small push up from Pablo. She carefully moved her right leg over until she was straddling the horse, then rearranged her skirts as best she could. Riding like a man was the only way she felt safe since she couldn't see the world at the top, bottom, and sides of her vision.

"*Gracias*, Pablo." Carmen extended a coin and the other orange. Then she clicked Angel into motion.

"Feeling okay?" Don Suárez called out. Carmen turned her head to find her father next to her.

"*Muy bien.*" She felt free, in fact.

All around them, the air was sweet and rich. There was the smell of dirt along with orange blossoms and linden trees, which all mingled with the savory aromas of roasting pork and garlic. Since the time of her ancestors, the Rio Pisuegra that flowed nearby gave the Castilian soil the perfect nutrients for growing wine. A wine so deep and rich that the Romans used to send ships to Spain to procure it.

Making wine was the oldest noble job. But it wasn't until after her mother passed away that Don Suárez threw himself into learning about vineyards and creating his own wine. While Carmen and Isabel were touring Europe, he would send them questions to ask the wine makers in Italy and France. Carmen liked learning from the people who knew the land as though it were their lover. Once she moved back with her father after Isabel was married and living in Toro with Jaime, she helped her father curate new wines. She had worked with the grapes for four years while waiting for Miguel to finish his schooling.

"Hyah," Don Carlos commanded, and his horse, Luna, trotted off faster towards the vineyards. Angel didn't wait for her command. He followed Luna into the rows of vines and up towards the village bodegas on the outskirts of town.

Three to four times a week, Carmen and Don Suárez walked up and down the vines to check for mites and fungus and learn how to create a better wine. They had made an excellent young wine just before her father was called up to serve as president of the province. Over the past two years, Carmen had experimented with different grape blends, searching for a magical combination to market. That was why her father was in such a good mood. Today was the day they would taste their wine.

A shiver ran down her spine as Angel slowed to a walk. They halted at a small, squat building nestled up against a hill. Inside, a door led to a dark, cool room in the earth where they stored their wine.

Don Carlos swung himself down easily, then came to her side to help her. "Come, hija."

Carmen slipped off as Marcelo, one of the Baldoa brothers, took the reins.

"*Buenas tardes*," she said to him.

Marcelo tipped his head downward. He had always been shy.

"Come out of the sun before you burn your nose," her father called from the entrance. Carmen scoffed, but hurried behind him.

Don Carlos lit a lamp before they descended into the earth. The smells of moss, mud, and fermenting wine wrapped her in comforting memories of mixing wines and attending annual parties in the village, of harvesting and choosing wines for a special occasion. "Here we are."

Carmen knew her father was holding a wineglass out for her, but when she groped for it, she only caught air. "Bring the light closer to the glass. I can't see it, Papá."

The light swung around until it reflected brightly off the glass, centimeters away from her fingers. Carmen curled them around its bulb. Don Suárez said nothing, merely shifting the lamp toward her chair and waiting for her to sit before speaking again.

"To my daughter," he told her. "This is our first experiment from five years ago. Do you remember it?"

"I remember," Carmen said, as they placed their noses into the glass and inhaled. A burst of blackcurrant and cinnamon and oak filled her nostrils. Then they sipped. Carmen allowed the wine to sit on her tongue. The tannins tingled the edges, and the taste of blackberry caressed her taste buds.

She sighed. They had created a delicious, full-bodied wine.

"It's beautiful. Full, smoky, and earthy, with a hint of black fruits. It's a beautiful wine, Papá. This is perfect for tonight."

Don Carlos grunted. His face and dark beard were illuminated, yet she couldn't make out his features to decipher his thoughts. "This was supposed to be your wedding wine."

Carmen swallowed, hoping to stay positive amid her father's sadness. They hadn't spoken about it since Miguel broke things off a month before.

Don Suárez's jacket sleeves rustled against the rough table surface as he leaned in towards her. "I would like you to marry, Carmen. You can only inherit the vineyard if you are married."

"Perhaps I still will, Papá," she said, though there certainly weren't any men lining up for her hand.

"Carmen," he said quietly. It was his way of leading up to a difficult conversation.

She could hardly imagine him as the military lieutenant he had been. He had never been harsh with her or Isabel and had never really disciplined them.

"I feel perhaps I have failed you when it comes to finding you a partner."

"Papá, you have not been lacking."

"To my credit," he continued. "Miguel Perez is a good man, and I had no reason to fight against your choosing him, though I was concerned he might take you away from the land you love."

Carmen bit her lip. More than staying with the land, she wished to be married. It wasn't that she wanted to leave Morales, but her father was only getting older, and she would eventually become a burden. Though Miguel didn't believe she would go blind, he couldn't predict how bad her vision would get. And besides, she wanted a husband and children. She had always envisioned herself having those things.

As though reading her mind, her father went on.

"I see, though, that my feelings are a bit selfish. I cannot keep you here. You must marry, and that most certainly will take you away from me and our home. Unless you are to marry one of the local men."

Carmen glanced up in alarm. Most local men were either already married or ancient. She relaxed when her father laughed.

"I am not serious about that, Carmen. But I am serious about you finding a compatible partner. With your permission, I would like to look for one."

Carmen sipped her wine as her father waited for her response. "I would like to marry, Papá."

"I will not marry you off to someone who isn't good for you. You will always make the deciding choice."

Carmen nodded, slightly relieved. She trusted her father in everything. And though she wasn't sure he would be able to find her a good match, her willingness to let him try would bring him some satisfaction.

"I will not get upset if you look for a match for me, Papá. Is that what you wish to hear?" she asked, reaching out for his hand. He caught hers and squeezed it.

"Very much." The air shifted as he straightened in his chair and released her grip. "But let's focus on the wine. Do you taste that lingering flavor? What did we do differently?"

"The oak barrels, remember? You had heard others speaking of it. We put the wine into the used barrels from France. It was a very smart decision." Carmen sipped the wine again, allowing it to sit on her tongue a bit longer. The oak mixed with hints of blackberry and olive perfectly, making a full-flavored wine. "Can we use the barrels twice, do you think?"

Don Suárez pulled the wine through his teeth, savoring the flavor. "I don't know. We could try it with a barrel or two. This wine, what a wonder. Now to find connections to export it to America and the Caribbean and England as well."

"Don't the English drink French wine?"

"Only because they don't know that this is here." He clapped thunderously and rubbed his palms together. "Now for the one I did on my own. Remember? Grafting the vines and seeing what kind of grape would come? Now is the moment to try it."

Another bottle appeared, and more wine flowed into their glasses.

"Cheers. To the grandchildren one day."

"Salud," Carmen agreed, her face heating at the thought.

The bulb of a crystal glass pressed gently into her fingers. She clasped it and took a sip. This wine was bolder, with far more tannins. It left a slight sting around the edges of her tongue, just as the full body of the grape bloomed in the middle of it.

"Hmmm? What do you think? Needs longer, no? Maybe two or three years?"

"Yes," Carmen said, her tongue pinched and dry from the wine.

"It will be a great reserva," Don Suárez said. "I think the Americans would like this one. It's far too bold for the English."

Carmen laughed. "The English will never leave behind their Madeira wine. They are so accustomed to that sweet flavor."

Don Suárez clicked his tongue. "Never say never, my dear. For now, we should go. Your sister will be angry if we're late."

Chapter 8

Thankfully, his head was no longer swimming in alcohol on Monday morning when Philip pushed off to sea for the first time. Once on the ship, Philip was far too excited to think any more about marriage or Viscount Hathaway's daughters. His declaration that he would marry seemed a bit silly in the sunlight, though he would have to do something. Meredith and Theodore weren't going to give up out of goodwill.

The voyage was simple and smooth, with no wind or rain. Philip enjoyed his sea legs and found he loved the open sea so much he had a dream about becoming a sailor. He was too old for that at this point in his life, and in the daylight, he thanked God for that. He knew his limits. Coming up against pirates would be one of them. Still, there was a certain sense of freedom when on the water that he quite appreciated.

Upon arriving in Portugal, he spent three days in Porto handling the wine and spice business before sending the ship to the south of Spain for the remaining cargo. Then, he took a riverboat from Porto to Zamora. Sailing along the River Duero wasn't as thrilling as the open ocean, but it had its own charm. He never thought he'd be so adept on the water, avoiding seasickness, and even joining the men to hoist the sails. Out on the deck, in the cool winter air, Philip practiced his Spanish with his shipmates and concluded that he hoped his cousin Jaime spoke English as well as he wrote it.

"You are too hard on yourself, Señor," José, the riverboat captain, told him as he hauled in the mainsail. "I understand you. You understand me. Good enough."

"I hope my cousin is as kind as you, José."

"You do not know yet?" José asked.

"Not yet," Philip answered. "This is the first time our families have met in several generations."

"Señor Daucer." It was young Alberto, a boy of about twelve, who Philip suspected was the captain's illegitimate son. They were mirror images of each other. "You see that? It is La Catedral del Salvador de Zamora. You see it?"

They were coming along a bend of dry farming land, but just ahead, a church bell tower stood taller than anything else.

"That is Zamora?" Philip asked. "Not much to it, is there? It's so old."

"A Roman city. Like London," Alberto said, shaking his head. His brown curls shifted back and forth. He had no idea, clearly, how many times over London had built itself since the Romans invaded. Zamora looked like the Romans had left the day before. "You never been there?"

"Not everyone knows Spain like you, Alberto," José chided gruffly, though he couldn't hide his affection for the boy.

"I like Salamanca best. Have you been?"

"No," Philip admitted. "Is it close?"

Alberto scrunched up his face. "Maybe. I went when I was a kid."

"You're not a kid anymore?" Philip asked, keeping his face very serious for his very serious question. Alberto straightened out his spine but didn't dignify Philip with a response. Philip tousled the wind-blown brown curls and laughed. "I'll miss you, Alberto."

"Then you come back soon." Alberto climbed under the thick anchor ropes and disappeared along the deck.

Less than twenty minutes later, Philip walked down the plank, having been told not to help the sailors. They were superstitious about who touched the cargo. Anyone not a sailor could bring a curse upon the ship.

"That man over there is looking for you," Alberto said, shoving a box bigger than his own body with a grunt onto a buggy.

Philip followed Alberto's gaze to a man in a cream suit speaking with another man near the docks. Their gesturing was escalating, as well as the volume of their voices.

"Does he seem angry?"

Alberto looked again, dusting his hands off on his pants. "No, he's just talking. They are talking about wishing the war would end."

Philip flipped a coin in Alberto's direction before retrieving his jacket from a pile of wine boxes. Taking long strides, he found himself next to his third cousin just in time to hear the end of the discourse.

"Jaime?" The man in the cream suit studied him from head to toe, surprise lighting up his face.

"Ah, my fellow cousin from England. Finally here!" Jaime exclaimed in almost perfect English. He pumped Philip's hand with vigor. Philip couldn't help laughing with relief, glad he wouldn't have to struggle through his Spanish. "How were your travels? And Portugal?"

"Travels were fine, and Portugal has the most beautiful women," Philip said.

Jaime burst out laughing before translating what Philip said to the man next to him. He also laughed. "You have strange taste in women, Philip, for Spanish women are the most beautiful. I will show you. Come! Up we go to the ancient streets of Zamora. But we cannot take too long here to make it to Toro by nightfall."

"How far away is Toro?" Philip asked. The climb up the hill strained his legs more than he wished to admit.

"We will ride on horseback. Maybe a few hours?"

Philip inhaled deeply, pretending he wasn't out of breath. "And that is where you live with your wife?"

"I have my office there as well as a house. And I have a house in Morales de Toro, where we will eat tomorrow with my wife's family."

"Will it take all day to ride there tomorrow?" Philip hadn't counted on traveling that much.

Jaime regarded him in surprise, then burst again into a chuckle. "No, no. I will show you around and then we will have lunch there."

"How early do you get up here? If we are to be sightseeing before lunch, that is," Philip asked through short inhalations.

"My wife's family eats at three in the afternoon, with dinner at nine. You are in Spain now."

"Nine in the evening you have your dinner? That's time for a brandy by the fireplace in England." Philip wasn't sure how his stomach was going to adapt to the new food schedule.

Jaime flashed his teeth. "I can get you whisky in Toro, but first, beer. And then I will show you a bit of Zamora."

"We are going to Toro tonight and then Morales de Toro tomorrow?"

"Yes," Jaime said. "Morales de Toro is a small village near Toro. My wife grew up there. The former king gave my father-in-law land there for his heroics in the War of Independence. You would know the war for the help your Duke of Wellington gave us, of course."

"We call it the Peninsular War. My father was in the military during that war, though I never heard him speak of a battle," Philip said as they made their way along the Roman-laid cobblestone streets, past the small market stalls and bars near the river.

Women stood framed in doorways and salesmen of wares and things unsavory rasped out offers to everyone who passed. Much like the river stops along the Thames.

"Your father was not a war hero like Wellington?" Jaime asked. "I thought the British were known for their soldiers."

Philip couldn't help laughing. His father had been a portly man who liked to wax poetically about what he would do in situations, but never found himself in any position requiring bravery. Except the day he married Philip's mother.

Philip grimaced. That was a bit crueler than he liked to be with his mother. She had good points, too, somewhere deep inside of her. But it wasn't kind to think ill of the dead. "My father was not the hero sort. He wasn't a bad man. Just rather average, like the rest of us."

They were at the top of the hill, half a mile from the river, and the shops gleamed with respectability. Just as in London, the further from the water, the cleaner the streets, shops, and people. Zamora was a quaint town, bustling with the ordinary activities of those contributing to society.

"I hear Lord Elliot is coming to negotiate the terms of prisoners and executions. At the request of Wellington, perhaps? Maybe he can convince Carlos and Zumalacárregui to end the war once and for all."

Philip kept his gaze on the town and shrugged slightly. He should have studied up on the local political situation before coming. Not doing so seemed stupid now, but it hadn't been at the top of his task list. "I do not work with my government, so I do not know everything they are doing."

He turned to find Jaime watching him. Jaime grinned and pointed to a small pub where several men milled around, speaking loudly as they gulped down glasses of beer. "Here, we will have a beer. It's a Spanish tradition."

Jaime left Philip at a small table while he went to speak with the bartender. Philip tried to make out what they were saying but could only deduce a few words.

"Take this," Jaime said when he returned. "Beer and a tapa."

"Tapa?"

"Yes, you know. A bit of food with your drink. Our king says it helps the public not get drunk."

"You have a queen now," Philip said, eyeing the "tapa" with suspicion.

Jaime shook his head with a laugh. "No, King Alfonso X. *El Sabio*. He lived, oh, maybe six hundred years ago. He is the one who tells us to eat a little each time we drink so we don't get drunk."

Since his cousin wasn't completely crazy, Philip popped the slice of bread topped with warm cheese and a thin slice of ham. The flavors melted on his tongue.

"We do not have this food in England," he said, understanding then why Cinch had stayed so long in Spain years before when he was setting up the business. The food was reason enough to never go back to England.

"*Jamón*. The delicacy of Spain." Jaime wiggled his eyebrows. "Better than a woman, yes? Well, an English woman, at least."

Philip couldn't help being amused. "I'm not certain it's a fair comparison, but the flavor is like nothing I've ever tried. Truly amazing."

"You're happy you came now, yes?"

"I'm happy to be here," Philip said, taking another small glass of beer. "I'm glad you wrote to me."

"Yes, my father heard of you. I'm not sure how. He thinks it is time to repair the relationship within our families."

Philip frowned. There would be no effort on his family's part besides his own.

"Your family doesn't agree?"

"My family," Philip mused. "Let's see, before my mother died, she asked that I forget about the family here. She believed this idea that England's Anglican church makes them higher than the Spanish, since you are all Catholics and ruled by the pope."

"You are not ruled by the Archbishop of Canterbury?" Jaime's eyes glistened with mirth. He did not laugh, but Philip did.

"I believe you and I share the same way of thinking. Business and God are separate. As well as family. My eldest brother, Theodore, assumes the God of the Anglican church approves of everything he does. Why else would he be firstborn?" Philip rolled his eyes, grateful for another glass of beer placed into his hands. "And he doesn't give a thought to the Catholic God since he doesn't care what He thinks."

Jaime clinked his glass against Philip's. "I am a Catholic man who can agree to keep the churches out of politics and business, but I believe family is interconnected with everything we do. At any rate, since our countries are forming a political alliance, one needed by Spain since our coffers are almost empty, I believe you and I are right to create our own alliance."

"Touché," Philip cried, raising his beer. "But England doesn't form an alliance for goodwill alone. I know it's possible you, too, are happy to see me for reasons other than family ties." Jaime raised his eyes at Philip, who gazed back, undeterred. "I value forthrightness, Jaime. Above all."

Jaime slapped the table with a laugh. "I like you, Philip. Yes, let's be forthright, as you say. Cold business."

It was a matter-of-fact statement, but Philip didn't back down. Getting to know a long-lost cousin could not be Jaime's only reason for writing to him after all this time and convincing him to visit.

"I asked you to come because there are a few things that must be discussed in person. Like your railway."

The statement caught him off guard. No one knew about their railroad save Cinch, him, and the lawyer they had contracted in the north of Spain.

"How do you . . ." Philip closed his mouth. Jaime was watching him, waiting, grinning. "Why would you say that?"

"I have my sources. You lost the railway in the north."

"We didn't lose it," Philip interrupted. "The war moved there, and we decided to let it be."

"And now you are building one from Madrid to Segovia. And then, where? Burgos? Leon?"

Philip shrugged slightly, unsure how much to tell Jaime.

"You do not wish to speak about it," Jaime said. "It is alright. Here is another problem for me. No matter who wins this war, my government is out of gold. They have taken much of the land held by the church and started to sell it. But this is a very touchy subject with the people."

"In what way?"

Jaime's dark eyes searched around the bar for a moment before he called for the bill. "Come. I will explain outside."

They entered a beautiful street leading away from the Cathedral and towards the ancient city wall. Beyond the city were rolling vineyards and farmlands, not as green as the hills in England. Around him, people chatted and laughed, selling their fruits and flowers and wares to those nearby as in England, and yet somehow it was more charming. The people seemed less harassed and possibly happier, though Spain was poorer than England. They certainly had their share of poor people, many of them left to rot by the government or the high society in London. And with the wet and cold, perhaps they were worse off than the poor he was seeing in Spain.

"If Carlos wins, there will be less reform and less of Spain," Jaime said, his attention out towards the vast Castilian lands. "I am with our queen and the liberals, but I know that war can change everything. The only thing I can do is to be ready to better the lot of my family and those closest to me. I would like to help this city and the villages nearby."

"You're a politician?"

"Civil servant. I am the mayor of Toro, and I work with the region as well," Jaime said. "My father is the third son of a viscount, but you know how that is. Eventually, without the ability to pass land on to the second, third or subsequent sons, they must find their own way."

"And you found yours in joining the bourgeoisie of Spain."

"It isn't a club," Jaime said, his wide grin still holding steady. Philip couldn't imagine smiling for that long. His English blood was too strong. Though Jaime's joviality suited him. "I admit that many of us wish to fight for the freedom of the worker and to take away some of the power of the central monarch. There is a movement toward countries ruled by the people, like America. I wish for Spain to move towards that without more bloodshed."

"And you believe siding with the new queen is the right decision?"

Jaime's smile faltered. "There are times when you must ally yourself with the one who will get your ideals one step closer. What I know is that Carlos will take liberation away from the people. He wishes to live again in the medieval ages where he can be the only ruler of the country and impose upon the people his iron will. Instead of taking Spain into the future, he will take Spain into the past. And I cannot be an ally of that thinking."

Philip considered his third cousin for a moment as they entered the local stables. "Okay, I understand your reasoning and see no illogic in it. But what does any of that have to do with the land and the church?"

Jaime tossed a coin to a boy near the stables. The boy ran off, presumably to fetch their horses. Philip groaned inwardly. He would have preferred to ride in a coach to wherever Jaime lived.

"The land is cheap because the government is desperate, but few Spanish are willing to buy it." Jaime paused for dramatics. Philip couldn't help leaning in. "They are not selling government property, they are selling private Catholic Church property. If a Spanish man buys it, his neighbors lose respect for him. They consider him a traitor. A bad Catholic. A bad man. I do not like the government taking land from the church and selling it, but it is happening whether I like it or not."

"You're worried about your reputation with the townspeople," Philip said slowly. The same happened in England. He himself made calculated responses when he did business anywhere near the family estate, not wanting to ruin the family reputation, for whatever it was worth. As much as Theodore annoyed Philip, he didn't wish to cause him problems.

Philip scrutinized him, looking past the grin. This was business. "An investment together."

"A family business." Two magnificent horses, both black, approached them, with the young boy hardly visible between the two. "It is getting late. We must ride to get to Toro before nightfall. Tomorrow, I will show you some of the land before we go to my father-in-law's house. With him present, I will explain more."

Jaime lifted himself with grace onto the horse. Philip tried to do the same, but he had never been a confident rider.

"You are okay to ride?" Jaime asked.

Philip rolled his shoulders back and steered his horse towards Jaime's. "Let's ride, cousin."

Chapter 9

CARMEN FOUND HER SISTER, who usually stayed in her room until the noon hour had passed, standing in the doorway of their father's house at ten in the morning.

"Jaime is due at lunchtime, sister. Why are you standing there waiting for him?"

"It's not that," Isabel said. Closer now, Carmen could see Isabel's eyes were closed, and she was breathing in and out very slowly. "Rosa said the world will stop spinning if I stand right here under the doorway."

"Truly?" Carmen watched her sister's lips pucker as she blew air out, the corners of her eyes wrinkling for a moment before they smoothed out again. "Is it working?"

Isabel opened her left eye, then her right, before she erupted into giggles. "Do you really think standing under the doorway would help a dizzy spell pass?"

Carmen huffed her indignation.

"I will never believe you about anything from now on," Carmen said, though she was laughing.

"Oh, come now. I am never clever with jokes. It's always you teasing me. At least let me celebrate." Isabel crooked her hand through Carmen's elbow. "Were you about to go out?"

"Yes, to the vineyards."

"I thought you weren't supposed to be out with full sun. It's midmorning already."

"That's in the summer," Carmen protested even as Isabel led her towards the back parlor room.

"Okay, but come have some mantecados with me. They are one of the few things I can keep down in the morning. Then I'll let you go before lunchtime. I promise."

"You know I don't require your permission to do anything. I am older than you by two years." Carmen gave her an irritated look, but her little sister knew she wasn't serious.

They entered the parlor to find the small table in the corner had been set with lemonade and a plate of mantecados already.

"You've just been waiting for me to come downstairs?" Carmen asked.

"Yes, partially. Though if Rosa had passed by, I would have taken her company as well." Isabel chuckled as Carmen let out a heavy sigh.

"It's nice to have you back here in the house," Carmen said, regaining a serious tone. Isabel's mouth was already full of mantecado cookie, allowing Carmen more time to speak without her sister interrupting. "I've missed you. I have thought about going to live with Tía for a while and decided that once the coming spring season of work in the vineyard is done that I will."

"Live with Tía?" Isabel repeated. "I can't say I'm surprised. There will be much more to do there than here, although Papá might be upset."

Carmen gazed out the window in the direction she knew she would find her father. "I don't think he will be upset. Sad, perhaps, but not upset." Carmen paused and gathered her courage for the next thing she wished to say. There was nothing she wanted to keep from her sister, but Isabel had strong opinions and could rarely hold them back. Carmen wasn't sure she was prepared to hear them.

"Isabel, there is something I want to tell you." Carmen picked up a cookie, then paused.

"What is it?" Her eyes narrowing, Isabel nibbled a crumbly cookie.

"I have decided to allow Tía to look for a husband for me."

The cookie dropped from Isabel's hand to the plate. Isabel's mouth hung open slightly, her eyes widening in surprise. "Whatever would you do that for? You're only twenty-four years old. You will meet a man on your own."

"With the war?" Carmen challenged.

Isabel chewed the pieces of her cookie thoughtfully. "I admit the war is a problem, but most men of our station are not in battle."

"But they are in Madrid or Barcelona," Carmen pointed out.

"She will find you an old man," Isabel complained. "You are too young for an old man. You don't want to be a widow. Don't you want to have children? Papá told me he was going to search for a husband for you."

Isabel clamped her mouth shut suddenly and drew away from the table, her skirts rustling.

"Papá and I spoke about that, Isa. And last night I told him perhaps it was time to send a letter to Tía. He is in agreement with me." Isabel relaxed and reached for another cookie. "I don't wish to marry a very old man," Carmen said slowly. "And Tía knows that. But I do wish to marry and there are only so many men on the market."

"And you're sure Miguel will not change his mind?" Isabel asked.

The question was not unexpected, but it still irritated Carmen. She found it bewildering that everyone expected her to take Dr. Perez back if he changed his mind. "No, he will not change his mind."

"I'm sorry, Carmen. I just can't understand it. He seemed to look at you in that way, the way Jaime looks at me. I was so happy he was to be my brother-in-law."

"He said he couldn't have a wife who has impaired vision. That it wouldn't give his patients any confidence in his abilities."

"Oh, bother. What a silly excuse." Isabel's small hands balled into fists. "You don't stop loving a person because of that."

"No, I suppose not. But if seeing me every day will only remind him that he couldn't cure me, then I'm not sure I want to marry him either."

"He can't cure you?"

"He said he couldn't. Which is why he didn't want me as a wife."

"I have been delaying on asking this, but . . . how long until you're blind?" Isabel's voice was small, quiet.

Carmen placed a mantecado in her mouth. The sweet egg-white coating melted almost instantly, giving way to the almond cookie inside. "He doesn't believe I will become blind. Not completely. But these black circles I see will never go away. And he can't say that my sight won't get worse."

The two of them sat quietly for a moment, watching the birds battle each other for crumbs Cook had tossed out the kitchen window.

"I should go to see what Papá is working on," Carmen said, pinching her sister's cheek gently as she stood.

"Carmen," Isabel called from her chair, her eyes still on the birds. "I understand you seeking Tía's help."

Carmen exhaled with relief. "Thank you, Isa."

"But I want to say one thing." Isabel turned to Carmen then, her eyes serious, her mouth set in a firm line. "Don't accept any man who isn't worth everything you're worth."

Chapter 10

THE WIND DRIFTED IN from the south, warm and dry, and still Rosa shivered.

"Rosa, for heaven's sake. It isn't cold out here," Carmen teased as she gently tugged on a vine. She examined it for fungus or mites, but detected only a young, healthy shoot. Perhaps that was a good thing.

Carmen cut the shoot, placing it with the others. What wasn't a good thing was that focusing on a small object brought tension immediately to the muscles right above her eyes.

"How many more will you cut? Eduardo is already done. He's going inside."

Carmen didn't bother looking for Eduardo. He had been working in vineyards since he was a child while she had not. There was no comparing their abilities or speed, so Carmen kept her attention on the vines as she passed them, fingering them as though she might memorize their needs with only her touch.

"I'm shaking from hunger," Rosa said, huffing slightly at Carmen's heels. "I'm sure it's time for lunch by now."

"Cook has not yet rung the bell, Rosa," Carmen said, stooping to examine a shoot with a brown mark on it. She pinched it and found it less dense than the others. "Let's finish this row. There is only a little left."

She neatly cut the shoot and held it behind her for Rosa.

"Rosa, take these," Carmen said over her shoulder, inspecting the vine further for any more problems. When Rosa didn't take the shoots, Carmen stood. "Rosa."

"*Perdona*." Rosa, once again beside Carmen, snatched the shoots from her.

"*Pero bueno*, Rosa, what are you doing?" Carmen asked. "I thought you wanted to learn this with me."

Rosa snorted, now closer to Carmen's ear. "I'm here to make sure you don't overwork yourself. Your father is coming down the lane now."

Far away, Carmen could see the outlines of three horses. "Who is with him?"

"Jaime, I believe. And possibly our neighbor, Señor Alzate?" Rosa said, lowering her hat on one side to block the sun.

"Señor Alzate? What would he be doing here?" Carmen asked, gathering the shoots from Rosa's arms and fastening them tightly into a bundle with red yarn, the same color yarn tied to the end of the row. Then she inserted it into the basket with the rest of her bundles.

"He's probably come to inspect your work," Rosa said, sniffing her mock disapproval.

Carmen ignored her. Rosa didn't like being in the sun and always became a bit obstinate about it. If her father intended to tell her to stop working, she wanted to finish her row first. She hastened away from Rosa, snipping small shoots from each vine as quickly as she could while trying not to appear careless. In case Señor Alzate really was with her father.

A shriek from Rosa caught Carmen's attention.

"I believe the other man is the English cousin," Rosa said, breathless. She had always been a romantic soul and slightly in love with every man she saw, despite being now close to forty.

"Is he handsome?" Reaching for the last stem, Carmen strained to pull it closer to her scissors.

"Quite," Rosa said, her voice suddenly closer. "Quite handsome, actually. And he's coming this way. Oh, Carmen, he would be a perfect match for you."

Carmen straightened with a huff. Rosa giggled. "What? You said yourself you want to marry. See for yourself."

Carmen snorted. The men were only a few feet away. They stopped close enough for Carmen to see their faces. The Englishman had a nice smile but appeared as though his pale skin had never seen the sun.

"*Buenas tardes*, Carmen, Rosa. This is my English cousin, Philip Daucer," Jaime said, first in Spanish and then in English. At the translation, the man tipped his hat backwards, giving her a better view of his face.

Carmen liked the sound of his name in English. The way the letter "p" popped at the end.

"He is handsome," Carmen told Rosa in Spanish. She fiddled with the tips of her dirt-caked gloves, trying to ignore her disheveled state. "For an Englishman."

The Englishman laughed aloud, and Carmen's heart fluttered.

"*Muy amable*," he said back.

Rosa joined the laughter as the men lowered themselves from their horses. Her father planted two kisses on her cheeks, saving her from the embarrassment of everyone witnessing their flush.

"You speak Spanish?" Carmen asked, striving to regain some dignity.

"*Un poco*," he replied. "But certainly not enough."

"It will be a wonderful way for you to practice your English, Carmen, speaking with my handsome English cousin," Jaime teased, knowing full well Carmen spoke better French and Italian than English.

"Perhaps, Jaime, one day you will learn proper manners," Carmen said, her heart still beating quickly.

Jaime seemed to be biting back a grin. Her father coughed, his eyes shifting between Carmen and Jaime.

"My name is Carmen Maria Suárez," Carmen said pointedly. "Nice to meet you." With her dirty gloves now dropped into the basket on the ground, she offered her naked hand to the Englishman.

Instead of shaking it, he kissed it gently while giving her a short bow. A spark lit within her.

"She is my daughter," her father said. He had attended Cambridge for a few years as a young man and knew the language helped him rise in rank during the War of Independence to become the official translator for the Duke of Wellington. Carmen knew this about him but had never before heard him speak in English. It sounded strange to her ears.

"The pleasure is all mine," Señor Daucer replied.

Carmen dipped her chin to hide her flaming face under the brim of her hat. She was too old to blush from a man's attention. Unfortunately, when she finally raised her gaze, she found Jaime watching her with amusement.

"What do you think about my cousin, heh, Carmen?" Jaime asked. "We share a great-great-grandfather."

"Great-great-great-grandfather," Señor Daucer corrected.

Carmen could feel his eyes still on her. When she turned to give a polite smile, she found she was right.

Carmen swiveled away from the Englishman who was handsome enough to capture her attention.

"We came to meet you," Jaime said, still grinning. "And I wanted to show my cousin our beautiful land."

Carmen fell for the bait. "It is beautiful, isn't it? Have you ever seen vineyards before, Señor Daucer? I don't suppose you have them in England. It's too cold there."

"England is a great many things and one of them is most certainly cold," Señor Daucer said in English.

Carmen smiled. Being part French, their mother wanted the girls to learn French, while Don Suárez insisted they learn English. The compromise was that the girls learned both. And for that, she was quite glad. The problem lay in that she hadn't practiced her English for three years. Before she could translate Señor Daucer's words, her father was already answering.

"We are in the midst of pruning as well as testing for fungus or mites," Don Suárez was saying. "It's something that needs to be done in March."

"I know a few things about that," Señor Daucer said. "Though not about vineyards, but my family estate has fruit trees, and I used to help prune them as well. I greatly enjoyed it."

"No, no," Jaime said, his lips curled up in disgust. "I cannot believe that my cousin likes such things. Hurry, we must go in for lunch before she wins you to her side." Jaime stared straight at Carmen when he said it.

Rosa laughed at the joke, as did Don Suárez.

"To your side?" Señor Daucer asked, his brown eyes dancing as he searched Carmen's face for an explanation. Carmen almost couldn't find the words with the way he was studying her.

"Being outside with the plants and flowers," Carmen said, waving her hand. When she glimpsed it flapping in the air, she suddenly felt silly and strangely exposed. She was babbling from nerves that had no reason to be attacking her. There was no reason to bring this Englishman to "her side" as Jaime had called it.

She dropped her hand and shut her mouth, hoping no one was noticing the slight tremble of her chin.

Jaime, not realizing Carmen's distress or kindly avoiding it, gestured back to the horses. "We can talk more at lunch," he said to his cousin. To Carmen he said, "Will you be joining us, Carmen?" Carmen breathed in, dizzy with the Englishman so close to her. "I was not planning on it today," she admitted, quite disappointed in herself. An emotion she had not expected to feel that day. "I'm to take this for testing and then I will go home. I believe Isabel is expecting us tomorrow."

"I remember now," Jaime said. "Rosa, will you be riding with me or staying with Carmen?"

"Riding with you, sir," Rosa said, hitching her skirts to mount the horse. "I don't wish to hear Señor Alzate's long, drawn-out lecture about fungus and mites."

Jaime's pointed look towards Rosa went unheeded by her, but Carmen saw it.

"Do your vineyards have mites? I find them quite healthy." The English man surveyed the area, squinting for problems with the vineyards. It was then she remembered Jaime's plan to convince his cousin to buy more land or something of the sort.

"Not especially. Señor Alzate does it every year. Despite the drought, we have healthy vineyards." Jaime tipped his hat to Carmen and climbed back up on his horse. "Be sure to hurry. Father Ruiz said he was going there as well. Said something about pests in the monastery garden."

"Father Ruiz is a pest," Rosa muttered. Carmen bit back a giggle. Father Ruiz was dubbed the dullest man in the county because all he talked about were insects and flowers and the fruit of the vine.

"My eldest brother used to call me a pest all the time, and I think I'm quite a lot of fun," Señor Daucer said. "Come to think of it, I believe my other brother also called me a pest. He wasn't much fun though and ended up becoming a minister."

Rosa's furrowed brow smoothed as she burst into laughter.

"Perhaps we should invite Father Ruiz to dinner then," Carmen said.

Rosa stopped laughing. "No, no, and no."

Jaime laughed at Rosa as he joined her on his horse and swung around towards the house. "Follow me, cousin," he shouted as his horse started off at a trot.

"See you soon." Señor Daucer raised her hand to his lips one more time, leaving her heart pulsating, then mounted his horse and followed Jaime. She watched his silhouette for a long time, her hand tingling where his lips had been, watching.

"He's handsome." Her father startled her so much she dropped the basket with all the bundles inside.

"Papá," she cried out, but he only laughed.

"Be careful, hija," he said as they repacked the basket. "He is only here for a few weeks. I don't want you to get your heart broken again so soon."

"I will not." Carmen huffed, snatching the basket from the ground. Her father said nothing more, but as she climbed onto his horse, she wasn't sure she was telling the truth. There was something about the Englishman that attracted her and triggered anxiety she hadn't felt since the day she expected Dr. Perez to propose.

Chapter 11

THE NEXT DAY, PHILIP and Jaime rode out to Don Suárez's house. A square, two-story home that appeared more French than Spanish. They entered through a vine-covered archway and circled around to a side door. The garden was quiet and smelled of turned-over earth, new blossoms, and whatever the cook was fixing for midday dinner. Philip had to admit, he liked the aromas of Spain better than those of England. Especially London, with the foul Thames River.

"After you," Jaime declared, holding the door open. It entered directly into Don Suárez's study. "My father-in-law is waiting."

Don Suárez was standing in the study, staring at the map spread out on his desk. Behind the desk was a wall full of books, some large, some small, all bound in leather. Philip secretly hoped the man had not read. Philip had always wanted to be a great reader, but never made time for it himself. He, too, had a full wall of books and he loved the way they looked, but rarely felt compelled to pick one up and open it.

"*Buenos días*," Don Suárez greeted.

"Good morning," Philip said. Every day in Spain, he felt more invigorated than the day before. The people were not as reserved as the English and didn't seem intimidated by Philip's energy. Jaime and he had spent the night talking, then rode horses that morning before coming to see Don Suárez. Usually, Philip felt obligated to slow himself down. But not in Spain. And that itself was refreshing.

"We must speak about some things I have found," Jaime explained, motioning for Philip to join them at the map. "You see here, this is the route you have already planned, according to my calculations."

Philip didn't want to admit it, but his cousin's calculations were exact. "How did you figure that out?" he asked. Sutton Enterprises had tried to keep this project a secret and clearly failed.

Jaime's eyes twinkled with amusement and possibly pride. Well-deserved pride, Philip would admit. "Do not worry. I doubt anyone else knows. I merely looked you up when we started corresponding, and because of my position as mayor of Toro, I have connections that others do not. At any rate, it will not work."

Philip crossed his arms. "Jaime, I'm sorry, but you have it wrong. We had engineers hiking through from Madrid to Segovia, and they told us it could happen."

"Not here. Not for a long time. The war has made progress in this country very difficult."

As Philip was about to protest, Don Suárez started placing small pebbles around the map; some in large groups, some in smaller groups.

"These are the soldiers, and these are the battles so far. And that is what I know up to now. If you are found by the Carlistas, they will destroy what you have built and probably kill you and your workers."

"Maybe," Jaime added. "Maybe not."

"I can't take that risk," Philip murmured. He stared at the map as though the circumstances might change if he so willed it. "I thought you wished to go into business together, but I don't see how if we cannot build the railway."

"Too expensive." Jaime waved, clearing the idea away. Then he moved the pebbles into sporadic spots in and near Toro and Valladolid. "You have land purchased here, to the north, near Leon. This is good, but not yet useful to us. I propose we continue to buy lands there when it comes for sale, and when this war is over, we will run a railway from Gijón to Madrid."

"A very grand idea," Philip interrupted, but Jaime wasn't finished.

"In the meantime," Jaime said, pushing forward with his pebbles. "We buy this land all over here. This is where we will build a flour factory. It is close to the river and therefore easier to distribute. You take it from

Cadiz instead of stopping at Portugal."

"That's quite far," Philip protested.

"But better than going through the war in the north or buying flour from the Americas. It goes bad from there. Here you can buy it cheaper than from Germany or France and then sell it cheaper in England."

Philip grunted. Flour could be an experiment between himself and Jaime, but it wasn't within the realm of Sutton Enterprises. There wasn't enough money in it.

"And here?" he asked. "More flour?"

Jaime's grin hovered back on his lips. "Copper. Here, here, and here. I had a man I trust scout it out."

That was very interesting. With the wave of electricity taking over every major city, the need for copper was rising every day.

"And here?"

"Lead, lead, and zinc."

Philip whistled.

"And these four are wine land. And mostly for the venture between you and me as family."

Philip peered at the map. The places surrounded the area they were standing in at that very moment.

"And this over here is a lead mine, also just for you and I as family. It will give us more money than the wine at first. But we will make good wine and soon be exporting, no?" "If it's good wine, then Sutton Enterprises would be happy to work with you on moving it," Philip said cautiously, still studying the map. "What you are looking for in me is an investor, then."

"No," Don Suárez said. "We have money to put into it."

"Well, yes, we do want you to invest and be part of it," Jaime said. "But we wish for you to purchase it, with our money being two-thirds, and keep it under a name we will choose together."

Philip glanced from Jaime to the map, then back to Jaime. "Why don't you purchase it, Don Suárez? It's Spanish land. And you are not in politics like Jaime."

Jaime shook his head, speaking for Don Suárez. "My father-in-law is a local hero. He still must play by the politics and superstitions of the *pueblo.* We both must attend mass with my people every Sunday and holiday. If we buy the land, we will look like traitors. But, if my English cousin buys the land and I benefit from it by managing the mines and giving men jobs they didn't have before, then perhaps they will forgive me for being part of the land sales."

"So, you want to form an alliance and buy it through me," Philip concluded. "But won't some have a problem with me being English?"

Jaime grinned. "An Englishman buying the land is not the same."

Don Suárez agreed. "The Pope will not go to war against England. So, we buy it at a good price. And then we use that good fortune to invest in the locals. It is more than the nobles would do if they purchased it all."

"Spain is different from England. We are not revolutionizing our industry yet because of wars. We are still stuck inside ourselves. I believe, and Don Suárez agrees, that for the good of our children, we need to go beyond Spain's borders with our products."

"If all goes well, you could become a hero to your people." Philip leveled his gaze at Jaime while awaiting his reaction, which was little more than a shrug.

"I am not against being a hero. If we win the war, then I probably will be seen as one by many people. But right now, I am thinking about the future of the child Isabel is now carrying and the people in my towns who have no jobs. I have good information that Madrid will confiscate these lands and monasteries and put them up for sale. If we have the right funding, Don Suárez and I can buy this land here, this here, and over here."

"And the rest of the land?" Philip asked. "It seems as though you will need that piece in the corner as well. Or at least permission to use it. Who owns it?"

Jaime exchanged looks with his father-in-law, but neither said anything. Jaime cut a cigar, rolling it between his fingers before lighting it. He didn't offer one to Philip, since Philip had refused five times before. Used to silence from Cinch, Philip settled in and waited.

Don Suárez scrutinized him. Philip could imagine he wasn't giving off the best impression. "I own that land, Señor Daucer. I assumed you knew that."

"And this up here, near this mine? We would need land from here to here. It is easiest when you own the land that allows access to the river.

Or railway."

Jaime examined the map and consulted his notes. "That land is privately owned, but we can work something out. We could travel to Valladolid and meet with a lawyer there I trust, Marcos Peón. Perhaps tomorrow or the next day? He knows all the families and will be able to advise us on the best next steps."

"Lunch is served, sir," said a young footman from the doorway.

The clock struck three thirty, tea-time in England. Philip's stomach growled angrily. He hadn't anticipated eating habits on the Iberian Peninsula to be so different from those in England, although he vaguely recalled Cinch mentioning something about it.

Philip followed his cousin from the study, his head filled with images of the map and calculations of what the different mines could mean to Sutton Enterprises. And to himself, of course, if he wished to partner with Jaime. As he calculated his available funds, a woman descended the stairs, so close he almost knocked into her.

"Pardon me," Philip mumbled, his mind slowly registering that it was the woman from the fields, the one with the dark hair and the laugh that had echoed in his head long after it disappeared. "Well, hello."

Chapter 12

OF ALL THINGS THEY could have eaten with a guest, garlic soup was that day's choice. The clear broth soup was a staple in the Suárez house and usually welcomed by Carmen, but only because she normally drank it from a breakfast bowl.

With a guest in the house, she would have to eat it from a dinner bowl like everyone else. With a spoon. Substantially increasing the chances of spilling it. The only way to keep her favorite blue dress clean was to gaze down while eating, concentrating more on not overflowing her spoon than the conversation around her.

Which got her into a predicament when Jaime said, "Don't you think, Carmen?"

She had no idea what he had been saying.

"Sorry?" Carmen raised her head, almost dropping her spoon. She gripped it harder.

Rosa's finger pressed lightly into her elbow, indicating not to put her spoon down. It was their signal that she would splash or somehow make a mess if she moved. Though she was focused on Jaime and couldn't see Rosa's other gestures, she knew the footman would be on his way soon to take the bowl and spoon, saving her from having to deal with them herself.

And before she had finished.

"I was telling Señor Daucer that if he thinks Zamora is beautiful, he would be greatly impressed by Avila and Salamanca."

"Carmen is our scholar of ancient Roman cities in Spain," Don Suárez said. Carmen marveled at how smooth his English had become in just the past day.

"I prefer Ávila." Carmen turned her head to speak directly to Señor Daucer. His amber eyes watched her with what seemed like intense interest, and every word poised on her tongue was gone.

That had never happened to her before. It must be nerves from needing to speak English after a long while. Carmen groped for something intelligent to say. She'd again forgotten the question.

"But isn't Salamanca's university world-renowned? Like Oxford or Cambridge?" Señor Daucer asked, as though to egg her on. His question helped her remember the topic.

"Carmen places Salamanca lower on her list, not because of its history or architecture," Jaime said. "She is simply biased against the practices of the university."

"How so?" Señor Daucer asked.

"They don't allow women," Carmen said, finding her tongue. She would have liked to study history at the university. Although her father had gotten permission for her to use the library, classes remained off-limits. The university was for males only. "When they allow women to study, then Salamanca will rise on my list."

She watched him carefully. Isabel shook her head to stop Carmen from testing the man, but she couldn't help herself.

"Well, then I would have to agree with your ranking," he said, smiling directly at her.

Carmen relaxed, pleased the Englishman was modern in his ideals.

"You believe women should be allowed in the universities?" Isabel asked.

"Why is that?" Jaime asked as the footmen served the roasted lamb chops.

"I know several women who are much more intelligent than I," Señor Daucer said, leaning in towards Carmen, "and Cambridge allowed me in. I don't feel it's just. If women want to study, they should study."

That deserved a toast. She raised her glass. "To one day allowing women in universities."

Señor Daucer responded with a tip of his glass back to her. Carmen would have to thank her sister for seating him directly in front of her for dinner. It was nice to be able to see his handsome face fully. She sipped her wine again and smiled. It was one of their best combinations.

"Well, Señor Daucer, you are quite the important guest here tonight," Carmen said.

"Why is that?" he asked, his eyes once again capturing hers.

Carmen tore her gaze away to salute her father. "Because my father has brought out one of his prized wines for you. One of our first combinations."

"Your combination? Do you mean to say that you've worked to create these wines?"

The question, the way he asked it, caused Carmen to pause. "Does your admiration of the female sex stop at university? Can we not also add to agriculture?"

Jaime shifted and coughed a warning, but Carmen wasn't going to back down. She waited, also ignoring Isabel's head shaking, which had started again.

"Not at all," Señor Daucer said, sipping his wine with relish. "I'm quite pleased to have met the Spanish Madame Clicquot. This wine is excellent." As though to prove his point, Señor Daucer took a long drink, watching her as he did.

Carmen couldn't stop the influx of pride that filled her at his statement.

When Isabel laughed, Philip looked between them with surprise. "Did I say something wrong?"

"No," Isabel said, reaching around Rosa to squeeze Carmen's hand. "It is only that I compare her to Madame Clicquot as well."

"And that the comparison is far from accurate," Carmen said. It was her usual protest. "La Grande Dame made her husband's business into a flourishing, world-known enterprise. Papa and I are at the beginning stages, trying to find the perfect combination that suits the grapes and the land we have. It isn't champagne—"

"But it's excellent," Señor Daucer interrupted. "And the food, Don Suárez, is also extraordinary. Even better than the fish I ate in Portugal."

Señor Daucer held her gaze until Carmen ripped hers away. Already she knew Isabel would pester her about how much time she spent ogling the English cousin.

"Of course it is," Don Suárez said. "Everything is better in Spain. If we are finished, we can move into the salon. We can teach our guest Ombre or Manilla. Those are Spanish card games."

"It's too hot for cards. Perhaps Rosa can play for us while Isabel sings," Jaime suggested.

"I'd be glad to," Rosa said as they stood. "Isabel sings like an angel."

Carmen paused, waiting for Rosa so they could walk together. When they had guests, she preferred to walk with someone to avoid mishaps, but Rosa took Don Suárez's arm. Carmen shuffled toward the end of the table, trailing her fingertips along the edge so she wouldn't have to look down. She arrived in time to watch Isabel take Jaime's arm.

"May I escort you?"

Señor Daucer was close, the vibrations of his voice traveling into her chest. The sensation was unlike anything she had felt before.

"Carmen?" He was extending his hand.

"Yes." Carmen feigned a cough. "Thank you." Señor Daucer tucked her gloved hand into the crook of his elbow and patted it.

He smelled of the outdoors, cloves, and orange, Carmen noted. And his arm was stronger than her father's. Something about his presence made her heart skip.

Miguel once had a similar effect, though not this intense.

Carmen kept her focus on the path to the salon. When Señor Daucer slowed before they reached the salon, Carmen turned to find why.

"This is quite a nice painting," he said, pointing to one she had done years before of Tía Merce's house.

"Thank you. I painted that," she said. "I painted that one as well."

"You have a nice touch." Señor Daucer sounded genuinely impressed, which caused an unusual flutter of pride in Carmen's chest. "Would you paint me?"

"I, well, I'm not very good at painting people," she said slowly.

Señor Daucer started walking again, but before they reached the salon, he leaned in closer and said, "I would be honored if you would try."

His words thrilled her. She hadn't painted in a few months, having grown frustrated with it.

"I would like to try. Perhaps in the afternoon. The light would be perfect then."

When they entered the salon, Señor Daucer lifted two glasses from the tray. Carmen used the opportunity to watch him.

"To you and your painting of me." If he were Jaime, Carmen would have teased him for that remark. Instead, she sipped her dessert wine. "What is this? It's quite good."

"Hierbas," Carmen said. "My father makes it himself. A recipe he keeps secret."

"Perhaps one day I'll share it," Don Suárez said with a chuckle.

"Do you sing, Señor Daucer?" Isabel called as she adjusted herself at the pianoforte.

"No, I'm afraid not," he said, chuckling. "I'm always asked to not sing when I attend dinners at home."

"It can't be that bad," Carmen said, pleased, strangely, at his sense of humor. She hadn't thought an Englishman would have one.

"It is," Señor Daucer insisted. "It doesn't help that my best friend married a woman who sings like an angel, so she is the one I'm compared to. Do you sing, Señorita Carmen?"

"Not very well," Carmen said. "And my playing is mediocre. But Jaime also sings beautifully."

"I'm flattered, sister," Jaime said, grinning as Rosa touched the piano forte's keys and Isabel started singing a lullaby. All Isabel thought of lately was the coming baby.

Carmen maneuvered her way to the small sofa, which she usually occupied in the evenings. It had a lamp that allowed her to see more and was next to her father's favorite chair. When Isabel finished, and they showered her with praise, Don Suárez motioned to Señor Daucer who was still standing near the doorway.

"Come, Señor Daucer," Don Suárez said as he sat as well. "Join us here near the window. The evening air aids one's digestion."

Carmen hoped her cheeks didn't show how hot they felt.

"May I sit here?" Señor Daucer murmured as Jaime and Isabel started a duet.

"Certainly." Carmen sipped her hierbas quickly to hide the way her voice was failing her with him nearby. "Why are you not called 'Lord

Daucer'?" she finally asked.

"Simple," Señor Daucer said, spreading his free hand. "I am not a lord. I'm the third brother. Once the brother inherits the title, the younger brothers, since my father was but a viscount, lose their 'lord' title. Not so for the sons of Dukes and such, but that doesn't matter. My father has passed, and my eldest brother is now the viscount, so I am simply Mr. Philip Daucer."

Carmen felt silly for the obvious answer to her question. She grappled for another topic to broach.

"Jaime said that your partner, Lord Candor, and you are interested in extending your business into wine. Is that right?" Carmen asked.

Señor Daucer seemed surprised at her question. Or perhaps at her knowing it, she wasn't sure. "Yes, we are looking into it. We have some business already in Spain and wish to expand further. Jaime and I were speaking today about what we could do to benefit each other in business."

"What is the business you have in Spain?" she asked.

Señor Daucer leaned towards her, only slightly. Not enough for anyone else to notice, but it made breathing difficult for Carmen.

"Last year, we started developing a bridge to the east with the idea of building a railway from Valencia to Madrid. Of course, with the war in that area, the project is on hold. To keep our investors happy, though, we can't just do nothing. They would think the whole thing has failed." He chuckled at his private joke. Carmen didn't understand it, but joined him in smiling. "Anyway, we have decided to buy the land your government is selling near Segovia and Vañadolie."

Carmen glanced at her father. He didn't seem to have understood Señor Daucer either. "Where?" she asked.

Her father suddenly burst into laughter. "Do you mean to say the city name of 'Valladolid'?"

Isabel stopped looking for music and laughed. Jaime, who had been whispering things that made Isabel blush, also joined the conversation.

"Repeat this," Jaime said. "Va-lla-do-lid."

Señor Daucer tried again. And again, it sounded like another language completely.

"I don't know how you are going to buy land there if you can't pronounce the name," Carmen said, her heart fluttering when Señor Daucer grinned.

"Perhaps you can give me more lessons," he said, his eyes searching hers.

"You will hear it quite a lot if you are coming with us next weekend to the ball," Isabel announced from the piano.

Carmen had forgotten all about the Benavente Ball. "That's right. Jaime, are you bringing Señor Daucer to the ball?"

"A ball," Señor Daucer repeated, his face alight. "I do enjoy a good ball. And to see a Spanish one would be quite entertaining."

Jaime stared morosely at his cousin, causing Isabel to laugh. "As you can see, my husband was greatly hoping you would not be up for it."

"We have business in Valladolid," Jaime said, looking like a child who had lost his favorite toy.

"Anyone you need to speak with will be at the ball," Isabel said, smoothing the music sheets she had chosen. "And you promised me we would go."

"The Benavente Ball is quite beautiful," Carmen told Señor Daucer, hoping to catch him up on the event. "My parents used to go. It's held in an ancient palace."

"One of the most beautiful in Castilla Y Leon," Isabel added.

"A statement I agree with," Carmen said.

"It's settled then," Philip said. "Jaime, you must take me to this ball. I'm willing to wager that the Spanish balls are much more diverting than the English ones. We have rather a lot of rules and such. I'm very eager to participate and compare notes."

Carmen beamed, the idea of spending more time with the English cousin giving her a sense of peace. Or perhaps it was the slow tinkling of the piano keys as Isabel played. "I'm pleased to hear you are laying railway through Valladolid. It's one of my favorite places. Though it is not as beautiful as Ávila or Salamanca, it was once where the Spanish court was held."

"Three hundred years ago, hija," Don Suárez said, shaking his head. "My daughter loves Valladolid, though I feel it has more to do with her favorite aunt living there than anything else."

"Perhaps," Carmen answered. "Valladolid could be more if given the chance. A chance Señor Daucer will be giving it."

"I'm pleased you approve of my plan, Señorita Carmen. But do call me Philip. I find the customary 'señor' to not fit me." He flashed a conspiratorial grin and Carmen couldn't help laughing.

"Alright, if you insist. And you will call me Carmen."

Isabel finished the song and promptly stood, interrupting Carmen and Philip's conversation. "I must excuse myself and retire. I'm quite tired."

Carmen stood to join her sister, but Jaime went instead. Much to Carmen's disappointment, Philip also excused himself, saying he had work to sort out back at the hotel. Within just five minutes, the only people left in the room were her, Rosa, and her father. Carmen settled back onto the couch, already imagining herself dancing with Mr. Philip Daucer, wondering how well he might lead.

Rosa gave a quiet snore from her corner in the salon, awakening Carmen out of her daydreams. Why did this man occupy her thoughts? She told herself it was because they received little entertainment, but the thought wouldn't stick. It was more than that.

Something about this man drew her to him.

Chapter 13

WHILE SITTING ON A cold stone wall, the uneven edges wedging themselves into places that no man should have anything wedged, Philip struggled to remember how he had agreed to this. He had suggested he sit in a chair. Carmen had insisted on the wall for the lighting.

He squinted as the sun shifted into his eyes. A soft sigh sounded from behind the canvas.

"Do be still," Carmen said, poking her head out from behind the large canvas on her black easel, the words slurring past the paintbrush she held between her teeth. Two rogue curls bounced in the wind, framing her face that was creased in concentration. The very image of her made him want to laugh aloud, or dance, or pull her to him.

He chastised himself inwardly. He should not be thinking about dancing or pulling his host's daughter towards him. Everything about it was inappropriate.

Philip squirmed again. She was so attractive that he almost swore aloud. Instead, he swallowed hard against the carnal thoughts plaguing his mind.

"You're worse than a child," Carmen teased. "I am almost done, I promise."

"My leg has fallen asleep, Señorita," he called back. "And I will need it for my trip."

"You are going by river," Carmen retorted, blowing the stray strands out of her face. It did little other than give her a few seconds of relief before the strands fell again. "So, you will not need the use of your legs. Only your mind and your pocketbook if you are going with my brother-in-law."

Philip laughed. "Are you referring to the suit he persuaded me to buy?"

He stretched his legs out and admired the local tailor's work. The fit was like the suits in England, but had a Spanish flair he couldn't quite put his finger on.

"Sit still!" Carmen said, attempting to sound serious. Her smile rendered her stern tone fruitless.

She would be an exemplary mother someday.

Philip hopped off the wall, the thought scaring him into activity. Observations about a woman's possible future mothering abilities were not usually in his repertoire.

"Mr. Philip Daucer, if you keep moving, I will not be able to finish this before you leave. I, at least, need the outline. I can fill in the rest later."

But Philip's body could not get back on the wall. Instead of sitting back down, he plucked a flower and strode towards her.

"I don't need a flower." Carmen sighed in exasperation.

A voice in Philip's head asked him what he thought he was doing, but he ignored it. They had spent the last few afternoons innocently flirting with each other, and if he stopped now, she could find it strange. Perhaps read more into him stopping than him continuing.

"Every woman needs a flower," he said firmly. "You, especially. Just wait."

He took the loose curls from her face, twining them around the flower stem before loosely weaving it into the back of her hair. Goosebumps rose on her skin as his fingers brushed against her. Carmen's quick intake of breath was also not lost on him.

But she was not a woman he could fool around with. She was a lady. And he was a guest.

He stepped back and cleared his throat. "There. Now, you can at least see what you are painting. I would not want my portrait ruined because of hair that would not obey."

Carmen touched the flower lightly as he retook his seat. "Thank you.

That was—kind."

Philip ignored the comment, pretending he was too busy arranging himself in the same position she had put him in an hour beforehand. He fought to concentrate on the plans he and Jaime had brainstormed, the vendor he still had to seek out, his upcoming trip to Burgos, or the trip to Valladolid afterwards. Anything but the woman standing in front of him. Her presence had floated in and out of his mind all day—a phenomenon he explained by the small size of Morales de Toro, leaving few other women to divert his attention. Plus, so far on his journey, he had spent most of his time amongst men—other vineyard owners, granite and coal miners, and even some factory owners, all of them seeking an investment.

Carmen was the only female company of an age and status he could flirt with. It was harmless. Or should have been.

Except that she had invaded his dream the night before.

"There you are." Jaime was rounding the corner, his navy-blue coat slung over his shoulders, his wide grin already active. "Where is Isabel?"

"She's resting," Carmen answered, accepting Jaime's kisses on both her cheeks without looking away from her canvas.

"She's making you more handsome than reality," Jaime remarked.

Philip grinned back, glad for the distraction. "You mean more handsome than I already am?"

Jaime clicked his tongue in disagreement. "I asked for some wine to be opened. I know you English have a teatime, but it's too hot for tea, don't you agree?"

"The weather is perfect. I'm relishing a bit of warmth. It's probably raining in England," Philip told him, but he wasn't going to refuse the wine. It would calm his nerves.

"How a country with such terrible weather could become so powerful, I will never know," Jaime said. "Carmen, would you like some?"

"Do you really think you need to ask?" she teased.

Carmen wiped her hands and her brushes before picking up the canvas and walking alongside the footman, who was just a step behind her. At the last instant, Carmen turned, spinning the canvas around, her body colliding with the footman and sending the tray of wine backwards before tumbling to the ground.

Philip reacted without thinking, dragging Carmen towards him and away from any glass that might fly into her. Unfortunately, that meant the two of them falling backwards into the bushes he was stationed against.

Only Jaime was able to keep his dignity, though the footman had enough grace and balance to stay on his feet as well. Both he and Jaime looked over the small wall into the bushes where Philip and Carmen were at a disadvantage against gravity.

Her whole body lay against his, but at first, he could only focus on the heat of her breath coming quickly against his neck.

"Are you hurt?" he murmured. Her hair threatened to choke him if he opened his mouth too wide.

"I don't think so," she said.

The caress of her lips against his neck threatened to overwhelm him. If he could choose, he might stay where they were. Perhaps tease her with a kiss. But Jaime's laughter from above reminded him that she was not a woman he could play with; she was his soon-to-be business partner's sister-in-law. "Jaime, help us up, would you? Ow!"

Struggling to push herself up, Carmen had placed her full weight onto her elbow, which just so happened to be on his chest.

"I'm so sorry," she said, sounding frantic. "I can't seem to find a way to get up."

Suddenly, the weight was off him, and only Philip was left on the ground.

"*Díos mío,*" Isabel exclaimed as she hurried over to the wall. "What happened?"

"A bit of a tumble," Jaime said. "Why don't you help Carmen get cleaned up, and we'll meet you over at the veranda for some wine?"

Philip watched Isabel whisk her sister away, the two of them speaking and fretting in Spanish much too fast for his understanding. He brushed what dirt he could off his jacket and trousers before starting on his hair.

"You have a small tear on your sleeve," Jaime said. "But do not worry. There is a woman in town who can fix it. I'll have it ready for you before you leave tomorrow."

"Thank you," Philip said, forcing himself to stop gazing after

Carmen's retreating figure. "Pardon, but are you not coming tomorrow as well? To make the introductions?"

Jaime looked where the women had disappeared, then indicated a small trail through the garden. "Let's walk. I wish to speak with you about something. Isabel's sister. She's pretty, no?"

Philip tried to control his grin. "Yes, she's pretty."

"She is not married or attached, you know?"

Philip sipped his glass of wine, an uneasy tick starting in his right eye. "What is it that you're saying, Jaime?" he asked.

"Listen. If you were to become my brother-in-law, there are many business ventures where we could partner together. But if you are not my brother-in-law, it will be rather hard. Too hard. There are things you do for family that you don't do for friends." Jaime spread his hands as though to show how hard it might be. Philip couldn't relate. He would do many more things for Cinch than he would for Theodore.

"You are marrying your wife's sister off to me?"

Jaime narrowed his eyes at the accusation, but only briefly. "I have spoken to Don Suárez about it, and he agrees. We like you. We think you are a good man. If you marry Carmen, then you are family. Business together, as a family, is stronger."

The words made Philip's blood freeze momentarily. Until he recalled Carmen's laugh. And how he didn't want to get up when she had fallen on him just a few minutes before. "How does Carmen feel about this?"

Jaime gave a little shrug. "Carmen has to marry someone, and she seems to like you. You also have to marry someone, and I have seen you looking at her. You like her. It is like God is willing it."

Philip wasn't sure if God cared about things like who was marrying whom. He pondered the idea of marriage again. The result was not the usual lightning bolt of fear. He considered it further, surprised he could see himself and Carmen in London, laughing and dancing. He pondered his problems with his house, his need to marry, and how he had considered wedding the next young woman he found appealing upon returning home.

Then he thought of Carmen. Her humor. Her beauty. How she spoke her mind.

"I should think she wouldn't want to marry an Englishman," Philip said slowly. "She'd have to move."

"You are thinking of marrying her then, eh?" Jaime asked.

Though he hadn't envisioned marriage with Carmen—his thoughts had been more carnal—Philip realized defending himself was futile. The longer he contemplated it, the more intriguing the idea became.

"It is alright, my friend. You can tell me the truth."

Philip drank his wine. "She is an attractive woman, Jaime, there is no doubt. But I have to leave for England in two weeks and I doubt your sister-in-law would be up for marrying an Englishman she just met."

"You leave that to me. You say the word that we become family, and I will make it happen." Jaime snapped his fingers in the air, the pop cracking through the background noise. "You give me your word, then I'll go back to Carmen, tell her the plan, talk to my father-in-law, and then you get married. Everyone is happy."

Philip eyed Jaime's hand. There was no need to feel obligated to marry a woman in Spain at the behest of his cousin. Yet a strange pressure to say yes engulfed him.

"I might be looking to marry," he admitted. A cold wave of nerves rolled over him as he said the words. Marriage. It was so final. If it weren't for the situation with his house, he wasn't sure he ever would have married. Now there was a pressure on him to do so more than a desire.

Jaime hissed his triumph.

Ignoring him, Philip continued, "And I find Carmen quite charming, but I do not wish to marry a woman without her being part of the decision." The very idea of negotiating behind Carmen's back made him ill. He doubted she was the type of woman to like it, either.

"Carmen told Isabel that she sent a letter to their aunt asking her to look for a husband for Carmen. You will see Mercedes, Carmen's aunt, at the ball. Wonderful woman, though a little crazy. She believes a woman should marry a man closer to his deathbed, but also one who is rich. Better to be a rich widow, she says."

The words hit Philip with sickly force. "Marrying me would be much preferable, I'm sure." He didn't like to imagine a man with spotted hands touching Carmen. A man who would see her more like a trophy than the funny, intelligent woman she was.

"Yes, I'm sure she would agree. You see, it is not just that it is most women's greatest aim to marry, but here in Spain the eldest daughter can inherit land upon her father's death, but only if she is married." Jaime picked up a glass paperweight and twirled it absentmindedly. The light caught the glitter inside it, casting bubbles of light and shadow over the room.

After a moment of silence, Jaime leveled his gaze at Philip. "So, you see? You will be marrying for the same reason. She to keep her land and vineyards when her father passes. And that way, too, the land we all buy together will stay between us and not go to the cousin who lives in Valencia. And you will keep your house. In London, isn't it?"

"Yes," Philip said slowly. "But I leave tomorrow for Leon and then I will go to Valladolid." Philip tried to calculate the days he had left in Spain. It didn't seem plausible to add in a marriage.

Jaime watched him, saying nothing.

Philip couldn't help continuing to consider what his cousin was proposing. If he were going to get married, Carmen wouldn't be a bad choice. Better than most of the eligible women he knew of in England.

"Perhaps while I'm gone..." His voice trailed off. Philip cleared his throat. "Well, perhaps you can find out if she is amenable to the contract."

"No need to be so cold," Jaime said, pouring more wine into their glasses. "I have seen how you look at her and it is not in a cold way." His mustache wiggled when he chuckled.

Philip hesitated, before saying, "I will seriously consider it."

Jaime laughed out loud, interrupting him. "Ah, yes. Yes! Wonderful. To marriage and family!"

"If you believe she is willing to say yes," Philip concluded.

Jaime clinked his glass hard against Philip's, sending a small vibration of anxiety, or perhaps excitement, through him.

Chapter 14

"Señor Daucer, are you listening?" Marcos Peón, the lawyer Jaime suggested, sounded irritated. They were standing in Señor Peón's office, where the sun was beating down on them. It was a cramped room on the second floor next to rooms where a crying baby wouldn't let up. The office reminded Philip of the one Cinch had for Sutton Enterprises before his brother died and left Cinch to inherit everything.

Philip was finding it difficult to pay attention. Not just because of the heat, but because he kept thinking about Carmen and the proposal Jaime had put forth before sending him off to Valladolid.

"I'm listening," Philip said tiredly. "You're saying that you haven't got the land we need."

Marcos shook his head, his black curls bouncing. "Perhaps not. No local wants to be the owner of land the church is forced to sell. We must just speak with the Fernandez family, who I have heard will be quite willing to give you the land bridge to the river."

"Then what is the problem?"

"This town here," Marcos said, pointing to the map. "They have started to complain that the train will ruin their town."

Philip massaged his forehead. Dealing with locals was the same in England as it was in Spain. "It's on the outside of their town. And it runs through the land we own, not anyone's farmland. Isn't that correct?"

"Yes. They're afraid it will ruin their crops."

"Proximity can't be helped," Philip said. "In no country can it be helped. Perhaps we just need to speak with them about how quickly they will be able to move their crops, which means more money for them."

Marcos stared hard at the map. He stood just shorter than Philip. The premature gray sprinkled through his black-as-night hair gave him an elegance that would have had the ladies in London swooning. Theodore would have been running about town to grey his hair were he ever to meet Marcos. And for the first time, Philip wouldn't have blamed his brother.

"No, the proximity cannot change, but we must convince them to our side. We do not need anyone to sabotage the railway."

"Sabotage?" Philip was now paying attention. "Will it come to that?"

"Passions are running high, Señor Daucer. The war, the past famine, everything is causing men to react in ways they wouldn't normally. And you are not Spanish, so it would be easy to create rumors about how these railways will not benefit this country."

"But they will benefit Spain."

Marcos let out a sharp breath. "It doesn't matter if the rumor says contrary and it's spoken by neighbors."

Philip had to acquiesce. Propaganda worked the same everywhere. "We cannot have sabotage as a worry. What do you suggest?"

"There's a monastery for sale here," Marcos said. "I believe part of the problem is that they believe you will buy it and turn it into the railroad."

"But we have no intention of buying it," Philip protested, but Marcos put a hand up to cut him short.

"But what if you were to buy it?"

"You're asking me to become the enemy of the Catholic Church in Spain?" Phillips asked. The last thing he wanted was for the church to be against him.

Marco met Philip's gaze. "What if you buy the monastery and allow the monks to continue living there? Then we can work out a contract wherein you rent part of the monastery to store the wine until it is ready to be shipped."

Philip couldn't believe that Marcos was both handsome and, quite possibly, brilliant. "Marcos, I think you might have just solved the entire mystery."

Marcos rolled the map back up. The midafternoon sun and the relentless workload were wearing Philip down.

"Do the monks know how to monitor the wine so that it doesn't spoil while being held there?"

Marcos tilted his head at Philip. "Your cousin's father-in-law. Don't you know he knows about wine?"

Don Suárez. Carmen. "Yes, of course," Philip said. Everything in his world seemed to come back to Carmen.

"Your cousin sent me a letter recommending a man. Perhaps it would be prudent to hire him? Perhaps the engineer will also be more apt to working with a man he believes is connected with you."

Philip sighed. "Fine."

Marcos grinned. "Good. Let's go."

"We're starting now?" Philip asked, barely able to grab his coat before Marcos strode out the door.

The next day, they spent their time negotiating the deal to buy the monastery. Since Jaime had most of his cash going to land already, it would be up to Philip to foot most of the bill. Usually, he would be an active part of the negotiation, but he found himself useless. Instead of arguing a deal, he was reflecting on Carmen, pondering the pros and cons of marrying her. Wondering if she would have him. Wondering if marrying her would save his house.

Even when they were doing the very thing Philip enjoyed the most, scouting out spots to build the train station, he was only marginally paying attention. Luckily, Marcos didn't seem to mind walking in silence.

"This building really is perfectly situated," Marcos said, suddenly halting. He stood admiring an abandoned building on the outskirts of the center of Valladolid. "We would only have to move slightly towards this way. But, of course, it would require buying this land and that area over there. But this would be the perfect place for the station."

Philip hummed his agreement. An abandoned building across the street caught his attention.

The sun glared off the broken windows at the back. Philip squinted. He could envision a six- or seven-story hotel with couples laughing on the balconies and coachmen helping people in through the large, arched doors. The lobby would have red, plush carpet and the dining room would boast the best chef in the area.

Without prompting, he pictured Carmen there, on his arm, smiling up at him. A dull ache pulsed in his chest.

He wanted to see her. He wanted to walk with her. They barely knew each other, and yet he thought of her more often than he had ever thought of another woman. The realization sent both unease and exhilaration flooding over his body.

"Everything alright?" Marcos asked.

"Fine," Philip said, clearing the emotion that had suddenly coated his throat. "What do you think?"

Marcos shrugged. "As I said, it is perfect for the train depot. You just need to buy that land I pointed out."

"No, what do you think about the building across the street?" Philip asked, pointing through the windows.

"For the train depot? It's so big. Maybe it would be good for a factory or something."

Philip thumped Marcos on the shoulders. "Or perhaps a hotel."

"It is too far from the main part of the city to be a hotel."

"Then we build more of the city near it."

Marcos gave him a look that said Philip was an arrogant Englishman who believed he could change a foreign city with the snap of his fingers. Which was true, of course. So Philip didn't bother to defend himself.

"I want to buy it, Marcos. Figure out who we need to talk to."

"And is this Sutton Enterprises who is buying?"

"No. Just me."

For a second, Marcos looked ready to protest, but in the next moment, he closed his mouth and nodded.

"Who is this running up here?"

A small boy dashed through the open doors of the building, his pants grimy and torn, his feet bare. He held out a letter, leaving small, black finger marks on the cream paper. The boy and Marcos exchanged a quick-fire conversation before the boy turned to Philip with his hands cupped.

"A missive for you," said Marcos.

"For me?"

The boy beamed as he extended the folded paper, smudged with his small fingerprints. When the boy bowed, Philip tossed him a coin that made his eyes widen in pleasure.

"Gracias, Señor!" the boy yelled before sprinting off again.

"You paid him too much," Marcos said, shaking his head. "This is not London."

"Little man deserves his payment. I couldn't run that much," Philip said, chuckling. They left the building, stepping out onto the sunny street, where Philip opened the missive.

I'm in Valladolid. Come to La Caracole with Marcos for us to sign the remaining papers. -Jaime

"Bad news?" Marcos asked.

"It seems my cousin is here and has papers for us to sign," he said, waving towards the map. "We are to meet him at La Caracole."

"Perfect," Marcos said, gathering the papers and the map. "I'm in need of a beer."

⁂

The Caracole was a small bar, but popular at midday. Groups of men milled around the bar and its tables, shouting, eating and drinking, when Philip and Marcos joined Jaime. After ordering a round of beer, the three of them settled at a table tall enough to accommodate them. There were no chairs or stools at any of the tables.

"This idea of standing to consume a beverage instead of sitting must be found only in Spain," Philip mused.

"It is so we don't settle for too long at the bar and then have very angry wives," Jaime said before laughing.

When the beers had come and another round ordered, Philip took out the map and smoothed it over the table as best he could. "This is the last piece we need, Jaime. Do you think you can manage to find the people needed for us to make the purchase?"

"Of course," Jaime said with a wide grin. "Señor Fernandez will be at the ball tomorrow. I will convince him then."

"The Benavente Ball?" Marcos asked. "You are taking Señor Daucer?"

"Yes," Jaime said.

"Do you know how to dance at a Spanish ball?" Marcos asked Philip. Philip looked to Jaime for help.

"Don't worry. I will teach him."

Marcos picked up his beer, shaking his head. "If you say so."

"Nothing is too difficult for Jaime," Philip said. "And besides, I'm an excellent dancer."

Jaime raised his eyebrows, ready to pounce on Philip's statement, but Philip changed the subject. "Do you know the building that is here?" Philip pointed to the map.

"No, should I?" Jaime asked.

"It's across the street from our future train station. I want to make that spot into a central shopping market. Indoors. I think you and I should partner up for it."

"Why do you want a place like that here in Spain when you live in England?" Jaime's dark eyes searched for the answer in Philip's face.

"This country has a lot of potential," Philip admitted. "I want to be a small part of the way it grows. If the war would stop, more foreigners would invest."

"I don't want foreigners to invest here more than Spaniards. I don't want Spain to change to the likings of the Englishman, but to stay for the Spanish man," Jaime said.

"You don't want to be part of my venture, then?"

Jaime shifted his gaze, looking suddenly uneasy. "That isn't what I said. I trust you."

"I, too, am uneasy about the foreign investment here. I can think of a few Englishmen who would buy the land just to let it rest fallow. After all, their loyalty lies with England's advancements, not Spain's."

"But you are not like them." It was a statement, but Philip still had something to prove to his cousin.

"I am not," he said. "I believe economic and political improvement in Spain will only help England. I want this area to thrive and prosper. This place has captured me."

Jaime's eye sparkled. "Perhaps it is a certain woman that has captivated you?"

Philip eyed Marcos, who seemed more interested in the conversation at the next table over than the one between Philip and Jaime.

"Well?" Jaime pressured.

A thrill pulsed through Philip as he realized he was about to throw all his chips on the table. "Have you spoken with her?"

"I have spoken with Don Suárez." Jaime sipped his beer, his face neutral. "He believes you might be a good match for his daughter."

"And Carmen?" Philip asked. The pulse of nervousness surprised him. He hadn't considered her not wanting him until that moment. Jaime broke into a grin.

"Don Suárez says you must be the one to speak with Carmen," Jaime said. "But my wife thinks Carmen likes you."

Philip breathed out, though relief flooded his veins. "Let's get back to business. I will speak with Carmen at the ball."

"Before we do, there is something I need to tell you."

Those words sent a flutter of anxiety through Philip. "What is it?"

"Carmen was almost engaged before."

The statement fell between them like a brick. Philip waited for more information, but Jaime offered none.

"But she isn't engaged now, correct?" he asked.

Jaime sipped his beer before shaking his head slowly. "No. The man never proposed. He broke things off because Carmen has weak eyes."

"Weak eyes? Is that why she uses those glasses outside?" Philip's mind raced. The very idea that a man would reject Carmen for such an idiotic thing made him fume, much to his surprise. "The man must not have cared that much for her."

Jaime finally looked him in the eyes and said, "The man was an eye doctor. And Carmen has something that affects her ability to see things in the peripheral. She can see, of course. You know that. But my wife is concerned about her being hurt again and thought it better that I tell you before you spoke with Carmen about marriage. In case you..."

Philip clenched his fists as Jaime's voice trailed off. "I'll admit a marriage between Carmen and me would not be built on what we might call love, but I have a great deal of respect for her. Enough that something like that wouldn't deter me from thinking she would make a good wife."

The relief on Jaime's face was evident. He sighed and clapped Philip hard on the back before calling for another round of beer.

"A round for everyone," Jaime shouted. "To celebrate this man

becoming my brother-in-law."
The bar burst into cheers.

Chapter 15

EVERY WINDOW IN THE old Castillo de Benavente held a large candle that flickered in the night breeze, creating the illusion that the castle was dancing against the darkening sky. Carmen couldn't see the castle and the color of the sky at the same time, but she could envision it together, the purple and pink streaked sky against the illuminated, ancient stones. She had visited Benavente one other time in her life, as a young girl of thirteen, back before the black ring infringed on her vision. She had spent the week pretending to be Queen Isabel of Castilla. An old suit of armor tucked in a corner represented her bright prince from the moment she encountered it. She remembered crying the day they left and hiding her tears from her mother.

They had gone there for a party, just like this one, though she had been too young to attend the festivities.

"I'm so excited I can hardly breathe," Isabel exclaimed as she rushed up to Carmen.

"Calm down before you faint," Carmen chided, though she also spoke in almost a whisper.

"Neither one of you is to faint," Don Suárez said sternly.

Though Carmen couldn't make out his facial features, she knew he was glaring at them sternly, recalling the times she and Isabel had fainted from over-tight corsets when they were younger.

"Where is Señor Daucer?" Carmen asked.

"He is in Leon," Jaime said.

Carmen blinked. Jaime said nothing more.

"Well, let's not wait then." Carmen sniffed, hoping to mask her disappointment from her family.

"Buenas noches." The deep, thickly accented voice could be no one but him.

Carmen whirled and found Philip only inches from her, his heat and bergamot scent filling her senses at once. Shivers crept down her spine.

"Buenas noches," she said, trying her best to sound cool and distant while breathing through the warmth spreading to her limbs. She shot a glare at Jaime, who was chuckling at his own joke.

"Good evening, Señor Daucer," Tía Merce said loudly, forcing Carmen to break away from her staring.

Philip snapped his heels together and kissed her hand. "You must be Carmen's aunt. I can tell where she gets her beauty from."

Tía Merce giggled behind her painted fan. She did look beautiful in her yellow dress with pink flowers in her silver hair.

"You are a charmer," Tía Merce murmured. "And for that, you can call me Merce, as my nieces do. And you will escort me inside. Lend me your arm. Carmen, take your father's arm. On we go."

Tía Merce, a woman who always got her way, snatched Philip's arm and left Carmen staring at them.

"Everything alright, Carmen?" her father asked, offering his arm.

"Yes," Carmen said. "It's all so beautiful. I was remembering Mamá and our time here at the castle."

Her father patted her hand with a sigh as her voice trailed off. "Life has unexpected trials, hija." The corners of his eyes pinched together as he smiled at her. "She would be very proud of you, I think."

"Thank you, Papá," she said. "I still miss her in times like these."

"She would want you to be happy," her father said as they continued towards the palace. "I also wish to see you happy. Jaime spoke to me about Señor Daucer. He believes he is looking at you as a prospective wife."

"Señor Daucer?" Carmen looked ahead, where Philip and her aunt were walking arm-in-arm. A tremor ran through her body at the sight of him.

"Isabel said she thought you found him quite amusing." Don Suárez paused before gesturing towards the entrance. "And I believe he will have your aunt won over by the end of this evening."

"Is he planning to stay longer in Spain then?"

Her father stopped walking and said quietly, "No."

They said nothing as the meaning sunk in. Carmen's mind raced with the implications, the changes, and what it meant for the future. Her father, her sister, her unborn niece or nephew. She sought out an answer in her father's face, but couldn't make out his expression in the evening light.

"Carmen," her father said, clasping both her hands in his. "It is your decision. Always. But I will say one thing. You were willing to place your future in my hands and in those of your aunt. There was never any guarantee that the man we would find for you would reside close by. Philip Daucer is a good man, I believe. And . . ." His voice cracked with emotion, bringing tears to Carmen's eyes. "I don't want to influence you. I don't wish to lose you, but more than that, I don't wish for you to lose the prospect of a good future."

He patted her hand that held his arm slowly, causing a rush of melancholy and fear to flood her. He had always been her anchor, even when she was traveling through Europe with her aunt and sister. She always knew she would return home to him.

They kept walking in silence. People shouted greetings to each other from across the way, breaking the spell between them, but not the questions that lingered in Carmen's mind. Don Suárez did his best to speak to everyone, but when the crowd surged forward, he restrained Carmen.

"Hija, listen to me," he said. "You must live your life for yourself, not for me. I believe that most people are made for companionship, not to be alone. But the decision is up to you. I want to give you the world, but I cannot live your life for you." He cupped her face and patted her cheek.

Carmen kissed his cheek, his beard tickling her lips and chin. "Thank you, Papá."

Together, they joined the rest of the family waiting at the front entrance. The light near the castle illuminated the guests' faces, allowing Carmen to distinguish Jaime by his posture and Philip from the way he threw back his head and laughed.

Carmen couldn't help smiling each time she saw the Englishman. His black suit, crisp, white shirt, and white cravat made him stand out. Not just as an Englishman, but as exotic and powerful. His hair was combed back, accentuating his strong facial features. Other women in the crowd paused to look at him. It was evident he was handsome, but Carmen's favorite feature of Philip's was his smile. It was so genuine it lit up his face.

Carmen's insides were a ball of nerves. Was he really considering a marriage proposal? Her heart leapt at the thought. She tried to calm herself, but found it difficult.

Philip grinned at everyone as the other guests passed, openly staring at him with slightly amused expressions. "Why is everyone looking at me?"

"You stick out like a sore English thumb," Jaime said, chuckling.

"You look very handsome," Isabel told him, swatting her husband with her fan. Jaime grumbled, but gave Philip a wink.

"Am I an embarrassment?" Philip asked Carmen, his mouth so close to her ear the rumbling made her shiver.

"No," she said quickly, moving slightly away from him. The one time she attended a dinner party with Miguel, he stayed with the men all evening. Not once did he get as close to her as Philip was now. She was unsure what to do with her hands and at a loss for words.

"This place is magnificent, don't you agree?" Philip asked, his long legs closing the distance in just two strides. Carmen cleared her throat and bumped into him when she turned. The black ring around her vision had blocked his presence to her right.

"Are you all right?" Philip asked, steadying her as another guest pushed past them.

"I'm fine," she answered, though she could hear her breathlessness. She wondered if Jaime had told him about her vision. "It's all just so beautiful, isn't it?"

He smiled and nodded. But then he continued to gaze at her, his smile fading into something more intense.

"You are more beautiful," he said, so quietly she wasn't sure he had spoken at all. She only knew he did because of the rumble that thundered through her like an avalanche.

Carmen gulped, trembling. "And you are very handsome tonight."

Philip caressed her cheek with his fingers. Ever so slightly. Only for a moment.

"You are the loveliest woman here," he said. When they elicited looks from a couple passing by, Philip cleared his throat and looped his free arm through hers. Carmen pretended her blood wasn't still running hot through her veins.

Philip led her towards the rest of their party. "This is going to be so much better than working in Burgos."

Tía laughed. "Do you enjoy dancing, Señor Daucer?"

"Please, call me Philip," Philip said. "And I very much enjoy it. In England, you're only allowed to dance so much. I usually leave a ball wanting to do more. Most of my friends dread balls, but I rather look forward to them." He turned his eyes on her. Carmen felt cold, then hot. Her hands tingled. "Do you like dancing, Carmen?"

Carmen hadn't expected Philip to say he liked it. No other man she knew liked dancing at balls.

"I do, though I don't dance as well as Isabel," she told him.

"No worries, my dear. You'll just follow me. I won't lead you wrong," Philip said.

"Except in the Jota," Jaime called from in front of them with a laugh.

Philip grimaced. "What is the Jota?"

"A dance," Carmen said with a laugh. "It isn't difficult."

"I hadn't thought the dances would be so different." Philip looked out at the crowd, a wrinkle of worry along his brow.

"You'll be fine, my dear," Tía Merce said.

"Always the optimist," Jaime said.

They entered through the giant doors that once were for keeping out an invading army from the north, but were now flung wide open for the guests. Hundreds of candles filled the hallway with light.

The ballroom was larger and more spectacular than Carmen remembered. The ceiling rose fifteen meters up, allowing for a balcony around the room on the second floor. Already, guests milled above the dance floor, talking and drinking sparkling wine. At each corner along the west end of the inner balcony were open doorways that led to an outdoor veranda, if she remembered correctly. But the most spectacular part of the ballroom was the ceiling. Before she could say anything about it, Philip tugged on her arm.

"Look at the ceiling, Carmen. Have you ever seen anything so magnificent?" Philip was unabashedly enthralled, craning his neck to inspect every nook and corner of the ancient castle.

She watched him in wonder. How the muscles in his neck moved, how his eyes glistened with curiosity. She remembered the first time she had seen the ceiling. She had lain down on the floor and gazed at it for what seemed like hours until her nanny found her and shooed her out into the garden.

The ceiling of Benavente Castle rose above the crowd in three levels until it peaked high above them, as though it had been used to create a mold of a pyramid. Tiny red and blue tiles, arranged in patterns echoing the Arab influence on Spain, adorned the first two levels. The last layer, closest to heaven, was created with stained glass windows. During the daytime, colored light poured in, dancing on the wood floors.

"Isn't it the most beautiful thing you've ever seen?" she asked Philip.

When he lowered his head, their eyes met. Carmen realized she was gripping his sleeve to keep from falling and dropped her hand quickly. His eyes followed her hand, then returned to her eyes.

"What is it?"

Philip cleared his throat as they continued ambling through the ballroom. "I guess I expected you to scold me. I've always loved buildings, but my mother hated it whenever I would inspect places. She stopped bringing me when I was young to others' houses because I would get lost for hours just looking at the details. I believe she thought I was being purposefully annoying, but I'm genuinely interested in buildings and architecture. But I'm so used to those around me being, well, embarrassed by my interest. Everyone except you."

His last three words, spoken softly, sent a shiver down her spine despite the stifling heat of the ballroom.

"Come." Carmen entwined her fingers with his and paused again. She had never been this conscious of a man's touch. Of his heat. Of his smell. She reminded herself of her breeding. She was a Suárez and needed to act as such. "We always meet the rest of my family at the refreshment table."

They strolled towards the refreshments, Carmen acutely aware of

Isabel's scrutiny. And Tía Merce's. Her cheeks burned, but she didn't release Philip's fingers. Everything was very confusing, more so than with Miguel. With Philip, though he could hold his own, she wanted to make sure he was comfortable in her country. Especially if they were to marry.

She wanted him to love Spain as much as she did.

"What do you think?" Jaime clapped Philip on the back, and they all took some champagne off the tray of a passing footman.

"More beautiful than my house," Philip said.

"You have a castle?" Tía Merce asked. The woman was incorrigible.

Philip laughed. "Hardly. But my family has an estate in the west of England, which is where I grew up."

"Like me," Carmen said, clinking her glass lightly against his. "In the west of the country."

"Yes, but England in the west is damp. Not quite the beautiful weather you have."

"But damp means it's green, doesn't it? Plus, you haven't been here for summer yet," Carmen told him. The sparkling wine was refreshing and sweet on her tongue. She drank it faster than was lady-like to cool her body. "You wouldn't think Morales de Toro is so nice in the summer. There are days you can do nothing but stay still and hope it will cool when the sun sets."

"Careful, Carmen. You haven't eaten much today," Isabel warned. Carmen ignored her.

"You need a tapa with your drink. Like your king says," Philip said with a grin.

"Or to dance," said Jaime as the orchestra started the first song.

"Yes, dance," Isabel agreed, snatching the glass from Carmen's fingers.

"All right." Philip said, holding out his arm as though asking Isabel.

A sudden, strange surge of jealousy fluttered within Carmen before she found his hand in front of her.

"Will you dance with me?" Philip asked. Without waiting for her answer, he grabbed her hand and led her out to the dance floor. But then his confidence waned.

"I don't know this rhythm," he admitted with a note of worry.

"It's pasodoble," Carmen said. "You'll pick it up."

Seeming unconvinced, Philip lined up with the other men. They bowed to the women, then stepped towards their partners. He made no attempt to hide that he was imitating the other men, who laughed and clapped, showing him where to go. The viola, guitar, and drums joined the trumpet as the women stepped forward and Carmen entered Philip's arms.

She tried not to focus on his warm hand cupping her waist or the one holding hers. She tried not to inhale the musky scent of orange that surrounded him as he led her forward and then around the room. She tried to focus on the dance, not on him, but her mind felt muddled, as if stuck in a fog. It wasn't until they had made a complete turn about the dance floor that Carmen remembered she couldn't see to the right or left of her body.

"Are you alright?" Philip asked as he danced her backwards once again. "You seem to have gone pale all of a sudden."

"I'm fine," Carmen said, allowing him to guide her. "I was just thinking that you were right. About your dancing."

Philip wiggled his eyebrows. "I told you I was the finest dancer in all of London."

"I'm not sure that is what you said," Carmen said with a laugh. Conversation was so easy with Philip.

As the music ended, the other male dancers surrounded Philip, showering him with congratulations on his dancing. He was saved from responding by the entrance of several female dancers dressed in deep red Flamenco dresses that fit slimly through their round hips before they flared out to give the dancers room to move. The men entered after the women, dressed in black suits with white lace sticking out of their cuffs.

"Are they going to dance for us?" Philip asked. "I had thought to dance with Isabel next."

"I don't know," Carmen said, feeling trapped suddenly.

Her heart quickened, despite her attempts to breathe calmly. A man appeared as though from nowhere on their left, startling her. She bumped into a woman to her right who made it no secret she wasn't pleased with the contact. Carmen froze as the woman huffed once more before stalking off for a better view of the dancers still congregating in the middle.

She dabbed at her temples with her handkerchief. "It's rather hot in here, isn't it?"

Philip gripped her arm and steered her towards the corner of the hall. "There is more room upstairs. Come."

She followed him out, grateful for the cool evening air hovering in the stone stairwell.

"Put your hands against the stone," Philip murmured, easing her palm against the wall. The heat in her body started to dispel.

Carmen closed her eyes and concentrated on her breathing, not wishing to faint. It was embarrassing enough that he had already seen her so weak. "Thank you," she said, slowly opening her eyes. "I don't know what came over me. I don't mean to be a burden. I felt so heated suddenly."

Gently, he tucked the curls at her left shoulder back into place, glanced around the empty stairwell, and blew a soft breath. Again, Carmen thought she might faint, though for a different reason. Never before had she been in so much agony. Never before had she felt so exhilarated.

"You are not a burden," Philip said, holding her gaze for a moment. Then, with one step backwards, he broke the spell. He glanced up the next flight of stairs and reached out his hand. "Come. The view is going to be better upstairs."

They made their way up the last staircase and arrived at the indoor balcony that overlooked the dance floor. She didn't notice his hand still on her waist until they were watching the dancers below.

The castañuelas clicked, the snapping punctuating the air. Philip nudged her further towards the edge of the balcony until Carmen could see the female dancer whip out a fan. Then the guitar strummed, and everyone in the hall quieted, their attention fixed on the dancers. The male dancers clicked their heels, and the women responded in kind.

Other guests pressed in closer to the balcony's edge, pushing Carmen and Philip closer to each other. Carmen heard Philip's breath hitch; his fingers gripped her tighter. Carmen turned her head, finding him only millimeters away.

"I'm terribly sorry. It's quite a crush up here. I can't seem to move." For the first time, he looked very much like an Englishman, with reddened cheeks and a slight discomfort in his expression. Another woman tried to wedge in between them, but Carmen leaned into Philip to keep her out.

As the guitar continued and the castañuelas snapped, Carmen could concentrate on nothing other than the feel of Philip's body aligned with hers, and how its warmth made her tremble. Her skin flushed at both her thoughts and the crush of the crowd. The air was stifling with so many people pressing in. She opened her mouth slightly and breathed slowly.

"Are you alright?" he murmured. His fingers brushed her cheek.

Carmen nodded. To keep her from being pushed by others trying to see the dancers, Philip encircled her waist with a reassuring arm.

The dancers below them twirled. Carmen inhaled slowly, her ribs pushing into Philip's. Then he exhaled, and she followed, her body temperature slowly falling. Below, the main dancer's fan beckoned to her partner, and he answered by spinning her until she was almost as close as Carmen was to Philip.

And suddenly, Carmen understood the dance more than she ever had before.

The dancer lifted the side of her dress; the frills cascading down like a red waterfall as the male dancers' shoes tapped faster and faster. Carmen's heart pulsed with the drum.

Then the room burst into applause. Philip's hand left her side as shouts for more dancing rose up. The dancers bowed and exited, and the crowd shifted.

Within seconds, Carmen had enough space to turn freely, with Philip now beside her instead of behind.

"That was beautiful," he exclaimed. "Nothing like what we have in England."

"I'm glad you enjoyed it. I love watching—"

"Carmen?" a familiar voice asked.

Carmen froze mid-sentence.

It was bound to happen eventually, but she wasn't prepared. Her body was still flushed from Philip's touch.

"Carmen," the voice said again. Carmen felt Philip turn and knew she must as well.

"Doc . . .Doctor Perez," she said, stuttering when she saw another woman standing close to Miguel. Carmen moved her focus until she identified Señorita Gavan, a beautiful brunette Isabel's age with one of the prettiest smiles in the county. Their mothers had once been friends, but it had been many years since Carmen had seen her. "Lucia. So nice to see you."

"It's nice to see you here, Señorita Suárez." To Lucia, Miguel added, "She is one of my patients."

"Encantado," Philip said, holding his hand out to Doctor Miguel. "I'm Philip Daucer. Jaime's cousin from England. And Carmen's fiancé."

Carmen dug her heels in to make sure no one noticed her smile wobbling. She clenched her jaw to keep her eyes from widening and kept her focus on Miguel and Lucia.

"Oh?" Lucia looked between Carmen and Philip. "We hadn't heard yet."

"Carmen." Miguel's brittle voice jolted Carmen out of her shock. "Are you well?"

"She became a bit overheated with the crowd," Philip said, drawing her closer towards him. "I was just taking her out for some air. Nice to meet you."

Within a second, Carmen could no longer see Miguel or Lucia. They were hastening at a clipped rate that left her breathless and the scenery a blur.

"Who was that?" Philip asked when they descended the stairs and sidestepped into the cool garden.

Carmen bit her cheek, then said. "That was the man I almost married last year."

<h1 style="text-align:center">Chapter 16</h1>

"THERE YOU ARE," Tía Merce said, bustling over to them as they descended the stairs. "We were looking for you. Did you see the dancers? Carmen, why are you so pale?"

Carmen opened her mouth, but no sound came out.

"We ran into someone Carmen knew," Philip said in his slow Spanish. "Miguel."

Tía Merce gaped at them both. "Are you all right?"

Carmen spoke quickly, so Philip couldn't keep up. "It was fine. I'm all right. He's here with Lucia."

"Well, come then. Let's go find the others. We can leave if you wish." Tia Merce gathered her skirts and motioned for them to follow.

"No, Tía, it's alright. I don't want to leave just yet."

Philip stepped up to her aunt. "Merce, please, may I speak with Carmen alone?"

A smile spread across Tía's face. She nodded vigorously as she waved them away. "Go on. Go out to the garden."

"Will you come with me?" This he asked of Carmen, who nodded, mesmerized by Philip's eyes as they searched hers.

Within moments, Carmen found herself through the doors and in the crisp night air, unaware of having walked there. Her entire body sizzled with uncertainty. He had introduced her as his fiancee.

"Carmen." Philip stepped closer to her, the air instantly changing between them. Inwardly, her heart started beating wildly, her breath catching. Suddenly, she didn't want him to speak. He was going to apologize; say it was a mistake. And for a reason unbeknownst to her, she knew those words would break her heart in two. It was easier to pretend nothing had happened. She could go back home and hide away, Philip could leave for England, and everything would eventually be forgotten.

"Look at me."

Carmen looked up. Anxiety pained his face so much that tears welled in her own eyes.

"I didn't mean to cause you distress just now," Philip said.

"You don't have to apologize," Carmen said, but her voice was scratchy and came out barely above a whisper.

"What I mean to say, Carmen," he said, scraping his fingers through his hair. "I meant to speak with you first, not just blurt something like that. It was incredibly obscene of me to do, acting as though you don't have a say in these things. I spoke with Jaime, and he spoke with your father. It isn't as though I haven't. I have. But this is 1836, and a woman has the right to decide if she wishes to marry a man or not. Especially if he's an Englishman and you'll have to go back to England with him."

Carmen watched Philip's lips, trying to keep up as his speech quickened. "What are you saying, Philip?"

"I'm making a mess of this, Carmen, I know. But what I'm saying, what I'm asking, is whether you would consider becoming my wife? I meant to ask you before, just now. Upstairs. I thought it might be romantic. But then that Miguel fellow appeared."

Carmen laughed. She couldn't help it. She covered her mouth with her gloved hand, but still her happiness spilled out of her. Her laughter stopped Philip. He peered at her, but soon her eyes were so full of tears that she could no longer see him.

"Carmen," he murmured. "Are you crying? Have I upset you?"

"No," she whimpered. "I'm not crying."

Philip clutched her wrists, peeling her palms away from her mouth. His eyes bore into her, and she found it impossible to look away.

"Would you consider marrying me?"

"Sí," she managed to say before his lips gently brushed hers. So softly she could have mistaken them for a flower touching her.

"That makes me happy, Carmen," Philip said. "I like you very much, and I think we can make each other, well, happy."

"I like you as well," she said, still smiling.

Looking back, although she had been courting Miguel for four years, she wasn't sure she ever fell in love with him. She did like him enormously and had wished to marry him, but as the days passed after he rejected her, she had come to realize they had never been near each other long enough for love to develop. Which was why she had told her father she was willing for him or Tía to look for a husband.

And they had found one for her.

"I think we could be happy together," she told him.

Philip slipped his hand around her waist and pulled her to him. Then he lowered his mouth to hers. And she responded. She lifted her body onto her tiptoes and pressed herself into his chest, winding her arms around his neck. It was as though they fit together like a vine grafted well onto another.

When Philip's lips nuzzled the soft crevice between her ear and her neck, she could barely think. The shivers in her body were so intense.

"You will come back to England with me?" he whispered in her ear.

Carmen drew far enough away to see his face again. "I will marry you, Philip, and go back to England with you."

He twirled her around, the cool air filling her senses. Carmen squeezed her eyes shut and laughed with happiness. She was going to be married.

Her entire world was about to change forever.

Chapter 17

OVER THE NEXT FEW days, Philip struggled to keep pace with the rapid changes. Jaime set about ordering everyone around while Philip finalized handshakes with the local men who were concerned about the mine deal details.

Marcos successfully negotiated for the purchase of the building that would become the train station in Valladolid and scheduled a meeting about the building Philip thought could become a hotel. All of which meant he returned to the city and left Jaime, Isabel, and his bride in charge of the wedding details. Not that Philip minded much. He was more in the way than helpful.

While he was away, Philip finalized railroad negotiations with men in Segovia and Leon. He rode a horse so much that he almost forgot how to walk. But the flurry of activity kept him motivated. With no plans to prolong his visit by more than a few days, he was under pressure to tie up loose ends.

Upon his return to Morales de Toro, dusty and exhausted, he booked Carmen on the boat back to Portugal the day after their wedding. A departure date that sent Carmen's family into an uproar.

"Why does Carmen have to go?" Isabel had demanded. "Why don't you stay here and finish the business you and Jaime are setting up?"

"Exactly," Tia Merce agreed, pounding her small fist against the table.

"I have an entire life and business in England," Philip said, but clamped his mouth shut when their faces hardened at his defense.

In the end, Carmen put the conversation to rest. "I want to go," she said firmly. "You all know I like to travel and have yet to see England. Besides, Philip will be my husband, which means our children will be partly English, and I should know his country."

"But you will inherit the vineyards here," Isabel argued back. "What will you do with them while in England?"

Philip never heard Carmen's response. Jaime pointed out that the vineyards remained Don Suárez's until his death.

"So when Papá dies, you will come back?" Isabel demanded. She didn't give Philip or Carmen time to speak before asking more questions. "And what of the children you will have? They won't speak Spanish if they don't live here. They won't know our traditions and our culture."

The mention of children had sparked an edge of anxiety in Philip. Like a cup of cold water thrown on him, it opened his eyes to the reality of marriage. For the first time since proposing, Philip wondered if he was being a hypocrite by entering a marriage of convenience, the type he had always scorned.

"That's enough questions for now," Jaime said, perhaps seeing Philip's nervousness. He clapped Philip on the back and led him towards the door. "I am taking the groom for the last-minute details while the women stay here in Morales de Toro. We will see you at the wedding."

Philip allowed Jaime to lead him away from the family, but Isabel's questions haunted him and unleashed even more worries. About the wedding, their marriage, their life in London and about the wedding night.

Not that he was nervous about the act of the marriage bed. He wasn't new to that sort of activity. Still, the question of how a man made love to a virgin he hardly knew kept running through his head. He'd never had to instruct a lover before. They were always quite experienced. What was he supposed to do with an innocent who had never been with a man? The night before returning to Toro, he slept little. As he glimpsed himself in the mirror the next morning, his horror and anxiety evident in his widened eyes and pale face, Philip realized there was nothing to do. He had committed to marrying Carmen. His absurd worries were clearly due to cold feet, having been a bachelor for so long.

Philip studied his reflection. It showed a man who looked drawn and tired. He wiggled his jaw to loosen the tension in his head and imagined Carmen standing in a wedding gown, waiting for him to join her. He smiled, his body relaxing as it always did when he thought of her. She was a beautiful woman with strong opinions on life, intelligent, curious. Everything he would look for in a wife.

"Carmen is the perfect woman to be your wife," Philip told his reflection. "So stop with your worries and get on with it."

Philip finished drying his face, then put on his jacket just as someone yelled his name from below his window.

"Philip, do you plan to come out?"

Jaime stood outside his house, awaiting Philip's carriage. When Philip emerged and entered the arched front door, an older gentleman dressed in the clothes of a Catholic priest greeted him.

"Hello," Philip greeted, eyeing the priest, who observed him with his lips thinned into a grim line.

"He's here to baptize you." It was said as though it were something Philip should have expected. He hadn't expected anything of the sort.

"Baptize me?"

"Laws about marriage and all," Jaime said. "It isn't valid unless you're Catholic. And there is no record of your baptism in the Catholic Church."

"It would be difficult for there to be one since I was baptized in the Anglican Church as a baby. In England," Philip mused in English.

Jaime sidled closer to him. "Don't say that in Spanish," he muttered. "You said religion made no difference to you. But it does to Carmen and our family."

Philip raised his hands in surrender. He couldn't back out now. He didn't want to. "Whatever needs to be done."

Within a few moments, water was sprinkled on his face, and he was prepared for the next day ahead. Despite the flip in his heartbeat that occurred each time he thought of it.

Chapter 18

"Are you quite sure about this?" Isabel asked. They were in Carmen's room getting ready for the wedding.

Carmen scowled at her sister in the mirror. Isabel continued fussing with the mound of curls on her head, oblivious to Carmen's irritation. "I'm sure of one thing. That a woman has more chances of happiness if she is married. And Philip is the only prospect I have. And before you claim that isn't enough for marriage, let me also say that he is handsome and kind and funny. We have seen nothing to give us pause these last few weeks, and he dances well."

Isabel opened her mouth, probably to protest, but Carmen continued "Today is my wedding day, and I'm determined to enjoy it. If you won't allow me to do that, I'll not invite you."

"You can't uninvite me!" Isabel exclaimed. "I'm your sister."

Isabel sank onto the settee with a sigh. One so heavy, Carmen regretted her words and the tone she had used.

"I'm sorry, Isa. I know you only have my best interests in mind."

"I do, Carmen," Isabel said, her tone earnest. "I want to make sure you are certain. Everything is happening so fast. You're about to leave us for months, perhaps years, at a time. And I'm—"

Her sister's voice trailed off.

Carmen rose from her chair and knelt in front of the person who had been her closest friend all her life. "I know, Isa. It isn't ideal, and it certainly isn't how I saw my life, but he's a good man and a good choice. This is best not only for me but also for the family. And even for Jaime and his work. Once this war is over and the railroad is built between the north and here, it will take only two days for me to be here. Imagine that!"

Isabel forced a smile, though it came out as a grimace.

"Come now, sister. Don't be unhappy on my wedding day. We must be strong."

"I am happy for you," Isabel said quietly. "But I do have one concern."

Carmen patted her sister's damp cheek. "What is it?"

"His Spanish is terrible!"

Their eyes met in the mirror, and both burst into giggles at the same time.

"He can learn," Carmen finally said, wiping the tears from her eyes. "If I can learn English, he can learn Spanish."

The maid came in with a coffee cart, and for the first time in hours, Isabel seemed to relax. Carmen wanted to reach out and hug her, hold her close and never let her go, but she didn't want Isabel to smell her fear. Not just after she had convinced Isabel that she wasn't afraid, that this was the right choice for her. But really, Carmen was terrified. Of leaving her home. Of being a wife. Of possibly losing her sight and wondering how Philip would react. All of it.

Isabel poured a cup for Carmen and dribbled a drop of milk into it. Already, the temperature was rising. The days were getting hotter and hotter and soon working past two in the afternoon would be impossible. Despite her apprehension, a cooler summer in England might be nice.

"Besides, you can't stay there forever," Isabel continued, as if they hadn't been interrupted.

Ignoring her sister, Carmen dabbed perfume on her wrists. She didn't want to ponder how long she would be staying in England and how quickly she might tire of the cool summer.

"Are you sure you have to leave tomorrow morning? What if you stayed for a few weeks more? Jaime has to go to London this year. He could bring you there once the baby is born."

Carmen glared at her stubborn sister, silencing her thoughts and fears to once again convince Isabel that, as the older sister, she didn't need looking after.

"You want me to get married and then not see my husband for a few months, possibly a year, after the wedding?"

Isabel shook her head emphatically. "I'm not sure it's good for a woman to travel after the wedding night."

The way she said it struck a chord of fear in Carmen, but she closed her eyes and told herself that Isabel was being dramatic. She would do anything to keep Carmen close by. Tía Merce said nothing about not traveling after the wedding night.

Maybe Isabel was afraid of childbirth. Perhaps that was why she was pushing for Carmen to stay. Her heart softened at the thought.

"How about this?" Carmen said, setting her coffee down. "I promise you I will come as soon as I can. But I do have to be careful with the war and all. Let's pray it all ends, and I can come back often."

The words soothed Isabel into a genuine smile.

"Besides, the war is the reason we have to leave now. Now there is little happening, but that could always change. Also, Philip needs to bring the goods back to England."

"You know," Isabel said, setting her cup down on the cart again and picking up a mantecado. "I could stop this wedding if I wanted to."

Carmen, knowing her sister wouldn't actually do it, played along. "How?"

"Well, he isn't Catholic."

Carmen laughed. "Most Protestants aren't, Isa. But didn't Jaime make him get baptized yesterday?"

"He did, but that means he isn't yet confirmed, doesn't it? I could ask Father Gonzalo his opinion about the validity of you marrying a Protestant."

Carmen tossed a pillow from her chair at her sister. Isabel shrieked, her laughter dissolving into hiccups.

"Don't you dare tell Father Gonzalo anything," Carmen said, gasping for air from her laughter.

Carmen had hoped for a Valladolid wedding, but her father's priest was away blessing the northern troops, and other priests refused to marry her outside her own parish. She had settled for a wedding in Morales de Toro, a small cathedral, with her childhood priest, Father Gonzalo, presiding.

"Can you imagine it? Father Gonzalo muttering and crossing himself against the English Protestant?" Isabel imitated the severe Father Gonzalo, her hiccups making her look more ridiculous.

"It's the reason Papá has kept him from coming over in the past month." Carmen chuckled at the image Isabel was painting.

"On a serious note," Isa said slowly to control her breath, "is Philip asking you to become Protestant? I assume there are laws in England the same as here. Perhaps if you don't, your marriage won't be recognized."

Carmen considered the question she hadn't thought to ask herself. "I don't know," she said, finally. "He hasn't spoken to me about it. But as long as I know I'm married, that's all that matters."

Isabel blinked. "No, no, Carmen. There are times you have to care what others think. This is the society your children will grow up in."

A noise outside the window caught their attention, cutting their conversation short. Though the last question nagged at the back of Carmen's mind, she was glad for the distraction. This was her wedding day, after all. Everything outside of getting married could wait.

"They're coming!" Isabel shouted from the open window. Carmen rushed to join her. Outside, beyond the adobe walls that surrounded their father's house, a parade of townspeople was coming down the road with Philip and Jaime at the front.

The idea of her marrying an Englishman was so foreign in this part of Spain that Carmen had worried everyone would stay home. And yet here they were, coming to celebrate with her. She had to breathe in and out slowly to keep from bursting into tears of joy.

It was finally her time to get married. This was her day. Due to the war and everything happening so quickly, the ceremony and lunch wouldn't be everything Isabel had, but it would be hers. And that was enough for Carmen.

"It's time!" Isabel exclaimed.

"Stop," Carmen cried, as her sister ran from the room. "Your dress is still loose."

She tried to tie the back of her sister's dress while they moved into the hallway. Rosa rushed out of her room, looking younger in her pale pink dress.

"Carmen, leave that to me. And Isabel, you should be looking after your sister, not the other way around. It is Carmen's wedding day," Rosa admonished, taking over the ties on Isabel's dress.

Isabel murmured an apology, but Carmen ignored it, weaving her hand through her sister's arm.

"You can't expect our Isa to change how she is just because today is different from yesterday," Carmen said, laughing. Isabel huffed in response, squealing when Carmen pulled her quickly down the stairs where their father was waiting for them, dressed in his former military uniform, his gray hair brushed back, his eyes glittering.

"Are you girls always going to behave this way when you are together?"

"We can't help it, Papá," Carmen said, kissing her father on his cheeks.

"Be glad you have daughters who love each other," Isabel said, smoothing her perfectly coiffed hair. "Are we ready? Have the men passed by already?"

"Don't worry about them. Jaime is at the helm. He'll tell Philip where to go. And once he gets to the church, Father Gonzalo will take over bossing everyone around."

Carmen giggled, her excitement getting the best of her again.

"Calm yourself, Carmen," Isabel said. "You don't want to giggle during the ceremony."

"Are you ready?" Don Suárez asked.

Carmen cleared her throat, shrugged back her shoulders, and nodded. "I'm ready."

She kissed Isabel on the cheek before taking her father's arm.

"You look very pretty, hija."

"Gracias, Papá."

They walked down the dim hallway and into the streets, where the servants were lined up to greet them. The women sprinkled lilac petals, and the men cheered as Carmen made her way past them to the church.

The other neighbors joined in the celebrations from their balconies or at their front doors. Her father's male servants trailed her, yelling "Viva la novia!" as the neighbors answered, "Viva!"

Carmen glanced at her father, unable to keep herself from smiling. Her insides were a trembling ball of fear and happiness.

"Happy, mi hija?" he asked her as they continued toward the cathedral.

"I am, Papá," she said, because it wasn't a lie. She was delighted to be getting married, just sad to be leaving her home. "He is a good choice for me."

They entered the courtyard in front of the church. After the ceremony, it would be filled with all the guests throwing rice and flower petals before following her and Philip to the old citadel for the dinner and dance. For the moment, she and her father entered through the side entrance and into a small room decorated with a red velvet chair, a brick fireplace, and a round table.

"Just give them a few minutes to enter the church and get seated," her father said. "Then we'll go in together."

Tears welled in his eyes, and suddenly her strong father seemed fragile and old. Carmen kissed him lightly on the cheek.

"You had the wine brought in, didn't you? The wine you had ready for my wedding?"

Don Suárez grinned, his tears gone. "Of course I did. And I can't wait to open it in your honor."

The church organ could be heard wheezing to life, jolting Carmen.

"I guess it's time, Papá," she said, wishing there was a glass of water for her to drink. She swallowed as best she could and lowered her lace veil over her face.

"It's time," her father repeated.

Chapter 19

THE DAY WENT BY in a blur of dancing, speeches, feasting, and drinking copious amounts of wine. The celebration was like nothing Philip would have had in England, and he was glad for it. In England, he would have been obligated to invite his brother's friends, the who's who of society, and generally a lot of people he didn't actually like. The ceremony and the dinner afterwards would have been a dour, serious affair to please Theodore and Meredith and to keep the family reputation intact. They were nobles, after all.

By contrast, everyone in Morales de Toro was invited to celebrate and almost all of them came—laughing and clapping Señor Suárez on the back, the women crying and congratulating Carmen. For a moment, as Philip sat at a table drinking the delicious wine his wife had created, he was saddened at the prospect of going home. The trip had exceeded his greatest expectations between meeting Jaime and Carmen, attending the Benavente Ball, succeeding with his business dealings, and finding a wife.

The biggest surprise of all.

Philip sipped his wine as he mused on his thought. No, the biggest surprise of all was that he was content with each of the things he had done, especially finding a wife. Not only would marriage allow him to keep his house, but he enjoyed being with Carmen. And he looked forward to building a life with her in his house.

He would miss Spain, but England was where his life was. Cinch and his family, the business, his dreams, his house, and everything else important to him were back in London. Now he could share that with Carmen.

"You alright?" Jaime's voice shook Philip out of his reverie.

"Very much so," Philip replied. "I'm married now to a wonderful woman."

They both glanced over to Carmen, who was bidding a tearful goodbye to some guests.

"My wife went inside to cry," Jaime said. "They've not left each other's side all evening. This part, saying goodbye I mean, might take a while."

Philip nodded before polishing off his wine. "I'll go be some support, then. Will you and Isabel be meeting up with us tomorrow morning?"

Jaime looked towards the house where Isabel could be seen through the windows talking with Rosa and dabbing at her eyes. Her belly was already rounder than when Philip first arrived. "I don't believe that will be good for Isabel's nerves. I'm hoping you'll keep to your word and let Carmen come back to visit as soon as it's safe."

The comment made Philip uneasy. The war wasn't the only reason he hesitated to let his wife travel alone by ship. There were still problems on the sea that he didn't want her to experience, like hostile foreign ships, slavers, and pirates. Not to mention storms and whales that could tip a ship over. He shuddered inwardly at the thought, but to Jaime, he smiled.

"I'll try my best."

The two of them joined Carmen. Only a few guests remained.

"Ready then?" Philip whispered to his wife, noting the goosebumps on her exposed shoulders.

"Yes," she said quietly, then reached out to kiss Jaime on both cheeks.

"Take care of Isabel," she told him. Jaime's eyes misted as Isabel reappeared in the garden. Her eyes were puffy, her nose red.

"One last hug and I'll have Jaime take me home," Isabel said.

The two sisters clung to each other for a long time. Philip marveled at the love they had for one another. It was a love he had witnessed between Cinch and his sister Emily, though, being English, there was less hugging. Philip had always admired their relationship and had never envied it until seeing Carmen and Isabel. He wondered what it might be like if he and his brothers felt that way about each other. At the very least, it would have stopped Theodore from threatening to take Philip's house.

But then, he wouldn't have been looking for a wife when visiting Spain. And he wouldn't have married Carmen.

It surprised Philip how sad that particular thought made him. Carmen and Isabel broke apart, and for the first time, he was grateful Theodore had raised the problem with the will. It had pressured him to make a good choice for himself.

With one final wave, Jaime and Isabel climbed into their carriage.

"There they go," Carmen said as the carriage rolled away.

"I am sorry to make you so sad," Philip finally said, unable to summon any comforting words to ease her melancholy.

Carmen faced him, her eyes glistening in the moonlight. "Don't be sorry. I knew I would have to move on when I married, since there is no husband for me in the village. Isabel is lucky she found someone close by."

Philip dipped his chin and kissed her lightly on the mouth. "Shall we retire? Tomorrow will be a long day."

The two of them left the garden, now empty of guests, and trekked up the stairs of the house. Jaime had informed Philip that they were to spend the wedding night in a wing generally reserved for guests. At the top of the stairs, they turned right and entered an airy bedroom with a walnut vanity on fluted legs, a French style four-poster bed draped by a blue canopy, white walls, and two double windows that showcased the vineyards.

"It's my favorite view," Carmen said, indicating the windows. "Sometimes, I come to this room at night and look out over it. The moon always gives the vines a haunting feel, don't you think?"

The moonlight did create an eerie effect on the vineyards, but Philip was more focused on his wife. He brushed his fingers over her high cheekbones, highlighted by the moonlight. She parted her lips as his fingers outlined her red, plump mouth, a staggered sigh escaping her.

"Carmen," he murmured.

He covered her mouth with his, pulling her softly against him.

She responded slowly, as though thinking through what actions were expected of her, until he let her go. He glanced at the bed, his body knowing exactly what it wished to do, but when he looked back at Carmen, she had turned pale.

It was then he remembered he was married to a virgin. Philip longed for a drink of whiskey, but he was not in his house, nor in his own country, and he wasn't sure if there was whiskey available.

Philip coughed. "Shall I help you with your dress?"

Carmen took a step backwards, her fingers trailing along her bodice as though feeling for the answer.

"I think I can manage." Her eyes darted to the privacy screen, a plain, wooden one that reminded Philip of shutters on a country house. "You can have some wine."

He followed her gesture to find a silver tray set with a bottle and two glasses. It took all of his control to keep from sighing in relief.

"It's a beautiful room," Philip said, pouring two glasses. Shuffling came from behind the privacy screen.

"It was my mother's room," she said, finally.

Knowing that didn't put him more at ease. Philip gulped half of his wine before filling his glass again.

"It's very beautiful," he repeated.

His palms were sweating, and his heart was beating too quickly. He was tempted to offer help again, but didn't want to come off as pressuring her. So, he sipped his wine and wondered what other men did in this situation. Not that he would have asked anyone the question, but he wished it would have come up in conversation.

Movement near the privacy screen caught his attention. Carmen stepped out, still in her dress, her hair disheveled.

"I need help," she admitted before turning around. She gathered the stray locks of hair now falling over her shoulders to one side.

"Certainly," he said in a gravelly tone. Philip cleared his throat, then assessed the button situation. When his fingers gently approached the bodice to commence with the button undoing, she stiffened.

Not a particularly good sign.

He pushed the first button through the looped thread, fumbling a few times before finally achieving victory. He gazed down at the line of at least fifteen more buttons on her dress and held back a sigh. Alice's buttons were usually decoration.

"You might need this," she said, her voice small, almost sheepish, extending a bone-handled buttonhook over her shoulder.

"How were you going to do this on your own?" he asked, accepting the buttonhook. He had meant the words in jest, but Carmen didn't laugh. She didn't even respond. Philip aimed the buttonhook under the loop and pulled the next button through easily. After a few moments more, the bodice was split open, exposing the almost transparent chemise underneath.

Philip's body stirred at the sight of her. His wife. Half naked in front of him. He nuzzled her neck, breathing in the scent of her hair. Carmen turned her head, but didn't move away. When she closed her eyes, Philip plunged his fingers into her hair and kissed her exposed neck. With a quiet rustling, Carmen's bodice tumbled to the ground.

In his mind's eye, Philip imagined himself sweeping her into his arms and carrying her to bed, but before he could move, Carmen dashed to the privacy screen and disappeared.

Philip returned to his wine. After finishing his second glass, he took off his jacket, then his shoes, his vest, and his cravat.

"Are there buttons on the skirt you need help with?" Philip called out.

"No," she answered, her voice just above a whisper. "I just need a moment."

After a few more minutes, Carmen crept out from behind the privacy screen, pausing when she saw him in his bare feet. Philip shuffled toward her, and she flinched with each step he took.

"Carmen." He motioned to the bed. "Do you know what to expect?"

Carmen nodded stiffly. "My aunt has informed me of the mechanics," she said.

Philip clenched his jaw to keep from laughing. The mechanics. This was not how he would describe it, nor was it what he wanted in his marriage. But clearly, they were going to have to start there. It was better than a wife who knew nothing.

"We don't have to do anything tonight, Carmen," he said. "It's been a long day, and we have to travel tomorrow."

He had thought his words would help her relax, but instead, her eyes narrowed.

"I am not afraid," she said.

"Carmen." Philip took her hand, circling her palms with his fingertips as he watched her. She stared straight ahead. "We can take things slowly."

Carmen snapped her focus to him. "It is our wedding night. I don't wish to be treated like a child."

"But if you aren't ready . . ."

"Tía says no woman is ever ready. That this is all for the man."

Philip opened his mouth to reply, but Carmen yanked her hand from his, marched to the bed and laid out on it, her nightgown covering her entire body. He swallowed hard, wishing he could explain how unenjoyable it was to him to have a wedding night of duty.

In fact, he wasn't certain he could do it.

When Carmen remained still, Philip sat on the bed and removed his shirt. Slowly, she turned her head towards him.

"You're very strong," she murmured. The words awoke his desires again, as well as his hope that the night wouldn't be awful.

"And you're very beautiful," he responded, before taking off his trousers. Carmen closed her eyes and her body went rigid.

Philip blew out the lamps and climbed into bed. Carmen didn't move. Philip stretched out next to her, listening to her breathing. When she opened her eyes and turned to him, he kissed her gently on the mouth.

"I don't want to pressure you, Carmen."

She nodded against his lips. "Are you not happy with me?"

"That is not the problem," Philip said, kissing the base of her jaw. "You are everything I would want in a wife."

He was glad it wasn't a lie. Far from it. Philip found he was happier with each passing moment. But the words did little to relax her.

"Then let's please get this over with." Her voice was low. "I am ready."

Philip had a mind to roll away from her, leaving it for another night, but he wasn't sure putting it off would help. A wedding night with a nervous bride was not unusual, he supposed. And to show Carmen that making love could be pleasurable for women as well as men, he would have to get her past the initial discomfort. That meant obeying her wishes.

So he did.

And Philip felt like a cad afterwards.

Chapter 20

CARMEN WATCHED THROUGH THE small, round window of her room on the ship as Philip and the other sailors heaved ropes, turned capstans, and ran about in an organized, though zigzag-like, fashion. The command Philip had as he spoke to those working on the ship and in the port sent her insides a fluttering. His strength impressed her. The more she watched, the more light-headed she felt. Carmen swallowed hard, pushing herself away from the window, memories of two nights before coming once again unbidden.

She felt her body flush again with embarrassment at her behavior. He hadn't tried to touch her since.

A dull throb pulsed through her lower belly, sounding an alarm as to what would be coming in a few hours. Carmen chewed her lip, mortified she had never asked Isabel or Tía Merce what a woman does during her cycles when married. Or on a ship. For a moment, Carmen imagined sharing a room with her husband and thought she might faint from panic. At home, she usually spent the first days in her rooms nursing her discomfort with watered down wine and warm compresses. She couldn't imagine a man being around to witness such a thing.

The door to her room banged open, startling Carmen. She jumped away from the sound to find Philip standing at the door.

"There you are."

Philip stood with his jacket off, his shirtsleeves smudged with black and his forehead beading with sweat.

"Here I am," Carmen replied, looking about the room. Anywhere but at her husband. "There is a wash bowl and towel just there."

Philip's heavy footsteps moved to the left. "Am I a terrible mess?"

"Yes," Carmen said, laughing nervously. She fingered her cuffs, her mind looking for something to do.

The sound of the water splashing gently against the bowl stopped.

"Carmen," Philip said. A young sailor pushing a tea cart through the door interrupted him. "Thank you, Martin."

The sailor snapped his heels together and scurried back through the door, slamming it closed behind him.

"Remind me to talk to him about the benefits of knocking," Philip said. "Come. Let's have some tea. I need to speak with you."

Carmen opened her mouth to defend the boy but thought against it. Instead, she positioned herself to serve the tea.

"I can pour it, Carmen," Philip said, reaching for the teapot. Her body froze at his touch.

She lifted her chin to find sympathy in her husband's eyes. "Jaime told you?"

Philip nodded. The mixture of musk, cologne, and peppermint sifted through the air. Carmen had a strange urge to inch closer to him, but instead, she moved away so he was in the center of her vision. "How much did he tell you?"

Philip dropped his arms to his sides and shrugged. "I was to become your husband, Carmen. Jaime told me Dr. Miguel Perez was your doctor, but he refused to marry you because your eyesight was poor."

Carmen clicked her tongue against Jaime and his meddling. She would have told her husband if he had just asked her. But of course, when it came down to it, even the men in her family didn't believe a woman could survive without them.

Philip brushed her cheek, trailing her cheekbones with his fingertips. "But you are not blind, are you?"

"My eyes are weak, but I am perfectly capable of seeing." She swallowed hard before she lied or exaggerated too much. "I can see that your eyes are brown, your nose is straight and that your hair is in need of brushing."

Philip's eyes narrowed briefly before he smiled.

Carmen lifted her chin in defiance at whatever it was he was thinking. "May I pour the tea now?"

"By all means," Philip said, waving her to the task and sounding relieved. "I'm glad we've cleared that up."

"Did it have you worried?" Carmen asked, her mind again wandering to the disastrous wedding night.

From the wash bowl, Philip looked over his shoulder at her. "No. I'm not the type to worry."

Carmen watched him even after he turned his attention back to his hair. She touched the spout with her fingers, then tapped the spout gently to the rim of the cups before tilting the pot up. Almost without looking. Rosa had her practice repeatedly during her last days in Spain, and she was grateful for it.

"Oh, lovely. Cheers, my dear," Philip said, his entire body relaxing when he sat and finally took a sip.

"Will we see your brother when we arrive?" Carmen settled into her chair with her own cup of tea. She was getting used to the English drink.

Philip blinked in surprise. "Heavens no. My eldest brother and the one causing me problems with my house, Theodore, will be off gallivanting about town and doing whatever it is that he does during the preseason."

"You really don't get along with him?" Carmen sensed his reluctance when discussing his brother, yet she wanted to know more. She couldn't imagine not getting along with Isabel.

"No. Not really. Here is one reason why." Philip took a large, white paper out of his jacket, cleared his throat, and then started to read. "Dearest brother, I took the liberty of telling Meredith to close up the London House. Not knowing if you were to be home anytime soon, I thought it best for all involved. Some members of the staff have chosen to be in our employ in Bath. As you have declared your return home so suddenly, I have not had time to make your arrangements. I hope this gets to you in time for you to do so. Your brother, the Marquess of Fillemore."

Philip passed the missive over to Carmen. "His signature took up half the space of the missive, see?"

Carmen peered closer at the neat lines of handwriting and then swooping lines that must have been Theodore's signature. His handwriting was elegant, but Philip frowned at it, as though a school master scolding a child.

"The man is purposefully trying to take away my inheritance. He tried to close the house without my permission, which would mean we have no proper place to stay in London. Thankfully, my butler is more loyal to me than my brother. He sent me a note as well, saying he and three of the best members of staff decided to stay in the house." Philip folded the letter again and stuffed it into his breast pocket. "Only three left. My cook, which is terrible, and two footmen. We should be alright with the four left."

Philip mused over the letter a moment more while Carmen watched him.

"We do have a place to stay, then?" she asked.

"For now, yes. But this means we will have to move quickly once we land in London. I had hoped to find a special license waiting for me when we stopped a few hours ago. But there was none."

"A special license?"

"For our Protestant ceremony. Since we don't have it, we'll be obligated to get one upon our arrival."

"Today?" she asked, the idea already making her weary.

"No," Philip said slowly. "But soon. We are married in the eyes of your church, but not yet in the eyes of England."

"We are not legally married in England?"

Philip stuffed his brother's letter back into his jacket pocket. "All Catholics must be married by the Church of England in England. To be legal. It's a silly rule they've gotten rid of, but the change doesn't go into effect until August. So, we must have the ceremony to be properly legal. All Catholics do it," he said, finishing the explanation with a shrug.

She swallowed against the bitter taste rising in her throat from the idea of marrying in the Anglican church. But Philip was her husband. And he was not asking her to convert. "It sounds as though you have everything set to right. Sit and have more tea."

Philip kissed her hands, sending shivers up her arms to her chest. "I admit I was a little worried about making a poor impression on you, what with this business with my brother."

Carmen's arm tingled from his kiss, and a strange feeling filled her midsection. She unleashed a steadying breath and said, "Perhaps we should host him and Meredith for dinner."

Philip drew back, his eyes wide. "Heaven's no. Why would we do that?"

"He's your brother."

"My brother would think I was pulling a prank."

"But you're not serious," Carmen said. Philip frowned. Or she thought he did. The clouds were darkening, sending the room into deeper shadows.

"Theodore and I see each other at social events and, of course, at family functions and holidays, but I make it a point not to stay too long." Philip laughed at Carmen's sharp inhale. "It must sound crazy to you, doesn't it? You have such a supportive family. Well, I shouldn't be unkind to him. I take back the rude words I was thinking against him a moment ago. At any rate, no, I do not think we should invite them for dinner."

"Tea, then." Carmen was sure if the two brothers just got together, they could be a family again.

"My brother and I have never gotten along, and there is no changing that," he said, his tone cool. "Especially now with him trying to take my house away."

"You never played together? As children?"

"Play? I daresay, no. He wouldn't know how to play anything. He abhors being dirty, always has. Which made it delightfully easy to prank him over the years. He also loves buying new clothes. The perfect combination for the nobles of today's England. They are soft gentlemen who spend more on clothing than our female counterparts."

"Nothing wrong with a man looking good," Carmen said, but Philip waved her comment away.

"Perhaps if the noblemen of my country would spend as much time on political and social issues that plague our society as they do on their clothing, I would change my opinion."

Carmen arched an eyebrow at her husband.

"What?" he asked, meeting her gaze.

"You are a gentleman," she said. "What made you different?"

"Accumulation of debt," Philip said matter-of-factly. "When I was still at the university, my father died, and suddenly the family fortunes were in the hands of my brother. A man who cared nothing about managing the land or investments properly. It was by pure happenstance that I found out my father had invested in bad stocks years before, allowed his land to go fallow, lost ownership of his mine in a card game gone wrong, and owed taxes. My mother was oblivious, of course, but Theodore knew and chose to ignore the facts and continue to live on credit. Which I was doing as well, since that was what I had grown up doing. It was when my own creditors started hounding me about it every day that I realized how wrong my father and our family system were."

"What happened?"

Philip sighed. "I went to work like every other poor Englishman. That's what I was, despite having grown up in a large house with servants. Thankfully, my friend Cinch was an ambitious man who had created Sutton Enterprises while living in Spain. His company was doing well enough to hire me on. There is little a gentleman is trained to do, but I was useful for traveling to his business points of interest, interacting with the captains of his boats, and inspecting the products that the ships brought in. Turns out, I'm quite good at healing relations between workingmen and those in London running everything." Philip cleared his throat. "I owe him a great deal."

Carmen liked the man named Cinch already. "Your family must be proud of you."

Philip spread his hands as though the answer might be there, but they were empty. "Trade, even for lower gentry, is not something most Englishmen want to be known for. My family is both landowners and nobility, though we've never been powerful or important. Still, my parents were staunch believers in a gentleman not getting his hands dirty. My brothers are carrying on that belief."

"I don't believe we were meant to be idle, nobility-born or not," Carmen said.

"Exactly right. I agree. But my family has a certain way of viewing the world that doesn't align with mine. Calvin, that's my second oldest brother, the minister. He won't want to get involved between Theodore and me. If he does, I'm sure his advice will be for me to give up the house."

Carmen leaned forward and threaded his fingers through hers. "I'm sure everything will work out."

Philip didn't answer. He seemed far away, though his eyes were still on her. The intensity of his stare caused her breath to hitch until she felt as though she'd been running.

"Carmen," he said, softly.

She'd never heard her name spoken like that before. It came off his tongue like silk, sending a ripple through her body she couldn't hide. This tremor was the feeling she had on their wedding night before fear overcame her. Frightened by the intensity building within her, Carmen dropped Philip's hand. Before she could sit back, he grabbed her arms and nudged her towards him until she was sitting on his lap.

Philip's strong fingers wrapped around the nape of her neck and pulled her into a kiss.

Her body seemed to burn from within as his mouth pressured her to open to him, his tongue dancing against her in a choreography she had never been taught. The pressure, the heat, the strange fluttering throughout her body made Carmen tremble until she was almost in tears. A whimper escaped her throat as the whirlwind of sensations became too much. She wanted him. Everything about him.

Until a sharp pain cut through her lower abdomen.

Carmen scrambled off his lap. She swallowed her embarrassment and tried to smile but was almost certain she scowled instead when her cycle pains reared again.

The noise of sailors shouting orders seeped through the door, alerting them both to a change outside.

Philip grabbed his coat and marched to the door. "We will be in London soon. When we get to port, I'll have to settle a few things. It can be chaotic, so stay in here until it's safe to leave."

Not waiting for her answer, he slipped out the door. Carmen stared at it for a long minute before marching through it herself. She huddled, hidden and safe near the stern, watching the city of London come into view. A sharp shiver ran through her as the cold wind blew harshly against her cheeks. The new city didn't stretch out its arms to her. Against the slate-colored sky, London stood tall and aloof, as though sizing her up and deciding what to do with her.

———— ❖ ————

After two hours in her room with little to do other than wait, Philip finally opened the door and declared it was time to leave.

"The carriage is here. Sorry for the wait," he said as he ushered her to the plank. "Let me go ahead, and you hold my hand. It's quite narrow."

Carmen wished she could refuse and stride down the plank herself, but the sun was setting, throwing off her sense of depth and space. And she was tired.

"Thank you," she murmured when they reached land. A large, black carriage carted by two brown horses rode up beside them.

"My apologies, sir," a man said, jumping down from the driver's seat. "We didn't think you were due until tomorrow."

The man stopped speaking when he saw Carmen and quickly bowed. He was younger than Philip, with keen eyes and ruddy cheeks.

"Nathaniel, this is my wife, Carmen."

"Nice to meet you," Carmen said, suddenly aware of her accent contrasting with the driver's. Nathaniel repeated the same, then turned to load the trunks. "How long will the ride take?"

"Not too long."

When he said nothing else, Carmen turned to the window and watched as the port disappeared, along with the stenches of the river. The sun dared to peek out from the clouds, even as it lowered into the horizon. A gentle breeze glided through the open window, though it came with the acrid stench of the city and not the sweet fragrance of vineyards and Toro.

Suddenly, Carmen shivered with the fear she might have made a mistake.

Chapter 21

WITHIN HOURS OF ARRIVING in London, Philip found himself having a light supper in his house across from his wife as though they were old hands at marriage. Down to Carmen looking weary. Philip fought back the memories of tense, wordless meals with his parents, reminding himself about Carmen's whirlwind trip from her hometown to London. This silence between them could not be an ominous warning. He refused to believe that.

"Is your room to your liking?" he asked after struggling for conversation with her.

"Very much." Carmen seemed to be shoveling chicken breast around her plate more than bringing it to her mouth. He had thought she would be impressed with the china dishes he had, but Carmen hadn't commented on them. She had barely said a word in the last few hours.

"My parents always had separate bedrooms," Philip said. "And I thought you might want some space." His voice trailed off. It was difficult to find the right words he wanted to say, that he wished to share a room with her and have an intimate marriage, but that he also wanted to respect her privacy.

"My parents did as well," Carmen said. She set her fork down and leaned back. He could count on one hand the number of bites she had taken.

"Are you finished? We could retire to the parlor. I'm sure Felix has a fire in there." Philip stood and waited as Carmen spread her fork and knife across her plate before rising. "We could have a glass of wine."

"That would be lovely," she said as she took his elbow.

Philip led her through the dining room and across the hall to the parlor. "Down the hall that way is my study. And past my study is the back garden. It isn't very large, but it's quiet. If you want to plant some things, this might be the time to do it. You can speak with Felix in the morning about it."

Carmen nodded, but didn't answer. Seemingly unimpressed. Philip ushered them into the warm parlor and poured two glasses of sherry. Carmen took longer than normal to arrange herself comfortably on the couch. He watched her from the liquor cart, downing one glass of sherry without her knowledge and pouring another. The wine would help calm his nerves and relax her. Except for the kiss earlier that day, he hadn't touched her since the disastrous wedding night.

The memory of it encouraged him to down his next glass in one go again. Then he joined his wife.

"Your wine, my lady," he said, offering the small glass to Carmen. She smiled stiffly and sipped it.

Philip grasped for a conversation topic, but his mind was stuck on a memory of his father frowning at him after he had fallen from his horse. "Get back on the horse, Philip," he had demanded.

It wasn't a pleasant memory, and Philip had no wish to link it to his marriage bed, but there it was. Now that a few days had passed, he feared something was broken between him and Carmen.

"Shall we go sight-seeing tomorrow?" Philip asked her.

Carmen looked at him in surprise. "I might want to rest tomorrow. Perhaps the next day?"

She gulped her wine, her body stiffening as he sat down next to her.

"Carmen," he murmured, brushing her hair back from her cheeks. Carmen jumped up, holding out her empty glass.

"I will go upstairs now."

Before he could reach for it, she marched away, still holding her wineglass, leaving him staring after her. He sat alone for a long time until the parlor door opened and Mrs. Brax entered.

"Mr. Daucer, I am retiring for the night unless you would like something else."

"No, no," Philip said. "Is Mrs. Daucer settled in?"

Mrs. Brax, who normally kept a stoic look about her, narrowed her eyes and tilted her head. "Yes, sir. She told me to tell you she was in bed."

"Thank you," Philip said, hope rising in him that he hadn't made a complete mess of everything. Without a doubt, he was unintelligent, having not read the clues before. But at least his wife didn't hate him. "Good night, Mrs. Brax."

Philip downed his fourth glass of sherry as he listened to Mrs. Brax retreating to the back stairs. Then he hurried up to the second floor, releasing a calming breath before knocking on Carmen's door.

She opened it in a nightdress and robe, her hair woven into a braid. "Philip," she said, sounding as though she hadn't expected him.

"May I come in?" he asked, suddenly feeling like a schoolboy talking with his first crush. He stepped his foot between the door, but Carmen didn't budge.

"No," she blurted. "I can't. Not tonight. Or tomorrow. I —"

"Carmen," Philip murmured, trying to soothe her.

"I cannot." She shook her head so hard her braid bounced across her shoulder. "Good night, Philip."

Before he could speak again, the door closed, leaving him alone in the hallway. And though no one bore witness to his rejection, a searing burn of shame filled him. Philip marched down the stairs and out the door.

———— ❀ ————

Still burning with shame, Philip stood in the entryway of his club. He jerked hard on his cuffs and prayed it didn't show on his face as he wandered through the rooms.

"Philip, are you still in town? I heard you were sailing away to Portugal or some such exotic land."

Lord Masterson called to him from the corner, his oily mustache making his bulbous nose appear even larger. Sir Calvin and Mr. Fredrick sat with him in a semi-circle of leather chairs.

"Yes," Philip said, catching a glimpse of Cinch in the far corner of the blue parlor. "Just arrived today."

"I salute you for being adventurous. If I were a younger man, I'd sail back to Portugal. Had a grand time there when I was younger." Lord Masterson clicked his tongue as though calling a horse. Philip felt slightly nauseous.

"I spent most of my time in Spain," Philip said diplomatically. Then he added, "Where I was married."

Lord Masterson sputtered, then gave his congratulations.

"Thank you," Philip said, hoping Lord Masterson would spread the rumor as quickly as possible. "Carmen and I had been corresponding for quite some time, and when we met in person, it was as though it were meant to be, you know?"

"Bah, poetic nonsense, Daucer." Lord Masterson gulped his drink before continuing. "That feeling doesn't last."

Lord Masterson's words stripped Philip back to standing in his own dark hallway just an hour before.

"Don't look so forlorn. You get what you can from your wife, and then you find yourself a nice mistress. It's a good way of life for a man."

Philip made a noncommittal nod. No need to insult the man. No need to agree with him directly, either.

"Where will you live?" Mr. Fredrick asked, joining the conversation before Philip could escape.

"In my house, of course."

Mr. Fredrick and Lord Masterson exchanged looks that they didn't bother to hide.

"I understood it's your brother's house," Mr. Fredrick said, his eyes locked on Philip's. "And that he had already moved half the servants out of there. Getting ready to sell it is the rumor."

"Good evening, gentlemen." The voice came from behind Philip and seemed to agitate both Mr. Fredrick and Lord Masterson. Philip turned to find himself face to face with Lionel Finley. "I'm wondering if I may steal Mr. Daucer from you? Lord Candor and I have business with him."

The other men murmured their greetings and hurried away, leaving Finley and Philip to approach Cinch.

"Look, Cinch, I procured Daucer." Finley clapped Philip hard on the back. Cinch grinned up at them from his seat in the corner.

"We thought you might need rescuing," Cinch explained as Philip settled into the last wing-back chair of their circle. Philip collected a glass of whiskey from the nearby footman and sighed with relief for the first time that evening.

"That doesn't sound good," Finley said.

"What doesn't sound good is your accent," Philip said dryly. "When is that going to go back to normal?"

Finley threw his head back and laughed along with Cinch.

"Be careful, Philip," Cinch said. "Finley here uses his accent as a distraction. He is ruthlessly worming his way back into London, and he'll cut you out if you aren't careful."

"From Sutton Enterprises?" Philip asked. "If you replace me with him, you'll have dug your own grave. No man's ear can stand listening to that all day."

Finley lit his cigar with a wink towards Philip. "I will try my best to remember my childhood dialect. Does that sound better?"

Philip winced openly at the jumbled accent Finley had assumed. "I'll drink more whiskey to soothe my ears."

The men laughed together. Philip reached for a cigar and found himself glad to be back. One question from Cinch broke his peace.

"How is married life, Philip?" he asked.

"Yes, I heard the good news. How is it to be married?" Finley asked.

Philip glared at Cinch. "What is this, Cinch? Are we letting Finley back into everything?"

"Calm down, Philip. It's Lionel. Just because he went to America doesn't mean he isn't our friend. When I came back from Spain after those few years, we went right back to the same friendship we always had."

Philip slid his focus from Cinch to Finley, who didn't appear even slightly put off by Philip's temper. It was what made Americans so disconcerting.

"But look at him. He's so American now. His hair is even cut like one."

"What's wrong with my hair?" Finley asked, touching his blond strands. "You're quite out of humor, friend. Which, for a man, can mean only one thing."

Finley snapped his fingers and leaned back in his chair. He and Cinch both tittered again as they sipped their whiskey and enjoyed their cigars.

"What?" Philip demanded. "What are the two of you going on about?"

"You're here at the club the day you arrived in London, Philip," Finley said, as though it were an explanation.

"Can a man not do as he wishes?" Philip asked.

"We both know you'd be warming your marriage bed if you had the choice," Cinch said.

A lump formed in Philip's throat that he tried to push down with more whiskey, but it didn't budge. "There—well, Carmen, she told me." Philip cleared his throat and started again. "She needs a few days. Travel and all that."

"A few days to recover from the travel?" Finley said. "Are you certain she wasn't speaking about that which plagues a woman each month?"

"Each month?" Philip repeated.

Finley frowned at him. "Surely you know about women and the signs of pregnancies and the like?"

"Marriage gives you a much more in-depth understanding," Cinch acknowledged. Philip waited for a better explanation. "Did your mistresses never tell you why they might turn you away?"

Philip sputtered a protest about never being turned away, cut short as the meaning of his friends' words struck him. He thought of Carmen blushing, of the way she had clutched at her robe, and at the way Mrs. Brax had narrowed her eyes at him. She hadn't rejected him. It was merely her female nature.

The realization gave him fresh hope.

He laughed with relief.

"You look as though you've discovered gold," Cinch said.

Now that it wasn't his male ego at risk, he found his good humor again. "To be frank, it's good to know my marriage isn't already becoming a bloody English marriage."

Cinch and Finley chuckled at Philip's expense as he refilled their glasses.

"If I could give you some advice, as a man who was married before you," Finley said slowly, glancing behind him before continuing. "Even if they are eager, they are, well, their bodies are more fragile. There are other things for them to worry about."

The words alarmed Philip. "Such as?"

Finley cleared his throat and looked to Cinch. Cinch waved the topic back to Finley.

"Well, er, my wife was not strong, but even still, at the beginning, it is best to keep things, er, perhaps every other night."

"That is not an issue, Finley, but I thank you for the concern." The minute the words were out of his mouth, Philip instantly regretted them. Cinch leaned in closer, the whiskey he had ingested making his eyes glassy, his mind eager for gossip.

"What's that, Daucer?" His grin irritated Philip.

"Forget it," Philip said. "I don't want to speak on it."

But his friend leaned in further and waited. Finley followed suit, probably remembering from school how many times Philip cracked under the pressure of silence.

Philip cleared his throat. "The first, well, after the wedding."

"The wedding night," Finley urged him on.

Memories of Carmen squeezing her eyes shut when he was above her flashed in his mind. But there was no use hiding it. In truth, he didn't wish to keep it a secret. He hoped one of his friends might have some encouraging advice.

Philip told a shortened version of the night, then looked at his friends and waited. They tried to hide their amusement behind their whiskey, but eventually, their laughter won out. There was no encouraging advice forthcoming.

"I don't know why I pour my soul out to you two," Philip said, flinging himself back into the chair, as far away from them as he could get without leaving all together.

"Don't be like that," Cinch said, chuckling. "I'm sure everyone has been there in some way."

Philip sat up again, uplifted by the suggestion. "On our way here, I realize I've only ever been with a woman who was already married. A woman who knew what was coming and knew what she wanted. I don't know what to do with an innocent woman."

"It isn't too different," Finley said. "Just do what you did with your mistresses."

"Right." Philip frowned into his glass. "But usually, and I'm not proud of what I'm about to say, but when I would visit Alice or women before her, I never had to think about what she wanted. I mean, Alice knew what she wanted and how to get it. But if Carmen doesn't know there is something for her to want, well, then what?"

Cinch clinked his glass against Philip's and said, "You have to teach her what she wants."

Chapter 22

"THE NERVE OF MY brother," Theodore huffed for the hundredth time since he'd woken up that morning. Meredith bit her tongue hard to keep herself from screaming. She had stayed on in London to help Theodore finalize the house and investment plans instead of attending her annual medicinal retreat in Bath, and the brittleness in her bones protested the choice.

At first, she had stayed to spite Philip. She wanted him to come down to the peg where he should have been roosting all along. He was third-born, after all. No third-born got anything. Not even second-borns got anything. And if you were a firstborn girl? Well, you still got nothing. Nothing but an arranged marriage to a man who couldn't figure out how to carry out the family lineage without his brother's financial meddling.

Meredith bitterly resented Philip telling them how to spend money. After all, if he had known Sutton Enterprises would do as well as it was, he should have invested the family money into Sutton Enterprises and then split everything evenly with the family. Half to Theodore, since he was continuing the family name, with the remaining half divided among Philip, Calvin, and their mother. It was only fair. But no. Philip claimed he was working and had full control over how to disperse the money he earned. It was just a power move, like any other. Philip had no real power in the world, so he got morsels of it from bestowing monthly stipends upon his family.

Now, though, things were about to change. And Meredith wanted to be there to see it.

"It doesn't matter that he married. The judge will rule in our favor."

Theodore stopped pacing and looked at his wife. "Why?"

Meredith shrugged, pretending to still read her book. "She is obviously Catholic, so his marriage doesn't count. He will lose the house because it is rightfully yours. The rumors have already turned in our favor. I have also heard that the bank backing the project Philip was starting with Lord Hemsworth no longer has the confidence to use the house as a lien against the loan. So, he is out."

Theodore's forehead furrowed, fraying Meredith's nerves even more.

"I didn't wish to set him back financially on anything. I didn't realize he wouldn't be able to build the hotel without the house."

It took great effort for Meredith to keep from closing her eyes in frustration. "Whatever Philip was saying or using the house for is on him, not you. It was never really his house. It is yours. And you want a house in Berkeley Square, do you not? Well, once we have this house, we can exchange it, just as we planned. Then you'll invest further in the India silk business. The dividends already give us a monthly income, and if they rise, perhaps we will have enough money to invest in other ventures that you will be part of because of your membership at the new club."

Theodore massaged his temples, squeezing his eyes shut. Meredith suppressed a sigh at his inability to keep up.

"Should I wear my new shoes today?" Theodore asked upon opening his eyes. It was a wonder the man had ever finished anything. He rubbed his hands together like a child at Christmas as he gazed fondly at his new leather shoes nestled in a velvet bag. The wrinkles in the middle of his forehead were now gone, and he wore a giddy grin.

There were times Meredith envied her husband's simplicity, the way he became excited for the small occasions in his life. She had thought she might feel excitement and happiness being a mother. But though she loved her children and wanted the best for them, she was perfectly content for them to stay with their nanny. If they were safe, there was no need to see them. The only thought that made her feel as happy as Theodore with new clothes was in her daydreams about becoming a lady so powerful in London that no one dared cause her distress.

Meredith smiled, serenity filling her at the image.

"You like them?" Theodore asked, excitedly turning and pointing his toes. "You don't usually smile at my shoes, but I told you these were special. I told you."

"Yes, dear, they are quite lovely." As far as shoes went. "Are you ready to go out? I believe the weather is holding. We can take a leisurely stroll, look at the houses."

Theodore slumped. The wrinkle between his eyes came back. "You wish to look at houses again? We can't choose one just yet."

"I know that." He was like dealing with another child at times. "Let's go now. I need some air. Just think of how many people will see your shoes."

Meredith tugged her gloves on and then held out her hand for her husband to take. He kissed it. As though she were a queen. It was one of the endearing things he did that she adored.

"I almost forgot to tell you. I sent a calling card ahead to Philip."

"Whatever for?" Theodore cried out, dramatic as always.

"Because he is back in town, and it's the proper thing to do."

"But I don't see why we need to call on my brother and his so-called wife."

"Because we are better than them," Meredith said matter-of-factly, "and we must follow etiquette and protocol. Without order, there is no nobility. And without nobility, there is no England."

That was something her father used to say over and over again. She hadn't understood it as a child, but now she quite liked saying it.

Chapter 23

Carmen opened the door to her bedroom and carefully stepped out into the hallway of her new home. Today was the first day of her new life. And she wasn't sure she was feeling up to it.

The hall was quiet. In fact, the entire house was still. Odd for how big it was. Her house in Spain always brimmed with warmth and activity.

She could not be homesick this early. There would be time to miss her sister and father and Rosa later. She should be excited. She was in London and a married woman. Every married woman had to leave her home to join her husband. Isabel had done it, though she didn't live so very far away from their father.

Images of her childhood home haunted her thoughts, along with memories of a recent talk with Isabel.

"You must be stern with the servants from the moment you enter the house," Isabel had advised. "They will respect you more when you show you understand your role and that you are now mistress. Do not abdicate the menu to the cook. Sit down and create it yourself. Do not tell them the decorations are fine as they stand. Make at least two to three changes in each room. It's a way of asserting your authority, and I am sure you will need to do so even more since you will be a foreigner. Do not think for a moment they will be gentle with you."

Carmen sighed. It all felt very overwhelming. She tiptoed down the hallway, wondering which of the other three doors might lead to Philip's room. She hadn't expected to sleep in separate chambers, though Tía had warned her it might happen.

"Those English are a bit strange, you know," Tía had said, squeezing Carmen's hand.

It was true that her mother had her own room, but she never used it for sleeping. Carmen's mother and father always retired to the same room at night.

Carmen pushed the thoughts of her family back in Spain out of her head, rolled her shoulders back, and surveyed her new home. Several massive paintings hung along the walls of the hallway of hills with sheep, a small village, and one of Mary and child. Halfway there was a long, narrow table holding expensive-looking vases. Carmen stretched her fingers along the sides of it, careful not to touch the painted vases and glass bowls, measuring the distance with the length of her arm.

When the table ended, she was only a few more steps from the stairs. At the edge, Carmen listened, still finding only silence. There was a small landing at the top of the main stairway which contained, if she remembered correctly, twenty-one steps.

Tall, narrow steps.

Carmen carefully moved down the two steps and stood on the small landing, tilting her chin down to gauge her place before moving forward. With another deep breath, she grasped the handrail, feeling each step with her whole body to acclimate herself to the descent.

The steps were narrower than those in Spain, but her foot still fit in the space. She took a deep breath for confidence and settled into a rhythm as she went.

"Good morning, Mrs. Daucer." Felix, the butler, stepped out of the shadows. She was concentrating so hard that he startled her, and she stumbled on the last step. Felix stepped forward as though to catch her, but Carmen straightened quickly, lifting her chin as though nothing had happened. "Are you alright?"

"Good mor-morning," Carmen stuttered. "Yes, I'm quite alright. It's quite dark in the hallway, isn't it?"

"I am sorry about that, madam. I will be sure to fix that today." Felix's voice was grim, but not unkind. His face expressed neither frustration nor amusement.

"Would you like to have your breakfast?" Felix asked.

"Oh." Carmen hadn't expected the question. She listened for the sound of Philip eating somewhere, but only silence returned to her. "Is my husband having breakfast now?"

"He is in the study. He usually works at this time of day."

"What time is it, please?"

"Ten in the morning," Felix replied.

"I had no idea. I don't usually wake up this late."

"Mr. Daucer told us not to disturb you. He wasn't sure you were joining us today."

Carmen bit her lip. She spent the day before in bed with her usual monthly discomfort. "I understand. May I see my husband?"

"Usually, he doesn't wish to be disturbed," a voice boomed from down the hall. Carmen squinted at the shadow making its way towards her. "But he would make an exception any time for his wife."

Philip stopped a foot away from Carmen. He tapped her nose. The act of endearment calmed her. She had been afraid he'd be upset with her turning him away the night they arrived. And for not coming down the day before. "How are you? Did you sleep well?"

"I'm sorry to come downstairs so late," Carmen said. "Perhaps I could have a clock in my room so I can better manage my time."

Felix snapped his heels together. "Very well."

"No need to apologize, Señorita Carmen," Philip said, taking her hand and pressing it against his elbow. His touch made Carmen's knees feel as though they were melting.

"I'm sorry you were feeling poorly yesterday," he murmured as he led her into the parlor.

His words brought her relief. "There are things to get used to as a married couple," she said slowly. "Getting to know each other and things about ourselves, I guess."

They arrived in the parlor, a spacious square room with tall windows that overlooked the front garden where lilacs, jasmine and roses were blooming. The white marble fireplace instantly made her feel more at home, with its ornate carvings of vines and grapes. Paper inked in shades of blue, lilac, and cream, with billowing pink ribbons trailing between each bouquet, covered the walls. Closer to the entrance was a low, wooden table with a chaise longue upholstered in a deep yellow and two Chippendale chairs.

She searched for something she would like to change, as Isabel had suggested, but she loved it already. "This room is so beautiful, Philip. Did you decorate it?"

Philip looked around as though he were seeing the room for the first time. "I guess I did, to some extent. I chose the chaise longue, at least."

Carmen laughed. When Philip's cheeks turned a dusty shade of pink, she cupped his chin with her palm. She couldn't seem to stop herself. When she touched him, his eyes melded to hers. Slowly, he dipped his head until his warm lips covered hers, pressing against her mouth until she was forced to part her lips. She pulled back, but her husband had no mercy.

He gripped her wrist and hauled her against his chest. All the while, his tongue explored her mouth. Carmen tried to keep up, tried to imitate what he was doing, but it was impossible. She had never, ever been kissed in that way. She couldn't think in words. Only in pressure and touch and feelings.

The sound of footsteps and then a doorknob clicking broke the spell. Within seconds, Philip and Carmen stood a foot apart, breathless and staring at each other as a young woman entered the parlor carrying a tray.

The maid stopped. "I'm sorry, sir," she mumbled.

Philip cleared his throat and gestured for her to come in. Carmen turned quickly to admire a painting on the wall, hoping her face was not as red as it felt.

The maid asked about wanting something else. At least, Carmen was almost certain she did. The accent was difficult for her to follow. Hoping her face no longer showed evidence of their kissing, Carmen turned and gave the young maid a timid smile, Isabel's voice once again in her head.

"That will do, Rebecca. Have you met your new mistress, Mrs. Daucer?" Philip asked, gesturing towards Carmen. Rebecca dipped an awkward curtsy.

"Hello. Nice to meet you," Carmen said.

It was clear from Rebecca's panicked expression that she didn't understand Carmen's accent, either. Philip translated for the young maid. The kindness he showed her gave Carmen a peace she hadn't felt before with someone. He was a good man.

"I see I might need to practice my English," Carmen said, once Rebecca had hurried through the door.

Philip gave her a wink.

A fluttering rippled through her heart.

"Rebecca hasn't been around many people from the continent. She'll get used to you. She's our cook now, too, in case you wish to change the menu or whatever it is you women do."

Carmen smiled at his sudden discomfiture as he ended the phrase with a wave.

Philip went on quickly, "Please, sit. Rebecca makes the best scones. And there is fresh tea."

As Philip paused to light his pipe, Carmen glanced at the layout of the chairs and low table, their edges just out of her sight. Carefully, she maneuvered between the furniture, choosing the plush, linen covered settee to perch on.

"I thought we might meet my friends today. If you feel up to it. What do you think?" Philip asked, sitting back on the other chair while puffing on his pipe. "They've invited us to lunch. We can work out the details about our Protestant ceremony during that time as well."

"That sounds lovely," Carmen said.

"Perhaps we can see London tomorrow."

"I would like that," Carmen said, her excitement building. "Could we drive past the palace?"

Philip laughed. "Of course. We can take the open carriage, and I will give you a small tour on our way to the dressmakers."

"You don't have to buy me more dresses. I have enough, I believe," Carmen said, taking a scone. Her stomach was finally eager for some nourishment. She hadn't eaten much since leaving Spain. She took a small bite, not wanting to appear unladylike, though it was difficult.

"You have beautiful dresses, Carmen, but fashion is different here. I want you to feel comfortable. Besides, I want you to have all the dresses in the world."

"Thank you," she said, hiding her grin with her hand. "I do love to shop."

Philip sank next to her on the settee. His smell of chicory and oak invaded her senses. Every fiber within her wanted to sway into his scent, to have his arms wrap around her and calm the buzzing in her chest.

"The season is about to start, which means London will be full of activities. Already we have an invitation to a music soiree. And I'm sure Rowena and Claire will take you to some teas and other things ladies do. Which will be excellent places for you to practice your English, if you wish to do so."

"Certainly," Carmen agreed, finishing off her tea. After seeing the panic in Rebecca's eyes, the idea of practicing her English wasn't very appealing.

Within less than an hour, their carriage arrived at a two-story house on the corner of one of the prettiest streets in London. Each house appeared new, with freshly planted trees, colorful flowers in the gardens, and painted black wrought-iron gates around each of them. At the house of number 1546, a tall man with dark hair, wearing a suit that was too expensive to make him the butler, grinned at her and said, "Welcome to Willowbrook House. And to England, of course."

Philip rushed up the steps and laughed. "I've never received such a welcome before. Carmen, this is my friend, Cinch." He turned to Carmen, whom he had left to get out of the carriage alone. "Oh, sorry, darling. Take my hand."

The man named Cinch laughed. Carmen smiled tightly, unsure if he was amused at her slow manner of descending the carriage or at his friend forgetting his wife.

Finally, she was on the ground. "Hello," she said in careful English. Lord Candor grinned at her before kissing her on each cheek.

"We're so glad to have you here, Carmen."

Philip pulled Carmen closer to him. "We aren't in Spain. Enough kissing my wife."

"Just making her feel at home, Philip," Lord Candor said, chuckling as he motioned for them to enter the house.

"Not too much at home," Philip retorted.

The house practically shimmered with light. The entryway was open, with high ceilings that had a stained-glass window at the top. The sun filtered in, throwing gold, red and blue shapes along the gleaming white-tiled floor. To the left and right were enormous rooms with large doors kept open, which added to the airy ambiance. Carmen was instantly in love with the house. Though Philip's house was beautiful in its own way, the hallways were dark. This house radiated warmth and sunshine.

"May I take your coat?" A footman was standing patiently next to Carmen, waiting for her to take notice of him.

"Yes, of course, thank you," she said. She handed over her blue wool coat that seemed simple and plain against the splendor of the house. The footman, of course, said nothing upon taking it. And Carmen had little more time to think on it before footsteps marched towards them.

"You're here," a firm female voice declared.

Carmen turned to find a slim woman in a muslin dress, her brown hair gathered loosely into a bun, beaming at Philip.

"This is my sister-in-law, Claire," Lord Candor said as Claire took Carmen's hands in hers.

"You are lovely. Much too lovely for Philip," Claire said.

Philip scowled, while Lord Candor and Claire laughed.

"And this lovely woman coming down the hall is my wife, Rowena," Lord Candor announced. Lord Candor's wife was plumper than Claire, though Carmen remembered Philip saying she had just had a baby. She, too, had styled her hair in a loose bun, but wore a less fitted dress in powder blue with a knitted shawl covering her shoulders.

"Come in," Rowena said, grasping Carmen's hand. "We're having tea in the back of the sunroom. It's a beautiful day for it. I have the baby there now with Eleadora."

"All Rowena thinks about is the baby," Claire said, walking alongside them. Rowena clicked her tongue. "I tell Claire that one day she will marry again and have a baby of her own, and then she will understand me."

Carmen smiled at the teasing. It made her miss Isabel terribly.

"I imagine it well enough," Claire said. "At the moment, I am quite busy with the day-school and convincing the local mothers that educating their children young is preferable. I have never been around so many children and babies in my life."

"That is such a lovely idea," Carmen said, feeling a kindred connection instantly with Claire. "I have always thought children should be educated, whether poor or rich, male or female."

"Exactly right," Claire said as they arrived at their destination.

The sunroom, as Rowena called it, had one wall made all of glass that looked out over the gardens. The other three walls were decorated with soft green paper that held delicately painted flowers. The wicker chairs and tables held cushions covered in a floral fabric that looked comfortable and inviting. Carmen was in awe.

"It's beautiful," she said.

"Well, when it's storming, which is often, it's frightening," Rowena said, leaving Carmen to march to the baby cradle.

Carmen forced herself to stop taking in the room and noticed a little girl of about five or six staring at her from one of the chairs. Her dark eyes and curly hair were reminiscent of many women in Spain.

"This is Eleadora," Claire said, sitting next to the girl and indicating Carmen should sit as well.

"You might not know, Carmen, that Eleadora is my husband's daughter. She's being a very helpful big sister, aren't you?" Rowena joined them, holding a bundle wrapped in blankets. Carmen peeked into the bundle of blankets to find a sleeping baby with fuzzy blond hair, a button nose and tiny pink lips. A pang of regret stabbed her as she thought about Isabel and the nephew or niece she might not see for years.

"I'm an excellent big sister," Eleadora said, her eyes still on Carmen.

"I'm sure you are. You look like you'd be an excellent big sister," Carmen told her, tearing her eyes away from the baby.

"My mother was Spanish," Eleadora said, her eyes staring up at Carmen.

"Eres muy guapa, Eleadora. I'm Carmen Suárez, though I suppose I'm now Carmen Daucer," Carmen said in Spanish.

Eleadora's face lit up. "I can't believe you speak Spanish and are now married to my Uncle Philip."

"Uncle Philip?" Carmen repeated, wondering if she had missed a family connection.

"I know he and Papa aren't brothers," Eleadora explained in Spanish, "but that's what I call him." She eyed Carmen. "Are you and Uncle Philip going to have a baby soon?"

"What did you say about me?" Philip asked as he and Lord Candor strode in.

"See?" giggled Eleadora. "Uncle Philip doesn't understand Spanish as well as he should. I've been teaching him for over a year, after all."

"Well, I understood that," Philip protested, his hands on his hips as he faced Eleadora down.

"Because I spoke in English, Uncle." Eleadora frowned at him, which made Carmen laugh and long for home at the same time.

"Eleadora, don't be telling fibs to my wife," Philip said in Spanish to show off. Eleadora responded by giggling. Carmen couldn't help joining her. The exchange between Philip and the child proved Philip would be a good father. That was a relief.

"You sound like you're still trying to speak in English," she said. "I learned to speak English without an accent."

"You came here when you were a munchkin," Philip said, pretending to pout. "What are you doing all day?"

"She's become the family's full-time portrait artist," Rowena said, smiling at Eleadora. "She draws a marvelous picture of her new brother."

"I wanted to capture how cute he was. I'm now working on one of Mamá and the baby. If someone were to invent a machine that could paint people, I wouldn't have to do this," Eleadora said with a sigh. "Alas, I must take responsibility for it. Uncle Philip, I could paint your portrait. For a fee, of course."

"You little scoundrel," Philip said, laughing.

"I like to paint," Carmen said, reaching for the painting. "Can I see yours?"

Eleadora beamed at her as Carmen bent over the painting. It obviously depicted Rowena and Claire, though the eyes were crooked and the noses too big and the lips were but two lines curved upwards. Still, it was good for her age. "I think you paint very well. I think you should ask for top dollar from your Uncle Daucer."

Their conversation was cut off when a footman came in announcing lunch. The dining room was as impressive as the sunroom, with high ceilings and tall windows dressed in green brocade fabric. Carmen was grateful for the light again as she discreetly studied her table arrangement. The sparkling bone china plate surrounded by gleaming silverware was easy to find and distinguish from the dark wood of the table.

"Darling," Philip whispered. Carmen looked up to find him studying her. "Cinch is going to make a toast."

"To the new couple," Cinch announced, his deep voice quieting everyone at the table. Carmen adjusted her posture and tried to understand all the words. "We are blessed to meet our new friend, Carmen." Lord Candor smiled warmly at her. "And glad to see someone willing to put up with our friend Philip."

"Hear hear," Claire said dryly. A burst of laughter and the clinking of crystal followed as the footmen entered with the first plates of the luncheon.

"We had some of your family's wine at dinner the other night," Claire said from across the table.

The comment delighted Carmen. She sat with the aid of a footman, eager to speak more about her family wine. "Did you like it?"

"It was lovely," Rowena said. "I only had a little, but it was some of the best wine I've ever had."

"I agree," Claire said. "Philip said you are involved in the wine-making process."

"I am," Carmen said, glad for a topic of conversation that highlighted her abilities. She glanced at Philip, who was devouring his green bean salad. "My father and I mix the grapes and come up with a plan for the wine. My sister isn't much interested in joining us."

"That sounds fascinating," Claire said, leaning in as though genuinely interested. "You must tell me about the process. Is it true that you step on the grapes to get the juice out?"

Carmen laughed good-naturedly. "We do not, no, though there are some wineries that do. My father and I place whole grapes into the barrels."

"Why?" asked Claire.

"It is the skin that gives our wine more tannins, that intense character you get on the edges of your tongue with our wines."

"Well, the wine we had to celebrate little Philip's birth was excellent," Lord Candor said, wandering into their conversation.

Philip snapped his attention away from his plate and looked between Lord Candor and Rowena. "You named the baby after me?"

"Calm yourself, Philip," Claire said in a bored tone, though Carmen could tell she was hiding a smile.

"Hold the presses!" Philip exclaimed, springing to his feet. Rowena and Lord Candor laughed with delight as Philip raised his glass of wine. "To Philip!"

"Which Philip?" Claire asked. Carmen couldn't help chuckling. Claire always seemed ready to tease Philip. She could see now why Philip had so easily slipped into the rhythm of her own family back in Spain.

"To any man, or baby, named Philip," Philip said, grinning from ear to ear.

Carmen's heart swelled in happiness at the sight of her husband so elated. This was Philip's family. She could see that now. Perhaps it wasn't conventional, but it was love. She was glad he had them as friends.

"To all the Philips of the world," Rowena said, still laughing.

Philip grabbed Carmen and kissed her hard on the cheek before taking his seat again. "Can you believe it? I have a little boy named after me."

"I can, Philip. I can believe it," Carmen said, her husband's laughter contagious.

"Perhaps you should have a boy of your own," Lord Candor said as more luncheon arrived. "Give Philip a playmate."

"I'll name him Cinch," Philip said.

"Oh, please don't," Rowena complained. "I still dislike that nickname."

The table erupted in more laughter as they cut into their pork loin with a gusto that surprised Carmen once she had tasted it. Though the food was nutritious, it was nothing like lechazo, or arroz a la zamorana, or a simple tortilla de patata that she enjoyed growing up. The realization hit her squarely in the heart.

"Shall we have dessert in the sunroom?" Claire asked as the table was cleared.

"I will excuse myself," Rowena said. "If I don't see you again today, it was lovely to meet you, Carmen."

"Where is she off to?" Philip asked as Rowena disappeared from the room.

"You have no idea the toll a baby takes on a woman, Philip," Claire said with authority. "She isn't even in society yet."

"Is she not?" Philip asked.

"Philip will be baptized next week, which will bring her time of confinement to an end. You'll learn of things like this soon enough." Claire saluted Philip with her wine and smirked.

"There is a letter just arrived, my lord," the butler announced from the doorway. "From Minister Percival."

"Cinch?" Philip said when Lord Candor didn't look up from reading the missive. "What is it?"

"Minister Percival claims he is unable to conduct the marriage ceremony. He says there is a problem, and he wishes to speak with Philip and me about it before we proceed." Cinch showed the missive to Philip, but didn't read from it while the others waited.

"Well," Carmen said, breaking the silence, "will he perform it?"

"I don't know," Philip said, his chair scraping against the floor as he stood, grating their ears. He tossed his napkin onto the table, clearly infuriated. "Cinch and I will find out."

Carmen glanced towards Claire, who gave her a reassuring smile. Philip's mood had changed so suddenly, she wasn't sure what to say or do.

"Shall we go to the sunroom? I can teach you to play a card game we like."

Carmen followed Claire, who reached for her elbow the minute they were in the hallway. "We'll find a way to entertain ourselves, won't we?"

Chapter 24

Alice.

Philip gritted his teeth, cursing the day he met her as he and Cinch rode straight to her house. After meeting with Minister Percival, a man that turned out to be Alice's cousin, Philip had decided to confront her. It was her fault there was a problem with the ceremony, after all, and he was too livid not to tell her his thoughts. Cinch had insisted on coming, probably to keep him from doing anything too stupid. No man could know for certain how a mistress would react the moment they were left behind, but he should have known Alice would not disappear quietly. Alice was a beautiful, dynamic, explosive, and passionate woman. All characteristics that drew him to her in the first place. But now, he needed her to go away without causing trouble. Ironic, that the very qualities that attracted him while she was his mistress now threatened his place in society and possibly his marriage.

Through the bay window of Alice's parlor, Philip watched Cinch smoke his pipe in the garden. Philip slapped his hat against his thigh impatiently as the seconds ticked by. He considered making himself a drink from the liquor she always had displayed on the mantel, but thought better of it. He wanted to be of sound mind when speaking with Alice. But if she made him wait much longer, he wasn't sure he could hold off.

Philip frowned at the room. A fine film of dust outlined the tables and mantel, the couch was threadbare in places, and the carpet appeared damp. Somehow, the room no longer felt warm or inviting. It was as though years had passed since he'd last been there instead of barely two months.

"Darling," Alice said as she swept into the salon. She gave a childish jump and giggle before launching herself into Philip's arms. "I expected you ages ago. I sent you letters, but you never replied. I figured that butler of yours wasn't giving them to you."

"Alice," Philip began as she peppered his face and mouth with kisses. "Alice, stop. I've come to speak with you."

Alice reared back immediately, and her mouth thinned into a taut line. "Speak?" Her eyes darted from his hand to the cart. "Sit. I'll pour you a drink. You must be fatigued."

"I don't want a drink," he said, but Alice ignored him. She sashayed towards him with two glasses, forcing Philip to sit on the couch. Then she sat on his lap. Something he used to enjoy immensely but now found rather uncomfortable.

"I missed you." Her pink tongue licked along the edges of her partially open mouth.

Another action that was once seductive, but now he found vulgar. Images of Carmen's lips in her wide smile, her laugh filling the room, her eyes sparkling with life, invaded his thoughts. He pushed them away when Alice impatiently pressed her own lips to his.

Alice's lips were dry, her movements rehearsed. Carmen's lips were supple and curious. Alice's overt eagerness to please now felt crass compared to Carmen's innocence.

"Alice," Philip grumbled, resisting her weight that was pushing him to lie back. "We need to speak. I need you to get off me and sit over there."

Alice jerked away so abruptly that Philip hardly saw her move.

"Speak? You came here to speak with me?" She tipped back the whiskey, her smile turning wicked.

"I came because you have disrupted my life in a way that is unacceptable."

Alice furrowed her brow and puckered her lips, a look that used to make her look innocent and childlike. Now, Philip could only see it as manipulation.

"I spoke with Minister Perceval today," Philip said.

Alice's deep, sultry laugh sent chills down Philip's spine.

"Are the rumors true, then?"

"What rumors?"

Philip watched Alice closely as she poured herself another drink. "I have friends all over this city, you know. Unlike you and the rest of the noble *ton*, I treat everyone the same. Anyone who can give me information, that is. And the information I have is that you and your wife didn't sleep in the same room while on the ship. That you slept with the men and gave her the cabin. A rather strange marriage, is it not?"

Philip cleared his throat, his mind racing. Who could be speaking with Alice about such things?

"I don't know who you are speaking with. . ."

"Don't bother," Alice said with a wave. "You're going to give me some excuse about treating her like a lady, are you?"

Philip shut his mouth.

"Yes, yes. The problem with that excuse is that no one treats a woman like a lady during their honeymoon period. Especially not a man like you with a wife who looks like that." Alice glanced at him, a smile rising in the left corner of her mouth. "Oh, yes, Philip. I've seen your wife. I was at the docks. I was there to greet you, but instead, I found you escorting another woman off the ship, talking to her as though she were a delicate flower."

Alice snorted. Philip imagined a sick donkey taking his last breath, though he knew that wasn't fair.

"Drink your whiskey." Alice pointed to the glass.

Thinking it better to stay alert, Philip ignored the order.

"I went back and spoke to some of your men after you left. They have interesting things to say about you," Alice said.

"Such as?"

"That you claimed to be married to this Carmen woman, but that you must have had the ceremony in Spain." Alice grinned, looking pleased with herself. "Didn't you wonder, when you spoke with Percival, how I could have possibly known?"

Nausea rolled through his stomach at her tone. "How did you get Percival transferred to my parish?"

"Oh, Philip, he's been there for a few months. You just never attend church. If you had, you would have noticed that I do. I understand I need atonement, and my cousin Percival is willing to give it to me." Alice shook her head. "If you had been a better Christian, perhaps you would have more power in this matter."

She leaned into him, planting her palms against his chest. He stiffened, but didn't move. His body betrayed him, clouding the reason he was there in the first place. Alice's palms slowly trailed down his body until they rested on his hips.

"If you want things to change, you only have to say so." Alice's fingers trailed the edge of his trousers as she licked her lips. "A man has needs. You have needs. We could start again where we left off."

The bodice of her dress slipped to her waist, exposing most of her large breasts. With only one step, Alice pressed them against his chest and snaked her fingers through his hair before pulling his mouth down to her for a long, lingering kiss.

Everything about her disgusted him. The way her body rubbed against his, the way her lips were too experienced, the way she had manipulated this very meeting.

His body stiffened.

"Alice, stop," he commanded.

The grin on Alice's lips gave him a chill. Before he knew it, she reached for him and wrapped her hands around the back of his neck. Suddenly, a hot, stinging sensation assaulted his earlobe.

"Damn it! Alice!"

She sank her teeth deeper still; the pain seeping into his neck. Only when he grasped her wrists that he still held in a twist did she release his ear. Philip pushed her away, covering the burning pain with his hands. Alice's lips curled as she stumbled backwards.

"I do not like being forgotten," she said. "I do not like being tossed aside."

Philip regarded her, saying nothing. The pain in his ear was slowly reducing to a pulse, but he was still furious. He just didn't wish to do anything rash.

Alice's eyes narrowed at his gaze, a pink tint covering her face.

"Why are you here?" she asked.

Philip extracted the letters he had found stacked on his desk when he arrived home. He had brought them to Cinch's house to ask Cinch to do him a favor, which he would have done. After meeting with Minister Percival, Philip decided it was best to return them to Alice in person.

"We are ended."

Instead of appearing hurt, Alice chortled.

"Oh, poor Lord Daucer." If humans could become animals, Alice would be a snake. She moved around the room as one, slithering and hissing her fury at him. "I sent that to remind you of your duties to me."

The threat turned Philip cold. He took out another envelope and threw it on top of the letter. "Here is enough to keep you fed and housed for one year. Consider it your payoff. My duties to you are summed up in that envelope there." He stepped towards her and lowered his voice. "You are still young, Alice, and you have many men in London waiting for me to leave. Let us separate amicably."

Alice picked up the money and glanced back at him.

"You are not to contact me," Philip said. "Not through letters, not in person. And you are not to contact my wife either." He stepped closer, glaring at her until she looked at him. "Do you understand?"

Alice nodded curtly, her eyes flickering to him for only a second before returning to the money. Philip didn't hesitate. He picked up his coat and marched to the door.

A soft thump against the closed door indicated a pillow had been thrown against it.

"All done then?" Cinch called out from a few feet away.

"All done," Philip said as wails seeped past Alice's walls. "There isn't much she can do now, and she won't speak with her cousin, but I believe that's the last I have to deal with her."

"Then let's go home, shall we?" Cinch summoned his carriage forward.

Philip rubbed his face with his palms and tried to think as they rode back to Cinch's house.

"What do you think about my chances of getting a special license?" Philip asked as they reached Willowbrook House.

"I'd say fairly good. I believe Finley and Henry have connections there."

Philip grunted.

"I will speak with Henry on Monday. Will you be coming here for our usual workday? If we get *The Emerald Mistress* into port tomorrow, I will need you there to make sure everything is offloaded properly."

"Of course," Philip said as they gave their coats to the footman, and Philip asked for his wife to be called. "What about Finley? Are we doing business with him in some fashion?"

Cinch waved dismissively as the tapping of female shoes came down the hallway. "I will speak to you about it on Monday. Claire, she doesn't like to speak about Finley."

"Claire?" asked Philip, but Cinch hushed him as she, Carmen, and Rowena appeared. Philip grinned at his wife. "Ready to go, then? I hope you spent a lovely afternoon with Claire and Rowena."

"Why are you speaking as though we are children having learned to play together for the first time?" Claire scoffed.

Cinch gave Philip a look that told him not to get into it.

"I had a lovely time," Carmen said as she slipped on her coat. Philip leaned in as though to kiss her. As he did, he smelled something very like Alice's perfume. Too late, he realized it was he who smelled of it.

Claire was looking at him, her eyes narrowed. "Did you clear things up with Minister Percival?"

"Sorry?" Philip blinked. He was watching for Carmen's reaction to the perfume, but she seemed not to have noticed.

"Minister Percival," Claire repeated with a tinge of irritation. Philip knew how this looked and how his friend felt about men who cheated on their wives. Claire tolerated it for many years from her former husband and then endured the shame of him dying in a duel.

"Yes, we spoke with him," Cinch said.

"We are working to get a special license," Philip said, taking over the conversation. "I thought it would be nice to have the ceremony more privately. Perhaps at my home."

"You should have it here." Rowena's eyes lit. "Or you could have it the day of Philip's baptism. The same day, wouldn't that be wonderful? The baptism will take place in the small chapel my father has at Tajir Villa."

"Tajir Villa?" Carmen was turning from one person to another. Philip found the movement quite distracting. His ear was pounding with heat.

Though he was glad to find it wasn't bleeding when he touched it.

"The name of my father's house. It isn't far from here and it's quite lovely. You would have a beautiful ceremony, I promise." Rowena clasped Carmen's hands in hers until Carmen nodded. "That's settled then. I will prepare everything. You just need the license."

Philip stepped towards the door to indicate they should be leaving. The way Claire glowered at him, he felt she might claw at his eyes at any moment.

"Carmen?"

"Yes, of course," Carmen said, hurrying through her goodbyes. Philip inched towards the fresh air where he hoped the fragrance of Alice's perfume would be blown away.

Claire and Rowena took their time sending Carmen off, Claire glaring at Philip whenever she got the chance, but finally, Carmen was free. When her shoes clipped against the brick of the doorway, Philip turned and held out his hand. But instead of taking it, she walked forward, her foot landing off the first step. Suddenly, her body flew forward, down towards Philip and the brick sidewalk.

"Carmen!" Philip shouted. He rushed to her, but there were only five steps up to Willowbrook House, and she was past him almost before he could move. She hit the ground hard, her arms flying out, the sound of fabric tearing filling the air.

Philip knelt over her, rolling her towards him, his heart thudding as though it might burst in his chest.

"Carmen, are you alright?" he croaked.

"Estoy bien, Philip," she said, twisting in his arm. "I'm caught in all my skirts, and my wrist and shoulder hurt."

"Call for a doctor at once," Cinch said as he rushed down the steps to her.

"I'm alright," Carmen protested. "More embarrassed. It will be best to take me home."

She looked at Philip with tears glistening in her eyes, and he was powerless to argue. When he picked her up in his arms, she muffled a groan against his chest.

"Send a message for the doctor to meet me at my house," Philip called over his shoulder as he eased Carmen into the carriage and joined her inside. Cinch hit the roof of the carriage, and it started with a lurch. Philip knew Cinch would come through.

Chapter 25

PHILIP AWOKE WITH A start, his body jerking backwards and almost completely off the chair he was half sitting on. His head had been lying on the edge of Carmen's bed where he had fallen into a restless slumber perhaps five minutes before or perhaps an hour, and now his neck ached when he turned to the left. At least it took attention away from his ear.

In the dim morning light, he saw Carmen still asleep in her bed, her hair billowing over the pillow like it had been blown by the wind.

He allowed himself to revel in knowing she was alright. But within seconds, the emotions and irrational terror that had consumed him in the night once again wrapped their cold, dry fingers around his chest until he had to gasp for breath. Almost as horrifying as the recurring image in his head of Carmen's fall was realizing his deep attachment to someone whose death he couldn't bear to fathom.

And it had happened so suddenly.

The horror and the confusion had kept him rooted to the terribly hard chair all night long. She could die and leave him alone.

And he was surprised to discover that the prospect of being alone now was like a boulder lodged on his chest. Death was not a stranger to him. Many people in his life had died. The last one was his mother, who he also sat up with, though he had left when she was deep asleep. With her it was the bond of duty and love between mother and son that kept him at the chair, reading over papers and glancing at her every few minutes.

Until the night before, he had never once in his life considered it possible to desire to sit with somebody all night.

When the doctor administered the laudanum, Philip remembered sinking into the chair and taking Carmen's hand in his. She had spoken about her home in Spain until her speech became Spanish, then thick and slurred as she fought to stay awake.

Even when she was asleep, though the doctor had said she would sleep through the night if not longer, Philip found himself anchored so fully to the chair that the very idea of moving for any reason disturbed him. He had sent Mrs. Brax to bed, leaving Carmen's side only once to relieve himself, but had been so panicked to get back to her he thought he might die of lack of oxygen. It hadn't mattered how many times he had told himself she was in a deep medicalized sleep and the doctor had said she was fine.

Philip rubbed his eyes and stretched his legs, still trying to work out what was happening to him. He couldn't spend his life worrying. There were things to be done. Being so connected with someone and still be successful seemed an impossibility. Before being married, his work with Sutton Enterprises as well as his dream of building the hotel had been enough to occupy his life. Now, sitting next to Carmen all night, neither of those things seemed to matter. Which made him feel further away, somehow, from his future. After all, what was the point of having dreamed and worked and planned before marriage if he were going to give it all up just because he now had a wife?

The feelings and thoughts were confusing. And he didn't like being confused.

Carmen wiggled under the blankets, then winced in her sleep. Philip knelt at her side as her eyes fluttered open.

"Good morning," he said.

Her eyes blinked slowly. She struggled to open them again. "Good morning. I feel—"

Her voice trailed off. The doctor had said there were no broken bones, but had recommended small doses of laudanum for the first few days. Philip didn't like the opium tincture. Too many people had become dependent on it in the past few years in London, but he didn't want Carmen to be uncomfortable, either. A little for just a few days shouldn't change Carmen into one of the listless users Philip saw throughout London society, with glassy eyes and little aspiration to live a conscious life.

"Are you in pain?" Philip asked, leaning in to kiss her forehead. He wanted to make sure she didn't have a fever. Every ailment was on his list of worries at that point.

"You are kind," Carmen said, her eyes still closed, her lips frozen in a smile. "So very kind."

Philip swallowed the lump in his throat. He wondered if she remembered he was nearest to her when she fell. He should have caught her, should have told her to take his hand.

The thought made him frown as her eyes fluttered open again. It was possible she hadn't seen his hand. And not because they had been saying goodbye, but because of her vision problems. He wracked his brain for the name of her condition but couldn't summon it.

"Philip, water, please." Her eyes were fully open, though they were glassy.

"Of course." He hurried to the pitcher Mrs. Brax had left and held the glass up to her lips to sip from. "Slowly. Not too much. Just a little at a time."

"My head feels strange," Carmen said as he guided her back to the pillows. She winced when Philip reached under her shoulder. "My shoulder is sore."

"I'm sorry." Philip moved away. Every cell within him wanted to pull her close to him, hold her, and keep her safe. But he didn't want to hurt her, so he sat back in the chair, his body protesting the position.

The question he wished to ask was, *Are you going to be alright?* But he didn't dare. In case he didn't like the answer.

"I should get up," Carmen said. "But I—I can't move very well."

"It's the laudanum. The doctor wants you to stay in bed for a few days. Make sure things heal properly."

"It's not that bad." Her brow furrowed. "I'm not in pain. Just sore."

"You're not in pain because of the medicine," Philip said as a knock rapped on the door.

It opened to reveal Mrs. Brax carrying a tray laden with food and a fresh pot of tea. "Mrs. Daucer, you're awake. Lord be, you gave us a fright."

Carmen smiled weakly.

"Let me help you sit up so you can eat something." Philip tucked his hands gently around her waist and lifted her into an upright position. "Are you alright?"

"Didn't hurt at all, thank you." Carmen cupped his face, sending lightning through him. Her nightgown, her bed, the way her hair flowed over her shoulders. His fingers ached to rake through her locks and smother her neck in kisses.

"I've come to relieve you, Mr. Daucer," Mrs. Brax announced.

The spell broken, Philip allowed Mrs. Brax to wiggle between them and set the tray on Carmen's lap.

"I better freshen up," Philip said, clearing his throat.

"You have someone coming to see you later this morning, Mr. Finley and Lord Candor." Mrs. Brax spooning medicine into Carmen's mouth, who took it without complaint.

"I'll go on then," Philip said reluctantly. He would have preferred to give Carmen the medicine, to sit with her all day and night again. But the call of life and duty were also strong. Everything about the situation was confusing.

"Well, go on then," admonished Mrs. Brax.

Chapter 26

PHILIP HAD JUST ENOUGH time to clean up and eat breakfast before Finley and Cinch were announced.

"Morning, Daucer," Finley said as he shed his coat in the hallway. The weather had turned on them after a full week of sunshine. The temperature had dropped significantly during the night, and the dark clouds kept one thinking it was almost night when it was but morning. "We thought we would come to you."

Philip nodded tersely, watching his friends. "I appreciate it. Though I would have truly appreciated not working at all on a Sunday."

Cinch chuckled. "You think that, but I'm betting you were already getting bored."

That statement didn't dignify an answer, so Philip gave it none. He simply marched down the hallway, calling for a fresh pot of tea from Felix when he had a chance. Within seconds, Cinch and Finley followed him.

"How is Carmen?" Cinch asked quietly.

"What happened to Carmen?" Finley asked loudly. The emptiness of the hallway emphasized each syllable.

Philip waited until they were seated in the study to answer. "She had a fall yesterday, but she's well. Her wrist isn't broken, although there might be a small fracture on her collarbone. Nothing to be done about it, the doctor says."

"Good heavens, that sounds awful," Finley said. "How did she fall?"

Philip turned away to pretend to stoke the fire. "Just a misstep. She really will be alright in a few days' time." He glanced at Cinch, who gave him an almost imperceptible nod. "She has some vision issues. It's hard for her to see in the peripheral. I wrote to Cinch about it while I was in Spain. It isn't a major issue. Perhaps it isn't even the culprit of the fall, I'm not entirely sure. Carmen can barely talk right now due to the laudanum."

Finley regarded Philip for a moment, then said, "I will only advise that you don't keep her on that stuff for very long. My late wife suffered from poor health and became rather reliant on the stuff. It isn't a good medicine, in my opinion."

"Nor in mine," Philp said. "And you are right, of course. I appreciate your advice."

"Good to hear Carmen is better," Cinch said. Philip and Finley turned their attention to him. "Because we have a bit of an issue."

Finley looked between the two men. "Don't be coy, Christophe Sutton. You most definitely have a problem."

Philip waited, but Rebecca entered with the tea set then. Cinch didn't speak until Rebecca had arranged it and left, closing the door behind her. Then he slid out a paper from his coat pocket and slapped it onto the table. Philip eyed him. Finley, too, said nothing.

"Yesterday, when *The Emerald Mistress* had only just landed, she was immediately condemned to being anchored. They won't let her leave the port. Or unload. There is little product on the ship, you know that. But it appears someone high up has an agreement, probably with an American or Portuguese who dislikes our clipper scouring the sea for slavers."

"The *Emerald Mistress* impeded five slave ships from continuing their route during her mission this past year," Philip told Finley.

Finley lit his pipe before responding, "Yes, I know."

That surprised Philip. He didn't understand how Finley could know so many things about their business doings.

"I believe one of those ships is the reason for her not being allowed to leave again," Cinch said.

"Have you petitioned to, well, whoever it is you petition to? You're in the House of Lords, Cinch. Why is it that you can't get this figured out?" Philip asked.

"I believe it's Lord Kent," Cinch said. "A bit of a revenge mission, possibly. So, the answer is no. I haven't yet spoken about this to anyone."

"I thought we were speaking of Lord Wellington's nephew?" Finley said.

Philip grinned. Finley didn't know everything then.

"One and the same," Philip said. "You see, Lord Kent has invested quite a lot in young Lord George Westchester's business, so to speak."

"And?"

Cinch took over from there. Philip was glad. Exhaustion gnawed at his temples.

"It isn't a proper business as much as it's a front." Cinch lowered his voice. "That bit doesn't leave this room. Lord Kent has the ear of very powerful men in London and can ruin anyone he chooses. I believe it is a way through which certain men in England pass money they might or might not have earned properly."

Finley's jaws visibly tensed. "Like the Poyais scheme?"

"Much like it." Philip downed his cup of tea and swallowed a scone in three bites. The nourishment was helping to wake him. "There's always a scheme or two running. Been like that since the beginning of time."

"Those who scheme on that level deserve nothing less than death," Finley said. When he caught Philip's eye, he stood abruptly and paced the floor. "My father was tricked into investing in the Poyais scheme. He lost thousands of pounds from it. He and his friends. And that General Gregor MacGregor never paid anything back nor ever went to jail. I'm lucky no one in my family went on the ships only to die of starvation over in the New World, but my family lost nearly all our land. Had I not been able to make money in America, we might have lost everything. I'm only just now able to buy back some of it."

"You're too modest," Cinch said, rolling the paper back and forth. "You had those publishing houses and the aluminum factory. Those kept your family going for the years before you made your fortune."

Philip patted Finley on the back twice. "I'm sure I'd love to hear that story one day, but today I was hoping we could finish the one about *The Emerald Mistress* being anchored illegally."

"Right. I have had a strongly worded letter sent to have *The Emerald Mistress* released, but you are the one who knows people. In the end, this is a decision to either get on our bad side or get on Lord Westchester's bad side, which might implicate Wellington."

Philip snorted. "You want me to sit down with all of them and have them make up and be nice?"

"More or less," Cinch said.

"I'll need some coins to pass around," Philip said, pondering how he was supposed to accomplish his mission.

"Done," Cinch said. "We are losing about a thousand pounds sterling a day with *The Emerald Mistress* stuck in Southhampton. I brought Finley because he had some issues with his imports that he's managed to iron out."

Philip regarded Finley, who didn't take the hint to let him in on the story.

"What am I supposed to do with you, Finley?"

The man shrugged. "I think this could be a beneficial friendship, Daucer."

"Finley's in with Sutton Enterprises now?" Philip asked, turning to Cinch.

He sighed heavily. "It's more of a mutual friendship. For the benefit of our company and his. We have agreed to buy the utensils coming out of his factories, and he has agreed to supplement our iron for the Spain project."

That was news to Philip. It must have happened while he was in Spain.

"Henry went out to the mine. I figured you wouldn't want to, being just married and all," Cinch said.

Philip spread his hands and said nothing. Cinch was the owner of Sutton Enterprises, after all. It was his call. "The men say there is less iron ore this year than there was last. And that's on top of the decline we had last year. This partnership with Finley's mine that doesn't seem to be giving out couldn't come at a better time."

"I guess I'll owe my bonus to Henry then," Philip said.

His friend laughed. "Well, if you're offering your bonus to him, I'm sure he'll take it."

"If he gets a bonus, I would like one, too," Finley said, winking at Philip. They both sniggered at Cinch's discomfort.

"You both have other things to focus on rather than take my money,"

Cinch muttered. "Namely, your women."

"Women?" Philip repeated, assessing Finley.

"Claire," Cinch said, receiving a shake of the head from Finley.

"Ho, ho, Finley, lad. Might as well get started then," Philip said, setting his lukewarm tea aside. "You can tell me about the trouble you're having with our Claire on the way."

Finley grunted uncomfortably as Cinch laughed. Philip grinned, letting him know there was no getting out of it. Damned if he was going to pass up the opportunity of knowing other men were having woman problems. Anything to make him feel better about his own.

Chapter 27

THE NEXT DAY, PHILIP wandered through London, again investigating who was responsible for the anchoring of *The Emerald Mistress*. Finley had meetings of his own, apparently more important, so they had agreed to focus on *The Emerald Mistress* later that week, but Philip didn't enjoy sitting still.

With Carmen still bedridden, Philip had slipped out of the house. Despite the mist that soon dampened his wool coat, he preferred to be out. The air cleared his head from replaying Carmen's fall over and over. Down at the docks, he almost forgot about his wife lying in bed, so focused was he on The Emerald Mistress.

By six in the evening, he was no closer to solving the problem, so he turned around and walked home.

Without a firm solution but with too much cold seeping into his bones, Philip entered the front door of his home. The foyer was dark, with just a weak light trickling from one lantern.

"Was your day satisfactory, sir?"

Philip jumped, his body involuntarily throwing itself against the door. "The devil hang you," he said, gasping for breath. "My god, you'll be the death of me, Felix. Of that, I'm sure."

"Yes, sir." Felix's face was serious as always. "But not before I take your coat, sir."

Philip shrugged out of his wet wool coat. "How is Mrs. Daucer?"

"She seems well, sir. She is in the library."

That was unexpected. "She is so well she got out of bed?"

"She came downstairs for lunch around one in the afternoon, sir." Philip glanced at the clock. It was just past seven. He had been gone all day, wasting his time, when he could have been home with Carmen. "She is feeling better, I take it?"

"She seems to be quite well, sir," Felix said. "Will you have some dinner, sir?"

"Something light, perhaps. But I'll take it in the library."

Felix turned on his heels and marched away. Philip calculated he would have a plate of cold meat pie in less than ten minutes. Before that, he wanted to see Carmen.

Inside the library, a steady fire burned. Carmen sat back against the couch, staring so intently at the fire Philip thought she might have fallen asleep. He stood watching the shadows from the fire bounce over her for a moment, breathing in the vanilla scent that hovered around her.

"Carmen," he whispered from the doorway. Carmen startled, her head snapping around towards him.

"Sorry. Didn't mean to scare you," he said. "Have you had your dinner?"

"No, I had some tea, but was waiting for you."

"Excuse me, sir," Felix interrupted from the doorway. "I brought up two plates, in case Mrs. Daucer is hungry, and a bottle of wine."

Felix set them on the low table near the fireplace and waited. "Will there be anything else, sir?"

"No, thank you. Please tell everyone they can go to bed. I'll make sure my wife is settled tonight." Philip paused and looked back at Carmen. "Unless you prefer to have Mrs. Brax stay up?"

"Oh, no. Of course not," Carmen said quickly.

Felix bowed and scuttled out of the room, closing the door behind him and leaving them alone.

"Come." Philip held out his hand. Carmen took it and sat in the chair he drew out for her. "You smell delicious."

"Do you like it? I took a walk today when Felix said you wouldn't be home. The shopkeeper said I could pay it later after I told her who I was." Carmen stopped suddenly. "I hope that's alright."

Philip sat across from her at the small table. "It warms me to know you bought yourself something pretty." He leaned closer and sniffed again. "The scent suits you."

Carmen relaxed. Silence hung amicably between them as they both bit into their meat pie and drank the wine.

"Are you in pain?" Philip asked. "You seem to be using your arm slowly, as though you are."

"My arm is still a bit stiff, and I do have some bruising, but I think it was scarier than it was harmful." Carmen took a sip of wine. "I don't want to take that medicine again. It gave me terrible dreams, and I felt rather dizzy when I woke up. After it finally wore off, I felt much better."

Philip nodded. Laudanum seemed to have effects on people that weren't ideal. Especially when they took a lot.

"If you're feeling well, I don't see why you should take it," Philip told her. "And a little wine will help with any lingering pain."

Carmen took a longer gulp. "This wine is nice. I haven't had it before."

"Italian. Sorry." She blinked at him, her mouth slightly ajar. "Well, it isn't Spanish," he explained.

"Spain isn't the only country that makes excellent wine, Philip," she chided. "I meant to ask if we will still have the wedding ceremony on Thursday? I mean, you haven't canceled it on account of me, have you?"

"No, I haven't canceled it." After a pause, Philip asked, "Would you like me to?"

"No!" Carmen exclaimed. "We must be legal here as soon as possible, Philip."

"I'll send Cinch a missive in the morning before I leave, telling him not to change anything."

"Where are you going?" Carmen asked.

Philip filled her in on the situation with *The Emerald Mistress* as they ate their pie. He realized just how famished he was. When the plates were empty and the story told, Philip stood. "Let's move to the couch. I'm starting to feel rather tired."

"I am sorry you've so much trouble to sort out," Carmen said as they sank into the plush velvet couch.

The fire crackled and danced in front of them, mesmerizing Philip and lulling them both into a peaceful silence. Once his wineglass was empty, Philip raised his legs over the side of the couch and laid his head in Carmen's lap. He hadn't thought about his motions until he was gazing up at her startled face. Her lap had seemed so inviting, and he had felt so tired that he had moved without thinking. This was the most intimate they'd ever been, but he didn't care. They were supposed to be intimate; they were husband and wife.

"Once The Emerald Mistress is free, I will show you the city, I promise."

"And shopping?" Carmen asked. Her voice was teasing, but the reminder hit him solidly in the chest. He had forgotten all about taking her shopping.

"Of course. And shopping. Possibly for a new necklace."

Carmen waved her delicate fingers in the air. "I don't require fancy things."

"But you deserve them." He caressed her collarbone, envisioning a teardrop sapphire or a string of pearls against it.

Carmen swatted at his head playfully. Like a cat chasing a mouse, he pounced on her wrist before she could snatch it away. Then he stared at her until she looked down.

"You're beautiful and a good wife for putting up with me. And I want to shower you with things that remind you what you mean to me," Philip said, the emotion that had built up in him the night at her bedside threatening to resurface. He kissed her hand and let it go. "I want you to have all the dresses and necklaces in the world."

"Fine, fine," Carmen said. "A compromise then. I will allow you to buy me a necklace."

Philip chuckled. "I didn't know how bull-headed you were."

"You should have known." Carmen scolded him with a click of her tongue. "I am the woman who was making wine despite what people said around me. I work the fields like the rest of them, harvest and press and mix the wine like any other winemaker."

"You sound like a formidable woman," Philip said. "I wonder how you could have ever ended up with someone like me."

Carmen chuckled, her breasts trembling directly above his nose. And suddenly he was no longer tired. Every cell in his body was awake. Philip grasped her bandaged hand and kissed it, his lips lingering. Her skin was soft, her perfume intoxicating.

If he closed his eyes, Philip could imagine they were in Spain again and everything was less chaotic.

"I am sorry for leaving you alone today," he said, hoping she could feel his sincerity. "Had I thought you would come out of your room, I would have stayed."

Carmen resumed her twisting of his hair as the light from the flames danced across her face. The glow illuminated her full lips and strong cheekbones. Philip's pulse raced, and his skin prickled at the thought of taking her in his arms right there.

"Carmen." Her name came out strangled. He cleared his throat and started again, pushing his mind away from seducing his wife. "I'll walk you upstairs."

He offered her his hand, and when she took it, he pulled gently until her weight collided softly into him; her breasts pressing into his chest.

Carmen straightened up, brushing away imaginary wrinkles from her skirt. "You're stronger than you think."

Thoughts of his hands on her undressed body assaulted his mind. He could barely move or speak, burning for her at a magnitude he hadn't felt for another woman before. He wanted her in his bed. Every night.

"Philip." Carmen's eyes searched his face in the glow of the fire. "Are you alright?"

Philip leaned in and kissed her gently, though it took all his willpower not to push her back onto the couch and make love to her there. First, he wanted her to want him just as much.

When he broke off the kiss, Carmen was breathless with her head tilted. Before she could move, Philip leaned in again, his lips enveloping her sweetly, slowly, his tongue licking her mouth until she opened it fully. Then he folded his arms around her waist and drew her closer, kissing her deeper as she tried to keep up.

"We should go upstairs. It's getting late," Philip said. Since she seemed rooted to the spot, Philip gently led her into the hallway, relieved when she didn't protest.

"Here we are," Philip announced when they arrived at the top of the stairs in one piece. He leaned close to Carmen to open her door, his pulse jumping again at her perfume. "It's nice to have a smaller house, isn't it?

We don't have to walk so very far."

"Yes," Carmen said.

Philip swallowed, feeling clumsy and innocent in a way he hadn't since he was a schoolboy. Not a flattering feeling, in his opinion. And strange that his wife would make him feel as such. His fingers itched to pull her close, but he wasn't sure how she would react. "Good night, Carmen."

"Philip."

"What is it?"

Carmen hesitated. He wished he could see her facial features better, but the hallway was too dark. "Would you help me with my dress?"

"Me?"

"You are my husband." Carmen said it lightly, but Philip detected a note of challenge. "And everyone else is asleep."

Certainly. He was her husband. And husbands did things like that for their wives. He cleared his throat and followed her into her rooms, waiting in the middle of her room like a boy who had never known a woman as she found her way to the lamp and lit it.

The light burst upon her, and Philip again realized how beautiful she was. Her hair fell to her shoulders in waves, with part of it still held up with pins.

"Your hair is lovely," Philip said. He had not meant it in jest, but Carmen's cheeks still blushed.

"My head was splitting before," Carmen explained, touching the loose tresses. Philip gently lowered her hands.

"You don't have to explain to me why you take down your hair," he breathed. He dug through her locks and found the remaining pins one by one. "If you are having headaches, perhaps you should see a doctor. An English doctor."

He could feel her eyes on him, watching his every movement as she thought about his suggestion.

"Is there a difference between an English doctor and a Spanish doctor?" she asked, tilting her head as he pulled the last pin out of her hair. There was enough of an edge to her voice that Philip knew to tread carefully.

"I am not sure about that, though I believe our doctors are at least as good." Gathering his courage, he met her eyes. "But perhaps seeing a doctor who isn't so closely connected with you would be beneficial."

Carmen chuckled. "I will think about it."

"Thank you." Philip was relieved to hear she would consider his suggestion. They sat as they were, eye to eye, in the firelight for a long moment. When Carmen finally turned away, Philip took the opportunity to kiss her gently on the neck. When a groan escaped her, he fought hard not to bring her mouth hungrily to his.

"Carmen. Turn around."

There was no need for her to answer. He pressed his palms into her waist and spun her towards him. Facing him with her hair over her shoulder and away from the dress was a line of what seemed like infinite buttons.

"Only half of them are buttons, the rest are decorative," Carmen murmured.

"Right." Philip lifted the button pick and started at the top, cupping his left hand against her shoulder for leverage. Carmen said nothing as her dress slowly released her body from its grip. With each button undone, Philip became more awake. "Carmen."

She twisted to face him, holding up the loosened dress. "Yes?"

He had no more self-will. With one sweep of his arms, she was against his chest, her lips against his. She gave no resistance, but opened her mouth willingly and wrapped her arms around his neck. Her dress fell to the floor, and suddenly there was little barrier between them. He drew her hips against his, his lips buried in her neck and the back of her ear, pulling tenderly against her skin until she whimpered.

Instead of moving away, she thrust herself closer to him, sending shock waves through his nerves. His instinct was his only guiding force. He was her husband. She was his wife.

Still kissing her neck, Philip scooped her up and carried her to the bed before realizing what he was doing. It wasn't until she was lying against the pillows, her brown hair spread as though flames above her head, that he paused.

"Don't leave." Carmen tugged at the back of his neck. "Kiss me."

Philip yanked his jacket off and complied with his wife's demands.

Chapter 28

Carmen awoke the next day to the feel of naked skin against the soft muslin sheets, a strange, yet pleasing sensation. Her body felt different, the way it moved, the weight of it. She thought of how silly she had been the night of her wedding, thinking too much about what was expected instead of allowing her senses to guide her.

When she stretched her arms across the bed, Carmen realized she was alone. She sat up, half-hoping Philip would be sitting in one of the chairs, but they were empty. And his clothes were gone. Every sign that he'd been with her that night was erased. Everything but the lingering sensation of his skin against her skin, his lips on her breasts, his hands on her hips. The last word he uttered before she fell asleep was a breathy, "Carmen."

In the dark, she had smiled at her name, thinking he pronounced it best. Though she wouldn't have minded staying a bit longer, Carmen slipped out of bed and set about getting ready for the day. One of the maids had placed a fresh jug of water at some point that morning. Carmen flushed, wondering if her naked body had been sufficiently covered. Not that it should matter, she supposed. She was married.

She breathed in deeply and rubbed her body with the damp cloth, reliving the night before, pleased to realize how right her aunt was. When married to a good man, the womanly obligations were no chore at all. Last night had been simultaneously pleasant and empowering. The way he touched her, how he whispered her name as though his body had an ache only she could soothe.

A knock at the door started her from her thoughts.

"Carmen? May I come in?"

A strangled cry was all she managed as she bolted for her dressing gown. But it wasn't enough to be heard through the door that opened just as Carmen struggled to slide her arms through the sleeves.

"Good morning," he said, his eyes roaming her half-naked body as she tucked the silk around her belly.

Her face flushed hot again. "Good morning."

Silence followed. Philip dropped his gaze. Carmen picked at the threads on the sleeves. She wished she could visit Isabel or speak with Tía Merce about how to act during the day. Things had come so easily the night before.

"Carmen, I wanted to see you this morning." Philip paused. "I wanted to make sure you were ...well."

"If I was well? I think I am. Should I not be?"

Philip stepped closer, then stopped. "I have heard that sometimes women are affected and feel..." Carmen couldn't hide her surprise at his concern. Or hold back her laughter. Philip finally looked up from the floor.

"There's no need to worry," she said, moving to sit at the vanity.

Memories from the night before flashed in her head, sending tingles down her spine. This was something no one ever spoke about at Tía Merce's teas. She willed herself to extinguish the fire of nerves and desire in her belly. "What will you do today?"

"I have to get *The Emerald Mistress* released." Philip paced behind her, rubbing his palms together. "I will be working with Lionel Finley."

"Who?"

"Just a friend. And business partner." His voice lowered to a level she could barely hear.

Suddenly, Philip stopped directly behind her, his eyes connecting with hers in the mirror. She stilled, captivated by his eyes, by the heat he gave off, by his scent of oak and chicory. She watched as he brushed her hair back. His fingers were gentler than she imagined a man's touch could be. The skin-to-skin contact made her lungs contract, her shoulders shuddering involuntarily.

Philip must have felt the change in her body, her lack of breath, her stillness. Slowly, he dipped his face down towards her bare neck and kissed her lightly. Her already starving lungs hitched. Carmen had to open her mouth to coax the needed air in.

"Carmen," he whispered, nuzzling his lips against her neck. She shuddered again, remembering where it all led the night before.

"Yes?" she said.

He traced his palms down the sides of her, pausing at her breasts, then continuing until his hands circled her waist. "I would like to visit you more often. At night."

Carmen swallowed a moan as his teeth nipped at her earlobe. "You know, in Spain, many couples sleep in the same room always."

"Do they?" He drew his teeth against her neck. Her knees buckled, but he was quick to grip her buttocks. "Would you like me to sleep here always?"

She couldn't answer. All voice, all rational thought, had abandoned her, replaced by a powerful sensation that coursed through her legs, midsection, and chest. Her thoughts were consumed by his hands and his lips. She wanted to press into him. She wanted him to cover her with his body. Nothing about her thoughts made sense. They were just feelings, emotions, and desire rolled into a tight ball that screamed for slack in the tension. For some release.

"Philip," she gasped when he rocked her head back and kissed her neck. He reached into the folds of her dressing gown.

"Carmen, I can't get enough of you," Philip whispered against her ear. "But I don't wish to distress you."

"I am not distressed." A flash of lightning jolted through Carmen's legs as his hands ventured to her hips. As though her body were not her own, it arched towards him, begging for him to kiss her lips as he had in the library.

Philip pulled her hard against him, covering her mouth in a demanding kiss that sent her into a haze where she couldn't speak or think, but could only submit to her yearnings and allow her husband to take her to the heights he did the night before.

Inside the haze, she felt her feet lift from the floor, Philip grasping her buttocks. She landed in the middle of her bed, and Philip stood over her, his hands on her shoulders, his knees by the sides of her hips.

"I believe we might be a match put together in heaven," Philip said, lowering his body over hers.

Chapter 29

ROWENA CANDOR'S FATHER OWNED a mansion, christened Tajir Villa, which he designed in the style of a North African palace. When he first built it, most people called it gaudy or lurid, but when he was named a baron by the king, Tajir Villa suddenly became fashionable. To Carmen, Tajir Villa was the most extravagant house she had ever seen.

From the moment they drove up the driveway of Tajir Villa outside of London, Carmen knew the day would be a feast for her senses. There were marigolds strung from one end of the doorway to the other, with bouquets of roses on every table, while jasmine crawled over and hung down corners and doors alike. As she walked through the entryway, into the parlor, and out onto the patio, it felt as though she were strolling through an enchanted garden. She breathed in deeply; the fragrance filling her senses, just as someone to her left sneezed.

Carmen jumped in surprise, jolting into someone half her size.

"Ow."

Carmen looked down to find Eleadora pinching her lips.

"Did I hurt you?" Carmen asked in Spanish, moving her head just enough to check the little girl over.

When she heard her native language, Eleadora forced a smile. "Just a little. On my toes. And you knocked over my basket."

"I am so sorry." Carmen searched for the basket in her field of vision and finally located it. "I didn't see you."

"It's hard to see this little girl. She needs to grow taller." Philip said as he joined them, holding a basket full of flowers placed haphazardly. "I put them back in. You might need to rearrange them, though."

Eleadora rolled her eyes but smiled again when Philip kissed her cheek.

"Go on, see if Claire can put those flowers back how they should be."

Once Eleadora had scampered off, Carmen fussed over her gloves and handbag to keep her embarrassment at bay. "I didn't see her," she repeated. Two more gloved hands enveloped hers, giving them a gentle squeeze.

"Are you nervous?" Philip spoke so low and close to her ear that it made a strange buzzing in her head. He stroked his palms up her bare arms, sending jitters down her legs. "Do you have cold feet, my lady?"

"It's too late for that," she said matter-of-factly. "We are already married."

He grinned at her like a boy who'd found the Sunday pies. "And we've already acted on that status several times."

Heat filled Carmen's cheeks. She wished she could see if someone had overheard them.

"You're blushing, my bride." Philip tucked a stray curl behind her ear. There was no chance of her keeping a grudge when he gave her that impish look.

She attempted to subdue him with her fan, playfully swatting at him, but her taps only grazed the air, encouraging his grin.

"Philip," boomed a voice farther ahead. It belonged to a man as tall as Philip, with broad shoulders and shockingly white hair. Though he looked and sounded English, his face told a story of years out in the sun. "It is so good to have you here. And is this your bride?"

"Mr. Brayemore," Philip called back, leading Carmen toward the man. "This is my wife, Carmen Suárez. Carmen, this is Rowena's father, Mr. Brayemore."

"Your house is beautiful," Carmen managed to say.

"Welcome," Mr. Brayemore said in Spanish. "Let me show you around. Or do you prefer to speak in French?" He changed languages with a wink. "I hear you are more learned than your husband in the art of language."

"I understand French," Philip complained behind them.

"Papa, the ceremony will start soon."

Rowena stood at an archway in a long cream gown with puffed sleeves, carrying what looked like a roll of lace. When the lace squirmed, Carmen realized she was holding the baby.

"We are coming. I am showing Philip's wife the house," Mr. Braymore said. "Do not worry. There is plenty of time. But I love my house and perhaps you will appreciate it as well. Where are you from in Spain?"

"A small place called Toro."

"Ah, I have never been, but I know of this place. So you are not from the South, but have you seen the Alhambra?"

"No, I have not."

"When Rowena's mother was alive, I worked for a few years in Madrid, and we traveled throughout Spain. After a few years in Spain, we went to Algeria where I worked as a businessman and helped my country speak with the French and Algerians. You know, things were a bit difficult there for a few years."

Carmen nodded, though she was unfamiliar with the history of Algeria.

"When I came back here, with my new wife then, I built this house with this entrance to remind me of where I have been." Mr. Braymore lifted his chin toward the ceiling. Carmen followed suit.

Above her, a mural depicted a seascape with ships approaching a land teeming with trees, fields, and people. The bright colors, along with the babbling sound of the fountain in the background, made it appear as though the waves were moving.

Carmen's breath caught in her throat at the sight. It was one of the most beautiful paintings she had ever seen, though she thought it a pity to have it on the ceiling.

"Do you like it?"

Carmen met Mr. Braymore's eyes again and nodded. "It's beautiful. I wish I had it on my walls."

"I shall have it cut it out of the ceiling for you, my dear," Philip interrupted. He took Carmen's hand, clicking his tongue playfully. "I think Rowena is getting nervous, sir."

Mr. Braymore laughed. "Can't start without the grandfather. Shall we?"

Carmen and Philip followed him through the archway and into a wide hallway that led to a room with yellow curtains and cream-painted walls. The minister, a thin frowning man, waited near the fireplace, blinking nervously as the family gathered and quieted down.

"I have to be near the baby," Philip whispered as Carmen sat. "I'm the godfather, you know."

He winked at her. His joy was so contagious. it vibrated through her bones.

The gathering was small. Perhaps a few dozen people to celebrate the baptism of Philip Sutton, the next Marquess of Candor. Though she didn't understand all the words, Carmen found herself emotional as she watched the minister wet the child's forehead and the parents declare how they would raise him. She thought of Isabel and the niece or nephew on the way. And the fact that she probably wouldn't be able to go back to Spain for the birth. Or baptism.

The reminder sent tears down her cheeks as Philip promised to help raise Little Philip properly in the way of their church. He sent Carmen a wink, and she imagined herself and Philip standing there with a baby of their own. The image froze her blood. They would have to baptize their child in the Anglican church. Not the Catholic church, as she had always assumed. As all of Isabel's children would be.

She hadn't considered it until that moment. Perhaps it shouldn't have mattered so much to her, but it did. Very much.

An ensemble of "amen" roused Carmen from her thoughts. The ceremony was over. Some guests were moving forward to kiss the baby boy, who looked on the verge of tears.

"Most of the guests will go into the library for the reception," Claire said, suddenly at her side joined by a woman who looked so much like Cinch with her walnut-colored hair and heart-shaped mouth that Carmen automatically knew she was his sister. "This is Emily, Cinch's sister. She came for the baptism."

"And your luncheon, Claire," Emily said. "Nice to meet you, Carmen. I have heard so much about you, mainly that you are too good for our Philip."

Philip, who had overheard, frowned at her, but Emily only laughed.

"Of course she is too good for me," Philip said. "Why would I marry a woman who was simply good enough?"

Claire and Emily admonished him for the statement, swatting at him with their fans while laughing, but Carmen found his argument endearing.

"What is this about the luncheon, by the way?" Philip asked. Claire's eyes rounded wide.

"You're joking, right?" Claire glared at Philip, but he didn't falter from his innocent look. "You remember I'm having the luncheon to raise money for the day school next Monday?"

"And what is it for?" Philip winked at Carmen before shaking his head at Claire. But she was having none of it. She had already guessed he was merely joking.

"This is what I find so intolerable," Claire complained. "You still get enjoyment out of acting like a child."

"Aren't you supposed to be somewhere now?" Philip asked. His eyes were wide and innocent. Claire glared at him.

"We are expected to stay here a moment for your ceremony. You need witnesses, after all. And it won't take but a few minutes."

"We want to make sure you go through with it," Emily teased.

"Little chance of me changing my mind." Philip rolled his eyes before pulling Carmen suddenly close to him and kissing her on the lips. "I don't want to lose her or my house."

Carmen wasn't sure what to make of his words, but no one else registered them. Philip changed the subject so quickly. "Emily, what are you smiling about?"

Emily was looking at baby Philip, an amused smile on her lips. "That baby is about to have a fit."

"Does the idea of it please you, Emily?" Claire asked, her eyebrows raised in suspicion.

"Very much," Emily said, crossing her arms against her chest. "Do you know Cinch used to say that I had the unruliest children? When they were babies?" She clicked her tongue at the statement. "Yes, he would deserve a nice baby fit right now."

Carmen would have laughed, but gasped instead as an arm stretched out from the cloud of darkness in her left eye and clutched Emily's shoulders.

"Don't you see you're scaring people?" Emily scolded as the full figure of a tall, dark-hair man came into Carmen's view. She chided herself silently for her reaction, blaming it on the nerves of the ceremony.

"This is Falcon, my husband. He does have another name, but there isn't much point in learning it as everyone calls him Falcon on account that he used to train them as a kid."

"That isn't even remotely true," Falcon protested as he kissed Carmen's hand. Sightly taller than Philip, Falcon had broad shoulders and a lyrical accent. His gentle demeanor made Carmen like him instantly.

"Yes, but it's much more interesting than the truth, since the truth is we have no idea how you got your nickname." Emily broke off long enough to take a breath and inspect Carmen. "That shade of green is positively radiant on you. Did you pick it out or did Philip? Don't answer that, I'm sure it was you. Your hair is lovely, too. So dark. Like an Irish woman I knew once, though you're prettier than her. I always wanted darker hair."

"Thank you." Carmen couldn't help being pleased with the compliment. Isabel had always told her the color that suited her.

"My goodness, Emily, you'll tire her out before the ceremony," Claire said, edging her way past Emily to greet Carmen. "Ah, finally. People are moving. Stay here, Carmen. I'm not sure where they want you to stand."

"I can't believe he isn't going to throw a fit," Emily said, her eyes back to Little Philip. The governess had arrived to sweep the baby away so the adults could enjoy the afternoon celebration tea. "It's absolutely unfair."

Falcon laughed at his wife, who huffed in what seemed like playful indignation.

"Come, Carmen. The minister is ready," Claire called out, waving Carmen forward. With so many people and chairs, Carmen had to navigate slowly. It wasn't that she was embarrassed about her vision problems, but she did have her pride. And she didn't wish to fall yet again in front of Philip's friends. "Carmen? Are you coming?"

"Yes," Carmen said. When she arrived at the end of the aisle, a tall man with chin-length blond hair and an intense air blocked her path.

"Finley. What are you doing here?" Claire asked.

"I was invited," the man named Finley said. Carmen tore her eyes from him to glance at Claire. She stood erect like a queen, her face impassive.

"Well, how lovely for you." Claire's heels clicked on the floor as she offered her hand to Carmen. "The minister is ready."

Philip took Carmen's hand from Claire and held her closely as the minister ran through the Protestant wedding ceremony. Irritation tinged the edges of his words, but it didn't diminish Philip's smile as they repeated their vows, this time in English. Carmen tripped over hers, forcing the minister to repeat himself.

Within a few minutes, the ceremony was done.

"Can I kiss the bride, then?" Philip asked.

The minister stared at him, stone cold, before saying, "You may do whatever you please."

Carmen bit back a laugh.

"Well, in that case." Philip grinned at Carmen as she waited for her kiss. But suddenly, Philip scooped her into his arms, lifting her off the ground.

Carmen shrieked, but the sound was cut off by her husband's kiss. The room erupted into applause as Carmen finally touched the ground again.

"Alright, love?" Philip whispered in her ear. A shiver ran through her body at the words, the tone, and his proximity.

"Yes. Though you're a brute."

Philip kissed her hard on the cheek. "I can't help myself. I couldn't be happier. We managed to get the ceremony done. It's all legal. Theodore can't continue trying to take the house." He clapped and laughed, and Carmen joined him with a smile, but the words tugged at her mind. No matter how many times she reminded herself of his attentiveness, there was a small part of her that wondered if, now that he didn't need her to keep the house, Philip might change.

There wasn't much time to reflect on the doubt before Lord Candor kissed her cheeks, launching a cascade of kisses and hugs from everyone present. Carmen brushed her worries aside and allowed herself to enjoy the afternoon of celebration. As her father always said, there was no sense in worrying for something that hadn't yet become a reality.

Chapter 30

CARMEN STOOD ON THE London streets, peering up at a red brick townhouse that rose up three stories. In each window, three per floor, she could see an electric chandelier handing from the ceiling. Carmen looked again at the address. This was the location of the afternoon tea she was expected to be at with Claire and Emily. She need only gather her courage and walk up the steps.

"Carmen! Hello!"

Claire and Emily were descending from a large carriage that had just arrived.

"I'm glad to find you outside," Claire said as they approached her. "Did you just get here?"

"I was just telling Claire that we should have picked you up from your house. It would have made more sense," Emily said, adjusting Carmen's hat.

She reminded Carmen so much of a Spanish woman—speaking all her thoughts out loud, instantly friendly, and always nurturing those around her. For that, Carmen was grateful.

"Did you walk here? All the way from your house? I must speak to Philip about leaving you alone to gallivant around London. It isn't safe, you know."

The only problem was that Emily spoke so quickly that Carmen had a hard time translating before someone else spoke.

"Leave her alone. I'm sure she likes to walk, as we do. And London isn't dangerous in this part of town."

"I came with the carriage," Carmen finally understanding the entire conversation. She pointed towards Nathaniel and Philip's glossy black carriage.

"It's beautiful. Must be new," Emily said, slipping her hand through Carmen's elbow. "I'm glad you came by carriage, though. You know, Claire isn't afraid of London like the rest of us. First, because she doesn't read the papers."

Claire huffed her indignation at the statement, though she gave Carmen a conspiratorial smile.

"And second, because she believes that if you simply don't agree something exists, it won't. Simple as that." Carmen stole a glance at Claire when she snorted in opposition.

"I know perfectly well that dangers lurk in London."

"Pish, posh," Emily said, waving away the words as though they smelled as bad as the wind from the Thames. "Did you know that Claire is very busy at any rate in one of the worst places in the city, building a day school?"

"It isn't the worst place in the city, Emily."

"I knew she was building a school," Carmen said. "But I did not know where."

Emily opened her mouth, but snapped it shut almost immediately. Claire was glaring at her with the icy look of a queen.

"The entire point of the project is to help the less fortunate. Women in poor neighborhoods must work. To keep their family fed. But working with babies is very difficult, or impossible, so I want to build a day school where small children can come, perhaps between the ages of two and seven, to get fed, play in a safe environment, have access to medical care and learn their letters."

"In Spain, a nurse or the grandparents usually do this."

"Yes, here as well, but so many people are coming to the city looking for work that they aren't always close to their grandparents anymore. And I'm talking about those who can't afford a nurse."

"How will they pay for it if they are poor?" Carmen asked.

"Oh, that's easy," Emily said, pressing the bell next to the giant doors of the house. "The rich pay for it. It's why she's having the luncheon. Claire is getting sponsors. Which means she's making all the rich people feel guilty for not helping the poor in London."

Claire scoffed. "They should feel badly. These people are coming here for work, which they are given, but their housing is in terrible conditions, and the pay they receive isn't enough to live on. But they can't complain because they will then be fired and replaced by someone else. The issue is that there are so many people looking for work and not enough jobs. They are expendable. Replaceable. And apparently not worthy of being paid or housed properly. We are on the verge of having an entire generation that has grown up in appalling conditions without a proper education. And I fear what that will do to England." Claire took a deep breath. "There you have it, Emily. I do fear some things."

The dream of a day school was impressive. Carmen had never seen a woman start something like that. She had never once thought on a larger scale what she could do for the poor in Spain. Probably because her life had been mostly about the people in Morales de Toro and her loved ones in Valladolid. Her next letter to Isabel would be about this day school idea and a question for her father about the wages they paid their vineyard workers.

"You and Philip will be coming to the luncheon, won't you?" Claire asked as they waited for the door to open. "Some of the doctors who have volunteered their time will also be there."

"I am sure we will be there, Claire," Carmen managed to say, past the lump of emotion that sprung up in her throat. She was glad for their friendly openness, but sometimes it reminded her so much of home that she ached. The door to the house opened with a creaking sound.

"Welcome," the butler said as he opened the door. Two footmen were ready to take their cloaks and guide them into a parlor with large windows that let in the London afternoon light. "It is up the stairs to your right." The footman gestured toward the stairs.

Despite the unfamiliarity of the house, the electric chandeliers lit the wide hallways so brightly that Carmen had no problem judging the distance between each step. No shadows jumped at her when a frame or corner appeared in her limited side vision, either.

Electric lights were a marvelous invention. She hadn't thought much about them until visiting Willowbrook House, but they did make a difference to her vision. While the black cloud around her vision never disappeared, the artificial light expanded her ability to see more depth and a broader space. If she had her way, she would request the electricity to be put into all houses from then on. Carmen wondered if Philip would be agreeable to adding the lights to their house, now that it was securely his.

"You aren't nervous, are you?" Emily asked as they approached the feminine voices floating down the hall.

Claire gave Emily a reproving look. "She probably wasn't until you asked her."

Emily's small hand flew to her mouth, and she mumbled an apology. "Sometimes I can't help but talk, even when it isn't beneficial."

"I'm not nervous," Carmen said. "Meeting new people isn't something that scares me." Carmen breathed in deeply, realizing she wasn't telling the entire truth. Meeting new people in Spain had never scared her, but in England her heart fluttered, and her hands trembled slightly at the thought of people not understanding her or finding her strange. Or outright not accepting her, though if the English women were like Claire and Emily and Rowena, she was worrying for no reason.

The three of them walked into a large room that appeared to have been created especially for entertaining. Large windows faced east and three sections of chairs were arranged in semicircles around low tables. Each table was set with scones and cakes for tea.

Carmen assessed the room for spots that might give her vision trouble. As she did so, she noticed all the ladies watching them. Emily led her towards the group.

"Hello, Lady Sutton, Lady Glanville. And you must be Mrs. Daucer," Lady Radcliff said. She was a short woman of Tía Merce's age with a gentle smile. Carmen noted the shade of her hair, brown streaked with silver, as a way to remember her. "So nice of you to come. Let me introduce you to the others."

Carmen left the security of Emily and Claire and allowed Lady Radcliff to guide her deeper into the room.

"This is Miss Elizabeth Rapport," she said.

"How do you do?" Carmen asked, appalled that her tongue suddenly felt thick and unwilling to move properly. The young Miss Elizabeth smiled thinly at Carmen before moving her gaze to the wall.

"And this is Lady Camille Burton."

Carmen dipped again into a curtsy while Lady Camille hid a smirk behind her teacup. Never would Carmen have guessed the English were as cold as this. Everyone had warned her, including her father and Tía Merce, but Carmen had envisioned the French attitude, not overly warm but polite and inviting while in public. This ability the English had to look through a person was somewhat of a surprise.

"Good afternoon," a woman said from the large, open doors. The room shifted. Heads swiveled between Carmen and the new woman framed in the doorway in a lavender dress and hat. Her voice carried a sort of triumph that made Carmen uneasy.

"Meredith, dear, we've just met your sister-in-law. Have the two of you met yet?" Lady Radcliff asked as she poured a cup of tea for Carmen.

Meredith, whom Philip never spoke kindly about, regarded Carmen with a smirk. "We have not yet had the pleasure, though I did hear of the news of Philip coming home with a Spanish woman." She marched towards Carmen like a bull charging a bullfighter. Carmen almost cringed and ducked out of the way.

"I'm Carmen Suárez," Carmen said. "Things have been very busy in the last two weeks since we arrived, but I have been wanting to meet you."

Meredith snickered. "Have you? I doubt Philip has."

"Why did you introduce yourself with your maiden name?" Lady Camille asked as Meredith moved to an open seat. "Why didn't you introduce yourself as Mrs. Daucer?"

"I supposed I should," Carmen said, enunciating each word carefully. "But in Spain, we women do not take on the man's last name. We keep our identity and pass our name to our children."

Eyebrows shot upward around the room.

"That's interesting," Lady Radcliffe said, though she didn't sound remotely interested. The conversation dwindled as ladies took up their teacups, and Clare, Emily and Carmen were ushered to three empty chairs.

Carmen landed on the seat of the chair without incident. When the footman served them their tea, she extended her hand a moment too soon, prompting him to place the cup directly into it.

"Lady Sutton," called out Lady Buton to Claire. "We weren't expecting you today. You've been so busy lately."

"Yes, how are things with your little project in the ghetto?" Meredith asked.

Carmen was beginning to see why Philip didn't get along with Meredith.

Claire sipped her tea before answering. "It's going well. Thank you for asking. It is not in the ghetto, though, my dear. It's in a middle to lower-middle class working neighborhood as it is to improve the lives of both children and mothers in the class underneath us."

"Goodness, me," exclaimed Lady Rapport. "When I have children, I won't want them at a day nursery where they could easily be kidnapped or murdered. How are you going to get any parents to pay you?"

"We have already a list of people interested in sending their small children to us for educational day teaching," Claire said with a confidence that left little room for arguing.

"Like a school," someone chimed in.

"Not quite," Claire said, "though I have found that it's the best way for some to understand the concept."

Lady Radcliff coughed into her handkerchief. "I'm sure we will all learn much more about it at the luncheon for the day school. We would like to get to know Mrs. Daucer more." She turned to Carmen and fired off the first question. "Where are you from in Spain?"

The room quieted, all attention fixed on Carmen.

"I'm from a town near Valladolid," Carmen answered, her stomach flipping.

There were murmurs from the women at the window, but Carmen kept her eyes on Lady Radcliffe.

"Not Madrid, then?" Lady Radcliffe asked.

"No," Carmen said, then quickly added, "Of course, I've been there. And Paris. But after my mother died, my father didn't wish to be in society much."

"He didn't wish to find you a suitable Spanish match?" asked another woman. Emily murmured to Carmen that her name was Mrs. Fredrick. "I was always of the opinion that people should marry within their own country. How do you and Philip communicate? He doesn't speak Spanish, does he?"

Carmen almost laughed. Claire sighed in irritation.

"What a ridiculous question, Mrs. Fredrick. You are speaking with Carmen in English, are you not?"

Mrs. Fredrick sniffed in response, her face growing pink. Carmen hastened to give an answer that might soothe the woman's feelings. "Philip speaks some Spanish. I know my English is not perfect, but yes, we speak in English."

"How did you and Philip meet?" Lady Radcliff asked.

"Yes, how did you meet?" asked a young woman.

"Philip went to Spain for business and to meet his cousin," Claire said.

Carmen nodded at Claire. "Yes, his cousin is my sister's husband, Jaime."

"D0 Spanish women normally spend time with a strange man there to do business?" someone asked. A burst of giggles followed from near the window.

"You must have made quite the impression on Lord Daucer," Lady Radcliffe said.

"I believe every woman leaves an impression on the man who decides to marry her, does she not?" Emily asked. "I know I made an impression on Falcon. And you must have on Lord Radcliffe as well."

"Perhaps she impressed him in a dark corner," a voice whispered somewhere in the room, loud enough for Carmen to hear.

Someone whispered back, "Or in an empty library."

Both women snorted and giggled, covering their conversation by clanking their teacups a little too loudly.

"Sarah and Mary, would you like to join the conversation?" Lady Radcliffe asked sternly, her face cold. The giggling stopped.

"Well, you can't blame the young women for being curious. After all, Carmen managed to convince one of London's most notorious bachelors to marry her." Meredith paused a beat, then looked at Claire. "You know my brother-in-law well. Don't you agree that he was a staunch bachelor, always claiming he did not wish to marry anyone?"

"I suppose he hadn't found the right woman before Carmen," Claire said. Carmen sipped her tea, grateful to Claire for taking some of the conversation off her hands.

"It wasn't the women," a woman said from the other circle of couches. Carmen wished she could sink away, disappear. Emily leaned in and whispered, "That's Lady Wilcox. And her daughter Miss Victoria Wilcox.

"There were many willing to marry Mr. Daucer," Lady Wilcox continued. "He is, after all, young, handsome, and rich."

Meredith scoffed at the last statement. Carmen turned to look at her, surprised at how much she wished to defend her husband, though she had no facts about who had sought his hand before.

"Carmen is charming and beautiful," Claire said. "It's no wonder Mr. Daucer wished her to be his wife. Besides, they've been corresponding by letter for months now, haven't you, Carmen? It's a wonderful way to get to know someone."

"Yes," Carmen said quickly, remembering that was the story she was to tell. It didn't matter that it wasn't true. All she wanted was for Meredith to stop mocking Philip. "We have been corresponding for quite some time. He didn't wish to announce anything until after the mourning period for his mother was over."

Meredith's mouth tightened into a thin line at the mention. "That is a surprise to all of us, even his family. There were no banns called, no announcement."

The ladies looked at Carmen for her answer, some of them nodding in agreement.

But Carmen was ready. "As you might know, my country is at war. When Philip came, we had corresponded about our plans to meet and if we found each other as agreeable in person as we did in letters, that we would marry."

"And of course you found each other quite agreeable," Lady Rapport said with a firm nod. "Mr. Daucer is a charming man. And quite rich."

Carmen didn't know if the last statement was meant as a judgment against her, but she decided to ignore it.

"You must have had a romantic, whirlwind courtship," Lady Edith said.

"Whirlwind romances are for novels," Lady Wilcox said.

Carmen blinked, tempted to laugh. But this wasn't Tía Merce's tea.

Unfortunately, it seemed that most of the English women in the room had very little humor.

"Quite so," Meredith agreed. "There are rules and traditions for a reason."

"Where were you married then, Mrs. Daucer?"

Carmen tried to find where the voice was coming from but wasn't quick enough. She answered in the general direction from which it came. "In Spain. With my family as witnesses. We found that while we respect tradition, the war made it difficult to predict when Philip could come back. We moved things along quicker than usual, as we wished to start our lives together."

"It's like the Scottish marriages," Lady Mary said, snorting into her tea. Carmen saw her then, noting she was little more than sixteen years old. Lady Sarah, her companion, glanced anxiously at Lady Radcliffe as she stifled a giggle.

"It is nothing like a Scottish wedding. Philip went to Spain on business and to meet the woman he had been corresponding with," Claire said firmly. "He went purposefully to see if they might be compatible for marriage."

Lady Victoria sighed again, joined this time by Lady Sarah and Lady Mary. Carmen said nothing, allowing Claire's version of the story to take root with the ladies.

"It's very romantic," Lady Victoria said. "He must love you very much."

Carmen hoped her surprise at the comment didn't show on her face.

"But is it legal to marry in Spain?" Lady Sarah asked, her question directed at Claire.

"They were married here as well in an Anglican ceremony, as required by law. Until this autumn when the law changes." Claire sounded like Jaime when he was talking about laws. There were a few nodding heads in response and one huff. Carmen identified Meredith as the one huffing.

"You traveled here directly after your wedding?" Lady Rapport asked.

"Yes." Carmen's energy was starting to drain from the questions.

"That must have been disappointing. Lord Benedict is taking me to Bath after our wedding," Lady Edith announced.

"It is lovely to think I might be a grandmother within the next year," said Lady Wilcox. Lady Edith's cheeks turned bright pink at the mention, but her mother didn't notice. "I think I became a mother just to become a grandmother."

That was the comment that broke the room into separate conversations. Carmen wasn't convinced she had passed. She dared to pick up her tea again, though it was cold, and sipped it.

"John, bring Mrs. Daucer fresh tea," a raspy voice said. She angled her body to the right enough to see the tiny old woman who had spoken. She sat straight-backed in a regal black satin dress with a high lace neck and several jeweled necklaces dangling against her bosom. "I'm Lady Keswick. You just take care of yourself and all will be right."

Carmen smiled weakly at her.

"There are others here who had reason to hasten their nuptials. And others who claim their babies were born early. We all nod politely, but we know." The woman imitated her words by raising her brows and nodding.

"No, no," Carmen said quickly, understanding what Lady Keswick was implying, but they were interrupted by the footman offering them more tea. Lady Keswick burst into a tittering laugh that felt both out of place and genuine. Almost like a child laughing.

"What is it?" Carmen asked. The older woman calmed down before taking a sip of her tea.

"It's just that I can see the pattern on the teacup. It's been a few years since I could do that."

Lady Keswick continued to enjoy her tea, but Carmen's curiosity was piqued. "What do you mean you couldn't see it?"

"Growing old is a terrible thing," Lady Keswick said. "I had cataracts that only grew worse. Do you know what it's like for the world to slowly become dim and blurry? No, of course you don't. You're young and strong. Although there are those who have to wear spectacles from when they are little, but you are not one of them, are you? You're too pretty to wear spectacles. And you know, I say that because I can see your face clearly. Before I would say that speculating on the person's voice more than anything."

She gave another joyous laugh that drew a few looks from others in the room. One woman with brown hair fastened in a bun, who looked to be a younger and taller Lady Keswick, stared at them.

"I'm very glad to hear you can see better now. How did you manage to get better?"

"Well, that might not be conversation for teatime, but my daughter found me a reputable doctor who specialized in eyes." Lady Keswick leaned in closer and whispered, "He had to remove the cataracts through a surgical procedure."

The older woman immediately righted herself as though it were something she never should have said.

"I find that quite fascinating," Carmen said, her mind running through the various ways she could ask for the doctor's name and address. Across the room, Carmen saw Meredith speaking with another and realized she didn't wish for her sister-in-law, or anyone else, to have more information to fuel the gossip fire.

"What is fascinating?" Claire stood suddenly in front of her and Lady Keswick. And the perfect idea came to Carmen.

"Lady Keswick was just telling me about her doctor."

"Ah, well, very interesting. Emily and I were saying our goodbyes and wondering if you were staying or going, Carmen."

"Of course. I'm coming." Carmen turned to Lady Keswick as Claire moved on with her goodbyes. "Would you perhaps tell me the name of the doctor? I believe the children at Claire's day school could benefit from an eye exam."

"How very true." Lady Keswick motioned towards her daughter. "What a truly wonderful thing Lady Candor is doing. Florence, dear, what was the name of the doctor who healed my eyes?"

"Dr. Kruger," Florence said. "Dr. Emil Kruger. He's German but speaks English very well and is very talented. He has treated several people we know in London."

"That's right," Lady Keswick said as Carmen repeated the name in her head. "He is near the Great Park, you know."

"Thank you." Carmen tucked away the name before making her goodbyes.

Chapter 31

"I was thinking while coming here that since he's my namesake, I should get little Philip for two weeks a year," Philip announced. He and Cinch were taking a break in Cinch's study, waiting for Finley to join them. "To teach him all I know and such."

"Absolutely not," Cinch said, though he was chuckling. "The last thing my son needs is to learn mischief from you."

"I will remind you that I had better notes at Eton, and you are not without your black years."

Cinch saluted him. "Touché. I will speak with Rowena. But you must wait at least until he can walk."

Philip paused dramatically. "Of course he must know how to walk. I wouldn't know what to do with a crawling baby."

"Well, and by then, I assume you'll have children of your own to occupy your time," Cinch said with a snort. "And you'll leave mine alone."

Philip wiggled his brows. "I'm working on it, though I wouldn't mind waiting a bit longer. It's too much fun just trying to make them."

"Well then, is it possible your marriage of convenience has become a marriage of love?"

Cinch and Philip turned to find Finley smirking at them from the doorway.

"Are you inebriated?" Philip asked.

"I have imbibed a bit in celebration that *The Emerald Mistress* and my own ship, *Carolina Star*, have been released on good terms with no fine," Finley said, giving them a dramatic bow. He swayed dangerously close to the cart holding the water carafe.

"Good man," Cinch said. "But do try not to tumble over. There are breakables in here."

Finley straightened up and grinned. "I'm not that drunk." He threw himself sideways onto a chair and plucked out his pipe from his jacket pocket.

"Is this what they do in America?" Philip said, indicating Finley's posture. "It's no wonder they are struggling to be taken seriously on the world stage."

Finley laughed, but didn't take the bait. Disappointed, Philip sat back down.

"How did you do it?" Philip asked. "Get the ships out?"

"Well, it took some negotiations," Finley said, squinting into the flame as he lit his cigar with a match. "Let's say, for simplicities' sake, that I had to buy some land from one man to sell it to another to get in the good graces of another to get a contract signed for his garment company to get the ships released."

Cinch laughed. "That sounds complicated."

"That sounds improbable," Philip said, frowning.

Finley shrugged. "Politicians and lords are still just men who want certain things. If you can find out what that certain thing is they want, and manage to get it for them, they are more likely to give you what you want." Finley puffed out smoke circles, clearly pleased with himself. And though Philip usually distrusted anyone who tended to be pleased with himself, he liked Finley immensely. "I was also able to get the contract resigned for *The Emerald Mistress* to go out again and catch slave ships. Truth is, that one was more difficult."

"Was it? How so?" The promise of a good story had Philip straightening up.

"Turns out, Lord Kent has a few things he doesn't wish to become public. Like a certain child of his born to a certain woman of ill-repute who he is paying to live in a certain place in London. More details of which I cannot tell you or you would know who and where. Even if it is written in a fictional story such as was set to go out in one of the novels my printing press was to publish. When faced with the release of the novel or working with us, Lord Kent chose his reputation."

Finley's grin widened as he savored his cigar.

Philip gaped at him, looked at Cinch, and then gaped some more. "That's blackmail."

Finley leaned in towards Philip. "I dislike that word for something like this. Though, honestly, I'm not against blackmail if it makes a stubborn man see the light."

"Are you not?" Philip asked. Finley's continued eye contact was beginning to make him rather uncomfortable.

"Sometimes there is little difference between explaining a business agreement that is beneficial for everyone and blackmail."

That didn't make sense to Philip, but when he glanced at Cinch for support, his long-time friend focused only on Finley.

"Let me put it this way. My editorial house, Faldrige Press, is one of the most successful novel and novella publishing houses." Finley paused to look straight at Philip. "I started it before I left England. I don't know if you remember. I was one of the first that saw the opportunity of fast story publishing."

"Yes, Finley, I remember," Philip said. "What does that have to do with Lord Kent?"

"Well, as you know, we are in the business of publishing short stories that appeal to women who find themselves in need of entertainment. My writers sometimes get their ideas from the real world either by listening to the gossip happening around them or reading the gossip columns. This particular writer came up with a very entertaining story based upon some gossip someone sold them. The names were changed, and the writer made certain to keep the story fictional, but there was the possibility that some people, especially those in society, might recognize Lord Kent." Finley paused again. Cinch leaned in, suddenly interested. Philip couldn't believe what he was hearing and blinked.

"What are you saying?" Cinch asked.

Finley grinned. "Being the good man that I am, I presented the story to him as a peace offering, asking him if he thought there was a chance he would prefer it not to be published." His grin grew wider. "Lord

Kent asked me how he could repay me, so I told him about *The Emerald Mistress.*"

Finley had the audacity to clap his hands and spread them innocently before him. Nothing to hide here, his actions implied. Philip shook his head but couldn't help chuckling. Cinch joined him.

"Well, as long as *The Emerald Mistress* is out, I will not ask any more details." Cinch settled back into his chair and relit his pipe. "We can now get back to harassing Philip about having fallen in love with his wife."

"A dangerous thing to do," Finley said, though he was still grinning.

Philip couldn't help himself. The words were out before he had thought about their consequences. "How so?"

"Love will make you do things you never thought you would. Might even make you change your principles."

Philip snorted. "If you change your principles, you didn't have them to begin with."

"You wouldn't kill for those you love?" Now Finley was serious. More so than Philip had ever seen him before. He glanced at Cinch, who was blowing smoke circles in the air.

"I haven't explored that question yet," Philip said slowly.

Finley nodded, giving Philip the distinct feeling that marriage, at some point, made a man explore exactly that question. He didn't look forward to that moment.

The three of them sat in amicable silence for a few minutes as their glasses were refilled. When they were alone again, Finley opened his eyes, which he had closed for so long, Philip had thought him asleep.

"There is a bit of bad news, Philip," he said.

"About what?"

"I spoke with Lord Hemsworth in passing. He was musing on what to do with a building I believe you were thinking of buying."

"What building?" There was only one building he had been considering, partly owned by Lord Hemsworth. Was Finley fishing for information?

"The building on Warwick Lane that he had thought to use for lodging but hasn't finished the building of? Isn't that the one you were looking to buy for your hotel idea?"

Philip gulped down his whiskey and his frustration. He didn't like

Finley, or anyone, knowing the details. The last thing he needed was competition.

"I saw Lord Hemsworth just yesterday at a dinner. Your brother was there as well. Before the cards were brought out Theodore was speaking animatedly with Wellington about a house and an investment. The names Grosvenor and Bailey could be heard."

"You what?" Philip paused. "Theodore was gambling?"

Finley narrowed his eyes at him. "And did quite well."

The comment, spoken so calmly, made Philip chuckle.

"Sorry. That was just very funny," Philip said. "Theodore was never a very good gambler."

"Well, he played well enough to invest more in some new business in India."

"He what?" Philip couldn't believe it. "What has happened in London since I've been gone to create a businessman out of my brother? I doubt the man even knows where India is."

Finley leaned back in his chair and closed his eyes. "I would seek a meeting with Lord Hemsworth if I were you. If you still want the building, that is."

Everything about the conversation made Philip wish to punch something. He clenched his fist over his whiskey instead.

"Before I do, Finley, why don't you be a good chap and tell me exactly why Lord Hemsworth was muttering to you, of all people, about not selling me the building? If he's fretting about it hanging around his neck, why would he decide not to sell it to me?"

Finley opened his right eye and said, "Because he doesn't believe you'll get the loan now. Since your house isn't something you can use as collateral."

"I beg your pardon?" Philip sputtered. "Why would I not be able to use my house as collateral?"

"Theodore keeps saying it is his."

Cinch, finally bored with his smoke circles, sat up and looked Philip in the eye. "If Finley says Theodore is still after your house, then he's after your house."

Philip shook his head. "But we have gone through all the ceremonies needed. According to the will, it's mine."

"Word on the street is that he is the owner, and everyone believes Theodore. Believing is power, Daucer. I'm betting you don't have much time to figure this one out. I would get to it straight away if I were you," said Finley

Philip tried to speak normally through his clenched teeth. "And tell me, in the meantime, are you planning on buying the building from Lord Hemsworth?"

Finley shrugged. "I haven't decided yet, but he seems insistent that someone buy it quickly, mentioning he would rather have it settled soon. He mentioned something about me not telling you. Pity for him that I feel more obliged to you than him."

"If this is what it's like to be your friend, I wouldn't want to be your enemy," Philip muttered, which only caused Finley to chuckle good-naturedly.

Philip eyed him a minute longer, his heart racing in his chest. But it wasn't Finley he should be angry with; it was Theodore. He might have to arrange a meeting with a solicitor to see what was going on, where the will was, and how they expected to evict him.

"I'll look into it tomorrow," Philip finally said, trying to speak evenly. "Perhaps with a little of your help?"

Finley nodded once before closing his eyes again.

Chapter 32

CARMEN LOOKED OUT THE small carriage window at the quiet street near Great Park. It was empty except for a few small children out walking with their nurses. Every house had a black iron gate around the small, well-kept gardens. Much like Philip's neighborhood, there was no shouting from boys selling newspapers or girls selling housewares or food.

Nathaniel opened the carriage door suddenly, allowing in a dizzying amount of light. Carmen squinted, trying to adjust her eyes quickly.

"It is the house just there, madame," he told her, pointing to the house three doors from the corner. "Would you like me to see if the doctor will see you?"

Carmen considered the question as well as Nathaniel. He was young with a thick accent that required her to pay close attention, but his eyes were kind, and she got the sense he was trying to help her without offending her.

She hoped he was as loyal to her as he was to Philip since she hadn't told her husband where she was going. He had burst into breakfast, claiming he had overslept and needed to leave right away to a place called South Hampton. Something about his brother and a hotel business. Philip had barely stopped to explain it to her. He told her he would most likely be gone until the next evening, kissed her forehead chastely, and ran out to mount his horse.

The memory made her cringe. She wasn't certain about anyone else's marriage, but she had not anticipated being talked at and left behind so often. In her hurt and frustration, she had remembered Dr. Kruger and decided to call immediately for Nathaniel to take her. Now that she was in front of the house without an appointment and without her husband knowing, she wasn't sure what to do.

"Is that the proper thing to do? You going to ring the door?" she asked. "If I were in Spain, I would have come with my aunt or sister."

Nathaniel nodded and trudged up the front steps without saying more. Carmen watched him from her seat, a south wind bringing the rancid stench of the Thames in through the open carriage window. She had not thought a city so powerful could smell so terrible, as though all the waste of England congregated on the river's banks. Each time the smell encroached on her space, she longed for the clean air of Morales de Toro. A movement at the house brought her attention back to the doctor. A tall man with white hair, from what she could tell, was at the door looking down his nose towards the carriage. Nathaniel was speaking, gesturing toward Carmen. After a moment, Nathaniel returned to the carriage.

"He says he will see you."

Carmen glanced at the house where the man stood stock still. She hadn't expected him to see her that day, though it was what she had hoped.

"Thank you, Nathaniel," she said. He helped her from the carriage and strode ahead to hold the small iron gate open.

"That is the butler at the door, my lady," Nathaniel replied. "He says he will take you to see the doctor. Would you like me to wait inside?"

"No, thank you, Nathaniel," Carmen said. "You can wait for me in the carriage."

Nathaniel nodded reluctantly as she passed by him and through the gate. The stairs were easy to walk up, as she had counted them when she was watching Nathaniel.

"Yes?" the butler drawled as though he didn't know who she was or what she was going there.

Carmen rolled her shoulders back and placed the butler's face directly in her circle of vision. "I'm here to see Dr. Kruger. I'm Mrs. Daucer."

"Your husband is not with you?" the butler asked.

"No," Carmen replied.

The man paused, then spun on his heels and went further into the house. "Follow me."

He led her to a room at the side of the house, decorated with leather chairs, dark red carpets, and a mahogany desk. A tall, thin man with a white beard to match his figure sat at the desk.

"A Mrs. Daucer to see you, sir."

"Come in, come in. Is your husband not with you?" the doctor asked, peering behind her.

Carmen swallowed. If Dr. Kruger had good news for her, she would bring Philip the next time. "No. He is out of town."

The doctor bit his lower lip, as if disappointed, before sitting at his desk. He indicated Carmen sit opposite him and folded his hands on his desk.

"I'll have tea served in just a moment. In the meantime, why don't you tell me about your sight yourself?"

Carmen reluctantly informed him of the first time she noticed the darkness encroaching at the sides of her eyes, the lines spreading until they were now fully encompassing her vision, her struggle with glasses not improving her sight, and her blurred vision.

"The blurred vision is mostly when I am fatigued," Carmen said, grateful for a cup of tea to wet her now parched throat. "The black circles never go away."

"And have you noticed a decline of vision more recently?" Dr. Kruger asked, holding a strange light contraption.

"No, the black circle has not expanded in the last year or so."

"Will you kindly lean your head back?"

Carmen took a deep breath, adjusted her skirts in the long chair, and pressed her spine against the hard back.

"Follow the light, please."

Dr. Kruger's face was so close she could have counted his whiskers; instead, she obeyed and focused on the light.

"Now, hold your eyes still and lift your hand when you stop seeing it."

Carmen did as she was told. The doctor grunted each time she told him when the light disappeared. His breath smelled of licorice. After the light test, Doctor Kruger continued examining her eyes with strange instruments, then tested her vision with different sized letters. When he was done, the clock claimed thirty minutes had gone by.

"What do you think, Doctor?" Carmen asked as she sat up, adjusting her skirts again.

Dr. Kruger sat again, but did not look directly at her. "I would really prefer to tell you with your husband present. I know he is Mr. Philip Daucer, is he not?"

Carmen gathered the courage to speak frankly. "He is very busy at the moment and away from London. It would be best to tell me, and then I can pass on the information."

Dr. Kruger's gray eyebrows almost touched as he frowned. "Very well, very well. From my initial analysis, I believe you could benefit from adding vinegar to your daily diet and acidic fruits when available. There is much study now about the benefits of these acids on the body."

"I was hoping there was a surgery. I met Lady Keswick, who said you healed her sight through a surgery."

Dr. Kruger froze, his teacup poised midair before he recovered. He sipped his tea deliberately, set it down, and assumed a tone Carmen would use with small children. "Lady Keswick suffered from cataracts. I'm sure you understand the difference between cataracts and what you have. I'm also sure Dr. Miguel, whom I've met and whose work I admire, told you that was the case. Just as I'm sure he told you then, there is nothing to cut in your eyes. There are no black circles that I could cut out, and I don't dare to dig out that which I cannot see. Perhaps it's not a question of something in the eyes so much as nerves dying around the iris. But frankly, I do not know."

Though it was exactly what Dr. Miguel had told her a year or more before, the disappointment weighed heavily on her. Speaking again required more effort than before.

"But you believe the vinegar and fruit will help me?" she asked.

"They will not heal you. There is nothing that will heal you. But it is possible the incorporation of these acids into your diet could keep the eye muscles from weakening as you get older and through motherhood. I have witnessed many women with weak eyes gain weaker eyes with each babe they had."

The conversation had ventured in a direction Carmen hadn't expected. Motherhood worsening her eyesight was not something she had considered.

"I will consult with other doctors about your case to see if they know something I do not. There is a convention happening here soon at the Royal Society this week where I can speak with many other doctors who are studying the eye in other countries of Europe and the rest of the world. I will send for you after I've had time to see my colleagues. It might be best if your husband is with you next time."

Carmen rose and thanked him. After the butler ushered her down the hallway and out the door, Carmen lingered, wondering what to do. The news wasn't any different from what Doctor Miguel had told her when he broke off their wedding. And yet it felt different.

She was incurable. And there was no changing that.

Chapter 33

THE HONORABLE MR. HUXLEY lived in one of the newer houses on Baker Street, a neighborhood for the families who were distantly related to noble blood but who owned no family estate or land. The second, third, and so on sons of titled families who worked as barristers and judges and the like.

Exactly where Philip should have a house.

Meredith stepped down from the carriage and suddenly felt conspicuous, as though everyone in a top hat were watching her, eyeing her, deducing why she was there. Meetings with barristers were matters usually left to the men, after all, but she had brought Theodore this far, and she deserved to be there. She could hardly believe her luck that Philip went and married a Catholic foreigner instead of an Anglican Englishwoman, a decision which made her and Theodore's argument more valid. It was a shame that they had to drag Philip and his marriage into the mud, since mud always splashed on the family closest to the person. To avoid all of this Philip could stop fighting and finally admit she and Theodore were right. But of course, he wouldn't.

And while society might have fun at their expense for a little while, other gossip would soon take over.

By that time, they would have sold the house to Lord Grosvenor in exchange for a coveted new house in Berkeley Square. And by the end of the summer, Theodore would be admitted into the new club, which meant more powerful committee positions and more access to other ventures such as the project to continue building homes for those in society in Hanover Square.

And she, Meredith, being a woman of Berkeley Square and already settled, would rise in status in the eyes of London society. As well she should.

With this new house and access to new investments, she and Theodore would soon have more income. Income that wasn't connected to Philip and his business dealings. Income that was more suited to them and their kind. Philip could go on working as though he were born in Liverpool, but he would no longer lay claim to how they spent their money in the slightest. What was more, Theodore could make sure that Philip continued in his proper place, preventing other men of the nobility from investing in his schemes. Like the hotel venture.

She shuddered at the thought. It was as though her brother-in-law stayed up at night conjuring new ways to embarrass their family. They were not the sort of people who should be known for running a hotel. Ships and the like were bad enough, but having the Daucer name associated with hospitality would be the end of her. She could never show her face in society again.

"Ready, my dear?" Theodore offered his hand, and she took it. This partnership between them in getting what was rightfully Theodore's, and therefore rightfully their children's, had brought them closer in a way they had never been before.

They were shown into the front sitting room, decorated tastefully. There was nothing garish about the curtains, colors, or paper on the walls. It had a modest air, though she suspected they made more money than many noble families.

"Lord and Lady Daucer, how very nice to see you this afternoon." His Honorable Mr. Huxley was a rotund man with a beak-like nose that made him look like a goose. But his eyes were clear, not watery like some men his age had.

She liked him instantly.

Though Meredith thought her silk dress a bit much for tea, Mrs. Huxley, with her simple hair and lack of jewelry, seemed rather boring. Thankfully, they were joined by Lord and Lady Farnborough as well as the Honorable Sir John Mason. The women were at one side of the table and the men on the other, trying their best to keep the smoke away from their wives.

Meredith glanced at her husband sitting a few feet away, masking her envy of his position with a neutral expression. There wasn't much she could do with her lot in life, that of being a woman. Previously, she'd accepted societal gender roles, even defending them to younger women, but now she questioned them. While Meredith was stuck discussing the new yarn and ribbon shop that was opening or how differently Lady Farnborough's cook made meat pies, the men discussed important topics such as the London to Greenwich railway, which would surely make the London air worse and crowd the city with poorer and disease-infested people, to the passage of the Irish Constabulary Act. Again, another mistake of Parliament. After all, if England was to be the most powerful country in the world, they should not be allowing Ireland to police themselves. Even she knew the Irish were incapable of doing anything properly.

Aware that she was staring too eagerly at the men, Meredith focused on Mrs. Huxley, who was saying, "Just wait until you're my age. Just you wait."

The phrase annoyed Meredith greatly. Mostly because it was frightening to consider that your body might betray you just because you reached a certain age.

She let out her breath when Mrs. Huxley excused herself to check on her children.

"Speaking of those passing on," Sir John said, directing the conversation as he said he would. Meredith clasped her hands to keep her nerves from showing. "I heard we might have another inheritance law come up through the parliament."

"I have not heard that, and I, for one, hope we do not," replied Lord Farnborough. "Why people want to change the way things have been done since the beginning of time is beyond me."

"Should the people not have the ability to write their wills and allow who they wish to inherit?" Sir John asked.

Meredith vibrated with anticipation. Mr. Huxley answered first.

"Perhaps," he drawled. "Though most do not have enough money left over to leave to anyone in their family."

"That is one point, but there is another. Many times, these sorts of things lead to the disintegration of the family."

"How so?" Lady Farnborough asked, her tiny sugar spoon clinking quietly against her cup as she set it down. "If a will is a legally binding document, there can be nothing for a family to dispute. It is simply the wish of the deceased."

Meredith cleared her throat, itching to argue. But it was Theodore who spoke next.

"My father," Theodore said after a shifting in his seat to gather attention, "had a will. I thought nothing of it at the time that he wrote it. I was just then happily married, and I supposed, wrongly, that he would be with us until much later in life. He died less than two years later."

"And did it cause harm to your family?" Lady Farnborough asked, her eyes wide with curiosity and perhaps some fear. Meredith couldn't have set up the conversation better herself.

"Actually, it has and continues to. My third brother received the house in London, which is a great inconvenience to Lady Daucer and I."

"But the country estate," Mr. Huxley asked. "That has stayed with you?"

"Yes, that, thankfully, my father had the sense to leave with me. My brother is a great lover of this city, you know, and would not likely have wanted to live in the country."

"You inherited the estate as well as the debt, I assume?" Lady Farnborough asked.

"There was not as much debt as one might assume," Meredith said defensively, though she didn't know how much they had. "The land is good, and the mines are still producing."

"No strikes or threats of strikes?" asked Lord Farnborough. "I have had a ghastly time trying to keep my workers happy without them taking advantage of me. They think that just because I live in a grand house, I have money to burn. It is one of the great misunderstandings between social classes in England."

"That is the truth," intoned Mr. Stuart.

"I wish our people would continue the grand tradition that has worked for centuries instead of making changes that will inevitably muck up the legal system," Mr. Huxley said. "For centuries not only in these grand Isles, but those countries on the continent have been content enough to pass on estates to the firstborn. We should all be content in the place we are to occupy, the space God, in His great knowledge, has placed us in. This idea of moving inheritance around is the same as forcing God's hand, of telling Him we know better. After all, if God wanted a man who is the third son, let's say, to inherit, He would have had him be born first. Or does God not understand our legal system? Is it not the same system as in the very Bible?"

Meredith could hardly contain her giddiness at the conversation, but she sipped her tea and kept her opinions to herself. A task that was difficult.

"That's precisely what I told my brother and my mother when we had to sit through the reading of my father's will," Theodore said. "It was such an unnatural thing sitting there, listening to the supposed will of a man who is already dead. We, the ones living, must continue with our lives. And at the moment he wrote the will, I had no children. But now that I do, I see that the will has not only caused us an inconvenience when we visit London but has robbed my children of a part of their own inheritance."

Lord Farnborough shook his head vehemently. "Is there nothing that can be done when it will rob children of their inheritance?"

Mr. Huxley puffed on his cigar in silence while Mr. Stuart leaned forward. "That would depend on what the will says. You don't carry it on you, do you?"

"That is not the kind of thing I keep in my pocket, Your Honor," Theodore responded. "But if you would like, I could send a copy to you. My wife, though, has it almost memorized. She has an impressive memory with things like that."

The three men then turned to Meredith, who had been anxiously waiting for her moment.

"Well," Mr. Huxley prompted. Meredith took a breath, then started reciting the will word by word. Of course, they wouldn't know for certain that it was until they read the will themselves.

When she finished, she restrained herself from sharing her thoughts on the will and the way it was written.

"What do you think about that will?" Lord Farnborough asked the two barristers. "It doesn't seem forthright enough for me. But then, I am partial to getting rid of wills and continuing the tradition of primogeniture."

"The words that catch my attention the most are those that say it is for your brother, his wife, and his subsequent children. Was your brother married at the time?" asked Mr. Huxley.

"No, your honor, he was not. But he is now." Meredith bit her tongue against scolding Theodore for saying Philip was married. They were trying to prove that he wasn't married, at least not under English law.

"Isn't it Philip who returned from the continent married to a Spanish woman? A Catholic?" Lady Farnborough asked.

"A Catholic?" repeated Mr. Stuart. "Then he is not married under English law."

"The Marriage Act passed and goes into effect in August," Lord Farnborough pointed out. "Soon every marriage of every religion will be recognized as equal to the Anglican marriage."

Lady Farnborough clicked her tongue. Meredith sighed, though she didn't care what the Catholics did if they stayed in their neighborhoods. Still, she was determined to cause some distress, regardless of the impact on Philip's marriage.

"According to the law, and that is what I teach and defend," Mr. Huxley said, "Philip is not married unless the woman has renounced her faith and become Anglican. Were they married in the Anglican church, Theodore?"

"I heard my brother scrambled to get a special license the other day. Probably didn't realize he needed to be married in the Anglican church until he returned home, your honor." Theodore shook his head wistfully. "This business of the will is tearing our family apart. All for a house. If my father had simply let the living sort things out, let the right person inherit and so on, perhaps my brother would not be trying to outwit me on the property."

Mr. Huxley and Mr. Stuart joined him in lamenting the situation, allowing Meredith to breathe out in relief.

"Still," Mr. Stuart said. "If he is properly married under English law, then the will is in effect, is it not?"

Theodore glanced at Meredith.

"But he was not married when the will was read, and he married only to tie the hands of the English law around the will," Theodore said. Meredith's heart skipped a beat as the men contemplated the situation.

"If I were the judge in this case, I would say the house is yours. It would have been yours from the beginning, since your brother was not married. At the time of marriage, though, if the property were still in possession of the family, I would assume your brother could petition it to become his, based on the will. Of course, this should have been done sooner to give yourself some time."

"I do not wish to cause strife in my family," Theodore said. The words were spoken with such sincerity that they caught Meredith by surprise. But then her husband went on. "I had not thought to question the will until I thought of my children and their future. And of course, my duty here. As I grow older, I see how much I am needed in the House of Lords here in London. And with that, a place to live. All things my father should have considered."

"Always question everything, Lord Daucer," Mr. Huxley advised. Mr. Stuart also nodded. "With regards to a man's rights, always question the motives of the humans who try to move the hand of God and the rights He has bestowed."

Theodore finally glanced at Meredith, and she gave him the imperceptible nod that was their signal for him to let it lie. The next step would be to spread the rumor that two barristers and Lord Farnborough did not recognize Philip's marriage as valid. If they were lucky, Lady Farnborough would join them in the work without Meredith having to say a word.

When they left thirty minutes later, Meredith heaved a silent sigh of relief. Everything had gone very well indeed. She was quite proud of herself. And Theodore.

"Rather poor weather we have today," Theodore said, grimacing as the sun shone down on them. He was sensitive to the sun's rays, turning red within minutes of being under it.

"It's nice to have some warmth," Meredith chided him, though kindly. She was feeling so awfully proud of them. "And just think of the crops. They need the sun as much as they need the rain."

Theodore wasn't convinced, just as she knew he wouldn't be. The crops never interested him. Nor did they hear, though she had a rudimentary respect for the crops feeding them.

"Shall we treat ourselves to some shopping?" she suggested, knowing how much Theodore loved buying himself something new. "All of our hard work is paying off."

"We could stop by and order you a new dress for the summer solstice ball," Theodore said. "And I could use a new cravat or two."

"Precisely, my dear," Meredith said, a bubble of relief and joy bursting within her. She was so happy she almost called Theodore 'love,' but stopped herself in time. No need to change everything about their relationship.

Chapter 34

THE NEXT DAY, JUST as the afternoon sunlight streamed through the windows in the parlor, the front door opened, and footsteps that could only be Philip's echoed through the quiet house. Knowing she planned not to leave the house, Carmen told Nathaniel to take the day off. Felix had gone to see his mother for the afternoon, and Rebecca had taken leave for two days to tend to her sick sister.

That left only Mrs. Brax in the house, and she was too busy in the kitchen to get the door. Carmen rose from the spot on the couch where she had been reading since coming home and went to see her husband.

"Oh, hello." Philip's eyes shone when he saw her open the parlor door and step into the entryway. "Where did you come from?"

Carmen indicated the parlor. Then she assessed her husband and chuckled. He was swaying slightly as Jaime and her father would sometimes. "Is it possible you've been drinking while working today, husband?"

Philip crept closer, his coat only halfway off his arms. "Call me that again, wife."

Carmen was forced to back up until she was against the wall as Philip advanced further towards her. He snuggled up against her neck, his lips dragging along the tender places behind her ears until Carmen gasped aloud. But when he tried to cup her chin and found himself caught in his coat, Carmen laughed.

"Come here, *idiota*." She yanked on his coat sleeve until his left arm was free. Philip twirled on his heel until he was facing her again.

"Did you just call me an idiot?" he asked, puckering his bottom lip as though offended. Carmen kissed it quickly, then stepped aside to hang his coat.

"If you act like an *idiota*, I'll call you *idiota*," she said, still giggling.

Philip watched her with hooded eyes, looking ready to pounce the moment she was done with her task. A thrill ran through her body. Now that she had an idea of what men thought about when they looked like that, she couldn't help thinking about certain things, too. Of his lips against her, his nimble fingers touching the most tender spots. Places she now knew shivered each time her husband caressed them.

Carmen took a staggered breath and finished hanging Philip's coat. It was midafternoon. Not exactly the time of day when lovers took to the bed. She was a lady and would behave as such.

"Where is everyone?" Philip asked, distracting Carmen from her self-scolding.

"I let Nathaniel have the day since I didn't need him. You let Rebecca go to tend to her sister, remember? And Felix told me that he normally visits his mother on afternoons when we have no plans to go out or have guests. I told him we had no such plans, so he left." Carmen spread her hands. "I've been home all day. All alone."

"Why didn't you go out?"

Carmen didn't wish to tell him that she had felt rather depressed about the news she received from Dr. Kruger the day before. "I was trying to be angry with you," she told him, pretending to take an interest in a stray curl hanging near her left eye.

"Angry with me?" Philip asked her. He looked her up and down. "Why would you be angry with me?"

"You left me alone," she told him. A spark flickered in his eyes at that statement.

"You wish I had been here?" he asked softly. "With you?"

Carmen shrugged one shoulder, unable to keep from smiling at him.

"Come here then, wife. I'm here now." The words came out as a growl as Philip tugged on Carmen's hand. She allowed him to lead her into the parlor again, the doors closing with a soft bang behind them. Before

Carmen could catch her breath, Philip cupped her face in one hand and pulled her tightly against him with his other.

His lips were cold, but his tongue was warm, swirling in her mouth, exploring her as though he hadn't done so already. Carmen pressed her palm against his hard chest, feeling his muscles move under his shirt. Remembering him on the ship, pulling the ropes with the sailors, made her stomach flip and a strange longing stir inside her.

"Philip," she said, trying to be stern. But her voice came out a whisper that sounded desperate to her ears.

"Yes, wife?" he whispered back. He leaned his forehead against her, rubbing her cheek with his thumb. It took a moment before Carmen could think of something to say.

"Perhaps we should call for tea," Carmen said. "It is but afternoon. The sun is still out."

Slowly, Philip backed away until he was near the windows. Without taking his eyes off her, Philip tugged on the curtain ties. One by one, he let them fall closed until the room was in semi-darkness.

"Philip," Carmen said, unsure of what to say. Half excited, half frightened by what her husband might be thinking of doing in the middle of the day, in the parlor.

"Come here, Carmen," he said. As though in a trance, with no will of her own to argue, Carmen floated towards him.

Philip quietly pulled her into his arms and promptly scraped his teeth against her neck until she could no longer stand on her own. Carmen moved her hands to his face, his hair. Shivers and flames of longing were licking her body both inside and out. There were no details registered in her mind, just touch, desire, breath, and kisses. Melted against him, his arms holding her up, Carmen gave in to the primal moves her fingers and body wished to do. She scratched at Philip's buttons. She pressed her lips against his neck. She gasped and panted and moaned.

It wasn't until the tips of his fingers stroked her bare breasts that she realized her husband had slid down her dress.

"Philip," she whispered. Or perhaps it was more of a whimper. "This... isn't...proper."

Philip chuckled against her chest. "Carmen, is anything a man and woman do together proper?"

She didn't respond. His lips lightly kissed her chest, scrambling her words.

"Would you like me to stop?"

Carmen concentrated hard as he continued to kiss her. It wasn't fair, really. Everything he was doing begged her to stop thinking and let go.

"No," she finally managed to whisper.

And it was the truth, as she had never told it before.

A knock at the front door awoke them a little while later. Philip sat up with a start. Carmen struggled to understand how her dress had entangled itself so terribly around her waist.

"Stay here," Philip said, tossing a blanket from the couch over her body. She scrambled to gather it around her bare chest, though her fingers continued to straighten out her dress underneath.

Philip drew up his trousers and buttoned his shirt before opening one curtain. Carmen squinted against the light. The afternoon had turned into a golden and pink sunset.

"It's a courier. I supposed Felix isn't home yet," Philip said as another knock, this time louder, sounded against the door. Philip gave up with his cravat, tugged on his jacket, and slipped through the parlor door.

Perhaps some women would have stayed where they were, but Carmen was too embarrassed now that her emotions were no longer swirling through her. While she trusted Philip, he might have seen incorrectly. Perhaps it wasn't just a courier. If there was even a slight chance someone else was at the door, Carmen wanted to be prepared.

It was her shame that pushed her off the floor. Years of practicing how to dress herself in the event she became blind helped her find the right way to set her skirts and button up her dress. Then she rushed towards the parlor door to listen.

"What is this?" Philip asked. Carmen peeked through the cracked door as she tied her bodice at the back. Her husband stood at the open front door, his shoulders stiff, looking down at something.

"Lord Daucer is requesting your presence in two days."

Philip snorted as papers were shuffled. "Is he asking for a reply?"

"Yes, sir."

Carmen retreated into the room as Philip pivoted abruptly on his heel. Two seconds later, the parlor door burst open. Carmen jumped back.

"What is it?" Carmen asked as Philip marched past her to the desk. He yanked open more curtains, then set about writing furiously on a piece of paper.

"My brother," Philip said curtly. "Apparently, we are to have a meeting with lawyers. He isn't giving up, just like Finley said."

"Is that bad?" Carmen asked. Philip didn't answer her. Instead, he went back to the courier and handed him the missive. When he came back to the parlor, his expression was dark, his brow furrowed.

"Are you worried, Philip?" she asked.

"I'm starting to see how much I hate secrets and . . ." Philip stopped, searching for words. "Betrayal, I guess. Theodore going behind my back, forcing us to speak with lawyers instead of just speaking with me, man to man. I hate it. He could just tell me as a brother should. But no, he must connive his way into getting what he wants."

Carmen took a breath. She looked around the parlor and tried to understand what it was about the house that had Philip's brother so interested in it. It was a pleasant house, a beautiful one, but she couldn't imagine Meredith living there.

"Why do they want the house so much?" she asked.

Philip shook his head, still staring at the letter. "He wants to exchange it for a better house. As leverage."

"Oh." Carmen had a vague idea of what that meant. "And your father left this house to you when he died?"

"Yes, Carmen. There's a will." Philip raked his fingers through his hair and sighed.

"I'm just trying to understand all of this," Carmen told him. Her emotions were getting away with her. There was no reason to be so upset with Philip's short temper, but she was upset. She was holding back tears, in fact.

"I know," Philip said, softer this time. He set the missive down and took her hand. "I'm sorry."

"If your brother manages to get the house, where will we live?"

Philip shook his head. "There's no need to worry about that. He will not win. I promise you." Philip kissed the tip of her nose and tried to smile, but it faded almost instantly. "I need to do some things in my study. Perhaps you should go freshen up in your room. We can have dinner together in an hour."

"Yes, alright," Carmen said, watching him walk away.

At the door, Philip called over his shoulder to her. "Don't worry, Carmen. I will take care of this."

Carmen stared at the door, wondering at her husband's words. She knew he wanted her to believe him, but his reactions and demeanor didn't demonstrate the same confidence.

The clock in the hallway struck five in the evening, waking Carmen from her thoughts. She was to take her vinegar at that time, according to Dr. Kruger. That was something she should have told Philip about, but it had slipped her mind before.

Carmen started her march up the stairs and decided she wouldn't tell Philip about the visit at all. He didn't need more things on his mind. After all, she wasn't any worse than before, and Dr. Kruger had offered no cure. Which might disappoint Philip.

Chapter 35

PHILIP WATCHED AS HIS wife slowly opened her eyes the next morning. He had managed to soothe his anger from receiving the missive by focusing on Carmen. She seemed to be able to make him forget everything when she looked at him with her wide, dark eyes.

She was so lovely when she slept. He would lay there and watch her all day, except that he couldn't stop thinking about the meeting. He would need to see Cinch and ask if he would accompany him to it. Cinch had the uncanny ability to make sure Philip didn't say or do anything stupid. Namely, yelling at his brother in front of a judge or other lord.

"Good morning," Philip said. "Would you like to sleep more?"

"Maybe just a little longer," she said with a sleepy smile. "What will you do?

"There are a few things that need my attention. Namely, to be ready for the meeting with my brother tomorrow."

"Tomorrow is also Claire's luncheon to raise money for her day school," Carmen reminded him. Philip hummed a reply as he lifted himself onto his side before slipping out of bed.

"Philip, I received a letter from Isabel yesterday."

"Did you?" he asked, only half listening as he washed his face with the water in the basin.

"She was asking me if I was coming home for the baby's birth."

Philip froze, then lifted the towel and dried himself. "Carmen, your home is here."

He watched her through the mirror. She had paled at his words.

"I thought there was a chance you would go back to Spain to overlook the project you started over there."

"No," Philip said. "That wasn't the plan."

Carmen gnawed at her bottom lip. "And if we lose this house to Theodore, what will we do? We could always go back to Spain. At least for a time."

That was not what he had expected her to say. A strange emotion akin to panic or abandonment surged within him.

"Carmen, what are you saying? I thought you were settling well here. You have friends in Claire and Emily and Rowena."

"Emily goes back to her home in three days, and Claire is quite busy with her day school. I haven't seen Rowena since the baptism."

The arguments against him were ticked off one by one, leaving Philip little to say.

"It might take some time, but I'm sure you'll settle, Carmen," he said, trying to sound reassuring, even with his own doubt evident.

"And if we lose the house?"

"We are not losing the house," Philip said more harshly than he meant. Carmen blinked. Then she nodded.

"As you say," she said. Philip noted a tinge of sarcasm, but didn't want to argue.

"Yes, as I say." Then he gave her a quick kiss and left.

———— ❦ ————

The meeting came a little over twenty-four hours later. Philip had hardly slept the night before and awoke in a very poor mood. When Carmen reminded him of the luncheon, he told her she would have to go alone.

"Will you come later?" she had asked him, which was not a question he was prepared to answer. To keep himself from snapping at her, Philip had paused and then shook his head. Then he had excused himself and retreated to his study without eating breakfast. It was strange to him that Carmen was more concerned with him going to the luncheon than to the meeting that would finally put to rest who owned the house. The house he and Carmen lived in.

When Cinch came by, ready to add his support, he found Philip on the warpath between his desk and the fireplace.

"Are you ready, Philip?"

Philip was deep in thought when his friend's question penetrated his brain.

"Sorry?"

"I think they're here," Cinch said as a knock rapped on the door.

"Lord Daucer and Mr. Sanders," Felix announced, opening the doors to the study wider.

"Good afternoon," Theodore said. He sauntered in as though he already owned the house.

Philip greeted them in his best business tone, biting back the words he wanted to say. Cinch shook Theodore's and Mr. Sander's hand as though they were gathering to play a friendly game of cards.

The door opened again.

"The Bishop of Winchester, his lordship Thomas Day," announced Felix. "And the Honorable Judge Watterson."

Bishop Day, a man of fifty with snow-white hair and eyes that judged more than God himself, marched into the room. Honorable Judge Watterson walked in behind him. The confidence the man had in his power sent an ominous shiver through Philip's shoulders that he couldn't shake.

"Good afternoon."

The bishop's voice held surprising force. Philip greeted the man of the church, kissing his rings when the gnarled hand was held out, finding it difficult to keep his face stoic as he rose from the strange stench on the man's fingers.

The rest of the introductions were short and to the point.

"How shall we proceed?" asked the bishop, taking a fresh cup of tea from Rebecca, who had quietly entered a moment before.

Mr. Sunder cleared his throat. Philip had to give his brother credit for calling the family barrister, wondering if he should have done so himself. The thought had crossed his mind, but he decided against it, not wanting to involve the man in a rift between the brothers. It had seemed an abuse of their long-standing relationship with him.

"There is a matter of a family will to settle, your lordship," Mr. Sunder started.

"I am here only as a spiritual advisor." Bishop Day sipped his tea again, then pierced Philip with a stony stare. For the first time in his life, Philip wished he had gone to church more.

"Yes, yes," Mr. Sunder said, clearly ruffled by the mere presence of the bishop.

"And I am here not as a judge but to answer questions about the law," Judge Watterson said. "This is not a formal court, and therefore I want to warn everyone involved that circumstances could always change."

"We appreciate you taking your time to give counsel," Cinch said in his best gravelly, lordly tone.

"Yes, I, too, would like to thank you for your time," Theodore hastened to say. It must have aggravated him greatly that he couldn't match Cinch's commanding pitch.

Philip dug his nails into his own palms to keep from rolling his eyes at his brother.

Bishop Day waved his hand slowly in a circle as though used to, and bored by, such accolades. "Who will present the issue in a precise manner?"

"I will begin," Mr. Sunder said, his voice cracking. "There is an issue with a will that we executed only a few years ago."

The man's voice never grew stronger, but did stop cracking.

"A will is a binding contract even in England," Judge Watterson said at the end of the account. Philip almost laughed with joy. If the will was binding, this would be a short victory.

"It's a rather preposterous thing, though, isn't it?" asked Bishop Day. "The other countries on the continent don't allow such nonsense."

Judge Watterson, who was perusing the will, didn't answer.

"The advice we have come to seek, your lordship," Theodore said, "is about the words stating that the house is for my brother and his wife and subsequent children. My brother, you see, took possession of the house directly after our father passed. Before the mourning period was over, in fact."

Theodore lanced Philip with a dramatic glare, the pause causing even the bishop to raise his head from the will in surprise.

Bishop Day fixed his icy eyes again on Philip. "You're too old to be gallivanting around town as a bachelor."

"My father died eight years ago," Philip said, struggling to keep his tone neutral. "I argue that the will allocates the house to me, regardless of my marital state, your honor, since he knew I was not married at the time." The bishop bristled, his shoulders stiffening, and Philip hastened to continue. "But you are correct, my lord, at my age and state of marriage. Which is why I was married just over a month ago. To Miss Carmen Suárez."

Mr. Sunder cleared his throat to bring attention back to himself. "Here are the facts as they serve. Lord Daucer was too distraught after his father died to study the will. Then he was married and had a child before the late Lady Daucer, Lord Daucer's mother, became sick and also died. Had these life events not kept him from reviewing the will sooner, Lord Daucer would have taken possession of the house in London for himself, as is his legal right."

"Again, I argue that the will gave the house to me regardless of my marital state," Philip repeated.

"I informed my brother of the correct interpretation of the will just before he left for Spain." Theodore grinned then, sending another ominous tremor down Philip's spine. "Since my brother came home from Spain with a bride no one has heard of and for whom he gave no notice he would marry, I contend that he, too, agrees with my interpretation of the will. That the house was for him only if he had a wife and children."

Judge Watterson peered at Philip over the rim of his spectacles. "Is it true that you agree with Lord Daucer's interpretation of the will?"

Philip glanced at Cinch. "I do not," he said, adding quickly, "but it doesn't matter, does it? I am now married."

"If you do not agree with your brother's interpretation, why then did you marry in such haste?" Mr. Sunder asked. "Why did you not come to England, call the banns, and marry as our rules dictate?"

"Yes, why not? I would think if you and your wife are to live in this country, that the proper thing to do would be to marry here. Do you not know the laws of marriage?" asked the bishop.

"Of course I do. I have my legal marriage documents right here."

Philip handed the special license to the bishop. "I was married by the special license the other day in the presence of Lord Candor and others."

Mr. Sunder read, his lips moving silently as his fingers passed over the words. He passed it to Bishop Day.

"But why not call the banns and have a proper celebration?" Judge Watterson asked again.

"Because she is Catholic," Theodore said, his voice booming over them.

Biting back the retort he would have fired if they were alone, Philip licked his lips. Instead, he gathered patience to defend himself against this brother's idiocy. "We were married in Spain first. With her family. We had a Protestant ceremony here. I believe we have done far beyond what most would do. I know several gentlemen who have married on the continent who did not feel obliged to have another ceremony here in England."

"Why did you feel you needed to do more?" demanded Theodore. "Because you did not believe it would hold up against the will? Because you were married in the Catholic Church there, in Spain?"

Philip held his gaze as he replied, "Our Parliament passed the Marriage Act, which is to go into effect in less than two months, which says that marriage in the Catholic Church is just as legal as marriage in the Anglican church."

"This is true," Judge Watterson said even as Bishop Day shook his head angrily.

"I do not understand what possessed our Parliament to pass such a law," said Bishop Day. "The English state has sanctified the Anglican Church as the spiritual guide of the people, and as persons of the nobility, you have an obligation to lead by example."

"Which he did," Cinch said. Bishop Day ignored the comment.

"There is nothing wrong with my marriage," Philip said.

Theodore's smile stopped Philip mid-track. Mr. Saunders cleared his throat, then extended another paper to Judge Watterson.

Philip squinted, but it was too far away to read. Even still, he could see clearly that the letter was in his father's handwriting.

"What is this?" Philip asked.

Judge Watterson grunted, then passed the letter to the bishop.

"What you might not know is that Philip married his bride in Spain," Mr. Sunder said.

"They know that because I just said it," Philip snapped.

"But you did not mention you were baptized as a Catholic before doing so," Mr. Sunder said.

Silence fell so heavily that for the first time that day, fear entered Philip's chest. "That was simply to follow the laws of Spain for marriage. I cannot ask my wife to leave her country as an unmarried woman alone with a man. We were married in the Spanish tradition, and then we came here and were married under common law."

"You could have moved her here with a maid. She could have resided at Lord Candor's house in the interim. There are many ways you could have gone about marrying her. You did not have to baptize yourself as Catholic."

Philip slowed his speech so as to not yell. But he didn't slow it so much as to be insulting, though he would have under other circumstances. "If you don't know, Spain is at war. While things are calm now, I thought it best for all of Carmen's family to participate in our nuptials, as most families would appreciate."

"Yes, Mr. Daucer," Mr. Sunder said. "But now you are in violation of the wishes of your late father. And therefore, we argue, you should no longer be considered in the will at all."

"What the devil? What are you speaking of?" he sputtered.

Cinch placed his hand in the air, a silent warning for Philip to calm down.

Judge Watterson waved the letter the bishop had given back to him. "This is a letter sent to Mr. Sunder dated before his death that states no son of his shall inherit if he becomes a Quaker or Catholic."

Philip reached for the letter with unsteady hands. There, in his father's handwriting he knew Theodore couldn't imitate, were the very words the judge had just spoken.

"But I am not a Catholic."

"It also says you will not inherit if you marry a Quaker or Catholic or any other religion," Mr. Sunder said.

"But I inherited years ago. You cannot take the house away now. There was no question of which religion I was when my father passed," Philip argued.

Judge Watterson rose, shaking his head. "Since the will is ambiguous in its meaning, though I can see where Lord Daucer got his interpretation and am partial to it, we do not know if the former marquess desired for the house to be given only if his youngest son married or if he also wished for him to inherit even in the event that he did not marry. That aside, with the question now put to us, we must also consider the fact that if he were alive, he would not bequeath the house to you now that you are married to a Catholic and have yourself become Catholic."

Theodore nodded, his smile now replaced by a grave, concerned, straight line. "I can tell you, as the eldest of the sons, that my father would have very much wanted my brother to marry. Our father saw marriage as the cornerstone to English society and the Anglican Church as the ultimate authority in our spiritual lives."

"It's what creates a strong union in our nation," Bishop Day said.

"Agreed," Theodore said, though he seemed off balance by the interruption. "And I cannot believe my father would have given an inheritance to a son who did not take the church seriously enough to stay allegiant to it."

Philip had to clench his fists to stop himself from punching him in the face.

"I will ask for a special license," Philip said. "And marry my wife again, if you all wish. We will even register as Protestants."

"Really?" Theodore asked. "Are you sure?"

Philip swallowed hard, remembering how Alice had convinced her cousin to take his name from the registry. He was, therefore, not registered in any parish. And he was certain Carmen would not be happy with him about becoming a Protestant. The whole situation was not going the way he had predicted that morning.

Theodore spread his hands innocently. "I believe there is little you can do with a special license now. Seems to me that even if you have not truly lied, you have not been completely honest so far."

Philip moved to speak but was interrupted by the bishop standing.

"I am needed elsewhere now," he said. "As a spiritual advisor, I am concerned about this situation. I believe the only thing you can do is recommit yourself to the Church of England, you and your wife, and write a letter begging forgiveness."

Philip winced inwardly. The bishop searched his face with his small, black eyes.

"I am not a legal expert. I leave that to Judge Watterson, but in my opinion, the house in question belongs to the firstborn of the family who is a member of the Church of England, as a nobleman of England should be." Bishop Day fluffed his robes and lifted his chin in an effort to look more regal than he was. "I will take my leave."

Philip bowed along with the rest of them. When the door shut behind the bishop, Philip turned to the judge.

"I will consult with my colleagues," Judge Watterson said. "But I will confess, it is not clear to me, Mr. Daucer, that you are to have the house now that you've been foolish. I will consult with my colleagues and come back with a decision when I can." Then, looking down his nose at Philip, he said, "Perhaps in the meantime you should think about getting your wife baptized in the Church of England."

With that, he rose and marched out of the room, Theodore following him, leaving Philip in a state of utter loss.

Chapter 36

THE HALL FOR THE luncheon was decorated all in white, giving it a heavenly feel. White cloths covered the tables and white blossoms filled white vases. Even Claire was wearing an ivory dress knotted with white lace at the neck.

"It's beautiful," Carmen said as Emily came to greet her. She tried to push back the worry she had about Philip and the meeting about the house. There was little she could do about it, after all. Whether or not Philip accompanied her to functions, this was her life now. Although it wasn't creating wine with her father, it was her choice to be in London, and she needed to make the most of it.

"Isn't it?" Emily looked about the room with appreciation. "I must say, Claire has an eye for these things, though I warned her that white might not be the color to choose for the school when she opens. Children tend to make a mess of white almost immediately upon seeing it, in my experience."

Emily giggled and dragged Carmen closer to Claire, who was speaking to an older man with a gray mustache. They both turned when Emily cleared her throat.

"Sir Andrew Tillman, have you met Mrs. Carmen Daucer, Philip's wife?" Emily smiled sweetly at the man who regarded Carmen cooly through tiny spectacles.

"How do you do?" he said.

"Nice to meet you," Carmen said.

"Well," Claire said, wringing her hands as she looked about the hall. "I better check on the last little details before the others arrive."

"I will accompany you," Sir Andrew said. "Remember, I cannot stay for the full luncheon. I have a few other things to do this afternoon, but you know that you have my full support."

Carmen and Emily watched them walk away, Sir Andrew still talking while Claire fussed over the flower arrangements and made signals to different footmen.

"I wish she wouldn't marry him," Emily said, clicking her tongue.

Carmen swung her body towards Emily to have her fully centered in her vision. "Claire? Marry him? But why?"

Emily shrugged wistfully. "I'm sure the proposal is coming, and Claire thinks it's expected of her, I believe. And the old man—. Oh, perhaps I shouldn't call him that. *Sir Andrew* is well respected in London." Emily chewed her lip as her eyes followed Claire and Sir Andrew. "But he's so very old and not fun at all. He has no sense of humor, which I believe is required for this life, don't you?" Carmen opened her mouth to reply that she did, but Emily continued on. "There is something about him. I can't put my finger on it, but I know she isn't supposed to marry him."

Carmen regarded Sir Andrew again, assessing him with the new information. He was much too old for Claire. And stuffy, as the English would say. She paused her thoughts, remembering how willing she had been to marry an older gentleman, as Tía Merce always suggested and felt a bit foolish. She wouldn't have liked being married to an older man, now that she understood more about marriage. Despite Philip's preoccupation with the house, she much preferred being married to him rather than an old man.

"My aunt is a strong advocate for women marrying older men, especially if they are rich, so that the woman can become a widow sooner rather than later. She says that the life of a widow is far superior to the life of a princess."

Emily stopped chewing her lip. "Are you being serious?"

"Completely," Carmen said. "But now I am not sure I agree with her."

Emily pressed her gloved fingers to her mouth, shaking her head as she giggled. "I doubt very much that is Claire's motivation. She is already a widow, after all. Though she is a poor widow in some sense of the word. Her husband, my brother, spent more than his allowance while he was alive. It took Cinch years to put everything back together."

"So, Claire isn't poor anymore?"

"Heavens, no," Emily said, steering Carmen out of the way of a footman setting up a ladder. "The family isn't poor. Cinch gives Claire over a thousand a year and has agreed to pay a dowry of three thousand if she marries again. He is being rather objective in her choice, saying he doesn't feel he should sway her one way or the other. Claire is very independent, you know. But the worry I have is that, well, I wonder if Sir Andrew is interested in her for her or just for the dowry and name."

"Surely you jest," Carmen exclaimed, scandalized by Emily saying those words aloud.

"Don't get me wrong," Emily said, leading Carmen slowly around the tables, just far enough from Claire to avoid being overheard. "Claire is a fabulous catch. So pretty and intelligent and creating something so wonderful with this day school project." Emily dropped her voice even lower. Carmen had to lean closer to hear her. "But there is something about Sir Andrew that makes me think he wants her more as a trophy by his side than for all of her wonderful qualities."

They walked in silence for a moment as more people filled the hall.

"I do hope you are wrong about that," Carmen said. "Do you have an idea of who she is supposed to marry?"

Emily brightened at that question. "I have an idea, yes. Have you noticed how she acts when Mr. Lionel Finley is around? They were interested in each other years ago, when Claire first came to London." Emily smiled conspiratorially at Carmen. "I have heard rumors Mr. Finley is here to convince Claire to marry him. And I do hope he wins her over."

Emily stopped when a woman approached them, clearly looking to speak with Emily.

"Lady Emily Glenville, how very nice to see you," exclaimed the woman. Emily stopped and smiled. The kind of smile one gave when being cordial.

"Mrs. Roberts, how lovely to see you again. Mrs. Daucer and I were just about to sit at our places."

Mrs. Roberts beamed at Carmen. "How wonderful to meet you, my dear. What a shame the late Lady Daucer could not have met you. I know how much she wished for Philip to marry."

Mrs. Roberts fluttered her hands as she giggled, the crystal champagne flute crossing in front of her body back and forth.

"It is very nice to meet you."

"Where are you from?" Mrs. Roberts asked, her champagne glass waving once again across her body.

"From Spain."

"Oh, how lovely!" Mrs. Roberts squealed. "There's another woman here from Spain. Her name is Lucia Perez, I believe. She doesn't speak as well as you do, but she is quite pretty." The sound of Lucia's name hit Carmen hard in the chest. It would be too much of a coincidence, surely. Mrs. Roberts rocked back and forth, turning her head to look. "There she is!"

Carmen followed Mrs. Robert's finger toward Lucia Gavan, who was sitting three tables away. Brightening, Lucia waved and half stood before remembering where she was. Carmen waved back, her mind swirling with questions. Mainly, why was Lucia Gavan called Lucia Perez?

Carmen was conflicted. She didn't wish to be married to Miguel, but she hadn't thought of him marrying less than a year after breaking things off with her.

Of course, she had married even quicker.

Her thoughts were cut short by Claire speaking.

"Welcome, ladies." Claire was at the front of the room, smiling brightly, with a paper clenched in one hand. "I am so honored to have you today at this luncheon for the Ambassadors Day School."

A smattering of clapping interrupted her speech.

"I named the school Ambassadors Day School because I truly believe that with our help, the children who attend will become true ambassadors to the world, contributing to it in a positive way instead of in a negative one."

Carmen tried to understand every word as Claire continued her speech, but was distracted by plates of sandwiches and small pies served at each table. The last thing she wanted was to draw attention by being in the way of a footman quietly placing a plate. When the speech ended, the applause startled Carmen back to the moment. Dr. Kruger was standing next to Claire, thanking her for introducing him. For a moment, Carmen was too surprised to think. She glanced at the door as though she might find Philip walking in at any moment, relieved to find that he wasn't. But if Dr. Kruger knew Claire, and possibly the rest of the Candor family, she would have to tell Philip about her visit. She didn't want him finding out from Cinch. Or from Dr. Kruger himself.

"Oh dear, you're quite pale, Mrs. Daucer. Are you not feeling well? It can be a telltale sign of being with child, this general pale feeling. And what a joy that would be." Mrs. Roberts couldn't help giggling at the mention of a possible child coming.

"No, um, no, I'm quite alright. Thank you," Carmen said quickly.

As Dr. Kruger spoke, Carmen ate the light lunch slowly, recalling his words about pregnancy and possibly going blind. Somehow, amid everything, she had downplayed the warning. But now, it was as though they were the only words she could focus on.

Despite her worries, she heard snippets of the speech. How Dr. Kruger promised to help the children at the day school with their eye health and fit them with glasses if needed. She supposed it was admirable, but she couldn't help thinking Dr. Kruger's stern eyes and lack of emotion might frighten the children away before he was able to help them.

"It's all very inspiring, isn't it?" Emily said to no one in particular when Dr. Kruger finished his speech. "I think I'll go speak with Lady Rutherford there before they serve tea. Are you alright here by yourself, Carmen?"

"Of course," Carmen said quickly. There wasn't anything else she could say, really. Emily left hardly without hearing the answer, but almost within seconds Carmen felt the vacated seat fill again. She turned to find Lucia's dark brown eyes staring at her, glowing as if she had just found a prized possession.

"Fancy meeting you here," Lucia said in Spanish, her words stumbling out and in a tone too loud for most English. There were sniffs and looks in response.

Lucia grasped Carmen's hand and squeezed it before continuing in a whisper. "How are you? It's a miserable city, isn't it? Well, no, I shouldn't say that. The city, if it weren't hated by the sun, is nice. But the food!

How awful! No wonder the English have that pale pallor about them. How are you, Carmen? How is your life here? Isabel begged me to come see you if I could. We just arrived two nights ago, and I haven't had the chance to even seek you out and yet, here you are! It's Providence, don't you think?"

"I'd have to agree," Carmen laughed as she finished the watercress sandwich. Lucia's talk of food from back home gave her a deep pain of longing for Spain in her chest. "And you are right about the food. I'm lucky, my husband's cook is more adept than many over here. She is talented, but I fear more talented in cakes. It's becoming difficult to keep my figure."

Lucia's eyes sparkled. "It is so good to see you. I was telling Miguel just this morning that we should call on you. He is so busy with his doctor things that I'm afraid I've spent quite a bit of time alone in every city we go to. In Paris, it was easier, because I speak French of course and because Paris is so beautiful, and the food is so delicious. Miguel insisted I come here to practice speaking my English, but already I'm thinking of leaving early. I simply cannot manage to speak this language. My tongue gets jumbled with every syllable. How are you faring with your English? It was already quite good before you came, though, wasn't it?"

When Lucia finally took a breath, Carmen ignored the last question and focused on the part she was most interested in. "Miguel?" she repeated.

Lucia waved towards Dr. Kruger. "You know Miguel Perez, your doctor. We were married the week after you were married. I would have liked to have you come to the wedding. I didn't realize you were coming to England so quickly. Isabel cried when she found out I was also coming to England. She said you could have stayed behind and come to England with Miguel and me. Which is true."

Miguel looked away from Dr. Kruger and locked eyes with Carmen at just that moment. He had the decency to look surprised and possibly uncomfortable. Just for a moment. Then he turned back to Dr. Kruger as though nothing had happened. As though the woman he was going to marry didn't happen to be speaking to the woman he did marry. Embarrassment snaked its way through Carmen's innards, sending her heart racing faster. Miguel had so easily cast her aside, something that still hurt her when she thought of it.

A nagging worry came into her head that maybe Philip would do the same. If the issue with the house didn't go in his favor, would he no longer wish to be married?

But no. Philip was different. Dr. Miguel had been thinking only about his reputation as a doctor.

"Yes, I guess-yes, I could have come with you," Carmen said slowly. She wished she could ask Lucia how that would have looked, the two of them traveling together, one married to the man who rejected the other. It was a pitiful scene in her head. One she was glad she hadn't actually lived through. "When are you going back home?"

"Oh, there is a boat leaving in about five days' time and I have a place booked already. Miguel is going to Brussels with Dr. Kruger instead of coming home with me. I am quite homesick and wish to see my mother, you know? Are you not homesick, Carmen? Not even for the sun?"

"I am a little." Carmen's heart skipped with dread as Miguel and Dr. Kruger made their way towards them.

"Lucia, I believe Mrs. Kruger is ready to go home," Miguel said, shifting his weight between his feet before finally looking at her. "It's nice to see you again, Carmen."

"You as well," Carmen said.

"Where is Mrs. Kruger?" Lucia asked in Spanish, craning her neck around the room. "We are staying with Dr. and Mrs. Kruger, you know. It's a beautiful house."

Dr. Kruger cleared his throat. No one in London liked it when foreign languages were spoken in front of them. Lucia blushed. "Good afternoon, Mrs. Daucer. Mrs. Perez, I will take you to my wife." He held out his elbow for Lucia.

"I will go to find Mrs. Kruger," she said in halting English. Before taking Dr. Kruger's arm, she kissed Carmen on each cheek and said quickly in Spanish, "Please, let's see each other before I leave. We could go to the new French pastry shop Mrs. Kruger was telling me about. My treat."

They strolled away through the crowd, leaving Carmen and Miguel alone. Near the door, Carmen saw Lord Candor enter the hall with another man on the far side of him. A pillar blocked the view of him, but Carmen was almost certain it was Philip. Her husband would rescue her from having to speak too long with Miguel. Just as he had rescued her at the ball in Spain.

"I hear from Dr. Kruger that you went to see him," Miguel said with a hint of reproach. Carmen stiffened. "You went without your husband. Is it possible he doesn't know about your condition?"

"Not that it's any of your business, Miguel," Carmen said, emphasizing his name without the label of doctor attached, "my husband knows about my condition and didn't think less of me for it."

Miguel's eyes narrowed slightly but, but he said nothing. "Dr. Kruger can't help you any more than I can, though he does have a concern I haven't brought up. That you could go blind if you become with child."

The words were like shards of glass cutting her chest. Carmen kept a steady stance, her face unchanging. She wavered between hoping Philip would come rescue her soon and hoping he would stay away to not hear the conversation. "Thank you, Miguel. You are no longer my doctor and mustn't feel obligated to give me the hard news. I will speak with Dr. Kruger about it."

"Carmen." Miguel stepped closer, raising his hand and then dropping it to his side. "We're friends, are we not?"

"Are we?" Carmen asked. "I am not sure we are. You served me well as a doctor, though it's true you gave me no cure or real treatment. But that isn't your fault."

She wasn't being completely fair, hitting him where she knew it hurt him the most, but she couldn't seem to stop herself. The hurt that passed on his face soothed her own wounds.

"I didn't mean to hurt you."

Carmen nodded. "Ah. Well, we rarely intend to hurt people when we do it, but there it is. We still do it. You left me and our plans behind because I was not in perfect physical condition. Then you married soon after breaking things off with me."

"Lucia is a good woman. She's hardy and able to travel with me . . ."

Carmen nodded. "She is a good woman. And Philip is a good man. Things worked out well for the both of us."

Miguel nodded curtly. Carmen, realizing it was true that she was better with Philip, accepted the kiss on each cheek from Miguel. As he walked away, Carmen watched him, not realizing Philip was behind her until he spoke.

"Carmen, I would appreciate it if you didn't kiss other men while in public at least," he said, startling her out of her melancholic thoughts.

She turned around to find Philip glaring at her. His eyes narrowed, his lips pressed tightly together.

"It's my culture's tradition, Philip." She peered at him, her words not getting through to him. "You know that."

Philip's eyes still followed Miguel. "I think it's time to go home."

Chapter 37

CARMEN SAT WITH HER hands folded in her lap as the carriage rumbled down the streets of London towards their house. Philip sat across from her, his face set, his eyes closed. They hadn't spoken since taking their leave from Claire and Emily.

"How was the meeting with your brother?" she ventured to ask. Philip didn't move.

"It did not go as I expected." His voice was flat, emotionless. Carmen pressed her palms together, waiting for him to elaborate. When he didn't, she let the jumble of questions in her head go.

Her mind wandered to Lucia and their conversation. *Are you not homesick, Carmen?* She shifted in her seat, a wave of sadness hitting her. Closing her eyes against the afternoon sun sifting in through the carriage windows, Carmen thought of her vineyards, of the dry, hot air, of Isabel's belly growing rounder. Of the dinners with friends. Of testing wines with her father. Of Rosa, always willing to complain about something but always saving Carmen from something she couldn't see.

Yes, she was homesick. Very much. The thought of drinking gazpacho on the porch as the sun set had her mouth watering. Food was what she missed the most after her vineyards. She stretched her fingers and looked at them. Stuffed into pale yellow gloves, they itched to touch the leaves and ground, to snip the bunches of grapes and hold a glass of wine she and her father had created.

Carmen couldn't help smiling at her memories, startling when the carriage slowed to a stop.

"We're here."

Carmen opened her eyes. Philip was staring at her, his face emotionless. Without another word, he leaned over and opened the door. Nathaniel was already there with the step and his hand to help her down.

"Could we have some tea served in the parlor, Felix?" Philip asked as he and Carmen shed their hats and gloves. "With something to eat. I'm famished." He glanced at Carmen. "Are you hungry, dear?"

The way he spoke the term of endearment without emotion hurt Carmen more than if he had simply omitted it. She tried to smile at Felix, not wanting him to think something was wrong. If Philip was putting on a brave face in front of the staff, she should as well. But an ominous feeling was rising within her. And more and more, she was convinced Philip was going to lose his house. There was simply no other explanation for his mood change.

"Shall we?" Philip gestured towards the parlor, waiting for Carmen to lead the way.

Carmen settled on the settee while Philip poured himself a drink from the liquor cart. She thought of afternoons with her father after a long, hot day, savoring a glass of wine as they discussed the different tannins or flavor points. Tears threatened at the memory, but she blinked them away. She had to focus on the sympathy her husband would need. The house meant almost everything to him.

She frowned. If Philip had married to save his house, would he wish to stay married if he no longer had possession of it?

"Word has gotten out that I was baptized in the Catholic church before marrying you."

"I'm sorry?"

Philip turned to face her, repeating himself. Carmen didn't know what to say.

"No one cares much, I don't think, except for Theodore," Philip continued. "He has a letter from my father that says he would leave nothing for his sons if they chose to become Quakers or Catholics."

"Oh." Carmen swallowed her offense, reminding herself that some

Spanish parents felt the same about their sons marrying Protestants. Still, she struggled to let it go, glad, though she knew she shouldn't be, that she wouldn't have to face her husband's father in this life.

"I know the priest did Jaime a favor, but I'm not sure you are really considered a Catholic in Spain," Carmen said. "You didn't go through any of the rituals of the sacrament as we do. So, I don't understand why the baptism was such a problem."

Philip sighed heavily. "Don't you see that it doesn't matter what the Catholic Church thinks? In the case of my inheritance from my father, it matters what the Anglican Church believes. It seems my last option to keep the house is to get baptized again in the Anglican Church. To prove my loyalty or some such nonsense."

Carmen cocked her head and opened her mouth to respond, but Philip wasn't finished.

"We *both* must be baptized."

Everything inside of Carmen stopped full force. Only those last words echoed. "I'm sorry. What did you—? Are you saying you wish for me to convert?"

"Carmen, there are certain factors about all of this that are beyond my control. To keep this house, my house from my father, we must make sure to obey the bishop. I am to rededicate myself to the church of England, and I need a wife who does the same. They made it rather clear that they were willing to add my father's letter to the will and reverse my inheritance, if not."

Philip raked his fingers through his hair with a sigh. "All of this because I was baptized in Spain." The pleading in his eyes broke Carmen a little. "I did that for you, Carmen. So, your family and countrymen would be satisfied you were legally and properly married. And now you need to do this for me."

"Betray my religion? My beliefs? I know religion is not important to you, but it is part of my identity."

"It's just a paper!"

"It is a declaration before God," she countered.

"I find the entire argument of Catholic versus Protestant ridiculous," Philip said. "There is but one God."

"You find my religion ridiculous?" Carmen demanded, her legs shaking. A warning alarm resounded in the back of her mind, telling her she was getting out of control, but she couldn't stop herself. Perhaps it would be better if she left the room, but Carmen was rooted to the floor, waiting to hear from her husband. The man she was to have children with. The man who she didn't realize had so little respect for her beliefs, thinking she could change them as quickly as she could blow out a candle.

Philip dropped his arms heavily to his sides. "That is not what I said. I don't understand the idea that one church is better than the other when we are using the same book and speaking of the same God. It doesn't matter to me if a priest or vicar marries us. Unfortunately, my brother cares enough to have found a letter that will persuade the courts to take this house away unless we make things right under the English law. It is all very stupid."

"Did you ever consider, Philip, that I take my religion seriously? That perhaps I do not wish to be baptized with the Church of England? That I do not wish to submit to it as the religious authority in my life?"

The air shifted when Philip stepped forward. She had seen sympathy in his eyes before, but that was gone now. Everything about his face was hard, set with determination.

"You are my wife."

"Yes." Carmen said nothing more as Mrs. Brax knocked softly and entered with a tray of tea and sandwiches.

Philip stared at the food as though he hadn't just asked for it. When the door closed behind Mrs. Brax again, he sat down, his movements stiff. He ate as though compelled to do so.

"A wife should trust her husband," Philip said softly.

"I didn't think my role as wife was in question, Philip."

He cringed and then continued to chew slowly. Carmen sipped her tea, allowing the bitter liquid to chase away her thoughts, its warmth renewing her as it filled her belly. Mrs. Brax's interruption managed to cut through the building tension in the room, for which Carmen was grateful. She was still angry, but also was more in control of her tongue and emotions now.

"You could think of it as a legal matter required of you in this country. I doubt very much your priest would mind."

"And if he does?" Carmen asked.

Philip swallowed the food in his mouth and followed it with a full cup of tea before answering. His eyes wandered to Carmen, then away again as he asked, "Do you regret marrying me?"

The question could not have been further from her thoughts, and it took a moment of repeating it back in her head for Carmen to grasp that he had said exactly what she thought he had said. "I beg your pardon?"

Philip pulled out his pipe, tucked some tobacco into it, and lit it. The smell reminded Carmen of her father and Jaime. Of evenings on the porch because the house was too hot. Of conversations and jokes and exchanging memories. Of Jaime teasing Isabel and her father's laugh.

"Do you regret our marriage?"

The spell of memories snapped. When Carmen tried to speak, she choked on her words. They came out in a garbled mess, requiring another sip of tea before she could repeat them. "Are you wishing for an annulment?"

Philip moved closer, chin tucked, eyes focused on her. "Is that what you are hoping for?"

His voice was low and even. It held no malice, but it also held no warmth. The question confused Carmen. She thought of her sudden longing for home and wondered if that was evident in her face, in her body. But even if it were, that did not mean she wished for an annulment.

"No," Carmen said slowly. "Not once did I think of it."

Philip's shoulders sagged. She closed her eyes as his lips found hers, softly gathering her into his arms.

No, she did not want an annulment. Every time she was in his arms, she could think of no better place to be. So, when he gently urged her up the stairs to her bedroom, of course she went. When she was with him, she didn't think in terms of words and phrases. Just with what her senses wanted. And all they wanted was the tips of his fingers grazing her bare skin, his lips pressed against the corners of her body only he ever saw, the weight of him against her. Carmen reveled in the way Philip made love to her, feeling herself let go of control more each time, and each time finding more pleasure.

So much so, she was beginning to understand the way she had seen Isabel look at Jaime, her eyes filled with love and secrets and trust. It was something she had longed to have when she was married, and she was almost certain, as Philip pulled her close to his chest under the covers, murmuring into her ear how beautiful she was, that she was indeed falling in love with him.

So when he asked her in the semi-darkness, after making her feel like the only woman in the world, "Do it for me, please, Carmen."

She said yes. And then she fell asleep in his arms.

Chapter 38

"You do not seem convinced you wish to do this."

The minister's words sliced into Philip's thoughts. "Pardon?" he asked and received a bland smile in return.

He and the minister were probably the same age, but Philip couldn't help feeling inept standing next to him. "It's what is expected of me," Philip finally said, noting how the minister's eyes pierced into his very soul.

Or so it felt. He squirmed under the scrutiny.

"Tell me," Philip said. "Do you think it matters if one attends the Catholic or the Anglican Church? Do you truly think that the God, who is the same for both churches, tells one to go to hell and allows in the other?"

Now it was the minister's turn to shift in place. Philip continued.

"And if you do believe it, which one is right? Since the Anglican came out of the Catholic Church and the reasons for leaving were rather, shall we say, carnal?"

"It is difficult sometimes to separate the law of God from the law of the land and to know which battle to incorporate into one's faith," the minister said finally.

A knock sounded on the study door, and Philip stood to answer it.

Carmen appeared in the doorway, radiant in a dark blue dress. The cap sleeve showed her slender arms, one of which was raised in an awkward greeting.

"Hello, wife, come in." Philip curved his arm around her waist and drew her into the study, where the minister stood at attention near the fireplace. Carmen marched out of Philip's arms towards him.

"Good morning," Carmen said, extending her hand in greeting.

The man cleared his throat, his eyes sliding for a second towards Philip before shaking Carmen's hand. "Good morning. I'm Minister Blakely. We are here to baptize you in the Anglican church. But I must know if it is of your free will that you do so. There are concerns that you do not."

Philip held his breath. Minister Blakely had not indicated any such thing to him.

"It is of my free will," Carmen said shakily. "I'm doing it for my husband and because some have left us no choice. But I do it of free will, Minister Blakely."

For a moment, no one moved. Then Minister Blakely nodded and opened his Bible. Philip bridged the gap that separated him and Carmen, but when he tried to take her hand, she resisted. Not enough for the minister to see, but just enough for Philip to notice. Enough to make her point.

And he couldn't help admiring her for it. This was a sacrifice for her, a sacrifice she was willing to make for him, which made him want to swoop up the world, the stars, the sun, and gift them to her. To set her up on a throne and shower her with everything he had planned to give her and more. The world, if possible.

She bent her head to receive the benediction and the water droplets over her head. And, suddenly, he knew that nothing he could ever do would be enough. She was too good for him. He would never be what she deserved.

But he would spend his life trying to be.

When the door shut behind Minister Blakely and his judgmental expression that never seemed to go away, Philip kissed Carmen lightly on the lips. A beautiful pink blossomed on her cheekbones.

"Thank you, Carmen," he said.

She relaxed against his shoulder and breathed in as he led her to the parlor. "Alright then?"

She lifted her head and nodded, bouncing a stray curl out of the twist she had put in her hair that morning. He had watched her do it, her long fingers taking several strands and wrapping them around each other, pinning them in certain places, and then twisting them around into themselves. It was a fascinating process to witness, and he had sat on the edge of the bed, transfixed by her movements.

"A curl has come loose," he said, his own finger reaching to caress it as she reached for the curl. When she didn't find it at first, he placed it against her finger.

"Thank you," she said, tucking the curl back as she went to the large mirror on the south wall.

"Could you not see it?" he asked.

Carmen laughed. "Of course I can see it. It is easier to fix it with a mirror. You see?"

Philip watched her work the pins and ribbon, and a sense of dread or guilt or something he couldn't quite put his finger on it, spread through his chest.

Carmen saw him watching her and turned, her blue skirts rustling gently. She planted her hands on her hips and cocked her shoulders to show her hair was just as it was before.

Philip nodded and gave her another kiss, pushing the cold tendrils of anxiety from his thoughts. "I want to thank you, Carmen. Again."

Carmen nodded, her smile drooping. "No more thanking me, Philip. What shall we do today?"

A loud knock interrupted them before Philip could answer.

"Sorry, sir," Felix said. "Lord and Lady Daucer are here. I showed them into the parlor.

"Thank you, Felix," Philip said.

The arrival of Theodore and Meredith caused such a pain in his chest that Philip was almost certain he now knew what it might be like to get hit with an arrow there. They marched in, Meredith looking around and frowning at the curtains. Theodore swirled a new, shiny, black cane with a brass handle so broadly he almost brought down a large vase sitting innocently on the table.

"Sorry 'bout that," Theodore said, chuckling as the vase settled itself.

Philip grunted. Theodore should have known not to stop by unannounced. Carmen rose to greet them.

"To what do we owe this visit?" Philip asked, moving forward to protect his wife from the cane. And Meredith's glare.

"Please sit," Carmen said, indicating the velvet high-backed chairs. She tugged the cord to call for tea, though Philip knew Felix would have already called for it.

"We have just been speaking with Judge Watterson." Theodore's smile stretched across his face and would have gone beyond it if physically possible. But the most concerning of all was Meredith, who looked so pleased that she almost appeared nice. "He wished to come and speak with you as well, but had a meeting. He said you could call on him if you wished later this week to discuss things."

"Discuss what?" Philip asked as Mrs. Brax brought in a tray of tea and cakes before quietly leaving again.

"He has consulted with other barristers about the will and this house," Theodore said, sweeping his arms about as though speaking on stage with a great audience. "He, or rather, they have come to a decision." He paused as though wishing for Philip to say something. Philip breathed out slowly through his nose. "They have interpreted the will and decided it is null and void. Considering both the ambiguous language, the fact that I brought up the issue before you were married, and also because you botched your marriage."

Philip then opened his mouth to speak, heat flaring in his face, but Theodore went on. "I believe it is the correct decision he could have made. If you wish to challenge the decision, we could all go to the Old Bailey and see what the public in London think of us squabbling over a house."

"I am not squabbling," Philip said, biting off each word carefully. "You're the one who brought up a suit on a house that you had no wish of having for years until you suddenly realized you could use it as an investment in Mayfair."

Theodore's eyes widened slightly, though Philip wasn't sure if it was the result of too much cake in his mouth or of realizing Philip knew the reason why Theodore wanted the house.

"Yes, Theodore, I know you are getting first choice on a house in Berkeley Square in exchange for giving this house over to Grosvenor."

"That isn't completely true," Theodore said, wagging his finger at Philip. "In the past few years, you will understand when you become a father, I have focused much on spending time with my wife and young children." Meredith coughed delicately. Theodore cleared his throat with a nod. "And getting things in order at the estate."

"Getting things–?" Philip couldn't finish the question without smirking. "I have been getting things in order at the estate."

Theodore's face turned red. "Perhaps with the creditors, but I am the one who lives there and has been taking care of Mother until she died. Our relationship with the town and the surrounding land gentry. Yes, Philip, yes. There is work there. You are not the only one doing things."

Philip clenched his mouth shut. It would not do to say what he wished to say. That is, that his brother considering drinking beer at the local pub comparable to what Philip did was laughable.

"You are just upset that I have some business sense as well, Philip. This investment in Mayfair is quite good. I heard of it just a few months ago, but after I investigated the will. Something I did on my own after thinking about it one evening."

Philip glanced at Meredith, knowing she was the culprit of his brother's thinking. She kept her attention on Theodore.

"Frankly, I'm surprised you didn't take Grosvenor up on the offer a year ago. Instead, I hear you wished to use this house as collateral for buying that run-down building to create a what, a hotel? You want to drag our family into the hospitality business as though we are poor commoners."

"It's disgraceful," Meredith said. Philip clenched his teeth so hard he was afraid he might break them. He forced them loose and took a deep breath.

Theodore nodded. "It is disgraceful. And this house should have been mine from the beginning. It is the law of England and God himself that the firstborn inherits."

"God wants you to have this house, Theodore?"

"Perhaps if you went to church more often, you would know the story of Esau and Jacob."

"The story of the brother who tricked his father into blessing him?" Carmen asked. Philip had forgotten she was in the room.

"Esau was the oldest and set to inherit everything, but Jacob tricked their father into giving him the blessing instead," Meredith said. "And you, Philip, aren't even the second born. You're the third. If anyone else were to have inherited, it should have been your brother Calvin."

"Are you saying I tricked my father?" Philip was finding it more and more difficult to control his anger.

"We can argue about your thoughts on the suit, Philip, or you can listen to what Judge Watterson had to say." Meredith was cool and calm.

"Do go on, Theodore," Philip said, picking up his tea to keep his hands from fisting. "I have work to be doing today."

Theodore rocked back on his heels before deigning to go on. "Judge Watterson says if you don't like this decision, you can refute it. But he warns that he and everyone he has consulted agrees."

"In other words, we would win," Meredith said. "And really, this isn't the worst that can happen to you, Philip. You have money and the ability to purchase another house."

"We lived for years now with the understanding that this house is my inheritance. It is only now that you have become selfish—"

"That is enough now, Philip. There is no reason to throw around insults. You should have considered that more likely than not, the barristers would rule in my favor," Theodore said, popping another cake into his mouth. "Our system thrives off of tradition, and traditionally the firstborn receives all properties upon the father's death."

Meredith smiled, nodding.

"Couldn't we purchase the house from you?"

Everyone turned to Carmen, again surprised she was there. Meredith started giggling.

"My dear girl, no. We are giving the house to Lord Grosvenor. Of course, you don't know who that is, but he is redistricting the City of Westminster." When Carmen blinked as though not understanding, Meredith sighed. "This area of London. We will, in exchange for this house, get a house in Berkley Square."

"Lord Grosvenor wishes to tear down these houses and rebuild new ones," Philip said, kindlier than Meredith. Carmen's shoulders slumped as she nodded.

"We are willing to allow you and Carmen to stay here until the end of this season. We are Christians, after all," Meredith said, looking pointedly at each of them. "That is, if you are willing to live in cohesion. We will also move in to save on expenses. Our house won't be ready until next year."

Philip didn't answer. The idea of living in the house with Theodore and Meredith as the owners turned his stomach. But he also had nowhere else to go, and he wasn't certain he could find a place to rent before they moved in, though he would try.

"If you have nothing more to say, we will consider this settled." Theodore stood and lowered the cord for his cloak. "We have tea with Lord Hastings this afternoon, Philip, so if you plan to take this further in the courts, please tell me now so we can prepare for it."

Philip said nothing. He wasn't going to fight this in the Old Bailey. He couldn't risk it. Losing publicly to Theodore would be too humiliating.

"Where is the will, then?" Philip asked.

Theodore grinned and patted his breast pocket.

"Must I sign something?" Philip asked.

Theodore belted a laugh. "Oh, how strange to have you admit defeat," he said, wiping his eyes. They were unusually moist. "There is nothing for you to sign because they have merely given their opinion that the will is void."

Meredith stood, looking very pleased with herself.

"And the staff?" Philip asked as they marched towards the door.

Shrugging, Meredith slid on her gloves. "Surely there is enough work in London for them. I know you'll give them a good enough reference. But really, Philip, that is not our concern. It is their lot in life, and this is a possibility for people like them."

Felix had come to help with coats and heard everything Meredith said. She didn't seem at all embarrassed, but Philip sank further in his defeat. He would have to find work for his staff, good employers who would treat them fairly. Perhaps Cinch could afford to hire Rebecca and Nathaniel. Or perhaps Finley needed a butler. That was, if he was staying in England.

"See you again soon, Philip," Theodore said as he slipped into his rain cloak Felix held out for him. "We will let you know when we plan to move in."

Philip stood staring at the empty entryway until the sound of Carmen's dress swishing alerted him to her moving.

"Where are you going?" he asked her. She halted midway up the stairs but didn't turn around.

"I'm going to lie down." She took another step but stopped when he ran up behind her, taking the steps two at a time.

"Carmen." She stiffened at his touch, but when she continued up the stairs and he followed, she didn't tell him to leave. At her door, he hesitated. "Can we talk?"

Carmen left her door open, making a vague waving gesture he took as a half-hearted invitation to come inside.

"I had no idea that was going to happen, Carmen. I didn't think Judge Watterson would—" Philip faltered for words. "I didn't know."

Carmen collapsed wearily into her chair and didn't look at him.

"I know you're upset," he said, treading carefully. "But it isn't too bad, is it? Being part of the church here?"

The blaze of fury that shadowed her face startled him. She struggled to suppress it, her jaw clenching and unclenching.

"Carmen . . ."

"It means something to me," Carmen murmured. "My religion means something to me."

"I know. I admire that about you. And I—I know that you were baptized today for me. That you only did it as my wife." Tears threatened to overwhelm him, but Philip choked them down, appalled at himself for being so emotional. "How can I make it up to you?"

Carmen looked directly at him and said, "I would like to go home and be with my sister as she has the baby."

Her words stabbed him in the heart. "You wish to go home?"

"Yes," she said. Then she lifted her chin and added, "I believe I deserve that."

"For how long?" he asked, his voice husky with unshed tears. "Just to see the baby being born." She glanced away from him. "I miss my family and my country."

Philip struggled to find something to argue against it. There was a growing warning in his head that if Carmen left, she wouldn't come home. Why would she? And to what home?

"What about the war?" he finally asked. Philip dared to close the gap between them, sinking to his knees in front of her. He laced her hands in his, though she refused to look at him. "Do you not think it dangerous to travel there on your own?"

"I know there is a ship leaving in two days. For Portugal. It is the same route we left on. I think I would be safe."

Philip caressed her palms between his thumbs. He thought of Dr. Miguel Perez kissing Carmen's cheeks at the luncheon. The first thing he had seen when he arrived.

If she knew there was a ship leaving for Spain, it must be because Dr. Perez told her.

He stared at her hands and thought hard. He could convince her to stay, just as he had convinced her to get baptized in the Anglican church. Carmen was his wife. He could demand she stay.

Or he could let her go.

"You could come with me," Carmen said.

"I have work to do here."

"Yes. You can find a home for us." Carmen released her hands from his grip, placed them against his cheeks, and searched his face. "When I get back, we can start again."

Philip, though he doubted she would be coming home, nodded and stood. "All right. I understand."

Carmen stood as well and kissed him lightly on the lips. "Thank you."

Philip hesitated a moment, wishing a moving speech would rise in his thoughts, but when nothing came to him and Carmen started organizing her things on the vanity, Philip turned on his heel and quietly walked away. At the door, he said over his shoulder, "I will tell Mrs. Brax to help you pack in the morning. And I'll send Nathaniel to secure a place for you on the ship. Perhaps you should write to your father, and I can see if there is a way to send the letter quicker than you will go."

"Thank you, Philip."

He gave a brusque nod, then went into the hallway, closing the door behind him.

Chapter 39

"Nice to see you tonight, Daucer."

Philip merely grunted and motioned to the nearby chair. He wasn't sure if he was annoyed Finley was interrupting his attempt to get drunk or glad the interruption would slow the self-massacre the alcohol would eventually cause. He had been at the club since two that afternoon and had no intention of leaving until he was drunk.

Finley gazed down at him while signaling a footman. "Half bottle as usual, Fredrik."

The footman nodded and rushed off as Finley settled himself across from Philip.

"What is wrong with tonight?" Finley asked.

"I sent my wife to Spain today," Philip said. His mind reviewed the day again: waking up after one last night of making love, saying little in the carriage on their way to the port because all he wanted to do was beg her to stay, walking up the plank, settling Carmen into her small room, speaking with the captain. And eventually leaving the ship alone. Philip flicked his fingers, stretching them against the emotional turmoil raging in his chest. That he was a failure in a way even his brother wasn't. As a husband.

"Mrs. Daucer is returning to Spain? For how long?"

Philip rolled his eyes towards Finley and managed to say, "A month. Or until her sister has the baby."

"Ah, women and babies," Finley said, accepting a bottle of whiskey and two glasses.

Philip's focus sharpened as he looked directly at Finley. "What is that supposed to mean?"

"Nothing." Finley handed a glass to Philip. "My late wife was always traveling to her sisters when they were with child. At least, until she was too sick to do so."

Philip hadn't thought it might be a maternal, female instinct to be with her sister. Perhaps, then, Carmen would be coming back to him.

He brushed the thought away. If he allowed himself to be hopeful, realizing she wasn't coming would be so much worse. "When do you leave for America?" he asked.

"I decided to stay." Finley looked over his glass of whiskey towards the corner of the room where Sir Andrew and three other men were playing whist. "There are a few things I want to straighten out here. I will be selling the business in America."

"Selling it?" Philip sputtered, his whiskey threatening to choke him. "Sorry. Just a surprise. Thought the American mines and all that made you rather rich."

"They did. And have. But there is more to life than money. There is something here that I've never been able to get." Finley's lips pressed together. "And I'm determined to get it."

Philip looked uneasily at Sir Andrew and back at Finley. "Which is?"

Finley's dark eyes moved towards Philip. "Convincing a certain woman to become my wife," he said.

Philip rolled his eyes and slumped further into his chair.

"You're better off without one. Men like you and me are not made for wives."

"Men like you and me? I didn't realize we were so similar." Finley downed his whiskey and poured another.

"Perhaps not in disposition or humor, but we are both businessmen and sons of impoverished noblemen."

"Does that make us unable to be husbands, then?" Finley asked. "I should have warned my first wife, then."

Clearly, the whiskey, fatigue, and his general losing streak were affecting him. "Right. You have been married before."

Finley grinned as though he had a magic trick card up his sleeve but was unwilling to share it. Everything about the smile grated on Philip. "Cheer up, Philip. I'm sure there are men more hopeless than you are at being a husband. Many men here don't care a whit about their wives. After all, most marry for convenience, money, or duty. Very few marry because they care about the other person."

Philip opened his mouth. Then closed it. The word twisting in his throat. He pushed his glass of whiskey away. Already his head was swimming, and he didn't like the dark hole he felt himself sinking into. "No," he finally said. "My actions were more noble than that. I mean to say, I was thinking about marriage. The possibility of it. I, well, I liked Carmen, too."

"Ah. I see." Finley's long fingers stroked his beard, reminding Philip of a wise professor determined to set his student on the right path. Philip drank more whiskey to ease his irritation. "But then, don't most men at least like their wife enough to marry her?"

Philip conceded the point. He thought back to the moment he met Carmen. There was something about her from the moment he saw her that told him he could be happy with her.

"You cannot rewrite history," Finley said. "And there is no reason to do so. You married for a purpose, and so did she."

"I liked Carmen upon seeing her," Philip said, though his protest was weak.

Finley nodded. "She is beautiful."

"It wasn't just her physical beauty," he said, now more energized to show he was correct and not like the other men. "It was her character. Her humor. Who she is as a whole. I could see it, and I thought she was perfect. The best match for me I had ever met. And I knew I would be lucky if she accepted me. I was not like other men around here who think it is the woman who is lucky to find them and their money."

He nodded with satisfaction at his words and that they hadn't come out slurred despite the whiskey.

"What is the problem, then?"

"I thought marriage would be different." Philip sighed, closing his eyes as the truth continued to pour out of him. "Maybe I thought I would be different."

"Cheer up, man. You'll manage through this. We all do."

"Well, listen to this. As you say, I married to keep my house, which I managed to lose. To my brother. But in an effort to keep the house, I asked my wife to reject her own faith and submit to mine."

Finley lifted an eyebrow and waited.

"To become a Protestant," Philip said, irritated that Finley didn't seem to understand the depth of it.

"Is that all?"

"No. While that was enough to make her quite angry, it is not all. Perhaps the worst of it is that her conversion ended up being worthless in the end." Philip lowered his head. "And because of it, she asked to go home."

"She chose to do something for you," Finley said. "Just because it didn't work in your favor, as far as the house is concerned, is not something you could have predicted. I would say she simply wants to be with her sister at the birth. It takes more than a squabble to push a woman into abandoning her husband."

"You don't understand. I asked her to do it for me. I—well, I managed to convince her when I knew she didn't want to do it. Her religion is much more important to her than mine is. I don't give a damn if someone is Catholic or Protestant. I honestly can't wrap my head around why it matters if it's the same God and the same book."

Finley considered him for a moment before saying, "You act as though she has left you."

The last words slipped through his chest like a recently sharpened blade. He breathed in cold air to temper the shock of hearing the words out loud.

Philip hit his fist against the chair's arms. "I think she has," he said, choking on the words. "Perhaps she agreed to be baptized for me, but it was all for naught. I still will lose the house."

"I heard. Doesn't surprise me, honestly, Philip. Society in England wishes for everything to stay the same as it always has been. The further your brother took this, the more chances he had that the barristers would recommend the will to him. He only had to keep pressing."

Finley was right. But the fact that he hadn't thought of that only made Philip angrier.

"It isn't any sort of justice."

"Of course it isn't," Finley said. "But it's done." He leveled his gaze at Philip. "You'll lose if you take this through the courts."

Philip sighed. "I believe that as well."

"Then move on." Finley nodded as though it was all sorted. Which, of course, it wasn't.

"I've lost everything else," Philip muttered, taking Finley's bottle and pouring himself another. Finley snorted at his insolence but didn't stop him.

"You have lost against your brother and lost the house, but that certainly isn't everything. You have your wife."

"Who left today for Spain with a man she was once to marry." Philip had to take a deep breath to get out the next words. "Dr. Miguel Perez."

Philip had expected sympathy from Finley. Instead, he cocked his head at him as though confused. "Dr. Miguel Perez? You mean she went on the boat Mrs. Perez went home on?"

"What do you mean?" Philip asked, now also confused.

"I accompanied Claire to the Royal Society today, where Dr. Kruger and a Dr. Perez from Spain spoke about illnesses of the eyes. Afterwards, we spoke, and I found out that Mrs. Perez left on a ship today bound for Portugal."

"Mrs. Perez?" Philip repeated. He remembered seeing Carmen at the luncheon. Alone with Dr. Perez. Him pulling her close and kissing her on each cheek. The kisses were not straightforward, but lingering. As though Miguel thought he might be able to take Carmen back.

Or was his memory tricking him?

"There is a Mrs. Perez?"

Finley shrugged. "That's what I've been told. But I know one thing for certain. Dr. Perez didn't leave for Spain today. He and Dr. Kruger leave for Brussels in a few days."

"For Brussels?" Philip jolted upright. "And do you know where Dr. Kruger lives?"

Finley shook his head. "But I would bet Claire does."

Philip stared at the row house from the carriage, debating what to do next. Part of him wished to storm in and demand whether Dr. Perez had been on that ship. Part of him wished to turn around and go home that instant.

The creak of the door unlatching made Philip shake himself out of his thoughts.

"That's the house there, sir," Nathaniel said as he waited for Philip to descend from the carriage.

"Right." Philip stepped down, an idea striking him. "Did you ever bring Mrs. Daucer here?"

"Yes."

The statement was so clear and unabashed it made Philip want to clutch Nathaniel by the throat.

"For what?" he asked, his tone no longer calm. "Why did you bring her here?"

"To see the doctor," Nathaniel said slowly. "Dr. Kruger. He's an eye specialist. It's not my place, so I didn't ask anything of Mrs. Daucer, but she mentioned you had suggested she seek out the counsel of an English doctor." When Philip said nothing, Nathaniel added, "Dr. Kruger is a specialist in cataract surgery."

"Is he?" Philip murmured, his anger dissipating, replaced by confusion. "That is all, Nathaniel. I'll walk home."

If he thought it odd, Nathaniel didn't show it. He merely bowed and went back to his place at the head of the carriage. Philip stood looking at the house until the carriage moved on, and the street became silent again. Then he marched up the steps and knocked on the door.

"I'm Mr. Philip Daucer," he announced to a grim-faced butler who stared through him. "I'd like to see Dr. Kruger."

"He is with a patient at the moment," the butler said, still looking through Philip.

"Then I'll wait." Philip took advantage of the surprise that flashed on the man's face to march forward into the entryway. He handed the butler his hat.

Philip was shown to a small, dimly lit sitting room and left to pace alone for a few minutes before the doors opened again and a woman greeted him.

"Mr. Daucer, what a pleasure to meet you," Mrs. Kruger said. "My husband is just finishing up, but he is eager to speak with you."

"Good morning," Philip said. "I am glad to hear Dr. Kruger has time to meet with me."

"I've asked for some tea. My husband will join us when he can. Please, won't you sit down?" She motioned to a high-back chair. With the amount of energy spurring through him, Philip didn't wish to sit. He wished to have answers. But he obeyed, sinking into the cushion just as the tea arrived.

"I believe a dear friend of my husband who is visiting us now is also someone you know," Mrs. Kruger said.

Philip was surprised by the statement. "Is that so?"

"Your wife is Spanish, is she not?"

"Yes." Philip considered where the conversation might go as he accepted a cup of tea from Mrs. Kruger. "My wife went back to Spain just the other day. Her sister is about to give birth, and she wished to be there."

"Yes," Mrs. Kruger said, nodding. The familiar way she answered shot more anxiety through him. "Mrs. Perez went home on that ship as well. I was glad when I heard she was not traveling alone. These days, one never knows who will be on those ships. It's best to travel with someone."

Philip ignored the woman's obvious anxiety about women traveling alone. "You are speaking of Dr. Perez and his wife?"

Mrs. Kruger, who had an attractive face for her age, with few wrinkles and soft brown eyes, regarded him quizzically. "Yes, Dr. Perez is the man I believe you know. And he mentioned you had met his wife, Lucia, while you were in Spain as well."

The door opened then, startling them both. A tall, thin man with a neatly trimmed white beard briskly strode into the room, his hand stabbing the air to shake Philip's even before Philip managed to stand fully.

"I'm Doctor Kruger. Nice to meet you," Dr. Kruger said, adding, "Finally."

Philip shook the man's hand silently. The doctor's grip was firm and cold. Philip sank into the high-back chair as Dr. Kruger joined his wife on the small settee.

"We were just talking about our mutual friend, Dr. Perez, dear," Mrs. Kruger said, offering her husband a cup of tea. Philip watched the man, feeling more and more like he was on the outside of something he didn't quite understand.

Dr. Kruger closed his eyes briefly as he swallowed his tea. A man who enjoyed the small things, it seemed to Philip. "Dr. Perez is a genius in our field. I am happy to call him my friend. He told me he met you briefly in Spain, and I'm sorry to say we haven't had time to call on you these past few days. He's been busy helping me."

"Ah," was all Philip could think of to say.

"His wife, Lucia, didn't find England very accommodating. Found herself homesick for Spain."

"I can't blame her, dear. Life certainly is different here, and she has been away from her family for over a month now." Mrs. Kruger sighed, her face looking more angelic with the gesture. "It can't be easy being so far from family."

Philip thought of Carmen and how she had been apart from her family for almost six weeks. While being so far away from his own would never affect him much, he thought of how close she was to Isabel, how she had still lived with her father, and they had dinners together on the regular. He breathed in slowly as he realized suddenly how very lonely she might have felt in London.

"Dr. Perez is staying with us and has agreed to meet with you if you need more information than I can give," Dr. Kruger said. Philip snapped his attention back to the moment, pushing aside his thoughts. "This loss of communication is why I told your wife I prefer to see my female patients with their husbands present."

"I'm sorry?" Philip stared at him, trying to piece together the information he was giving him. "Carmen has been seeing you or Dr. Perez?"

Dr. Kruger paused. His blue eyes pierced Philip with an icy stare. "Dr. Perez arrived only last week in London and is not seeing patients." His narrowed eyes practically disappeared under his heavy eyebrows as he continued staring at Philip. "Did you not know your wife was coming to me for treatment?"

Philip shifted, looking at Mrs. Kruger, who had a serene, innocent look about her and was clearly unable to help Philip navigate the predicament he found himself in. "I must confess, I did not know my wife was seeing you for anything. I only just found out she came here once with my coachman."

"I told Mrs. Daucer I don't care for treating men's wives without them present, though of course it isn't always the case that the husband can come. Still, I believe you have the right to know, and I am unsure if Mrs. Daucer can explain everything in the same way I can."

Dr. Kruger waved his hand in the air, his stare no longer directed at Philip. He stood and paced four steps towards the window and four steps back. Philip found the movement distracting. "Dr. Perez did all he could do, but I told your wife that I agreed with his final diagnosis."

"And that was?" Philip asked. He had forgotten what Jaime had told him, though he remembered Carmen assured him she wasn't going blind. Now, with Doctor Kruger, he wondered if that wasn't correct.

Dr. Kruger turned on his heel, and once again directed his steely gaze at Philip. The door to the sitting room opened, and Dr. Perez came sauntering in. So, it was true. Dr. Perez was not on the ship. That eased pressure from his chest, but it was instantly replaced by a return to the topic at hand as Philip greeted Dr. Perez and sat down again.

"I was telling Mr. Daucer the specifics of his wife's vision problems."

"I thought you would have known all about her diagnosis before the wedding," Dr. Perez said. "It wasn't a secret in Spain."

"Jaime told me she had some vision issues that happened from sun exposure. Or perhaps it was that it worsened in the sun," Philip said, pausing when Dr. Kruger snorted. The man took out a handkerchief to blow his nose. "And Carmen explained to me that she has black circles, dots I guess, on her field of vision, but I never saw her greatly affected by it."

That wasn't entirely true. The day when Carmen fell down the steps at Cinch's house entered his mind's eye, as well as the time she ran into Eleadora, but he didn't correct himself aloud.

"Carmen doesn't have black spots or dots. She has a black ring around her vision that inhibits her from seeing up and down and to the side, as you and I do," Dr. Kruger said grimly.

"It is as though she is looking through a tube," Perez said, his voice lighter than his colleagues'. He nodded as though his input might help Philip further understand.

"Is there a chance you have misdiagnosed her?"

The doctors exchanged looks, Dr. Kruger pressing his lips together as though offended by Philip's question, Perez giving more a look of pity.

"There is not," Perez said gently. "She has been struggling with this condition for a long time."

Philip nodded. "Yes, I suppose Jaime said as much." He regarded Perez before adding, "She also told me it's the reason you refused to marry her."

To his gratification, the Spaniard blushed. Dr. Kruger's eyes darkened with anger.

"I will have no accusation thrown at my guest," he said, but Perez interrupted.

"It is true. That is what I told Carmen." Perez nodded at Philip. "I did not wish to hurt her so, but I did not feel we were compatible. I had met Lucia and, well, I fell in love with her."

Philip rolled his eyes. He couldn't help himself. But he didn't argue further. After all, while he disliked the man for treating Carmen the way he did, he was also glad Perez hadn't married her, leaving her free for him.

"Before we end our visit, I want things to be very clear for you, Mr. Daucer," Dr. Kruger said. "I think it is only fair that a man understands his wife's health."

"Certainly," Philip said. "What is the treatment, then?"

"There is no treatment," Perez said, shaking his head. "There is no cure."

Before Philip could fully grasp the meaning those words held, Dr. Kruger added, "We do recommend she stay away from direct sunlight, always wearing a hat. That she only read and do needlepoint with ample lighting. And that she eat nourishing food."

"Is that all?" Philip asked.

"These recommendations will not change what has already been done, but it could slow down the progression of the black circles," Perez said.

"But your wife is very young, and you have not yet had children," Dr. Kruger interjected. Mrs. Kruger squirmed in her seat, then settled again when Dr. Kruger's attention slid to her. "I have found that being with child can change a woman in many ways, and sometimes it changes their eyes and eyesight. Forever."

Philip swallowed hard. "Do you mean to warn me that my wife will go blind if she becomes with child?"

Perez shook his head. "No, but what we are saying is that it isn't out of the realm of possibilities."

Chapter 40

"I thought I would find you here," Cinch said, strolling into Philip's study a week later as though he owned the world. "Why have you not come out to the club or over to have lunch?"

Philip grunted a nondescript response. He waved at the paperwork in front of him as though Cinch should know what he was doing. "Why do you think? There is work to be done."

Cinch picked up an empty whiskey glass he found on Philip's desk and sniffed with judgement.

"I'll call for tea if you have gone soft," Philip said, crossing his arms.

"Has your wife died?" Cinch stared at him, waiting for an answer.

Philip stared back. "No."

"Well, then," Cinch said, replacing the glass. "Stop acting like you're mourning."

"She left me for Spain and didn't tell me she was seeing a doctor about her vision." Philip picked up his pen and returned his attention to the tax documents. "Is that not enough?"

The sound of Cinch sinking into the chair by the cold fireplace grated on Philip's nerves. He put the pen down again and steepled his fingers.

"I am neck deep in doing the taxes for our ships going to Canada, and next, I have the correspondence dealing with the railroad in Spain. Once again, we've come up against a problem of supplies."

"And that is the project I've come to talk with you about," Cinch said, removing his gold watch from his pocket.

"Is it?" Philip asked. "I'm surprised you know what is going on."

Cinch gave a pause, as he sometimes did right before insulting a man. Philip leaned back and waited, a grin twitching on his lips. "I am still capable of handling Sutton Enterprises."

Philip merely shrugged. It would irk his friend more than a verbal jab.

Cinch cleared his throat. "It is not a problem with supplies."

"What do you call not having the material for the men to do the job?"

"I think it is an issue of management. We need eyes on the project."

That sobered Philip. "We have eyes on the project in three different forms. We have the engineer, Mr. Van Haussen, our lawyer, and we have our spy, my brother-in-law."

His longtime friend nodded but didn't appear pacified. "None of which are managing the project well. I don't believe your brother-in-law is there often enough to understand what is happening. The lawyer certainly isn't, and Mr. Van Haussen is clearly angering the local men."

Philip grimaced as he thought about Spain. About Jaime and Isabel, Señor Suárez and Carmen. He wondered what the family thought of him now that Carmen was back home. He wondered what she was telling everyone. He wondered if she was able to sleep or eat. Ever since she left, he hadn't been able to.

"Come on, let's go," Cinch said, standing once again. "We can talk about the railway on our way. You have just enough time to get dressed."

"Dressed?"

"Luncheon. Little Philip will be there, and Claire said I am not to take no for an answer."

Philip waved him away. "No, I have no time for a luncheon. I've just gotten back from the docks. We sent out *Glory* to Canada. There were favorable conditions this morning."

Cinch eyed him.

"What?"

"*Glory* could have left on its own. You didn't need to be there. Captain Brisbane is well experienced." Cinch stopped speaking, though he probably had more to say. And the silence hit Philip more than the words ever would have. *Captain Brisbane knows more than you.*

Which was true.

"I know what you're thinking, Christophe."

"What is that?" his friend asked.

"That I'm working to avoid my stress or some such nonsense."

"Is it nonsense?" Cinch asked. "You're a good worker, Philip. And you know it. But you get into these fits of overworking yourself. Our men know what they're doing. Most of them have worked for us for years now. The business is not in the same place as it was five years ago when you and I needed to supervise every shipment."

"I know it," mumbled Philip. "It's just this whole mess with the marriage and the house."

"Come then, we'll talk about the railway situation, and you can complain about your house."

A female voice echoed in the hallway. Philip paused to listen. "Who is here?" His heart skipped a beat as he dared to hope Carmen had come home early. "Who is talking out there?"

He maneuvered around his desk to get quickly to the door. Just as his hand clasped the doorknob, Cinch called out, "It isn't Carmen, if that's what you're thinking."

Philip stopped, still reaching for the door, when Cinch patted his shoulder.

"I sometimes wonder if she'll decide to stay there," Philip confessed.

"If you are afraid of that, why do you not go there?"

The idea hadn't occurred to Philip. He glanced at his desk, then back at Cinch. "Go to Spain?"

"To get your wife," Cinch said. "Run after her. Women love that."

"What do you know of women?" Philip scoffed, but he was already thinking of the proposal, and Cinch knew it. "Could Sutton Enterprises afford for me to leave? It might take a month."

"I am hoping it will take longer than that."

"I beg your pardon?"

Cinch threw an arm around Philip's shoulders and led him out of the study. Down the hall, Claire and Rowena could be heard. Before reaching the end, Cinch said, "I think you should go there and oversee the railroad. That's why I came. I realize you miss Carmen, and I also realize we need help in Spain. It seems like a simple solution."

They began walking again, reaching the women before Philip had processed what Cinch was saying.

"You look tired, Philip," Claire said as she kissed his cheek in greeting. "What has your brow so furrowed?"

Philip noticed Finley looming behind Claire, shooting Philip a dark glare. "I doubt my brow is as furrowed as Finley's."

"Ignore him," Claire said. "He's in a mood."

"I am not."

Philip regarded Claire, then Finley. The way the two of them argued indicated something more than merely two people who didn't get along.

"No arguing during the picnic," Rowena said, managing to squeeze between Claire and Philip to kiss Philip on the cheek. "You look as though you need sun. Oh, thank you, Mrs. Brax. Your cook was kind enough to add to our already copious lunch."

"Thank you," Philip said, to which Mrs. Brax gave her usual nod and stepped out of the way.

Philip managed to grab his hat with Felix's help as they left this house and clamored into separate phaetons. He entered the one with Claire and Finley, who was still grim.

"Did the sale not go as you planned?" Philip asked.

Finley's mouth opened in surprise. "Sale?"

"Of the business in America."

"No, the sale went fine. What is it you're getting at?" Finley asked, his brow once again deeply creased.

"He's asking you why you look like a child who wasn't given a piece of cake," Claire said, laughing lightly. "You might as well tell him."

"It's nothing."

"Oh, for heaven's sake." Claire turned to Philip and whispered loudly, "He has rented a house, but the staff have refused to stay. He suspects it's because the last person spread rumors about him or his family."

"More precisely, my father. And I don't suspect anything. The butler, Mr. Thompson, told me it was the reason before he took his leave."

Claire shrugged. "A man has a right to work where he pleases."

Finley pounded his fist into his other hand. "I am a perfectly good man to work for." Claire sighed loudly at the declaration. Finley merely slumped lower in his seat.

They rode into Hyde Park in amicable silence until just before the carriage stopped.

"Cheer up, Finley, I believe I have the staff for you," Philip said.

Felix marched into the study, his eye warily glancing behind him.

"What is it, Felix?" Philip asked.

Felix narrowed his eyes at the question.

"It's the American accent," Felix said. "There's something unnatural about it."

Philip grinned, then cleared his throat to hide his amusement as Finley walked into the room.

"Hello again, Felix," Finley said. "Mrs. Brax and Nathaniel are on board, as well as Rebecca. Have you decided yet?"

"I am honored to be given the opportunity, sir." Felix gave a brisk bow, then turned on his heels and marched away.

"Little guy doesn't like me much," Finley commented, once the door closed again.

"Call him 'little guy' within earshot of him, and you might be out a butler," Philip warned. Finley acquiesced with a small bow. "And while Felix is ornery, he is the best butler I've ever had. Wish I could bring him with me."

The idea wandered around his mind for a moment before he discarded it.

"I'll have to figure out how my valet, who is also my butler, will fit into the hierarchy," Finley said.

"Please do not insult Felix. If I ever make my way back, I would like to have him back on my own staff."

Just then, Felix burst into the study again, holding a large metal tray with a bottle of wine and two glasses.

"Here's to a long relationship," Finley said, plucking his glass from the tray. "And to you, Felix. You and Mrs. Brax working with me will help me immensely in my plans here."

Felix grimaced even as he blushed. For a moment, Philip thought the butler would say something or cry, but instead, Felix bowed and marched away.

Philip sipped his wine, the taste reminding him of Carmen. A dull ache pulsed in his chest.

"When will you leave?" Finley asked.

"These early summer storms make it difficult to leave now, but I've been told they will clear in two days' time."

"I have to put up with you until then?"

Philip chuckled.

"But to speak seriously, I do appreciate you recommending me your staff. Things were looking rather bleak for me a few days ago." Finley twirled the glass between his fingers. "It would have been difficult to impress the woman I wish to marry without a full staff."

Philip studied him for a moment before saying, "If Claire is the woman you speak of, I believe you would be better off telling her how you feel rather than trying to impress her."

"I am in competition with Sir Andrew," Finley said.

"I rather thought she had let that chap go." Philip sipped, shuddering at the thought of Claire marrying Sir Andrew. "I expect you to rescue my friend from that ghastly idea *tout de suite.*"

Finley saluted him. "The very thing I am trying to do."

Returning his salute, Philip laughed. "I will warn you that wooing Claire will be complicated. She isn't like the other women."

Finley grunted, a smile escaping him. "I fell in love with her the moment I saw her over ten years ago. I wanted to marry her then but was tricked into leaving long enough for her father to convince her to marry Richard Candor. Now, I just hope she will listen to me long enough to forgive me."

Philip winked at his old friend. "Since you know my own situation with my wife, I feel I shouldn't give you advice, but I have faith you will get what you want. And I'm convinced you will find happiness together."

"Have you sent a letter to your wife telling her of your plans?" Finley asked as dinner was announced. The two men rose together, finishing off their wine before making their way to one of the last dinners Philip would have in what he still considered his house.

"No. I decided on surprising her. I am landing in the north and will look in on the railroad project first, as well as pick up the plans for the hotel in Valladolid before heading to see Carmen."

"You think the hotel idea will be of interest to her?"

Philip glanced at his friend as they entered the dining room and took their seats. "I certainly hope so," he said. More than anything else in the world, he hoped so.

Chapter 41

THE SUN BIT AT her skin underneath her muslin dress, but Carmen ignored it as she filled glasses of wine for the vineyard workers in celebration of her father's birthday. They always celebrated with the workers and their wines in the vineyard.

"Gracias." The workers came one by one, accepting their glasses with smiles.

"Todo bien, Carmen?" Rosa asked, passing by with an enormous empanada. Carmen's mouth watered at the sight of it. She had been back for two weeks but still hadn't satiated her appetite with enough Spanish food.

"Todo bien, Rosa," Carmen called back, glancing at Isabel, who was seated under a pine tree, her growing belly rounded like a melon under her skirts. Carmen's stomach growled as she pictured the melon slices wrapped in Spanish ham that awaited her at the lunch table.

"Everyone has a glass of wine now, yes?" Don Suárez asked, standing on a tree stump. When the crowd, a small but pleasant one, replied affirmatively, he caught Carmen's eyes and winked. "First, a toast to my daughters, both of whom are here today. And to my new grandchild, who is soon to be here."

The crowd cheered for Carmen and Isabel. Isabel turned pink as she scrambled to standing. Carmen curtsied as she was used to doing in London, laughing along with the neighbors she had grown up with when they whistled and called out her "English" customs.

"Let us hear the blessing over the meal," Don Suárez said, raising his glass as Father Cortez stood. The prayer was short and simple, but for some reason, it brought Carmen to tears. Lately, she had been much more emotional than was necessary for the silliest things. It was a frustrating phenomenon she assumed was due to her missing Philip more and more each day. Not England, but Philip.

Her chest tightened as memories of her husband's face, and laugh flitted through her thoughts.

"Now, please, drink in honor of our benefactor, Don Juan Carlos Suárez. Feliz cumpleaños!" shouted Señor Lopez, thrusting his wine glass high.

The rest of the crowd matched his enthusiasm. Carmen, too, raised her glass in honor of her father, then took a drink with the workers. The moment the wine hit her lips, she knew it wasn't their day-to-day wine at all, but one of their experiments. She glanced up in surprise as her father joined her.

"I thought it was time we shared with others what you can do with some grapes," Don Suárez murmured, clinking his heavy glass against hers.

"This wine is delicious," Isabel told them, her eyes wide and watery. "I want to keep drinking it, but I'm afraid it will make me fall asleep if I have too much. I don't know if it's okay to drink with the baby."

"It will make the baby strong," their father argued, but Isabel didn't look convinced.

"I'll get you some food," Jaime said hurriedly, eyeing his wife's belly as he went.

"The way that man feeds me, you'd think I was carrying two babies." Then Isabel hurled her arms around Carmen and kissed her on the cheek. "I'm happy to have you home, Carmen. This has been the most wonderful month."

"I'm glad to be home." She clinked her glass to each of theirs just as plates of empanada, tortilla, melon wrapped in ham, and tomato salad passed to them. They filled their plates and ate in happy silence, laughing when Jaime arrived, holding two large plates full of food.

"I received a letter today asking me to go up to Burgos in a few days to check on the bridge for Sutton Enterprises," Jaime said as he sat down again.

"You received a letter from Philip?" Carmen asked, trying to hide her vexation. She hadn't received a letter from him. Not that she had expected one. But if he had written to Jaime, he could have written to her as well.

"No," Jaime said with a cough. "From Lord Candor. Just a routine check. They are sending a new engineer and want someone to make sure he is settled."

"But why should you go?" Isabel demanded, her alarm clear.

"Your sister is here to help you," Jaime said. "And I promise it will be but one night."

Carmen laughed. "Perhaps I will go to Valladolid with Jaime, just to prove how sure I am that you will not be having this baby anytime soon."

Isabel's objection was more of a shriek than words.

"No, Carmen, I need you to stay here with this nervous one," Jaime said. "I'll take you to Valladolid once you have become an aunt. Although I could stop to pick Merce up and bring her here."

"Would you?" Carmen asked, forgetting her sister's complaint.

Jaime chuckled and said he would. Isabel lifted her chin towards Carmen, their signal that someone was in Carmen's peripheral.

"Would you come dance, Señora Carmen?" someone asked.

Carmen turned to find Alberto, one of the young men who worked in the local mine, offering his hand.

"Of course," Carmen told him. "You must come dance as well, Papa. It's your birthday celebration."

"Later, hija."

Carmen barely had time to smile back at her father before Alberto drew her into the circle of dancing people. They lined up for one dance, then gathered in a circle for another. Carmen was dismayed at how much she had forgotten in such a short amount of time, but the more she danced, the more all the steps came back to her. It was good to be home.

———◈———

As Carmen and her father left the bodega a week later, the clip-clop of horses trotting down the road caught their attention. Carmen tied the ribbon from her hat around her chin while she angled her vision to get a glimpse. The visitors were men, by the way they rode.

"Who's coming, Papá?" she asked as Don Suárez struggled to close the door. He squinted towards the setting sun before shrugging.

"It's Jaime."

Carmen squinted until the two figures were close enough for her to see that the cut of the other man's suit wasn't Spanish, but English.

"Philip," she gasped, half-startled, half-alarmed at his presence.

Carmen stilled, her heart thudding at the sight of him. Somehow, he had grown more handsome.

She glanced at her father and tried to calm her nerves.

"Do you think he's come to take you back to England?" her father asked grimly. Carmen knew he would fight to keep her in Spain if she just said the word.

"I don't know, Papá."

Before she could say more, Philip was sliding off his horse and running towards her.

"Carmen!" he shouted a few yards away. Within seconds, his arms were tight around her waist and he was twirling her in circles.

"Philip, you'll make me sick." She laughed, her stomach flipping.

"I missed you, Carmen," he murmured against her ear. She breathed in his scent of chicory and oak as he cupped her chin and brought her lips to his. His mouth was warm and soft and just as demanding as ever.

A cough from Don Suárez brought their kiss to an end. Suddenly, Carmen was standing on her own, her cheeks flushed and her body tingling, while Philip was shaking her father's hand.

"I'd say they are rather happy to see each other," Jaime mused from his horse. Carmen's father chuckled.

"Sorry, sir," Philip was saying. "I missed my wife."

For the first time, Carmen saw pink blossoming on her father's cheeks.

"Good to see you care for her," Don Suárez said after he finally cleared his throat enough to speak. "We were just headed back to the house for dinner. Will you join us?"

"That is something I came to discuss with your daughter. I thought she and I might walk together back to the house."

Her father glanced at her, but spoke again to Philip. "It's a long way. Over two kilometers."

"It would be good to spend time with my husband, Papá," Carmen said. "And the breeze is pleasant this evening."

"I'll send Raul for the horses later," Don Suárez said, kissing Carmen lightly on the cheek before mounting his horse. Already his countenance was heavier with the assumption that Carmen would leave again soon.

Once Jaime and Don Suárez turned their horses towards the house, Philip gave Carmen his arm. Carmen found herself without much to say. The realization scared her.

Philip broke the silence first.

"How have you been?" he asked.

"I have been well," she finally said. "The days have been hotter than in London, but we have survived. Isabel will have the baby soon." She tried to study him without moving her head much, but of course, all she saw was the blackish cloud. "You will not make me leave before then, will you?"

"I'm not here to take you away from your sister, Carmen. You came to be here for the birth. I wouldn't force you to leave before that happens."

"I'm glad of that, Philip."

After a few steps of silence, Carmen broke the quiet. "But then, what did you come here for?"

"Is it a long way to visit my wife?" Philip teased. "I don't think so. A man would go to the ends of the earth for his wife, I should think."

Carmen didn't know what to make of the statement.

"It's a beautiful view, is it not?"

Carmen nodded.

"I spoke with Dr. Kruger," Philip said slowly. "You could have told me you went to see him. Even if he didn't have good news."

Carmen swallowed, the gritty dust of the dry Castilian land catching in her throat.

"I'm sorry. I should have. But things became so muddled and busy and. . . I didn't want you to worry. And I went only to see if Dr. Perez was right. There was a chance he was wrong." Her shoulders hunched as she remembered the visit with Dr. Kruger. "But Dr. Perez wasn't wrong. The problem with my vision is called—"

"Retinitis Pigmentosa." Philip grasped onto her hands and tugged her so close to him she could hear his heartbeat and feel his breath against her cheek. "I'm sorry you felt you couldn't tell me, Carmen."

"There was so much going on already with the house and me fitting into your circle in London." She paused before saying the next words, but decided to tell the full truth. "To be honest, I wasn't sure you hadn't changed your mind. About marrying me."

Philip tugged her the last few millimeters closer, his lips covering hers in a kiss that tried to say all the words he couldn't seem to find. Carmen was breathless, but couldn't pull away. She closed her eyes and grasped him at the nape of his neck, her physical desire for him growing at an alarming rate within her. She pressed her mouth closer, wishing to be as near to him as possible. Her tongue danced against his, exploring him again. After the weeks of separation, she thought her body might explode for want of him near her.

Suddenly, without warning, they moved apart far enough to breathe. Philip rested his forehead against hers, still breathing heavily. Carmen closed her eyes, trying to regulate her own breathing and heart.

"I haven't been a good husband, Carmen," he whispered. "I'm sorry. If you'll have me, I would like to start again. Could you forgive me?"

He stepped away. And this time, he was close enough for her to see his anguish.

"I can forgive you," she said. "And can only hope that you can forgive me."

Philip wrapped his arms ever more tightly around her, his stronger fingers dipping into her hair, bundled at the nape of her neck.

"There is no need to forgive you," he murmured. Then he kissed her, gently, his lips moving ever so slightly, before tucking her hand into the crook of his arm again and guiding her towards her childhood home.

———— ❖ ————

"Philip! It's nice to see you again," Isabel said, pattering to greet them. Don Suárez and Jaime were not far behind. "Are you well, Carmen? You look a little pale."

"I am fine, Isabel," Carmen said with a laugh as Philip gave the customary kisses on Isabel's cheeks.

Carmen's eyes found her father's gaze and suddenly, she had to swallow back tears.

"Will you be leaving us soon, then?" Don Suárez asked Philip.

"Not just yet," Philip said. "I've been in Spain for a week working and now I plan to spend some time here."

"You've been here for a week?" Carmen asked. She couldn't believe he hadn't written to her.

"Don't be mad, darling," Philip said softly as they all settled on the cool veranda where a tray of wine waited for them. "I've been working hard to finish some things."

When Philip caught her hand in his, a small shudder ran down her spine, dispelling her hurt. She had missed him, even if she had been happy to be home in Spain. She had missed him, especially at night.

"What things?" Isabel asked from her spot in the corner.

"I bought the old manufacturing building in Valladolid. I want to bring the train directly there, so I'll be making it into the train station. I received approval just yesterday."

"I'm glad for it," Carmen said slowly. "But wasn't that already done?"

Jaime nodded. "Well, there was no reason to think it wouldn't get done, but it was finalized yesterday." Jaime and Philip exchanged a look Carmen couldn't interpret before he continued. "Your husband bought another building in the center of Valladolid and finalized that this past week as well."

"Another? In Valladolid?" Isabel repeated. She glanced at Carmen who shrugged, not knowing any more than her sister.

"One he wishes to convert into a hotel, even though our lawyer says he is crazy."

Philip laughed. The sounds squeezed Carmen's heart. She had missed hearing that sound.

"I believe the hotel will do well there," he said. "Though only time will tell."

Don Suárez lifted his wine glass towards his sons-in-law. "Cheers to Jaime and Philip, for investing in the new Spain."

A torrent of emotions welled in Carmen's chest. Philip was investing in her favorite city. It was better news than him having bought them a new house.

"Yes." Carmen swallowed the tears welling up in her. "To Philip and Jaime."

Philip kissed the top of her head. "It's been my dream for a long time to build a hotel and I am excited to develop it here."

"If this war ever ends, Philip, you must bring Carmen home often," Don Suárez said. "After all, you'll have a place to stay."

"Yes! Building the hotel means you must come here quite often, does it not? To run it, I mean?" Isabel asked. The hope in her voice broke Carmen's heart, knowing she could never come home enough to satisfy her sister or father.

"We will not have to come here often, no," Philip said slowly.

"But you will need to come sometimes, won't you?" Isabel asked, her voice having shrunk in her own distress. "Can't you promise you will bring her home sometimes?"

"I can do better than that, Isabel," Philip said.

"What is better than bringing me home?" Carmen asked.

Everyone's attention moved to Philip. Slowly, he withdrew a paper from his coat.

"That looks like a deed," Isabel said, peering at it from her corner.

"Did you buy the house back from Theodore?" Carmen asked, her mind racing to understand what her husband was saying.

Jaime snatched the paper from Philip's hand and twisted away from him so Philip could do nothing but let him have it.

Philip laughed and contented himself to sip his wine. "At first, I thought of making a show of it, but couldn't come up with an appropriate way," he said.

"An appropriate way for what?" Carmen asked, half frightened by what her husband was trying to say.

"Did you purchase this?" Jaime asked. His eyes were wide, staring straight at Philip.

"Of course."

Jaime looked at Carmen. Then at his wife.

"What is it, Jaime?" Isabel tried to stand but found herself without the energy to get to her feet.

Everyone waited, but Jaime didn't seem able to find the word to explain.

"What does the paper say, Philip?" Carmen asked.

Her husband spread his arms, looking very pleased with himself, and said, "I bought the apartment next to your Tía Merce."

The room shifted with a collective gasp.

"In-where? In Valladolid?" Don Suárez stuttered.

"Please, don't tease me," Isabel said. She clutched her neck, her eyes wide. "Are you serious?"

Philip looked only at Carmen. "We are moving to Valladolid, Carmen."

Isabel and Rosa squealed. Don Suárez laughed aloud with pleasure.

Carmen leapt from her chair and threw herself into Philip's arms. She kissed him hard on the cheek before drawing back to look him in the eyes. It wasn't a tease. He was telling the truth. His eyes were bright and proud. And he was looking at her as though she were the only person who mattered.

"You are willing to move to Spain? With a war? A country that isn't yours?" she asked.

Philip cupped her face and kissed her softly on the mouth. "I love you, Carmen. I want to make you happy. You're happy here, and I realized that the happiest I ever was in my life was here. With you and your family. We will expand Sutton Enterprises in Spain with a little help from Daucer-Suárez Enterprises, and we will create our own happiness. Maybe even give our niece or nephew a playmate."

Carmen burst into tears. Valladolid. They were going to live in Spain. Near her family. She couldn't think of a greater gift her husband could give her.

"That means she's happy," Don Suárez said quickly, as he and the rest of the family burst into congratulations.

"I can't believe we will live so close by," Isabel squealed., pulling Carmen in for an awkward hug over her belly. "Our babies will know each other! Jaime, did you hear?"

"Yes, darling." When Isabel also burst into tears, Jaime pulled her away from Carmen and into his arms.

Carmen laughed at her sister as reality sank into her.

"You really are alright with this?" she asked Philip again.

Philip grabbed her hands in his and nodded. "I wouldn't have proposed it if I wasn't."

Carmen breathed in a staggered breath before throwing her arms around Philip's neck again. She and Philip were going to live in Spain.

"Will you not be embarrassed of me and my terrible Spanish?" Philip asked quietly in her ear.

Carmen nuzzled his neck and whispered back, "I think I can help you improve your Spanish."

Philip pulled her in for a kiss on the mouth, despite her father being nearby. For one long moment, her entire world was just Philip and his embrace.

"So then. Are you happy? Will you live with me here?"

"I will and I am," Carmen said, before reeling him in for another kiss.

———————

Did you enjoy *Stepping Across the English Channel*? Please don't forget to leave a review Goodreads, Bookbub, Amazon.

WHILE ACIDS WERE RECOMMENDED for various things throughout history, there is no evidence they can do anything to slow vision problems.

Want to know when *Stepping Across the Thames* (Claire and Lionel's story) will be out? Join Kat's mailing list to be the first to find out! https://katcaldwell.com/readers

Stepping Across the Desert

Chapter 1

Tiaret, Algeria, May, 1832

The wind blew softly through the trees as Rowena dropped the dress back into the sudsy water. From downriver, she could hear the soft chant of the male slaves resting against the cedars. No time to rest for her.

Rowena closed her eyes as she ran her calloused hands up and down the cloth, the movement slow and gentle. While the garment must surely be out of style in Paris by now, it was still one of Mistress Nadira's favorites. The fine silk had to be washed with care.

Selma grunted loudly from where she was pulling wet clothes out of the river—a warning to focus. There were guests tonight at the grand house and under no circumstances could they delay with the clothes. Rowena considered the dark-skinned woman her adopted mother, but love as a slave was harsh. No one was willing to take a beating for another person's badly done work. Selma's love could include swift slaps to the face, but a warning slap from Selma was better than a whipping.

Rowena unconsciously touched her cheek, remembering the first slap Selma had given her, then wrapped her thin, muslin scarf over her head as a shield. Her heart began to race, and she noticed the throbbing in her feet again. Gently she pushed the silk dress back into the water, singing to herself in hopes she could calm herself down. There was no need to waste energy on anxiety.

"Slow, methodical," Selma said in Berber, the language they both had in common. "Breathe. I'll tell you a story."

Rowena looked up with a smile for her adopted mother. "About your brothers?" she asked.

Selma grunted in mock disapproval but began the well-worn story of her brother the warrior as Rowena hung the yellow dress from a tree branch to start the time-consuming task of wringing out the water.

"Come, sit down here," Rowena said in Berber when she saw Selma stretch out her back. "I will finish the wash while you tell the part about your brother saving your mother from the lion. Sit here and wring out the water."

Selma started to protest, but shouts down the river cut her words short. She turned her head with pursed lips and narrowed eyes, but sat down in the seat without a word. Rowena tried to concentrate on the shouted words as she picked up a long, black silk vest embroidered with gold thread.

"Hurry, child," Selma said wearily. Her story now forgotten, she started to hum a tune in her mother tongue.

"What are they saying?" Rowena asked.

"Keep your eyes down, Fatia," Selma replied sharply. "It doesn't involve us."

Rowena obeyed immediately. The afternoon was still young, and the sun would only get more intense. They must work faster to get the clothes dried and pressed before dinner; Rowena willed her fingers to go quickly as she delicately rubbed a stain out of the embroidery. When shouts floated to them from the river again, she stole a glance at Selma with concern, but Selma simply continued singing.

It was a sad song about a child being taken away—a story that rang all too true to both women. Rowena shook her head sharply and stared at the water. With even breathing, her heart had slowed, and the tears that threatened finally receded.

Thanks to persistence and a little luck, the stubborn stain in the embroidery started to fade. Two years before, when she had begun living here, the tips of her fingers would tingle at the end of the day, sometimes cracking and bleeding. Now her callouses worked much like hardened sponges without nerves.

A sigh escaped her as she rolled back her aching shoulders. Selma clicked her tongue to chivvy her along, but Rowena didn't need it. She was already dipping the tunic back into the water. Nadira had beautiful garments, just like those Rowena had once worn. They were all made of silk and dyed to perfection. Nadira's legendary beauty did not keep Saed from having other wives, but it was clear that she was his favorite, his first. The only wife that had ever traveled to France for her clothes.

"Have you thought on Sara's offer?" Selma asked in Berber.

Rowena looked sharply at her, but Selma didn't take notice of her glare. "I will not become a concubine."

"It is more secure."

"No."

Selma gave one nod, then continued with her work.

Now that Nadira could not have any more sons for him, Saed seemed to expand his harem every month. Just a few days ago Sara, Mistress Nadira's personal maid, had offered to train Rowena into being a concubine, an offer that she had received with horror.

As grotesque as it seemed to Rowena, with her English upbringing, entering Saed's harem was considered an honor. Some woman tried to be chosen well past their prime years. Selma encouraged her to enter it, saying it would provide a luxurious life. But it also meant no escape. No one ever left the harem.

Still, if Rowena was to be a slave the rest of her life, Selma argued that she should not risk going to the slave market. To Rowena's fortune, she had been privately bought and sold since the moment she had been kidnapped five years ago. The slave market was something she had never experienced and never wished to.

"*Balik A'brid!*"

The fierce command echoed through the trees. Surprised, Rowena scrambled to obey. She grabbed the basket and threw herself onto the bank before realizing that the command was not for her. Instead, it was directed at Saed's head slave, Mohammed, by a tall man with shoulders twice as wide as even Saed's personal guards. He appeared from the forest as though by magic, his red burnous flying about him like a sandstorm, yet never daring to hinder his long, determined strides. Mohammed obediently fell into step behind the man, trying to maintain long enough strides to keep ahead of the other slaves. An aura of panic surrounded the entire group. Even the lowest slaves could not seem to focus on their tasks.

Rowena squinted, trying to find the reason for such strange behavior. Some in the group were house slaves, which added to the incongruity. Selma gasped just as Rowena's eyes fell on the bundle the man carried. In them was Youssef, Nadira's eldest son. The boy bounced like a limp fish to the rhythm of the stranger's steps, his eyes closed, his soaked clothing leaving Rowena and Selma to think the worst. Youssef was nearing his fifteenth birthday, but in this man's arms, he looked like a child.

A long stick poked into her ribs. Rowena turned around abruptly to find Selma looking steadily at her.

"It is none of our business."

Rowena sent a silent prayer towards the boy before reluctantly turning back to her work. As she did so, she noticed the stranger was wearing black, English-style boots over tight brown riding trousers underneath his burnous.

For the first time in years, tiny bubbles of excitement popped within her. If an Englishman was here, it was possible—but—no. No. She shook the hope away. Even if the French soldiers were here, they would not bother to rescue slaves.

When Selma and Rowena arrived that evening, the entire household was buzzing with the story about Youssef. He had been thrown into the river by his horse, and before Mohammed had been able to do anything, the stranger in red had appeared from nowhere to fish the boy from the rocky waters.

It was a miracle Youssef was alive, and for that Saed wished to celebrate. Already the smell of lamb and couscous and dates wafted through the air, along with honey cakes and strong tea. Rowena entered the female baignoires, where she slept with forty-four other female slaves, and heaved a sigh. Her stomach growled as she listened to the story being told once again, the weight of her exhaustion intensifying the moment she sat down.

"Fatia! Come! Mistress is asking that you perform for the man who saved Youssef's life. You must bathe!" commanded Sara from the tent opening. The urgency in the command pushed Rowena to her feet.

"Coming!" she called out in Berber, grabbing her soap before running from the tent towards the female bathing house. Before she went far, Sara grabbed her hand.

"Mistress wished you to bathe in our quarters. You are to put on perfume and a silk dress. I was told to make you look as beautiful as Venus."

"A-a silk dress?" Rowena sputtered. "I have no such dress."

Sara smiled. "Come. You must hurry."

Rowena kept herself only one step behind Sara until they entered the cool, marbled bathroom reserved for Nadira's personal maids and slaves. She slowed to take in the sight. The green marble seemed to transform the room into a stone pond. On the eastern wall hung a life-sized oil painting of the mistress with kind, golden eyes.

Truthfully, Nadira was the kindest woman Rowena remembered knowing, though she knew that might be due to her not having known very many women in her life. Although everyone described her as a jealous wife, Nadira radiated an energy of kindness and love to those around her. Every Saturday she gave out dates and cakes to the slave children, and she always made sure each worker was given proper clothing. Often, she spoke with the elder slaves to make certain the pregnant women didn't work past their eighth month or that every child saw the doctor when they fell sick.

To those who had never known anything but misery or cruelty, Nadira's kindness was easy to accept—but Rowena had known luxury. She knew there was more to the world than working for Nadira, and she couldn't give her heart to loving the woman who owned her, who kept her from going home, who kept her from the future she was entitled to.

Or rather, had been entitled to a long time ago.

"You should practice. Perhaps if tonight's performance pleases Mistress Nadira she will move you permanently into the house quarters."

"Yes, Sara," Rowena said, managing to suppress a shudder.

Swallowing hard, she began to warm her voice as her vocal teacher had once taught her. Like bees, the other slaves swarmed around her, carefully removing her dirty clothes, clicking their tongues at the line that divided her skin into two very distinct colors. Rowena continued her scales, closing her eyes against the veiled women who washed her body and hair. She stopped her practice only to wash her face, beginning again as oil was poured over her hair and an ivory comb ran through the strands.

"Come now with the dress," Sara commanded a young girl as Rowena stopped her voice exercises. The slave combing perfume through her hair stepped away as a pink silk, empire-waist ball gown was presented to Rowena. The style must have been about twenty years out of date, which was why she was allowed to wear it.

Still, as she stepped into the gown and that unmistakable rustling of silk reached her ears, Rowena could not help feeling beautiful. It took much of her strength to keep from crying at the familiar touch against her skin as she smoothed the silk down her concave abdomen. Sara molded her hair into a spiral, smiling at her from the large mirror. Rowena smiled back, knowing Sara couldn't possibly understand the pain that silk against her skin caused her.

For years, she had denied herself the pleasure or pain of remembering her old life. Carefree afternoons in the garden; dinner parties where she sang for her father's friends and business partners—it seemed a world away. But now the memory of standing in a pale blue dress with her hair pinned in ringlets was too vivid to dismiss. It was her seventeenth birthday, and she had her future planned out down to the very moment when all of London would shiver with awe at the sound of her voice.

The image that now looked back at her was nothing like the pampered girl she remembered. Instead, she was a woman in an overworked body with darkened, callused hands and gnarled feet.

A self-pitying sigh escaped her as Sara finished the placement of her hair. The older servant raised her brows in a warning. It was an honor to perform for Saed and his guests. An honor to wear a silk ball gown. Rowena didn't bother explaining herself. She hadn't spoken in confidence to anyone in so long that she wasn't sure she knew how anymore.

"You look very beautiful," Sara whispered with finality in Arabic.

"*Shokran Gazillan*," Rowena answered. Her Arabic had improved greatly since Saed had bought her, but it was still heavily accented. Berber, the language she had used to speak to her own servants, was what she spoke in the baignoires. Sara used to speak to Rowena in French, proud that she knew the language fluently, but since the invasion of the French army, Saed had forbidden it from being spoken in his house. Not even Nadira dared to speak it, though it was her mother's language.

"Master Saed wants you to sing only European songs tonight," Sara instructed her. "He wishes to impress this man."

She stepped away to admire Rowena, scrutinizing her with a critical eye. When Rowena received approval with a firm nod, she once again warmed her voice, this time with a song. The bathhouse fell silent as Rowena sang *Ave Maria*. It was the last song she had learned before her life had changed forever.

Audible sighs of pleasure filled the room. Rowena closed her eyes, pretending she was singing in an opera house in London, with her father watching from the front row. As the last note rang out, she felt something cold placed around her neck. She recoiled and opened her eyes. Sara smiled at her again through the mirror.

"But why?" Rowena asked as she gazed at the heavy, intricate detail of the traditional Algerian necklace. The necklace contained four large rubies, each surrounded by small diamonds. Rowena had never worn anything like this, not even when she had performed for Saed's brothers just a few months before.

"Nadira told me you should wear it," Sara answered. "Now, it is time to go. Are you ready?"

⁂

"The most beautiful voice you have ever heard is right here in our very own home," Saed announced. "And she is here tonight to honor you, my friend."

The words gave Rowena no pleasure. Saed would say anything to impress his guest; it did not mean he thought anything of her. She was a slave, here to do his bidding.

At Saed's signal, the boy slave standing near Rowena tapped his large stick. Immediately, Rowena raised her head and began *Auld Lang Syne*, the first song her German teacher had ever taught her. As she sang, the young boys sat together on the floor eating dates while the two men smoked. Their manners were relaxed. The Englishman seemed at ease with the local traditions of eating with fingers and passing food to one another, something she had seen many Europeans struggle with when coming to Northern Africa.

Saed was dark, slightly taller than Rowena herself, and although he was strong, there was little build to him. He reminded Rowena always of the men her father used to describe after coming home from a boxing fight. The Englishman was much taller. His skin was tan, and he had a build that was more like those of the slaves who did the heaviest labor. For a moment she found herself lost in the difference of the English man, which caused her to repeat too many verses of an opera she couldn't quite remember. Noticing a flicker of amusement in his eye, she quickly focused on the top of the curtains as she finished the ballad and began a different song.

After just three more songs, Saed made an impatient gesture for her to stop. He looked grim, which was never a good sign.

"Mr. Sutton, we are honored tonight not only by your presence and company," he said gravely. His voice lifted the sleepy silence from the room, instantly bringing the family to attention. "But also because you have, by the grace of Allah, saved my first son."

Saed placed his hands on the young boy's shoulders and squeezed them with love.

"You have honored me, Saed, with your hospitality and your generosity. I did only what one does for a brother."

While no one paid attention to her, Rowena dared to look again at the stranger. When she heard his English name, her heart raced. With so much adrenaline running through her veins, she had to fight the urge to faint.

"I grow weary of this concert because it is not enough for what you have done, my friend," said Saed. "Nadira wishes to give you a gift. One we hope will please you and comfort you, as we are comforted with our son safe and alive."

He flipped his robes back dramatically. Mohammed stepped up, holding a small, golden box towards Saed. Rowena shrank back, but found a man standing directly behind her, forcing her to stay put. Saed presented the box to Mr. Sutton with ceremonious words that Rowena had trouble understanding. Then Nadira stepped forward, kissing Mr. Sutton's hands.

Something pushed her forward. She tried to plant her feet firmly onto the floor, but a second later a large staff struck the back of her knees, forcing her to kneel.

"In gratitude, my wife would like to present to you the most beautiful virgin of all our slaves. It is a small payment to the enormous debt that we owe you," Saed announced as Rowena tried desperately to scramble to her feet, to get out of the way before someone noticed her clumsiness. It was not until Mohammed swiftly kicked her in the side that she understood.

She was the gift.

Anger built up in her chest, but she ground her teeth against it and continued to stay still. Five years ago she might have screamed at them, shouting that she was not cattle to be given away as a present, but now she knew it was of no use. From her kneeling position, the flicker of light from her silver bracelet reminded her she was not Rowena Brayemore now, but Fatia, the slave.

"I am honored by these splendid gifts, my brother," Mr. Sutton said. A coldness in his voice that hadn't been there before sent a shiver through Rowena.

Saed laughed. "Tomorrow we will talk more about the business. For now, we should all rest."

With that, two men whisked Rowena away through the opposite door, where Sara waited.

"Sara!" Rowena gasped as the other woman dragged her through the hallways towards the servant's quarters.

"Hush," Sara commanded as they entered the green marbled bathroom.

"*La afham!*" Rowena whispered. "I don't understand!"

Sara gently took the pins from Rowena's hair before quickly pulling a comb through it. Rowena swallowed hard against her tears, but could not stop shaking.

"Stop," Sara said forcefully. "You are not to cry. Allah has sent you here. This is your life now."

Rowena shook her head, snatching her chin from Sara's fingers. "I do not believe in Allah, Sara."

"Whoever your god is, he has sent you here and made you Saed's slave. And now Saed has given you to this Englishman. Now! Listen to me!"

Rowena focused her attention on Sara's stern brown eyes. The severity in them kept her from fainting.

"Listen to me," she repeated. "You make sure this man likes you. Make sure he understands you are not to be left behind. Saed has given you to him, and if he doesn't take you with him Saed will see it as a disgrace. He will think that you did something to displease this man and will probably sell you."

"But I do not want to be this man's slave. I do not know him."

"Listen, Fatia! Do not allow fear to swallow you. Think about if this Englishman takes you with him. Perhaps he will take you back to Europe with him and then you will find your life again there. Perhaps he is kind and will do that for you. Won't he have no choice but to set you free?" Sara turned Rowena around and took up her hair again. "Do whatever you must, Fatia, to make certain this man takes you with him."

The plan was so clear it shocked her senseless. Perhaps being given to an Englishman as a concubine was not how she had planned it, but it was the only option she had. This was her chance to go home.

———— ❖ ————

Get *Stepping Across the Desert* from your favorite bookstore!

About the author

Kat is a novelist and short story writer. She writes everyday and can't seem to stick to a genre, having dabbled in historical fiction, contemporary family drama and romance, as well as speculative fiction. Kat is the creator of the Pencils&Lipstick podcast, a podcast for writers with author interviews, craft talk and insight into the publishing world. She is also an accredited Author Accelerator fiction book coach. In between conducting interviews for her podcast and writing, you can find Kat traveling the world, reading, or volunteering with her church—always with a cup of cold brew close by.

You can find out more about Kat:

On her website https://katcaldwell.com

On Instagram @author_katcaldwell

On Facebook @katcaldwellauthor

On TikTok at @katcaldwell.author.

Find her short stories by subscribing to her mailing list at https://katcaldwell.com/readers

www.ingramcontent.com/pod-product-compliance
Lightning Source LLC
Chambersburg PA
CBHW021032310726
48969CB00006B/1622